53LETTERS
for my
Lover

—⟩◉⟨—

LEYLAH ATTAR

PITCH73 PUBLISHING

10 9 8 7 6 5 4 3 2 1

ISBN: 978-0-9937527-0-4 (pbk.)

Printed in the United States of America

PITCH73 PUBLISHING
TORONTO, CANADA

This book is dedicated to anyone who has ever tried—

"Fly,
dammit,
fly!"

CHARACTER LIST

SHAYDA'S FAMILY:

Ali Kazemi (Baba) - **Shayda's father**
Mona Kazemi (Maamaan) - **Shayda's mother**
Hossein - **Shayda's brother**
Adele - **Hossein's wife (Shayda's sister-in-law)**
Hossein's & Adele's kids - **Kayla, Ethan & Summer**
Khaleh Zarrin - **Mona's sister (Shayda's aunt)**

HAFEZ'S FAMILY:
Kamal Hijazi (Pedar) - **Hafez's father**
Nasrin Hijazi (Ma) - **Hafez's mother**

SHAYDA'S & HAFEZ'S KIDS: Natasha & Zain

TROY'S FAMILY:
Henry Heathgate - **Troy's father**
Grace Heathgate - **Troy's mother**

OTHER:

Pasha Moradi - **Kamal Hijazi's friend**
Bob Worthing - **Shayda's mentor**
Elizabeth Worthing - **Bob's wife**
Jayne Worthing - **Bob's daughter, Shayda's best friend**
Matt Cavelry - **Jayne's husband**
Jayne's & Matt's kids - **Brady & Sophia**
Ryan Worthing - **Bob's son, Jayne's brother, Troy's college buddy**
Ellen Worthing - **Ryan's wife**
Ryan's & Ellen's kids - **Terri & Alyssa**
Nathan - **Natasha's boyfriend & (later) husband**
Farnaz **(Hafez's cousin) & her husband,** Behram
Marjaneh - **Hossein's ex-wife**
Amu Reza - **Marjaneh's father**

LETTERS

1. HERE WE ARE

June 18th, 1995

THE THIRD TIME I SEE HIM, TWELVE YEARS AFTER THAT hot, sticky night in July, he's kissing Jayne. My hand freezes on the door knob as I watch their silhouettes embrace against the brilliant arch of the window. I step back, not wanting to interrupt this private moment between bride and groom. But something keeps me riveted. Matt doesn't make the air crackle like this. He doesn't send long, dark tentacles, tempting me out of the shadows and into the light. No, not Matt. Troy. Troy Heathgate, kissing my best friend minutes before her reception.

And just like that, I'm at war—two sides of me charging down the hills, clashing and clanging in a valley about as wide as the sliver of the door I'm peeking through. I want to barge in, to rescue Jayne from the captivating black-magic knight that's him, but I waver at the threshold, clinging to a tattered banner of self-preservation.

The dusty sneakers and sweatshirt are gone. A formal jacket outlines shoulders that are impossibly broader.

The tousled, shaggy hair has been tamed with a suave, sophisticated cut. All the same raw-boned ruggedness, poured into a hard, polished presence. I flinch, dropping my hand from the door. This. This foolish, heady pounding of my heart. This is what destroyed Maamaan and Baba, what sent Hossein running, and left us scattered like four points on a compass. I grip the gold band around my finger. I will never let this darkness touch my home.

I watch as Troy's fingers circle the back of Jayne's neck, weaving into her hair. He pulls her face away and says something in her ear. For a second, she stares at him. Then she blinks and slaps him hard across the face. The resounding smack barely affects him. Amusement lurks in the corners of his mouth as he takes the hand that lashed out and kisses it. Then he straightens his jacket and heads for the exit.

I duck behind the door, squeezing myself flat against the wall as six feet of solid male whips by me, leaving the unmistakable blast of power and expensive cologne. His shoes click across the smooth marble floor as he walks into the banquet hall, cool, confident and completely unruffled. I lean my head back against the wall and let my breath out.

"Shayda? Is that you?" I hear Jayne calling.

Damn. I pull myself together and enter the room.

"You have no idea what just happened." She engulfs me in a hug.

"I saw. But now's not the time." I turn her around so she can see her mum and dad approaching.

"Sweetheart." Elizabeth clasps her daughter's hands. "It's almost time."

"I can't believe it." Bob hooks his arm around Jayne and pulls her in affectionately. "My little girl."

2

I swallow, wishing I could conjure up some memory of my parents from my wedding day.

"Dad!" says Jayne, wriggling away from him. "You're ruining my hair."

"Me?" Bob laughs. "Looks like someone already beat me to it." He tugs a piece that's sticking out.

Jayne and I exchange a look. We know who's to blame. "It's barely noticeable," I say. "But we need to retouch your lipstick."

"I'll get it." Elizabeth reaches for Jayne's purse.

"And I better get back to our guests," says Bob. "Care to join me, Shayda?" He offers me his arm.

I look at Jayne.

"I'm fine." She reassures me. "You two go inside."

BOB LEADS ME THROUGH THE ELEGANTLY APPOINTED reception hall, to the family table.

"Are we the only ones here?" he asks Ryan. All the other tables are filled with people, talking and mingling.

"For now," says Ryan. "Ellen's in the back, doing whatever maids of honor do. I thought it'd be you for sure, Shayda."

Decked out in a suit, Jayne's brother is the splitting image of their father.

"I'm not one for crowds or speeches," I reply. "Your wife saved the day. How was the drive from Ottawa?"

"Great. The kids slept most of the way. We're paying for it now." He points to the two girls spinning circles on the empty dance floor.

"Wow." I laugh. "They've grown."

"They certainly have. What about yours?"

"Well, Natasha is now eleven and Zain is nine."

"You didn't bring them?"

3

"They're with my mother."

"And Hafez?"

"He's out of town," I reply.

"Still the same, crazy hours?"

"Still the same."

"Shayda, have you met Ryan's college buddy?" asks Bob. "Where is he?" He looks around. "Hey, Troy. Troy!" No. Please no. But he's already waving him over.

I stare at the monogrammed favor box on the table. "J & M" it says, in cursive silver. The hair on the back of my neck stands when Troy Heathgate stops behind my chair.

"Troy, meet Jayne's friend, Shayda. Also my brilliant protégée. She started off as my assistant and is now one of my top realtors."

I paste a cardboard smile and stand.

"Dad, they've already met," says Ryan. "Canada Day fireworks. Remember, Troy?"

"Yes." Something flickers across those brilliant pacific blues. "I remember." His smile falters the tiniest bit before he takes my hand.

Our palms barely connect before we pull back, like we've touched a live wire.

"Troy has just moved back from New York," Bob is saying...

It doesn't matter.

It doesn't matter what anyone is doing or saying. I wish Troy Heathgate would stop looking at me like that. Time has intensified his gaze into a laser beam that zaps hazy memories of him into a cloud of smoky grey. Poof. Gone. Dissolved. Disintegrated. What chance do black and white rainbows have against full, blazing technicolor?

"They're here, everyone!" Elizabeth sweeps in.

We turn as Jayne and Matt make their entrance. I watch over the back of Troy's shoulder, acutely aware of the way his hair grazes the top of his collar. He shifts, putting his hand on the small of my back, and guides me in front so I can see better. It's the lightest touch, but every part of me bristles. How dare he kiss Jayne? How dare he stand behind me and cheer and clap as if he hasn't betrayed years' worth of her family's trust?

"There you are." Long, red talons claim his arm as a chestnut haired beauty sidles up to him. "Did you forget about me?" she purrs.

Of course. A date.

"Heather." He smiles. "Where's Felicia?"

"Right here, darling." A honey hued goddess coos, leaving a neon pink lip print on his cheek.

Huh. Two dates.

The clapping stops. It's time for us to take our seats. Thank god. I wish he would just leave.

He walks his dates to the other side of the table and takes the empty seats next to Ryan.

No. Nonononono.

We sit across from each other, through the speeches and dances and toasts—me with Bob on one side and Ryan's little girl on the other; him, flanked by twin bombshells.

"So explain to me what it is that you do," says Bob as we're finishing dinner. "This 'internet' that I've been hearing about."

"It's quite simple really," replies Troy. "A system of computer networks that connects people around the world. It's been around for a while, but it's just starting to get interesting. My company designs and implements security protocol for businesses that want to establish their presence online, so that sensitive information exchanged on the internet stays secure."

"It's really taking off," says Ryan. "Troy's firm is doing so well, he needs to set up offices here in Toronto to cover the Canadian side of his operation."

"Well that's great," says Elizabeth when Heather and Felicia leave for the ladies' room. "What I want to know is, when are you going to settle down?"

"Oh no, no, no, Mum." Ryan holds his hands up. "Did you *see* those girls? Troy, buddy, live it up. For the both of us, man." He clinks glasses with him.

"I'm just saying," Elizabeth continues. "It's all fun and games until someone steals your heart from right under your nose. You should think about that, young man."

"I don't know," replies Troy, twirling his glass. "What do you think, Shayda?"

He says my name like he's been holding it in his mouth for a long time, savoring it, letting his tongue taste each vowel, each consonant, before releasing it with a warm 'ahhh'.

Am I the only one hearing this? Seriously? Shaydahhh.

I lift my eyes and find him watching me. Intently. Like I'm some specimen he's pinned to a cork board with brightly colored thumb tacks.

"Hey." Jayne and Matt stop by our table. "Why isn't anyone dancing? Come on guys. Let's go, let's go!"

Jayne seems relaxed, like she's really enjoying herself. I steal another look at Troy. No reaction. It's as if I imagined the whole thing between the two of them.

Ryan and Ellen take the kids and follow the bride and groom to the dance floor. Heather and Felicia return, giggling. Nothing like a trip to the ladies' room for some female bonding. They drag Troy away, one on each arm.

Elizabeth declines, pointing to her half-finished plate. "Why don't you take Shayda?" she tells Bob.

"No thanks," I reply. "I prefer to sit and watch."

"Suit yourself," says Bob. "But Milton Malone is making his way over and I have a feeling it's not me he wants to dance with."

"Oh Bob! Why would you invite him?"

"I invited a lot of our clients."

"Let's go." I grab him, and we scoot off to the dance floor.

"She picked the perfect venue," says Bob.

I nod. In spite of the extensive renovations inside the mansion, the graceful estate that Jayne chose for her wedding retains the glamour and romance of the 1920s.

"This is where I'm going to get married," she said when the proprietor showed us the sunken garden. "And this is where we'll have the reception."

The room looks even more beautiful at night, with twinkling chandeliers and creamy damask curtains.

"Was this intentional?" asks Bob.

"What?"

"You match the decor."

I laugh. I'm wearing a knee-length dress that reflects the soft, blush tones on the wall.

"I think you should get Elizabeth for this number," I say when the DJ switches to a slower beat.

"Liz has her partner picked and it looks like she's having way too much fun for me to cut in."

"Where is she?" I laugh, turning around, and find myself staring straight at Troy Heathgate.

"Mind if I cut in?" he asks Bob. It's more of a statement than a request. "Thank you for saving me a dance, Lizzie."

"Oh no. Thank *you*." She fans herself. "I hope you can keep up, old man," she tells Bob, and is promptly rewarded with a smack on the bottom. They dance off happily.

Troy clasps my fingers in one hand while the other circles my waist. Jon B's dulcet tenor mingles with the cool vocals of Babyface. 'Someone To Love,' they croon. He leads me flawlessly, in a slow, lazy rhythm. The jacket has come off. I can feel the warmth of his body through the crisp cotton shirt—every turn, every twist, every flex of hard muscle beneath. My eyes are level with his collar, staring at the undone buttons, the tie that's been loosened as though he can't stand to be restrained. I keep my eyes on the silver cross resting in the groove between his collarbones. Some things never change.

"So." His breath lifts the tendrils off my neck. "Here we are, Mrs. Hijazi."

"You remember..." The words spill out before I can stop myself.

"Of course." Like anything else was unimaginable. "Was it a girl, with sunset red in her hair, like her mother?"

"Yes," I reply. "But she looks more like her father."

We move silently, thinking of that other night, when we danced under fluorescent lights, between rows of magazines and toilet paper and chewing gum.

"Are you happy, Shayda?"

A second. That's all it takes. A single beat of hesitation on my part.

When Natasha was a year old, Hafez and I had gone to see 'Fright Night'. Jerry Dandridge was the dark, seductive vampire who couldn't cross the threshold unless you let him in.

Here I am, ten years later. Troy Heathgate is at my door.

Let me in.

I falter.

Sometimes I wonder how many worlds unfurled in that one second.

"Roses." He smiles and shakes his head. "I smell roses."

"I'm not wearing any perfume."

"I know."

My heart quickens as his eyes roam my lips, pausing over the faint silver scar.

"Your dates are waiting for you," I say.

Heather and Felicia have turned their chairs and are following our every move.

"Let them wait."

We cover the floor, mingling with other couples. Dancing with him would be effortless. If I could relax.

"What?" I ask when the weight of his stare became too much.

"That's what I'm trying to figure out," he replies. "What. What is it about you, Shayda Hijazi? There's nothing remarkable about the shape of your eyes or your nose or your face. And yet, when you put it all together, something extraordinary happens. Everything clashes. That cool rosebud mouth sets off whatever is percolating in your turkish-coffee eyes. Your eyebrows. Such a proud arch to them. Completely at odds with this demure nose. And when you look away, it's as if some soot is going to fall off your lashes and smudge those chaste cheeks. You're a mass of contradictions, Shayda. All these delicious curves, wrapped around a rod of steel."

"It's called a backbone, Troy. And you don't seem to have one. Or do you just have a thing for married women?"

"I have a thing for women all right." He laughs. "Delicious creatures, every one of you. Married? Maybe one..."

"Just Jayne then?"

I have to hand it to him. He doesn't flinch. Or falter.

"You saw that, did you?" His eyes gleam with hidden mirth. "Did it offend your sensibilities, Shayda?"

"You think it's funny?" My temper flares. "I wonder what Ryan or Bob would say if they knew."

"I wouldn't mention it to anyone if I were you." His fingers tighten painfully around my waist.

The song ends, but the air continues to thrum between us.

"I'd like to sit down now," I say.

"You know what I'd like to do?" His grip shows no sign of relaxing. "I'd like to loosen this tight little up-do of yours and let your curls fall free. I'd like to see what you'd be like if you weren't so ruthless with yourself, Shayda."

I shrug his hands off. "Stay away from me, Troy. And stay away from Jayne."

I turn and head for the table, feeling him hot on my heels.

"Where do you think you're going?" Heather intercepts him and leads him back to the dance floor.

"He's got that whole alpha-male vibe going on, doesn't he?" says Felicia as I collapse into my chair. "If Troy Heathgate locks in on you, you're done for. Even when you know he's so, so bad for you, it feels so, so good."

Unbelievable. The Troy Heathgate Admiration Society.

"How do you do it?" I ask. "How do you...share?"

"Look at him," she says. "Wouldn't you rather have a piece than nothing at all?"

We watch as he leans in to catch something Heather is whispering in his ear.

"I'm going to get a drink." Felicia gets up.

A woman doesn't like to share, no matter how well she's convinced herself otherwise.

I see Milton Malone making a beeline for the table. It's too late to make my excuses so I say no to the dance and suffer through the conversation. Bob rescues me a little later.

"Jayne and Matt are looking for you," he says. "Hey, Milton. How've you been?"

I escape to the head table to say my good byes.

"What? No way!" says Jayne. "We're just getting started."
She pulls me back to the dance floor. It's fun until
I notice Troy Heathgate's eyes on me. Every time I turn
around, there he is, following me with brooding eyes.
Having shots at the bar, looking at me. Listening to his dates,
looking at me. Toying with his drink, looking at me. Like a
hunter stalking his prey. Watching and waiting.

By the time everyone returns to the table, my legs feel
unsteady.

"I have to pick up the kids," I say, gathering my things.

"Don't forget to take the centerpiece with you." Elizabeth
points to the ivory orchids in the glass vase.

"I thought the centerpiece goes to the person whose
birthday is closest to the wedding date," says Ryan.

"Yes. That would be Shayda," replies Elizabeth.

"No, that would be Troy."

"Shayda."

"Troy."

Elizabeth sighs. "Shayda's birthday was yesterday."

"No shit! Troy's was yesterday too." Ryan slaps the table
and laughs. "You guys have the same birthday?" He looks at
Troy and then at me.

Troy watches my discomfort with tipsy amusement. Or
maybe that's just how he looks when he's completely sloshed.

"What do you say, Shayda? Arm wrestle me for it?" He
reaches across the table.

His 's's are shlurred. Um, slurred.

"How about we go by birth year then?" suggests
Elizabeth. "Troy?"

"1962."

Nineteen shixty two.

"Shayda? You don't have to say. Just before or after?" She
asks with a sensitivity that makes me smile.

"Same," I reply.

Elizabeth sits back. "Now isn't that something?"

"My grandma used to say that people born on the same day are two halves of the same soul," says Heather.

"You hear that, Shayda?" Troy props his elbow on the table and rests his cheek on his palm. "We're shoulmates."

Everyone laughs. He sounds like Sean Connery on Her Majeshty's Shecret Shlurrvish.

"Well, I'll be on my way," I say.

"Please." He picks up the orchids and stands, surprisingly steady on his feet. "I prefer prickly roses."

I reach for the flowers.

"I'll walk you out," he says, holding on to them.

"That's not necessary."

"I insist." He points to the door.

Milton Malone is checking his breath.

He's not a bad guy. Really. Troy is much worse, except he could charm the tux off a penguin.

God. I miss Hafez.

Troy leads me to the coat check and waits while I pick up my wrap.

"Here." He puts it around me as I juggle my keys and purse.

His knuckles graze my nape, lingering there, a fraction longer than necessary. And then I feel something else, something soft and warm on my skin.

I spin around, clutching the back of my neck.

"Did you just...?"

"Sorry. My lips may have..." He points to his mouth and then to my neck.

"You're not sorry at all!"

"No, not really." He grins. It's completely lop-sided.

"You're drunk." I can still feel my skin tingling.

"Guilty." He raises one hand.

"Hey, Shayda. Are you leaving?" Milton Malone catches up with us.

"I am. Good night, Milton."

"Yes. Good night, Milton." Troy picks up a mint from the counter and hands it to him.

"I can take it from here, Troy," I say.

"As you wish." He hands me the vase and holds the door open.

I step outside, thankful for the slight chill in the air. He follows me out.

"I *said* I can take it from here." I glare at him.

"Just getting a smoke," he replies, holding out a pack of cigarettes.

A shmoke. I roll my eyes.

I cross the parking lot, acutely aware of his eyes following me, and don't let my breath out until I get in the car. I hope it's another twelve years before I see him again. Maybe he'll have tobacco teeth by then. And thick, bushy hair growing out of his ears. And, please god, a beer belly. Yes, a beer belly would be quite nice.

I round the exit and catch the red glow of his cigarette. His dark silhouette watches me from the stairs as my tail lights disappear into the night.

2. NOVEMBER

June 19th, 1995

It's past midnight by the time I get to Maamaan's.

"They're fast asleep," she says as we check on the kids.

I stroke their hair. They smell of innocence and trust and fluffy teddy bears.

"Why don't you just stay over?" asks Maamaan.

The thought of sleeping next to my mother, sandwiched between tightly tucked floral sheets, fills me with dread.

"I'll pick them up in the morning. Do you think you could have them ready for school?"

Maamaan shrugs. She's never been one to worry about details. Things always fall into place, people always do her bidding. Including Baba. Until she divorced him.

"I don't have to put up with it here," she said, a year after they moved from Tehran.

Of course, she had been counting on Hossein. He would stay with her, he would look after her.

Maamaan pours me a cup of coffee, regal, even in her curlers and ankle-length night gown. The orchid centerpiece sits unacknowledged on the counter. It's more Maamaan than me. I feel like November around her, dull and colorless. We sit in silence as the grandfather clock ticks the seconds by. The lamp over the table casts a pool of yellow light around us. The rest of the house creaks in weary darkness.

"You should find yourself a boyfriend," says Maamaan, snipping a coupon. "You need chicken? It's on sale."

I choke on my coffee. "What?"

She taps the paper. "Chicken. Boneless, skinless."

"Not that."

"The boyfriend? Why not?" She puts her scissors down and looks at me. "They do it to us all the time. Every man I've known. My father, your father, your brother."

"And look what happened." I push my chair away from the table. "Hafez is nothing like them."

"And you think that will keep you safe?" The bitter laugh of a woman whose face is lined with disappointment. "Your father and I, we were something, you know. We burned so bright, the stars grew jealous. But maybe you know something I didn't. Maybe if you don't allow yourself to shine, you never burn out."

"I didn't really have a choice, did I, Maamaan?"

"Well, you have it now."

I know she's only saying it because she thinks I'd never act on it. It's her way of trying to shake off some sense of remorse, for using me to secure the family's move, to leave behind the life she couldn't live anymore. Had I not married Hafez, we would still be in Iran. But she didn't do it alone. I'd played along. There were so many things I had kept from her. What was the point in sharing dark, ugly secrets best left in the past?

"I have exactly what I want, Maamaan. Hafez makes me happy."

"Hmph. Of course he makes you happy. You'd be happy with practically anyone. You've never believed anyone owes you anything."

I sigh wearily. "What do you *want* from me, Maamaan?"

"Nothing." She goes back to her coupons. "I don't want anything from you."

I look at my aging mother across the stark wooden table. She's right. She's never wanted anything from me. Not me. She always looked surprised when the nanny took a day off, like she'd forgotten I was there.

"Well." I get up. "I'm all you've got." I walk to the sink and start washing my cup. The water goes from icy cold to blistering hot in seconds.

"Would you just leave it?" Maamaan grabs the sponge and pushes me out of the way. "It drives me nuts. You can't even have a cup of coffee without cleaning up after yourself."

I push down the familiar prick of pain and wipe my hands. "Thanks for having the kids over this weekend."

"Wait." She gives me a yellow envelope stuck to the fridge with pink daisy magnets. "They made this for you."

Inside is a lined sheet of paper, folded in half to make a card.

'Happy Birthday Mum!' it says. Four stick figures with giant heads hold hands in front of a crooked house. They're standing on green spikes of grass under a crayon yellow sun.

'We love you.' Natasha's careful print, the kind she reserves for important projects, scrolls across the sky.

"What is it?" asks Maamaan.

"Nothing." I smile, folding the waxy paper back into the envelope. "Did Hafez call?"

"No. Were you expecting him to?"

"I thought that maybe—never mind."

Hafez has never been one to remember birthdays or anniversaries.

"I'll see you in the morning." I head for the door.

"Come early," she says. "I want you to call Hossein."

My brother, her baby boy.

I am the secretary between two VIPs.

"HOSSEIN, MAAMAAN WANTS TO SPEAK TO YOU." THAT'S how it goes.

I can always feel his misery, picture him squaring his shoulders for the guilt trip that's about to hit him.

Maamaan had chosen the prettiest girl for him, the flower of Tehran.

"Give me lots of grandchildren," she said.

But things fell apart. Hossein fell in love with someone he wasn't supposed to. He left his wife, said goodbye and moved to Montreal. He has three kids now. He sent us a picture of his first born five years ago. We are like shadows from another life to him.

"Maamaan, he loves you," I say in the moments her heart is breaking.

"What good is love if you don't show it?"

3. KISS ME

....

June 21st, 1995

"Troy Heathgate, line 3." Susan buzzes me.
I stare at the flashing red light.
Don't pick up. Don't pick up. Don't pick up.
"Good morning, Shayda Hijazi," I say in my most
professional voice.
"Shaydahhh." So lazy, so raspy, so I-just-woke-up that I
can almost see him in bed. "I'm looking for a place. A condo
or loft. Downtown. I'd like you to help me find it."
"Sorry, Troy." I press down hard on my pen. "My client
list is pretty full right now."
A long pause.
"Let me get this straight..." His voice turns steely. "You're
refusing to work with me?"
"I...uh..." I wind the telephone cord around my fingers,
wishing I could throttle the connection.
"I see."
The line goes dead.
I unclench the phone from my hand.

That was easy. I look at the line again.

Too easy.

AN HOUR LATER, HE STRIDES INTO MY OFFICE AND SHUTS the door behind him. V-neck t-shirt, worn-in jeans, silver belt buckle—looking like he's walked straight out of a Levis ad.

"Wha...what are you doing here?"

"I get to you, don't I?" He leans back against the door and folds his arms, unnerving me with point blank scrutiny.

"What are you talking about?"

"The only reason you didn't take me on is because you're afraid." He takes two steps towards me.

"That's ridiculous." I give thanks to whoever thought of putting wheels on a chair.

"Bullshit!" His palms slam down on my desk.

I grip the edges of the folder I'm holding.

"Kiss me, Shayda." His voice is thick, like slow-pouring molasses. "It can't possibly be as good as it is in my head. I'll walk out of here and we'll both be free."

He leans in, his hands spanning the width of the table. I notice twin tattoos circling his biceps. The blue-black barbed wire reminds me of a crown of thorns. I bet he hasn't had to sacrifice a thing in his life. In spite of the cross dangling around his neck. I scoff and meet his eyes.

Big mistake.

This is what it must feel like, being sucked into the dizzying spiral of a deadly tornado. One moment I'm spinning in the absurdly dark rings around his electric blue irises, and the next, everything fades into the smoldering sensuality of his mouth.

How many heartbeats does it take to cross ten inches? To close the buzzing, zinging, charged up field between us?

He waits, not moving, not breathing.

I move, not thinking, not caring.

Anything to break free of this insane, intense connection between us.

That first brush of our lips—I think it's going to be like a white-hot current zapping through me, but it's not. It's soft and still and very, very quiet.

Ha! I rejoice. I can do this. I can break this spell.

My smugness lasts for all of two seconds. Until his arms come around, cradling my face. And he kisses me back.

All of that dancing, cheating, lying-in-wait energy explodes between us. It swirls through my blood and surges inside me. I reel back, but he doesn't let go, holding me immobile as his mouth devours me. A hot, awful joy bubbles in my veins as he drags me through a twisting-turning tempest. My fingers start to loosen their grip on the folder, greedy for the texture of his hair.

And just as I begin to melt, he backs off.

My eyes bolt open.

"Thank you. That's all I needed." He turns and walks out the door.

A few minutes later, I hear him in Bob's office, cool as ice, asking him to show him some properties.

God. I twist my wedding band until the skin beneath turns white. How could I? How could I, knowing he kissed Jayne with those lips? And Heather. And Felicia.

My eyes sting with tears.

What is it about Troy Heathgate that just won't let me be?

4. EARTH AND SKY

....

July 23rd, 1995

"Welcome back." I hug Jayne. "You look amazing."

"Like my tan?" She holds out her arms. "Greece was fabulous!"

"This place isn't too bad either." I look around. A sprawling log cottage, tucked away in a secluded cove on Lake Of Bays. The water sparkles through the majestic pines lining the shoreline.

"It's been in Matt's family for three generations. I'm going to love spending the summer here."

"And then what?" I ask.

"And then there's so much to do! We have to find a place of our own. Then I'll be busy decorating. Oh, and Matt's mum wants me to help with her charity. Can you imagine? Me, a sophisticated socialite?"

"You're going to do great."

It's true. There may be just four years between us, but Jayne and I are worlds apart. She loves the glamour and glitter, the dinners with influential people. I prefer quiet nights at home, the simple rituals of tucking the kids in, of putting away a freshly washed load of laundry; the smell of homemade soup. We turn at the sound of rubber on hot gravel. A car pulls into the driveway. It's impossible to mistake the driver's silhouette, the narrow waist, the long muscular thighs. I suck in a lungful of air. It's been a few weeks. His skin is darker, like he's been playing in the sun. He starts walking towards us, with that lazy gunslinger stride, a power keg dressed in snug jeans and a black t-shirt.

"Troy, you made it!" Jayne abandons the lunch we're setting and runs to greet him.

"Friends?" She kisses him on the cheek.

"Friends," he replies.

His eyes skim the long table under the oak tree and fix on me.

"Nice," he says, but he's not looking at the rustic lanterns on the table, or the mason jars filled with bright sunflowers.

He takes me in, from the red bandana holding my hair back, to the white summer dress, to the bamboo sandals on my feet.

"Hello, Shayda."

"Troy." I nod and busy myself with the table.

"Oh good!" says Jayne as a van arrives. "Ryan's here. Troy, would you mind rounding everyone up? Mum, Dad and Matt are in the kitchen with Shayda's kids."

His eyes swing my way.

Yes, Troy. Kids. I had another one after the girl.

"I can't believe you invited him!" I say as soon as he's out of earshot.

"Troy?" Jayne looks puzzled. "Why?"

"Really? The man who had the audacity to kiss you on your wedding day?"

"Oh that. Well..." She smiles. "He didn't kiss me. I kissed him."

"What?"

"Don't look so shocked, Shayda. You know I've always had a killer crush on him. He came in to congratulate me and I figured it was my last chance. Ever. So I kissed him."

"And?"

"And nothing." Jayne shrugs as she arranges the cutlery. "He gave me cold, dead lips. It was rather awkward, to say the least."

"Then why did you slap him?"

"Because!" She puts her hands on her hips. "He said, 'You want me to get the ice again, squirt?' He still thinks of me as Ryan's little sister from that summer. Squirt. Who calls the bride a squirt? Really!"

I laugh. Jayne has always managed to get exactly what she wants. Her pick of the best clothes, the best schools, her choice of men. Her exasperation is understandable.

"He let me think he forced that kiss on you when I brought it up," I say.

"You took it up with him? Are you serious?" She laughs. "Well, I'm not surprised he didn't enlighten you. He's always been chivalrous in spite of his womanizing. A gritty integrity beneath that brazen exterior. He's also very...discreet." She giggles. "In any case, he helped me get it out of my system."

The rest of the family comes out, with Zain and Natasha running towards me at full sprint.

"Mum! Troy says he can take me out on the boat! Can I go? Please? Pleaaase?"

"Me too," says Natasha. "I want to go on the boat."

"Not now. It's time for lunch," I reply, feeling a little betrayed by my own children. They just met Troy and already they want to run off with him. Is no one immune to this Troy Heathgate epidemic?

"After lunch then?" asks Zain.

"We won't have time for that. It's a long drive back."

The kids look crest-fallen.

"Why don't I pack you a basket? You can have lunch on the boat," says Jayne.

"That's not necessary," I reply.

"Nonsense. It'll be fun. Who wants to help?" Jayne heads towards the house with the kids in tow.

"Mmmm. Everything looks delicious," says Bob, holding out a chair for Elizabeth.

"No fried chicken for you," she reminds him.

Bob eyes the basket. "I hope you're not going to be like this on our cruise."

"Where are you headed?" asks Troy.

"They're hitting the Mediterranean this year," replies Ryan. "Their annual getaways get fancier every year."

"We've worked hard for it," barks Bob.

"Don't forget your annual getaway to the pharmacy before you leave."

"Rascal." Bob throws him a bread roll.

"Boys, our son-in-law is going to think we're a crazy bunch," says Elizabeth.

"He might as well find out sooner rather than later, right Matt?" Bob slaps him on the back.

I smile. Being around Bob and his family makes me forget my broken links with Maamaan, Baba and Hossein. Of course, it could be much worse. Like Hafez and Pedar.

"All set." Jayne returns with a basket full with goodies.

"Let's go!" Natasha tugs my dress.

"Why don't you come with us?" I look around the table. Someone? Anyone? Troy and Zain are already heading for the dock.

"Go!" says Jayne, giving me a little push. "Have fun."

There's no graceful way around it. I take Natasha's hand and follow Troy to the boat. He lowers the kids in, climbs inside and holds his hand out for me. I stumble as the boat sways. His arms grip my waist, steadying me. Then he lifts me up and sets me down slowly, letting me slide down the entire length of him.

"Welcome aboard." That devilish smile when my feet touch the deck. "I hope this is more to your liking than that rusty old canoe."

I think back to that night, the white orchid moon, our clothes plastered to our bodies.

Dear god. What have I let myself in for?

I busy myself with the life jackets, fussing over the kids. Zain squeals with delight as we pull out of the bay.

"Sit tight." I strap them into the cushioned seats.

"First time?" asks Troy when I join him at the helm.

I nod. They've never been on the water before. Troy, on the other hand, looks completely at home manning the boat.

Strong, tanned arms span the wheel as we turn into crystal waters, flanked by majestic forest on each side. The blue horizon melds into the endless expanse of the lake.

"Beautiful, isn't it?" He removes his glasses and tucks them into his t-shirt.

I don't know which I prefer—his naked eyes, intensified by the clear sky, or the disconcerting screen of dark shades.

Shades on, I decide, as his gaze lingers on my lips. I don't need his thoughts revealed as he recalls our kiss. The kiss he walked away from.

"Ready for some action?"

"What?"

"I was asking the kids," he replies with a twinkle in his eyes.

Zain and Natasha beam as he powers up.

"Hold on tight!" He swings the wheel from lock to lock, carving tight turns across the lake.

I look back, watching the zigzag trail of foam and the sheer joy on the kids' faces. Later, when their cheeks are flushed and their noses cold, he circles a rugged outcrop and drops anchor.

"Lunch time, mateys. Let's see what Aunty Jayne packed for us."

Gentle waves lap up to the boat as we dig into the basket.

"Ah, there's a cold beer in here," he says. "Must be for you, Zain."

Zain giggles.

"No? You want it, Shayda?"

The kids giggle even louder.

"Mum doesn't drink, silly," says Natasha.

"Natasha!" Since when does she act so familiar around strangers?

"It's okay Mum. Troy's cool," she replies.

"Yeah, Mum. I'm cool." He pulls the tab.

Instead of a smooth ssssst, there's a loud explosion as beer foams all over him.

"Fuck!"

I clear my throat loudly, hoping to drown it out.

"The Captain said the f-word," says Zain, between fits of laughter.

"Damn!" Troy waves his arms, shaking off the droplets.

"Here you go, Captain Cool." I hand him a towel, trying to suppress a smile.

"Oh yeah? You think it's funny?" He covers the can and shakes what's left inside.

"No, Troy!"

"What do you say, mateys?" There's pure mischief in his eyes.

"Get her!" they shriek.

It's not long before he corners me in the cockpit, his eyes gleaming with a wicked glint. But in the two seconds that it takes to close the distance, the childlike fun disappears. We stand there, heaving and out of breath, aware of something much bigger than the both of us. My heart thunders like the hooves of a thousand wild horses. He steps back and lowers the can.

"Your mum's lucky she's wearing white," he tells the curious audience of two. "But we can't have this go to waste. Who wants to get sprayed?" He pretends to go after them.

Somehow he makes it look like they got him with it.

"Mercy. Mercy!" He lets them wrestle him to the floor and soon the three of them are rolling around on the cushions.

"Zain, Natasha! Back in your seats. It's time we head back." For some reason, I'm choked over the fact that they're bonding with him.

"But we haven't had the brownies yet," protests Zain.

"Brownies?" says Troy. "We can't leave without dessert."

Natasha hands him a saran wrapped square from the picnic basket. He pulls his wet t-shirt off, sits back and takes a big bite, closing his eyes to savor the rich, fudgy taste.

"Are you a rock star?" asks Natasha, eyeing the tattoos and the rosary around his neck.

"A rock star? Heck no, I'm Captain Cool." He winks at her.

She melts. "You want another one?"

"I'd *love* another."

"Mum made them," says Zain.

"She did?"

With his shirt off, he's even more intimidating, like he's suddenly grown and filled my whole field of vision.

"Uh-huh. We can't give you the recipe," Natasha declares solemnly. "But we can make another batch if you want."

"Oh, I want." He looks at me as he lets his teeth sink into the last piece. "I have quite an appetite for sweet things."

My cheeks burn with a mix of exasperation and embarrassment. Flirting in front of my kids.

Not. Cool.

"And there it is," he says quietly as he notes the color rush into my face. "I think we've gone far enough today." He gets up and takes the wheel.

I wish he'd put his shirt back on. Or his sunglasses. Anything would be an improvement over the smooth expanse of bronzed muscle disappearing into his jeans. There's just too much naked. Naked shoulders, naked chest, naked back.

"Ready?" He looks back and checks on the kids.

"Aye, aye Captain!"

This time, he cuts a path straight across the lake at full throttle. The world rushes by in a blur of rainbow drops and trees and sunshine.

"Hey, Shayda?"

"What?"

He tugs on my bandana.

"No!" I say as he pulls it free, but it gets swept away, a startling red, floating free against the vivid blue sky.

The wind whips unrestrained curls around my face. I try to hold my hair down with my hands.

"Let it be." He flashes me the most brilliant smile.

Stay mad. Stay mad. Stay mad.

But I can't. Not for long. It's exhilarating, skimming over the lake, feeling the wind rush through my hair. I close my eyes and tilt my face up to the sky. My hands reach out, touching the air as it whizzes by; my tongue tastes the spray from the lake.

By the time we get to the dock, we are sun-kissed, windswept and cracking up over absolutely nothing. I squint at the lone figure on the dock. The sun is in my face, but Zain makes it out.

"Dad!" He waves.

My heart drops like I've been caught driving the wrong direction on a one-way street. I start smoothing my hair as best as I can.

"Thank you, Captain," says Natasha before Hafez helps her out.

I'm about to follow, when Troy pulls me back by the strap of the life jacket.

"Oh, sorry." I fumble for the clasp. Hafez is already helping the kids take theirs off.

"Hold still." Troy reaches around me. His fingers slide the vest off, grazing my arms.

I tell myself the goose bumps are from the lake air.

"You made it," I say, as Hafez gives me his hand.

"The line up at the border wasn't too bad today," he replies.

I feel a stab of guilt. He looks worn and tired, his face brown from wind and sun and dry, dusty roads. The stubble he left with has grown into a full beard, and his clothes smell of diesel and coffee shops. He has none of Troy's polished veneer, his attraction built on the craggy isolation that surrounds him, the kind that makes you want to dig beyond the dark brown depths of his eyes.

"Hey, Troy!" Bob and Elizabeth walk down the pier. "You think you could take a couple of seniors out for a trip?"

"Hop on," replies Troy.

"Shayda, make sure you feed Hafez," says Elizabeth. "He rushed straight here to find you."

She pauses, looking from Troy to Hafez. "Have you two met?"

I hold my breath as she makes the introductions. *Troy, meet Hafez, Shayda's husband. Her anchor, her rock, her safe harbor. Hafez, meet Troy, the current that sweeps her so far ashore, she forgets which way is home.* They shake hands—the solid, down-to-earth man and the restless, unpredictable lightning in the sky. I feel like a tree exposed to the elements, my roots clinging to the soil, my branches flirting with heaven.

"Nice to meet you," says Hafez.

"Likewise," replies Troy.

"Oh Shayda, I almost forgot," says Bob before he gets on the boat. "I told Troy that you'll look after him while I'm away. Show him a few places, will you?"

A dart of terror shoots through me, but I nod.

"Thanks." He waves as the boat pulls out.

"What's that, Dad?" Natasha and Zain clamor around Hafez.

"Something for Mum." Hafez hands me a white gift box.

"Open it!" says Zain.

I rummage through the foam noodles and uncover a bubble wrapped package. Inside is a family of four porcelain figurines, joined at the base. The matte ivory finish captures stylized silhouettes of a mother, father, daughter and son.

"It's beautiful," says Natasha, admiring the details.

But it's more. So much more than she could ever understand.

I turn away from the sight of Troy, as he sets course for the shimmering mirage of the horizon, and squeeze Hafez's hand. His gift is a reminder of another time, a time before Natasha and Zain, before porcelain shards mingled with blood and left pin prick splinters in our hearts.

5. BOARDWALK

....

PAST

July 10th, 1982

WHAT I REMEMBER MOST ABOUT MEETING HAFEZ IS HIS smile. Not the one he greeted me with, but the one I caught later, when he thought I wasn't looking. It was two months after I had arrived in Toronto. I suspect *Khaleh* Zarrin had planned it even before my flight touched down. She was Maamaan's younger sister, and a notorious matchmaker.

"But I don't know anything about him!" I said when she told me she had invited Hafez and his family over for dinner.

"Think of it as a starting point," she replied. "If you don't like him, you never have to see him again."

I left the house early that morning. I needed a sign, an omen, a crystal ball into the future. It was clear enough— you could see for miles into the blue sky. I sat on the grass by the boardwalk and watched the world pass by. The whirring of bicycle wheels, oiled bodies playing beach volleyball, melting ice cream cones, babies in strollers.

What a beautiful, wondrous country.

A golden retriever came up and licked my face.

"Hey, you." I laughed as he slobbered all over me.

Then I heard it. The joyful burst of laughter. It was a young couple on neon roller skates, their faces hidden under shiny helmets. She was obviously a learner, but it only added to their sense of adventure. He held her gently, but firmly as she pushed off one foot and then the other, confident he wouldn't let go.

He pulled a camera out of his backpack, looking for someone to take their photo. I started getting up, but an elderly gentleman intercepted. The roller skating duo removed their helmets and leaned in. I saw the backs of their heads as they held still for the camera. Suddenly, the guy scooped the girl off her feet. She squealed and threw her arms around him, half delighted, half terrified. I hoped that was the moment the camera captured. They thanked the man for taking their picture and took off, hand in hand.

That's what I wanted. Him. Them. Someone I could walk with, and laugh with, and hold hands with the rest of my life. I had my sign. I smiled and got up.

MAAMAAN HAD CALLED WHILE I WAS AWAY, AND *KHALEH* Zarrin was happy to regale Hafez's parents with the latest gossip from home. Kamal Hijazi looked disinterested. He was a small man who picked at the motor grease under his nails and spoke only when he had to. His wife, Nasrin, had a round face and a thick neck. She breathed heavily as she regarded me over her cup.

Hafez sat across from me. His face was reserved and so perfectly symmetrical that I found myself staring. He reminded me of the imported bars of chocolate that sat behind locked shelves in Tehran, the kind that Baba would get for Hossein and me if we'd been very, very good. His hair was the color of cacao beans, roasted and husked, and he wore it slicked back from his face, leaving his eyes in stark focus. They were sweet and intoxicating, but with a bitter aftertaste, like two round drops of dark liqueur. He knew he was being paraded and cool resentment rolled off his caramel skin like the layers of shiny packaging we ripped off our chocolate bars when we finally got our hands on them. When I caught him checking his watch for the third time though, he looked suitably contrite. I shrugged. It wasn't exactly a picnic for me either. After that he stole small sips of glances. When *Khaleh* Zarrin's neighbour stopped by, he said hello, but his eyes came right back to me, as if he hadn't noticed her starlet red lips or juicy cleavage. At dinner, we sat side by side, painfully aware of being scrutinized—him by my aunt, me by his mother, us as a couple.

"Why don't we let the kids clear up?" said *Khaleh* Zarrin after we were done.

"This is so awkward," I mumbled when we were alone.

"Your first time?"

I nodded.

"My third," he said. "It gets easier."

Our fingers touched as we reached for the same bowl. We jumped back simultaneously. I liked his laugh and the way he looked when he let his guard down. It was as if a little boy had been frozen under lock and key, and he was finally free to come out and fly kites and build sand castles. I was so taken with the transformation that I didn't notice the rice dish by my side, and elbowed it right off the table. It shattered on the floor with a loud crash.

"Shayda? What was that?" *Khaleh* Zarrin asked from the living room.

It was one of her favorite dishes, part of a set she had shipped from Iran. I stared at the pieces, horrified.

"Sorry," replied Hafez, after a tense silence. "I broke one of your dishes."

There was a pause.

"It's okay, dear," said *Khaleh* Zarrin. "I guess Shayda will just have to keep you out of the kitchen."

We heard laughter from the living room.

'Thank you,' I mouthed.

The teasing went on. I turned a bright shade of red as Hafez helped me clean up the mess.

When he proposed two weeks after, I said yes. It wasn't until much later that he told me he'd never intended to get married. We both had our reasons—mine was my family, waiting in the wings for a new life, and his were the ghosts he was trying to keep at bay.

August 3rd, 1982

A WEEK AFTER WE SET THE DATE, *KHALEH* ZARRIN TOOK ME to see Dr. Gorman. He gave me three discs.

"These are samples. Use one pill every day for twenty eight days. When one pak finishes, start the next. Understand?"

I nodded. "Do I insert them in the morning or at night?"

Dr. Gorman looked at me as if I had just landed from another planet.

"My dear." He smiled. "You don't insert anything. These are to be taken orally. Swallowed, like this..." He opened his mouth and pretended to drink a glass of water.

I turned scarlet. How naïve of me to assume that everything to do with babies had to do with down there.

"Here's a prescription. Get it filled before you run out."

"Thank you."

I found *Khaleh* Zarrin waiting for me outside. She gave me a sly wink and slapped my bum.

"Now buy me some mint tea and I will tell you how to drive your *jaan* wild."

How different she was from Maamaan.

October 9th, 1982

MY FIRST NIGHT WITH HAFEZ, I DIDN'T USE ANY OF THE advice *Khaleh* Zarrin had given me.

I had moved into his parents' place, a crowded one bedroom apartment. Hafez usually slept on a mattress, but they had bought a pull-out couch for the living room, and made a great fuss presenting it as our wedding gift.

"We won't be disturbed," said Hafez.

"Can we..." I fumbled. "Can we wait until tomorrow?"

I was exhausted. It had been a long day. *Khaleh* Zarrin had been the only familiar face. I felt like I was being swallowed in a sea of strangers.

"Of course." He looked almost relieved. "Good night."

"Good night," I replied.

I wished he would put his arm around me, but he slept facing the other way. I missed my cozy pajamas. It felt strange lying on the lumpy couch in the silk nightgown that Maamaan had sent. I held my hand out in front of me and surveyed the gold band around my ring finger. My skin glowed orange from the street lights.

I'm a Mrs., I thought.

October 10th, 1982

HAFEZ WOKE ME AROUND DAWN.

"I have to leave." He was already dressed for work. "I'll call you. Around noon?"

I nodded self-consciously. It was the first time he had seen my morning face.

"Just one thing..."

I thought he was going to kiss me, but he held up a box cutter and sliced his finger.

"What—?"

"Shhh." He squeezed until a stream of liquid red pooled to the surface. "It's not deep. Make sure Ma sees this, okay?" He rubbed the blood on the sheet. "I'll see you in the evening."

I reached for him, this man who had cut himself to prove my honor, no questions asked. I took his bleeding finger into my mouth and sucked it.

He drew a sharp breath. "That's not...necessary." But he let it stay, regarding me with soft, thoughtful eyes.

"We don't have all day," Kamal Hijazi snapped from the door.

Hafez flinched. It was an odd relationship. Father and son barely spoke to each other, but they went to work together every day.

Ma woke up a few hours later. She told me to call her 'Ma' and Hafez's father 'Pedar', just like he did.

"We your parents now," she said.

I debated about making her breakfast, but didn't know what she liked or where to find it, so I pretended I was still sleeping.

"Today, I will show you," she said. "After, you make the breakfast every day for us."

She insisted on speaking English with me.

"It good for my learn," she explained over lavash with feta cheese and fig preserves.

I washed the dishes as she made up the couch. After a while, she came and kissed me on both cheeks.

"Good girl. We must do laundry." She laughed and held up the blood stained bed sheet.

By noon, we were ready to receive Hafez's cousins and aunts. They were immaculately dressed in shoulder-padded blouses, with big hair and bright lipstick.

"Nasrin!" They hugged Ma.

The younger ones pulled me aside. "So?" They teased. "How was it? Your first night?"

"I'll go get the tea." I excused myself.

"She's shy!" They laughed.

I poured sweet tea in glass teacups and served it with a tray of cookies.

"We know Hafez and Kamal have to work, but it's Thanksgiving weekend and we were hoping you'd join us for lunch." The aunts informed me.

I glanced at Ma. Lunch meant money, and I had none.

"Farnaz and Behram own a restaurant. You must go," she said.

"What about you?" I asked.

"*Khaleh* Nasrin doesn't like to go out," said Farnaz, one of Hafez's cousins. "The doctors say it's her heart."

"I don't like go out because I don't want put feet in shoes," said Ma, pointing to her swollen ankles. "You go."

WE SQUEEZED INTO FARNAZ'S CAR AFTER SAYING GOODBYE to Ma. Farnaz insisted that I sit in front with her.

She slid me a sly glance. "I can't imagine getting much privacy in that place. When are you off for your honeymoon?"

"We haven't planned anything. Pedar says the shop is too busy."

"It will always be too busy. Hafez is his best mechanic. You don't think he's just going to let him go, do you? You'll have to fight for him, my dear."

She pulled into a parking lot behind a Greek restaurant. "You've met my husband, Behram." She waved to him as she led us to a table.

"*Salaam*." He greeted us, looking a little flustered. "*Jaan*," he said to his wife, "I could really use your help. We're short staffed."

"What happened to the girl we hired?" asked Farnaz. "She was supposed to start today."

"She never showed."

Farnaz rolled her eyes and disappeared into the kitchen. She returned with plates full of souvlaki sticks, pita bread and salad.

"Eat up, ladies. I'll be in the kitchen if you need anything."

"You need help?" I asked.

"Sit down," hissed one of the girls. "You're making the rest of us look bad."

"Oh." I took my seat and lowered my head.

Uncomfortable seconds ticked by. When I looked up, they were all rolled over, trying to keep themselves from laughing.

"Welcome to the family," said the one on my left, ribbing me with her elbow. "We're the not-so-serious side."

"Let the poor girl eat," said Farnaz's mum. She filled my glass with water. "I thought I would see Mona at the wedding. How is she?"

"Maamaan is fine. They couldn't get their papers on time."

"Tell her Farideh sends her regards. I visited your summer home many times when I was there."

"You did?"

"Yes. And what a grand place it was. Your mother threw the most lavish garden parties. And you father..." She laughed. "A handsome devil with a silver tongue. You must have been very young. I don't recall seeing you or your brother."

"We used to fill our plates and sneak off to the lemon groves," I replied. It had been my favorite place in the whole world.

"I was sorry to hear about what happened," said Farideh. I nodded and picked at my food, trying not to think about the smell of burning lemon trees.

WHEN I GOT BACK, MA WAS DUSTING THE GLASS CABINET that stood gleaming like an exclamation point in the drab apartment. Hafez had told me that it was her pride and joy.

"They're beautiful," I said, peering into the collection of porcelain figurines on the shelves.

"You like?" Ma beamed. "Many years it take."

There were different shapes and sizes, some hand painted with gold accents, others the kind you'd find at a garage sale, but each was grouped into a family—mother, father, a kid, maybe three or four, a pet, sometimes a house.

"This us." She handed me a set of three, painted in soft colors. "I get when I have baby. Me, Kamal and little boy Hafez."

"Very nice," I said. "Now you need to fit me in there."

"No." She returned her miniature family to the top tier. "This mine. You need make own." Ma laughed and patted my belly.

At the time, thinking about having kids with Hafez had filled me with both apprehension and anticipation. A family of my own was something I had always turned to in the corners of my mind, whenever I was trying to muffle the shrill arguments coming from Maamaan and Baba's room.

Looking back now, I was grateful that Hafez and I never had those, that Natasha and Zain were never witness to their parents fighting. No. We were a different kind of broken. The quiet, silent kind that gets swept under the bed or stuffed in the linen closet. And we had become good, really, really good, at leaving those spaces undisturbed.

6. ALMOST THERE

August 4th, 1995

"Perfect," says Troy. "I'll take it."

"But you haven't seen the rest of it." I'm standing before the wide glass doors, ready to lead him to the private rooftop pool.

"No need." He stops behind me and catches my eyes in the reflection. "I like it." His voice drops. "A lot."

My breath fogs up the pane. A lifetime ago, I had turned to him as we stood like this.

I think perhaps that had been the beginning.

"Why are you doing this?" I ask.

He picks up a curl and plays with it. "I'm dying to kiss you."

But he doesn't kiss me. I lie outside the circle of free, single girls. He wants me, but he wants me to open that door, fully empowered, fully aware.

Let me in.

I turn away. "Should I draw up an offer?"

"Please." But he says it in his bedroom voice.

I picture him under me, waiting for the brush of my lips, my fingers, my tongue.

Please.

My hands are unsteady as I pick up the papers and skim over them. This is the sixth property we've seen since Bob left for his cruise.

'*Carved from a century-old warehouse, with twenty foot exposed wood beam ceilings, sandblasted brick walls, motorized window coverings, heated floors and an elevator to a private garage, this two bedroom penthouse loft, with a custom built gym and library, is one of the largest and most spectacular units in the city.*'

I remember reading the listing and thinking it would be perfect. And maybe, just maybe, I'd be free of Troy. Every hour we spend together intensifies my awareness of him. The scent of his skin, the shape of his nails, the subtle inflections in his voice—the savvy businessman, the charming bad boy, the sensual lover. Watching him eat, talk, smile, tease, it's easy to see why women come undone around him. That insatiable appetite for life, the intrinsic confidence, the dark, dangerous allure wrapped in layers of genuine playfulness.

"Okay then." I start turning the lights off.

This is it. We've found him a place. I'm almost there, still intact.

We take the private elevator down. Small spaces are the worse. Cars, laundry rooms, guest bathrooms, walk-in closets. I've been in them all with him, showing him this, inspecting that. Soon, I'll be able to breathe freely.

"I leave for New York in three days. If we could have this wrapped up by then, it would be great," he says when the doors open.

"The closing isn't for another two months. That's if they accept our offer."

"They'll accept. I want it. Whatever it takes." He walks me to my car before saying goodbye.

I get in and shut the door, massaging my temples. The stress of holding it together when I'm around him drains me. I jump at the knock on my window. He's circled back. Now what?

"I just realized that I'm officially living in the city," he says. "I think that calls for a celebration."

"I can't, Troy."

"Can't?" He looks at me for a moment. "I like 'can't'. Much better than 'won't.'"

"Can't, won't. What difference does it make?"

He straightens, but his smile is oddly unsettling. "See you when I get back, Shayda."

7. BEETROOT BUTTERFLY

....

September 29th, 1995

"BYE, SHAYDA. HAVE A GREAT WEEKEND."

"You too." I wave back at Susan, set the code for the alarm and lock the door behind me.

A dark sedan pulls up beside me. The driver unrolls the passenger side window.

"Shayda."

I peer into the car. "Troy? What are you doing here?"

"Get in." He unlocks the door.

"I'm on my way home."

"This won't take long."

"Is there a problem?" I ask. The closing on his loft went through without a hitch.

"No." He dangles the keys in front of me. "Just picked them up from the lawyer. Now will you get in before Hulk Hogan back there decides to have a go at me?"

I glance at the driver of the car waiting behind him. The thought of Troy's impeccably fit six foot frame being tossed around like a Saturday morning cartoon is a bit far-fetched, but amusing.

"Why do I get the feeling that you'd enjoy seeing me get roughed up?" he says.

"What do you want?" I ask, getting in.

"I have something for you," he replies, indicating the back seat.

I see a round mesh box, wrapped with a satin ribbon.

"What is it?"

"Something that needs our immediate attention." He pulls out of the parking lot and takes the highway.

"Where are we going?" I ask.

"Would you quit with the twenty questions and just relax?"

I sit back and look out the window as the fall foliage whizzes by in spectacular streaks of red and yellow. It's easier than dwelling on how good he looks in a leather jacket. He takes the exit a few minutes later and turns into a quiet park.

"Come." He grabs the box and walks me to edge of a big pond that mirrors the blazing colors of the trees around us. We follow a path up the hill, where a slight clearing gives way to a breathtaking view of the ravine.

"Wow." I take in the meandering silver of the Don River as it cuts through the valley, flanked by golden oaks and maples and birch. "It's like we're not even in the city. How did you find this place?"

"I come here for my daily run," he replies. "Here." He hands me the box. "A little something for you. Make a wish before you open it."

"What?"

"Close your eyes, make a wish and then open the box."

"This is silly," I reply.

"Do it."

I take a deep breath and close my eyes. Then I untie the ribbon and peek inside.

A brilliant flash of red flutters inside.

"Oh my god!" I snap the lid shut. "Is that...is that a butterfly?"

He smiles at my obvious delight.

"What am I supposed to do with it?"

"You're supposed to release it."

I peek into the box again. "It's a Monarch! I've never seen one this color before. Where did you find it?"

"I happened to be frolicking through a field of wildflowers and there it was. And wouldn't you know it? I just happened to have my handy butterfly net."

"Troy."

"I made a few phone calls." He fesses up.

"But why?"

"Remember that first time we met? By the sidewalk outside Bob's house?"

"Yes?"

"I lied. There was no butterfly. I made it up."

"Why would you do something like that?"

"Because you were about to bolt and I wanted you to stay."

My heart stops, and then slams hard and fast against my chest, my thoughts racing back to that sunny morning in June.

IT WAS A LONG WALK FROM THE BUS STOP TO BOB'S HOUSE. My hands were heavy with the contracts he needed for the day. I heard someone running behind me. Two girls, walking in the opposite direction, all long legs and bouncy hair, passed me by. They smiled. I smiled back, but quickly realized they were smiling at whoever was behind me.

"Morning, girls." The tone was bold, appreciative and wickedly playful.

The girls giggled and walked on. The footsteps behind me slowed, then started up again.

The next instant, I felt myself being knocked off my feet. I landed on my knees, papers flying everywhere.

"Whoa! Are you all right? I didn't see you there."

Of course not. Why would he? He was too busy checking out the girls over his shoulder, enjoying the rear view.

He chased down my papers before kneeling next to me. Dusty sneakers, grey sweatpants, a 'University of Waterloo' sweatshirt, and then—the most startling pair of blue eyes. They reminded me of the cut outs I had saved in my wish book, of the places I wanted to visit. Blue like the water that surrounds the islands in the South Pacific. I felt like I had been picked off the pavement and plopped smack dab in the middle of it. I floated there for a while, suspended in its endless horizons as it held me for long, still seconds.

The chut-chut-chut-chut of an automatic sprinkler transported me back to the suburban street. I blinked and started getting up.

"Shhh. Don't move," he said. "Not a muscle."

"Huh?" I had the most peculiar urge to flee. My cheeks were already burning like I had run a long way.

"Don't move. There's a butterfly. On your shoulder."

I froze. I don't know why. I couldn't even see it.

"What color?" I asked.

"Red."

"Red?" I felt that molten blue stare on me again.

"It's the most beautiful thing I've seen," he said.

I dared not breathe.

"You know," he continued, "there's a Native American legend which says that if you want a wish to come true, you must capture a butterfly and whisper your wish to it. Since it makes no sound, it won't tell the wish to anyone but the Great Spirit. By making the wish and releasing the butterfly, your wish will be taken to the heavens and be granted."

"Are you...are you going to try and catch it?"

"Only if it wants to be caught."

I squeezed the bundle of papers in my hand to stop them from shaking. His gaze dropped to my lap, breaking that electric contact. When he looked up, his eyes were different.

"It's gone."

"What?"

"The butterfly."

I nodded, letting my breath out.

"Are you all right? You're not hurt, are you?" he asked.

"No." But every second he looked at me, he zapped through another layer of my safe, calm cocoon.

"I'd say I'm sorry for running into you, but I'm not really." He smiled as he handed me the rest of the papers.

It wasn't fair. Having a smile like that.

I looked away, my eyes focusing on the silver cross that hung from a rosary around his neck.

"Need some help?" He held out his hand.

"I'm fine."

He paused for a beat, then he turned and took off, the steady thump of his footsteps fading into the summer morning.

I looked at my watch. 9:05 a.m. I was late. And all the forms were out of order. And my heart was beating like I'd jumped over a thousand hurdles. I rounded the corner to Bob's house and rang the doorbell.

A second later, I was staring at the blue eyed stranger through the criss-cross mesh of the screen door.

Of course. Bob's son. Home for the summer. How could that have slipped my mind?

"Ryan?" I asked, turning red as he appraised me from head to toe.

"I'm Ryan." A head popped up beside him. "He's Troy. Who are you?"

"Coming through, coming through." Bob's familiar voice. "Oh hey, Shayda." He stepped out and held the door open for me. "Boys, this is my assistant. Be nice." He gave them a stern look. "I've left some notes for you, Shayda, but I'll be back in a couple of hours."

"Okay." I put my head down, parted my way through two hard, muscular bodies and marched into the office.

"Holy crap. My dad's assistant? She's smokin'!" said Ryan.

"Lay off, man. She's married." I heard Troy reply.

I dropped the papers on the desk. My wedding band. He'd noticed. And run. Literally. I smiled in spite of myself.

"Oh my god. Oh my god. Oh my god!" Jayne came into the room and shut the door. "Did you see Ryan's friend?"

"I did." I laughed.

It was way before noon, but Jayne was up. Her hair was combed and she had on a dab of mascara.

"So he was washing his car yesterday. No. Shirt. Eeeeee!" she squealed. Then she opened the door a crack and peeked out. "He's so cute!"

"Hey, Jayne?" I asked. "Have you ever seen a red butterfly?"

"A red butterfly?" She turned around. "Does that even exist?"

"Sure does." Troy poked his head into the study. "I saw one just this morning."

"Yeah, right," replied Jayne. "What's it called then?"

"A Beetroot Butterfly."

I STARE AT THE RED MONARCH BEFORE ME NOW.

"You made it up? There's no such thing as a Beetroot Butterfly?" I ask over the sound of blood rushing in my ears.

"Oh, but there is." He catches the color wash over my face. "And I'm looking at her right now."

The seconds stretch out indefinitely, leaving me suspended, floating mid-air, weightless, breathless.

That's when the butterfly decides to come out. It perches on the edge of the box, wings folded flat, with white spots that stare at us like fake eyes. The majestic valley calls, but the butterfly clings to its mesh cage.

"Fly, dammit, fly!" says Troy.

The Monarch spreads its wings, taking in the warmth of the sun before touching them together and flying away. It rises before us, a fragile wisp of crimson against the vast valley.

"I wonder if she'll make it," I say.

Every year, Monarch butterflies migrate south by the millions, a round-trip journey of many thousands of kilometres.

"No one butterfly completes the whole trip," he replies. "It takes four or five generations."

"That's sad," I say. "And beautiful. If she stays, she dies. If she goes, she dies."

We watch it glide lower, and lower still, until it disappears into the backdrop of autumn leaves.

"We all die, Shayda." He turns and looks at me. "It's about how we choose to get there."

"Is that what this is about?" I ask. "You want me to choose?"

He pulls the edges of my coat together as the sun begins to set and a coolness settles in the air. "It's not about what I want. Or what anyone else wants. What do *you* want, Shayda?"

"Don't," I say, feeling tiny headed flowers of hope push through long-forgotten graves. "Can't you see what you're doing?"

"When it comes to you, I'm blind, Shayda." He lifts my chin. "I just see you. Not a mother or a wife or a co-worker or whatever. Just you, Shayda."

With the setting sun in his face, Troy's eyes look like the tops of two blue umbrellas with dark pin point centres and spokes of gold. The glints in his hair soften his features, making him seem infinitely more vulnerable.

"You just see what you can't have," I reply.

"Maybe. Or maybe I've carried you with me for so long, there's no room for anyone else."

I suck in my breath. "You've made me out to be something I'm not. It's all in your head."

"That theory went out the window the moment we kissed. And you know it too."

"It's just physical attraction, Troy. Nothing more."

"Fine." He lets out a ragged sigh. "Then let's have a wild and crazy affair. Get it out of our system. Anything would be better than this. This half-living. This damned yearning." His thumb traces the curve of my lips. "I can't stop thinking about you—your touch, your taste, your smell."

I close my eyes as he runs his finger down my neck.

How do you deny a living, breathing feeling? How do you hack it and kill it and bury it so that it never surfaces again?

"Stay away from me." I wrench myself away from him. "I don't want anything to do with you, Troy."

8. NOT LIKE THIS

....

October 9th, 1995

"Happy Thanksgiving, Shayda." Jayne hugs me at the door. "And Happy Anniversary!"

"Thanks. Happy Thanksgiving to you too."

Hafez, Natasha and Zain follow me inside. I take the brownies to the kitchen.

"Smells wonderful, Elizabeth. Thank you for having us over."

"Oh good! You brought my favorite." She beams.

"Shayda, Hafez." Bob calls us into the living room. "Good timing. Troy was just about to leave."

I freeze.

Troy?

"Come look at these plans." Bob unrolls a large sheet of paper on the dining table. "I was just showing Troy some commercial properties for his new office."

"I really have to get going, Bob." Troy puts his glass down. "Nice to see you again, Hafez. You too, Shayda."

I get why he's leaving, and it twists my gut.

I don't want anything to do with you, Troy.

In a white-button down shirt, navy sweater and tweed jacket, he's a far cry from the laid back t-shirt-and-jeans Troy I've come to know, but just as devastating. Even more so with the cool distance in his eyes.

"Come on, Rachel," he says.

I notice her for the first time, a leggy blond lounging on the sofa, in a chic black turtleneck and pants.

"Are you sure you can't stay?" asks Elizabeth.

"We're spending Thanksgiving with Rachel's parents."

Okay. So maybe I was wrong about why he's leaving. It has more to do with Rachel. Less to do with Shayda. And that would also explain the more conservative outfit. It's 'meet the parents' night. The knife in my gut twists deeper.

"Troy!" Natasha and Zain zero in on him.

"Hello, mateys!" He picks up Zain and refrains from ruffling Natasha's hair, which earns him bonus points.

"Captain." Zain gives him a smart salute.

"You're not leaving, are you?" Natasha follows him to the door.

"Afraid so, princess." He puts Zain down and helps Rachel with her coat.

"Wait." Natasha rushes into the kitchen and comes back out with something wrapped in a paper towel. "We made brownies."

"And you remembered?"

"Uh-huh. You like them."

"Thank you, sweetheart." He kneels and takes them from her.

"I'll follow up on the downtown unit," says Bob.

"That would be great. Talk to you soon." I hear before the door shuts.

Elizabeth peeks out from the window "Wow. Thanksgiving with the parents. Is it serious?"

"Stop spying, Liz."

"I'm not spying." She lets the curtain fall. "I just hope that boy finds someone nice."

"I think he rather enjoys playing the bachelor," says Jayne. "He moved back, what—three, four months ago? And his social life is already off the charts. He's made it into more gossip columns than I have in as many years."

"Lots of buzz in the business section too," adds Matt.

"Are we going to sit around talking about Troy all night or are we going to get some dinner?" Bob starts putting the papers away. "You know," he says to me, "he's thrilled with the loft. I'm surprised he didn't come to you with this."

"He was your client to begin with," I say.

Bob smiles and pats me on the shoulder. "You've got a great gal here, Hafez."

Hafez lights up. I don't get to see that face too often, but every time I do, it aches like an old wound on a rainy day.

THAT NIGHT, I PULL OUT A LACE BABY-DOLL FROM THE back of my closet. It feels daring and sexy. The bright pink complements my skin and brown eyes. I spritz on some perfume and step out of the bathroom, feeling a little self-conscious.

The lights are off and Hafez is already in bed. I slip between the covers and snuggle up to him.

"I'm so glad you made it home for our anniversary."

"Me too," he replies.

"I've missed you." I nuzzle closer and let my hand slide lower.

"Hmmm. You *have* missed me." He turns to look at me with soft wonder. "How did I get so lucky?"

I can't remember the last time we had sex. Months have turned into years, and the years have melded into a hazy point beyond recall. But tonight I want to burn for him. I want to drive away thoughts of anyone else but him. I want it here, where it belongs, where it's good and right and pure.

He slides my panties off and turns me on my tummy.

"No, not like this," I say. "I don't want it like this any more, Hafez."

A pained expression crosses his face.

I've asked for too much. I know. But I need this. I really, really need this.

And so he takes me, face to face, but he hides his eyes in my neck.

Look at me. Please. Look at me, I want to say.

When it's over, he slides off me and curls up on his side.

I put my arms around him, wanting to absorb his pain, trying to hide my own. "Maybe it's time we see someone."

"You mean like a therapist?"

"It might help."

"You've never mentioned it before."

I prop myself up and look at him. "It's not just about this. You've never talked to anyone about what happened."

"There's nothing to talk about. It's behind us now."

"But it's still in here." I put my hand on his heart. "Don't you think it's time you dealt with it?"

"What do you want me to do, Shayda? Do you want me to sit on a couch and tell some stranger that I can't make love to my wife because every time I look at her, I see that monster?"

I let his words sink in.

That's not what I want. What I really want is something else, *someone* else, and in my bid to run away from that, I'm putting my husband through hell.

"No," I reply, suddenly exhausted. "Let's go to sleep, Hafez. You're here, I'm here, the kids are fast asleep in their rooms. That's all that matters."

We cling to each other, two souls from broken homes, determined to keep it together, to never let the claws of the past rip our family apart.

9. POSEIDON

December 27th, 1982

PASHA MORADI. I REMEMBER THE EXACT MOMENT I HEARD the name. My whole world was about to tip over and I stood, warm and clueless, in a beautiful crimson coat that Hafez had just bought for me.

It was a season of firsts. First winter, first Canadian christmas; the first time Hafez and I had three whole days to spend together.

We bought two slices of scalding hot pizza and stopped by a playground behind the apartment. Hafez brushed the dusting of fresh snow off the bench and smiled as I lined it with a napkin before sitting down in my new coat.

"You like it?" he asked.

It was more than he could afford. I was worried what Ma would say when we got home.

"It's lovely."

It felt a bit ridiculous, being tongue-tied around the man I'd been married to for over two months. But today, as he picked the red onions he knew I didn't like, off my slice, I felt a curious warmth flood my heart. With that simple act, Hafez pushed aside all the doubts and anxiousness I had about us.

I bit into the doughy crust, the taste of melted cheese and tomatoes more delicious than anything I could remember. He did care. He cared for me. It was there in his eyes, a slight lifting of the gates, just enough space to let me crawl through to carefully guarded grounds. I wanted to sit there forever and watch the twinkling lights on the balconies.

"Do you roller skate?" I asked.

"Roller skate?" He looked amused. "No. Do you?"

"No." I laughed. "I was just thinking about this couple I saw on the boardwalk, the day we met. They looked so happy."

He took my gloved hand and held it quietly. "Shayda, I know we haven't...I haven't..."

The words wouldn't come so he took a deep breath and tried again. "I know there are things you may not understand, but I *do* want us to be that couple. When I look at you, I see things I never dared imagine before. I want to give you everything that's good in me, Shayda. I promise I'll do whatever it takes to make you happy."

My heart swelled. I felt like a big, red balloon, about to float away.

We walked hand in hand past the dumpsters behind the building. The warm blast of scented dryer sheets from the laundry room greeted us as we took the elevator. Hafez pulled me close and nuzzled my neck. I liked the feel of his stubble on my skin.

When we got to the apartment, Ma was so excited, she didn't notice my new coat.

"Pasha Moradi, he call. He got papers. He move to Toronto! Stay here until he find place."

"When?" asked Hafez. "When is he coming?"

"In two weeks," said Pedar, smiling from ear to ear.

It was the first time I had seen anything but bored indifference on Kamal Hijazi's face.

"Who is Pasha Moradi?" I asked, not noticing that Hafez had slowly let go of my hand.

January 8th, 1983

PREPARING FOR PASHA MORADI WAS LIKE UNLEASHING A whirlwind into the tiny apartment. We bought steak and chicken and whole snapper and lamb. Every night would be a feast. Pedar spent hours installing new parquet flooring and Ma polished her glass cabinet until it danced with rainbows in the light. I mopped and vacuumed, and buffed the faucets, and tooth-brushed the bathroom grout with bleach.

One evening, Hafez drove us to Honest Ed's to buy new bedding. He stood by, detached and distant, as we sorted through the sets.

"What do you think?" I held up the ones we were considering.

"Get whatever the hell you want." It was the first time he had been short with me.

MA CROCHETED A BEDSPREAD IN ZIGZAG COLORS. PASHA Moradi would have their room. Hafez and I would use the mattress, and Ma and Pedar would sleep on the couch.

"He very powerful man. No wife, no family. If we good to him, he change life for us," said Ma.

Money. So that's what it was about, I thought, trying to decipher the looks of resentment Hafez threw his parents as they gushed over the man on the phone.

Yes, yes, yes, we are coming to pick you up.
What would you like to eat on the first day?
Of course, we will go to Niagara Falls!

"Call your parents," Hafez said to me, after they got off the phone one night.

"It expensive." Ma was not pleased. Pedar rolled his cigarette between stained fingers.

"I don't see why she can't talk to her family when you spend hours of long-distance with him."

"It's all right," I whispered to Hafez.

"Call them." He handed me the phone.

That night, the night before Pasha Moradi's arrival, Hafez turned to me. He had been withdrawn since our day out, like a curtain that closes before the show even begins.

"This will be our last night alone for a while," he said.

We were never really alone, but the living room was our space at night. My heart lurched as I felt his arms around my waist.

My husband is going to make love to me, I thought.

But his eyes were far away as he stroked my hair.

"If it weren't for Ma, I would have left a long time ago," he said. "I thought we would be free once we moved here." His chest trembled as he spoke, but with anger or anguish, I couldn't tell. "Stay away from Pasha Moradi. Do you understand, Shayda?"

I didn't. But I nodded because of the intensity in his words. A worm of fear crawled over my flesh and left tight little goose bumps on my skin.

Hold me, Hafez, I wanted to say.

But he turned away, wrestling his own demons in some dark corner of his backstage.

February 25th, 1983

A GREY WIND SLAMMED GRITTY SNOW AGAINST THE windows. February was furious, pounding the glass panes until they shook in their frames. I lay on the mattress, clinging to the warm indent that Hafez had just left. It was barely dawn, but he was out the door. He had been doing that a lot lately. Last one in, first one out. I listened to Pedar snoring on the couch, thankful for the long, heavy snorts that kept me up most nights, because it meant that I wouldn't have to wake Pasha Moradi up today.

I hated going into his room after Hafez and Pedar left for work. It smelled of him, like overripe fruit fermenting in whisky. He was the complete opposite of Pedar—big and boisterous, with pink cheeks and fat lips that he smacked loudly whenever he ate. He sucked on his fat sausage fingers when he was done, coating them with saliva instead of getting up to wash his hands. It didn't matter whether we were at home or treating him to dinner at a restaurant we couldn't afford. Pasha Moradi didn't give a damn what the world thought of him. I think he deliberately let his penis protrude from his pajamas, under that round, hairy belly, while he lay in bed, waiting for me to wake him up. But that was something I kept to myself. Ma and Pedar worshiped the ground he walked on. Pasha Moradi could do no wrong.

"Of all the places, you had to move to this god forsaken piece of frozen land." He cursed as he stuffed his fingers into Pedar's gloves.

Pedar laughed and buried his cold, bare hands in his pockets.

"You taste like yesterday's lamb." Pasha Moradi smacked Ma's bottom and kissed her on the lips.

Pedar laughed and refilled his drink.

"Really, Kamal. My driver's shack is bigger than this hell hole. I can't spend another night here. Dirty elevators, cockroaches, stinking hallways. Find me a real place."

Pedar laughed and called a realtor.

I LIKED BOB WORTHING AND WHAT HE DID. HE WAS AROUND Baba's age, and his job was to match people with their dreams, to fill empty spaces with families that belonged. I gawked at the beautiful homes he showed us. A stately brick manor snuggled amid towering trees; a gated estate with soaring ceilings; a cozy bungalow with walnut floors and a stone fireplace.

Stepping into Bob Worthing's van was like taking a trip to a world I had left behind, when everything safe was contained within sturdy walls and the air was fragrant with citrus blossoms. After every outing with Bob, I played with the tail end of possibility, the chance that Hafez and I could build our own nest, and there, perhaps, I'd find the part of me that had fallen out the day Maamaan, Hossein and I ran up the hills.

"You take the front, Kamal." Pasha Moradi insisted that day, as we got into the van. "I hate making small talk with these people." He added the last bit in Persian, 'these people', meaning Bob.

He slid into the back seat next to me. I inched closer to Ma, trying to get away from the feel of his pudgy thighs pressing into mine. Ma smelled like rose water and garlic, more so when Bob cranked up the heat.

"How old are you, Shayda?"

I felt Pasha Moradi's sweaty stare on me.

"I turn twenty one this summer."

"A baby." He put his arm around me and squeezed. "A sweet, little baby."

His hand stayed on my shoulder, fondling me in small circles. I felt his whisky breath in my ear, but there was nowhere to go. Bob caught the exchange in the mirror. It wasn't the first time he'd noticed my discomfort.

"What do you and your husband do?" he asked as we stood at the entrance of a new townhouse later. Ma, Pedar and Pasha Moradi were in the kitchen, checking out the appliances.

"Hafez works at his father's auto shop. I stay at home."

"Your English is very good. Have you thought about getting a job?"

We talked about my qualifications. High school, yes. Experience, no.

"You know, I'm looking for an assistant—answering phone calls, looking after the paper work, simple stuff. It doesn't pay much, but it would get you out of the house." He didn't have to say it, but I knew he was thinking about Pasha Moradi's hand on my shoulder.

"Thank you," I replied. "But my father-in-law wouldn't approve of me working outside the home."

"I have a daughter, a few years younger than you," said Bob, as if that explained the concern. "Here's my card. In case you change your mind."

I slipped it into my pocket as Pasha Moradi came out of the kitchen, shaking his head.

"No good. What's next?"

Bob crossed one address after another off his list. Nothing pleased Pasha Moradi.

"Too close to the road. Too much traffic."

"What do I need such a big backyard for?"

"Too much light."

"Too little light."

White neighbours. Chinese neighbours. Black neighbours. Indians. No. No. No. No. Too far from the bus stop. Too close to the bus stop.

"He's never going to leave," said Hafez.

Every day, he looked more gaunt. And strained.

Ma and I took on sewing jobs to pay for extra groceries. Pasha Moradi did not eat left overs. He wanted lamb every Friday, and eggs every morning. And every night, Pedar opened another bottle of whisky.

"It's okay," said Ma when she pricked her finger. "You wait. See. After he buy house, he looking for big business. Making Kamal and Hafez a partner. After that, everything is all right. Everything is all right."

I put a pillow under her ankles and we continued sewing.

That night, Pasha Moradi came into the living room. It was well after midnight. I watched from the mattress as he stood over the couch, swaying over Pedar's and Ma's sleeping forms. Then he went into the bathroom. A few minutes later, Pedar got up and followed him. They met in the dark hallway, green ghosts glowing against the night light. Pedar stroked Pasha Moradi's face. Pasha Moradi took him by the hand and led him into the bedroom.

March 21st, 1983

"BE READY. 6:30 P.M.," SAID HAFEZ.

My heart soared as I put the receiver down. For the first time in months, I had caught the glimmer of a spark in his voice. Instead of spending Nowruz, the first day of the Persian New Year at home, Hafez wanted to take me out. I knew that Ma and Pedar wouldn't be pleased when they got back, but dinner was ready and there was just enough time to do the dishes and hop in the shower.

I hummed as I cleaned up. It was rare to have the place to myself. I hoped the friend that Pasha Moradi was visiting insisted that he stay the night. Maybe two or three. Preferably forever.

Yeah, right. I shook my head. Wishful thinking.

My eyes rested on the beautiful Haft Seen, the traditional table we had prepared for Nowruz. It symbolized the arrival of the spring equinox and the rebirth of nature. In the middle were seven items starting with the letter 'S' in the Persian alphabet. The candles that Hafez and I had lit together were burning over an elegant arrangement of mirrors, eggs, coins, nuts and pomegranates. Perhaps Ma was right.

"The candles bring good. Warm. Spring come," she said. "Evil go. Winter go. But they burn till finish, okay? If blow out, bring bad luck."

I felt foolish, having her explain things that I should have learned growing up. The Haft Seen had been something that the help set up, and later, Maamaan had done it silently, grudgingly.

Ma and I got along. I tried to imagine her, married to Pedar at sixteen, her hair lush and flowing around an unlined face. It was tough to picture her like that. Ma's face was set in a permanent scowl that was directly proportional to how swollen her feet were that day. The one thing that transported her away from it all was the glass cabinet. I gave it a light dusting, wondering what dreams lay frozen in the porcelain families that made her smile.

I hopped in the shower, feeling a stir of anticipation. Hafez had kept his distance, but perhaps tonight...I reached for the shampoo, recalling the hushed conversations Salomeh had shared with me about boys. Maybe it was the lack of privacy, like Farnaz had suggested. Maybe if Hafez and I went somewhere alone—I flushed as I wrapped the towel around my body and stepped out of the shower.

With one foot on the ledge of the tub, I started rubbing lotion over my legs. I knew my husband wanted me. Sometimes it was so fierce, that look of longing, but always he turned away, as if he'd hit an invisible wall.

A puff of cold air hit my neck.

Then I smelled it.

Whisky.

I spun around and froze.

Pasha Moradi was standing in the doorway, watching me.

Fondling himself.

A thousand thoughts rushed through my head, but none of them mattered.

He lunged for me, his eyes red and greedy, ripping the towel off me. I fought, my nails clawing at the shower curtain. Ping ping ping. The metal rings bounced off the ground. The jolt of my bones colliding with cold, damp tile emptied my lungs. Pasha Moradi pinned me to the floor. Or against the wall. I couldn't tell. I had no idea which way was up. All I could feel was his breath on the back of my neck, his hands grabbing my hips, the metallic taste of blood in my mouth.

I kicked. I tore. I hit. I bit. I could feel the thick, wiry hair on Pasha Moradi's arms as they tightened around my rib cage. He yanked me off my feet and slammed me, face down, against the sink. My feet slipped as they beat against the floor, sliding on a slick layer of spilled lotion. I choked on the sweet scent of lavender, my cheek smashed into the porcelain bowl.

No, I cried. It's Nowruz. I'm having dinner with my husband.

But Pasha Moradi couldn't hear my silent screams. He grabbed my hair and pulled so hard that I was staring at his twisted face in the mirror, still foggy from my shower. His other hand reached for his pants. I could hear the zipper unfastening, the sound of my dreams being sucked down a rusty drain. I screwed my eyes shut, locking out the thought of his ugly, purple penis pushing into me.

My hands flailed out, like a drowning man trying to keep afloat. The plastic tumbler by the sink tipped over. Toothpaste. Comb. The soft bristles of a toothbrush. My fingers closed around a cold, ring shaped handle.

Scissors. Hafez's tiny, cuticle scissors. The ones I laughed at whenever I caught him trimming his nose hair.

I could feel Pasha Moradi's beefy knee between my thighs, forcing them apart.

I gripped the scissors and drove the pointy end straight back. Pasha Moradi hissed as it punctured his big balloon of a body. But it wasn't enough. His grip remained iron-tight. I dislodged the scissors and stabbed him a second time, with all the desperate, sobbing force I could muster. This time he screamed and staggered back.

I was shaking so hard, I could barely push myself off the sink. My soles skid on a wet mess of blood and lotion. I broke free, dragging a dead shower curtain along with me. I could see the front door. My heart hammered with wild relief.

I was almost there when he grabbed my leg.

I clutched at the shiny parquet tiles as Pasha Moradi dragged me into the living room by my feet. When he rolled me over, the first thing I saw were the scissors sticking out of his eye, like some horrible cartoon parody. And then I saw his face. Rage-blinded, with red devil tears streaming down one cheek. He slapped me twice. Each time I felt my teeth rattle, my still-wet hair spraying drops of water everywhere.

Then he wrapped his hands around my neck and squeezed. I clutched at my throat, my legs thrashing against the floor. He could have killed me then, but he was enjoying it too much. So he eased up and let me gasp a lungful of air before tightening his grip again.

I felt myself fading as darkness overtook me, but then I saw his bloated face through the haze and started laughing. He looked pathetic, a big, swollen puffer fish with scissors jiggling in one eyeball, like a knife stuck in jello.

"Jendeh!" He slapped me again.

He didn't like me smiling, but I couldn't stop.

A huffing, puffing blowfish was blowing my house down.

"You want pain?" He fumbled with his flaccid penis. A sharp object in the eye can do that to a man's libido.

I laughed harder.

I was in a different place, removed from myself, wrapped up in a cocoon where everything was muffled. Still, my entire body clenched at the thought of it. How many times does a girl think of her first time? How many perfect, golden scenarios? I laughed at the irony of it.

"Shut up!" He spit on me, his face red with exertion, still trying to get himself hard.

Blood collected around the silver rims of the dual metal loops sticking out of his eye, and plopped down on my face. I wondered if his slimy, convoluted brain would spill out if I unplugged the scissors, and laughed harder still.

My lip split open with that slap. Or maybe it was from before. I couldn't be sure. All I knew is that when I felt Pasha Moradi's body being pulled off me, I felt so defiled, I wanted to hold on to its stifling weight, to have the life squashed out of me.

"You fucking bastard!"

Hafez's voice. Followed by a volley of grunts. I turned my head and saw their feet. Giants with far-away faces, smashing and pounding at the world. Something crashed. Or someone. Pasha Moradi was clutching his eye, trying to contain the stream of blood pooling behind his palm. The scissors lay on the floor. Hafez swayed over him, his knuckles bloody and swollen.

Pasha Moradi grabbed the gold cloth that covered the Haft Seen table and heaved himself up. His purple penis bobbed like a withered eggplant. A shower of coins fell from the table and jingled off the floor. The front of Hafez's shirt was stamped with red hand prints, like a kindergarten art project.

Pasha Moradi seized the mirror on the Haft Seen table and swung it at Hafez. The sprouted barley that Ma and I had started growing a few weeks ago turned upside down. Hafez ducked the first time, but Pasha Moradi got him in the back of the skull as he came up. Silver shards exploded everywhere. Hafez reeled back, clutching his head. His other hand gripped the table as he fought for balance.

"You want more, little boy?" Pasha Moradi sneered, wiping his bloody nose with the back of his hand.

Hafez froze. Something flipped inside him. When he straightened, his face was set with a crazed ferocity. He lunged at Pasha Moradi with a savage cry. They trampled the pastel colored boiled eggs that had rolled off the table, into a rainbow mush. Like a caged animal let loose, Hafez pummeled Pasha Moradi to his knees.

That's when Pasha Moradi's fingers clenched around the candlestick. He waved the smoking flame in Hafez's face. Hot wax splattered on Hafez's skin. Pasha Moradi got up, keeping him at bay.

"You think you're a big man now, huh?" He laughed, an awful, shuddersome cackle. "You can't even protect your woman."

He took a step back towards me, but tripped over the pants around his ankles and fell back, crashing into Ma's glass cabinet.

The shelf wobbled precariously. For a moment it looked like it might right itself. Then it tipped over, smashing Pasha Moradi under it. The glass panes slid out, cracking open over his half-clad body. Shiny miniature families shattered in a million fragments around him.

The front door creaked open. Pedar stopped mid-sentence. The candlestick rolled from Pasha Moradi's outstretched arms and the flame snuffed out. He lay face down, one grotesque eye staring at us, his body slashed like the jagged grid of a tic tac toe, in an expanding pool of crimson blood. Ma's purse hit the floor with a dull thunk.

"What happened?" Pedar's face was the color of ash.

"The filthy bugger attacked her." Hafez wrapped me in the torn shower curtain and carried me to the couch.

"Mind your tongue!" Pedar stepped over the glass shards in his polished Nowruz shoes. *"Jigar?"* He tried to rouse him, but Pasha Moradi wouldn't respond.

"What are you waiting for?" Pedar yelled at Hafez. "Call an ambulance!"

"He's gone. And I hope he rots in hell."

"Hafez!" Ma found her voice. *"Be pedaret goosh kon!"*

"Listen to him? Why should I? He never listened to me. Did you, Pedar?"

Pedar ignored him, frantically dialing the phone.

"Even now," laughed Hafez. "Even now you don't listen." He swept the phone off the stand in a violent sweep of his hands. It clanged to the floor with a jarring crash.

Pedar stood still, holding the receiver in one hand, his mouth hanging open.

"I came to you. I told you. And you did nothing. Nothing!"

"It was a long time ago. You were imagining things."

"And this?" Hafez pointed to me. "Am I imagining this too?"

"She brought this on herself."

"You're a coward." Hafez's voice was shaking. "You can bury your head in the sand. You can tell yourself whatever the hell you like, but you know he did this. Just as you knew he was abusing me."

Some words, when spoken, are like spells that unleash demons from carefully nailed coffins.

"Hafez—" I tried to speak, but no words came out.

"Do you think I didn't know?" continued Hafez. "What a farce the two of you played all these years."

The sound of Pedar's palm stinging Hafez's cheek echoed in the ensuing silence. Ma's mouth opened and closed like a fish out of water.

"Here." Hafez picked up the phone and handed it to Pedar. "Call them. Tell them your son just killed your lover."

June 10th, 1983

BOB WORTHING HAD A SMALL HOME OFFICE WHERE I SPENT the day taking calls, booking appointments and looking after the paperwork. He offered me the job after the investigation cleared Hafez and me of Pasha Moradi's death. The police ruled it as accidental, and our actions as self defense. Bob Worthing's statement, about what he had witnessed of Pasha Moradi's behavior, may have helped. Working for him was not something I did just for the pay check; it was also an expression of gratitude for his kindness. Not only did he introduce me to his answering machine, his fax and his typewriter, but also his home, his wife and daughter.

"He's gone?" Jayne padded into the office with her sleep-ruffled hair, tank top and shorts.

"Your father's at a lunch meeting."

"But it's barely—" She looked at her watch. "Oh."

It was hard not to like Jayne. She sat across from me, legs drawn in, and rested her chin on her knees.

"Ryan's going to be here in a few weeks." She grinned.

"You must be excited about seeing your brother again."

"Yes..." She hesitated, then trailed off with a sly smile.

"But...?"

"But I'm also looking forward to seeing his friend."

"Ah. The friend."

"I know, I know. You're sick of hearing about him, but Shayda, he's soooo dreamy."

"I've told you before Jayne, he's too old for you," her mother said from the kitchen.

Jayne rolled her eyes. "He's twenty one. How is that too old? And can you not eavesdrop?" She got up and shut the door. "Swear to god, she hears everything."

"Not everything." Elizabeth opened the door and peeked in. "I'm just saying. You're in high school, he's in college. Plus I don't see him going for his best friend's sixteen year old sister."

"Seventeen!" Jayne folded her arms and looked at me. "What's the age difference between you and Hafez, Shayda?"

Six years. But I didn't want to get involved. "I think I'll have my lunch now," I said.

"Ooh, that looks good." Jayne eyed the greek food I'd brought from Farnaz's restaurant.

"Jayne. That's rude," said her mother.

"No, it's fine. Would you like some?" I asked.

"Uh-huh."

"Really, Jayne." Elizabeth shook her head. "I hope you like shepherd's pie, Shayda, because I insist you join me for lunch."

"Shepherd's pie sounds lovely," I replied.

I was tired of eating leftovers from the restaurant. Hafez and I worked there at night. Behram and Farnaz had been kind enough to let us use the store room after we locked up. We planned on moving out as soon as Hafez found a job.

I FINISHED AT BOB'S AND GOT TO THE RESTAURANT BY 6 P.M. Locking the restroom door behind me, I freshened up for the evening shift. Washcloth, soap, warm water. On Mondays, when the restaurant was closed, I washed my hair in the sink. I still saw Pasha Moradi every time I looked in the mirror, his twisted face staring over my shoulder. I put on my apron and took a deep breath, thankful that the restaurant was still empty. It wouldn't be long before the Friday night crowd started coming in.

The door chimed as I was setting up the tables.

"Hi, Farnaz," I greeted her.

Then I saw the woman standing behind her.

"Ma!"

She held out her arms.

In the three months since Hafez and I had walked out of the apartment, she'd shrunk. Her eyes were deep hollows and the lines on her face were etched deeper. I pulled out a chair and sat her down.

"I'll be in the kitchen," said Farnaz, disappearing behind the doors.

"I ask her...to bring me." Ma wheezed.

"Are you all right?"

"I come to see Hafez."

"He'll be here soon."

Classifieds, interviews, employment offices. It's what he did all day.

"I wait," she said. "How are you?"

"I'm fine."

She must have seen through it because she slumped into the chair and closed her eyes.

Look, I wanted to tell her, my face has healed up. The bruises are gone, the cuts mended. All that's left is a scar where my lips split open. I'm fine. Really.

But I couldn't find the words to comfort her. What could I say to make a mother feel better about the awful truth she had learned that day?

I excused myself as a couple walked in. I had just handed them the menus when Hafez came in.

"I got it," he said.

There should have been more excitement in his eyes, more victory in his voice, but everything was less. Pasha Moradi's death should have freed him, but every time he looked at me, he was reminded.

"I thought you'd be safe," he'd said as they cleaned up my wounds that night. "I thought he was into boys. Men. But it wasn't about that. It was about power." Hafez wore his guilt like a layer of self-loathing, even now when he should have been celebrating his new job.

"The truck driver position?" I asked.

"I need some training, but they liked the fact that I can fix cars. I start next week."

"That's great." I felt a small bubble of relief.

We needed this. To feel good and worthy. To have hope for tomorrow.

"Hafez..." I pointed to the back. "Go talk to her." I left him with Ma and went back to the customers.

When I returned, Ma was distraught.

"You make him understand," she said. "He say no. He say no to me."

"Ma." Hafez took her hand. "Now is not a good time, but it won't be long before we have our own place. I have a job now. I promise. I'll come and get you."

"Now. You take me now," she cried. "I can't live with him. I stay here. I stay. I sew. I cook. I help." She started to cough, gasping for breath in between.

"*Khaleh*, it's time to go." Farnaz touched her shoulder gently.

Ma looked at Hafez.

"Soon, Ma," he promised.

She walked to the door slowly. I could only imagine how painful her bloated feet felt.

THE EVENING PASSED IN A BLUR OF FOOD AND CHANGE AND loud music. When everything was locked up and we were ready for bed, I set mouse traps around the mattress. It was the only way I could fall asleep after the horror of the first night.

We lay back to back on the makeshift bed. I understood now why Hafez slept facing away from me. There was a vulnerability in sleep, those unguarded hours when you didn't want anyone to see your face, when grotesque shadows rearranged its contours as they roamed your dreams.

The shrill ring of the phone woke us up. Hafez stumbled to the kitchen to answer it.

I looked at the time. 3:15 a.m.

When Hafez didn't return, I went looking for him.

"It was Farnaz." He was sitting at one of the booths in the dining room, barely discernible in the dark.

I started shaking because I knew it was bad.

"Ma..." He kept his eyes on the salt shaker, sliding it on the table, from one hand to the other. "She's gone."

"Where?" I thought of her trapped in that tiny apartment, staring at the empty spot that had been her glass cabinet.

"She's dead, Shayda. The doctors say her heart finally caught up with her. What do they know?" Hafez laughed. It was a bitter, hollow sound. "It was me. I'm the one that failed her."

"Don't do this to yourself," I said.

Across the street, the traffic lights changed. Red, amber, green, each one casting an eerie glow on our faces. The streets were empty and still they continued, flashing to a pre-set pattern.

"When's the funeral?" I asked, after a long stretch of silence.

"Pedar doesn't want us there."

"She's your mother. He can't stop you."

"Maybe it's for the best. If I see him, I'll kill him."

"Hafez—" I reached for him, but he flinched.

"The day we first met, I just wanted to get Ma off my back. I thought I'd say, 'There. I met her. I don't like her.' I'd done it before. I couldn't tell her that I was damaged, that no girl deserved that." He stopped playing with the glass shaker.

"But I liked you," he said. "You were sweet. And innocent. I thought that if I could hang around you long enough, I'd become less...dirty. So I put you on a pedestal, like those figurines that Ma loved. I wanted to keep you pure and safe. Instead I dragged you into the mud. I let you down, Shayda, just like I let Ma down today."

I watched him lay his head on the table. He was surrendering, letting waves of guilt and shame toss him around. The painting of Poseidon, hanging across the restaurant, mocked me. I saw Pasha Moradi, rising from the depths, ready to spear Hafez with his trident.

No.

He had taken the boy. He was not going to get the man.

I held Hafez. I rocked him. I brushed the hair away from his face. I gathered the drifting pieces and stuck them back on. When he finally looked at me, I kissed him. When he turned away, I kissed him. I kissed away the layers of stuck-on grime so he could feel clean again. I gave him all the things I wanted for myself. Love and tenderness and a place to belong. And slowly, he turned to me in the dark, resting his forehead on mine.

I slipped the straps of my nightgown off my shoulders and let him look at me. Red, amber, green, my skin glowed. I took his hand and placed it on my soft, warm flesh. He gasped, finally allowing himself to breath.

"Shayda..." He wrapped his arms around me and lifted me off the table.

We made love for selfish reasons, clutching at each other. He needed to claw his way out of the pain and I wanted to be needed. We shared a bond beyond our gold bands. A common predator haunted us, and I knew, even as Hafez shut out my face when he took me, that we were always going to be.

10. TANGLED

....

November 11th, 1995

I REACH FOR THE CRIMSON COAT THAT HAFEZ HAD GIVEN me that first winter. It's frayed around the edges now, but it reminds me of hot pizza and new dreams.

I head to the community centre with the kids. Zain has just switched from swimming to guitar.

"I hate it!" he said of the beginner's aqua class.

"It's an important life skill. You have to learn."

"Next semester. Pleaaase?" He pulled puppy dog eyes. We caved and bought him a guitar.

Between his music, Natasha's art classes, and my open houses, weekends are a blur of activities. I head to the grocery store after seeing the children off.

"$84.56, please."

I hand my card to the cashier.

"Shayda?"

I look at her for the first time.

"Marjaneh." Hossein's ex. My one time sister-in-law.

She seems embarrassed as she hands my card back. "I just started here."

"How are you?"

"Good." Her eyes move to the line forming behind me. "How is Maamaan?"

She still calls my mother 'Maamaan', but I know she's asking, 'How is Hossein?'

"Fine," I reply.

The man behind me coughs, not too discretely.

"Good seeing you." I pick up my bags.

"You too."

I WALK OUT OF THE STORE, THINKING ABOUT HER.

Marjaneh, the girl whose fate I may have stolen.

Our fathers had been business partners in Tehran. The plan was to send Marjaneh and me abroad. Every month, they put aside money for airfare. When there was enough to send one of us, they held a big picnic to celebrate. All of our extended family joined in.

We ate and played games, and then it was time to decide which one of us would go.

"We'll toss a coin," says Baba. "Hossein, get my wallet from the car."

"We don't need a coin. We have these." Marjaneh's father, *Amu* Reza, pointed to the pebbles on the ground. "We'll use two—black and white. Black means stay, white means go."

"You're older," Marjaneh said to me. "It's only fair you get to pick."

Everyone gathered around, laughing and talking. I was the only one who saw *Amu* Reza get the pebbles from the ground. He chose two black ones. It didn't matter which one

I picked. He had just made sure his daughter would be the one to go.

Amu Reza closed his palm over the stones and held his hands out.

"Go ahead," he said. "Pick one."

Calling him out would humiliate him before everyone, and a man's honor is his everything. So I took a deep breath and tapped his right hand. As he went to turn it over, I lurched forward, knocking it off his palm. It fell and mingled with the other pebbles on the ground.

"Sorry," I said.

"It's all right. We'll try again." *Amu* Reza reached for another pebble.

"There's no need," I said. "Just look at the one in your hand and you'll know which one I picked."

Amu Reza's eyes narrowed. He knew I knew. We stared at each other for a moment.

Then he turned his other palm over.

"It's black!" exclaimed Baba. "That means Shayda picked the white pebble."

"Congratulations." *Amu* Reza looked at me with grudging respect.

"I'm happy for you." Marjaneh hugged me.

AND NOW HERE SHE IS, STRUGGLING TO MAKE ENDS MEET. When Maamaan told me she was marrying Hossein, I had felt relief. She was going to make it to Canada after all. How different would her life have been, had I let *Amu* Reza play out his plan that day? How different would mine?

I get in the car and glance at the clock. I don't have to pick up the kids for a while. I take the highway and find myself at the park Troy took me to. The golden leaves are gone, turned colorless and brittle under my feet. I sit on the bench, staring at the reflection of cold sky and bare branches.

My watch beeps. Remembrance Day. I had set it for 11:00 a.m. I close my eyes to pay a silent tribute to all those who fell for the freedoms I have today, but all I see is a red butterfly, a blue sky, a valley on fire.

My mind keeps going back to Troy.

Somewhere in the fabric of all these years, our lives got tangled, like unruly threads pulling and snagging into impossible knots. How could we have known that one night would stay with us so long? I remember it like it was yesterday.

11. FIREWORKS

....

PAST

July 1st, 1983

"That was delicious" I said as I cleared the dishes. "Jayne did such a great job of setting the table."

"She's quite the little party planner, isn't she?" Elizabeth smiled.

We stood back to admire her work. Even with the dirty plates and messy napkins, the Canada Day set-up looked beautiful. Place cards, held by pine cones, now rolled over like sated guests on the red table cloth. A white table runner accentuated wine bottles holding bright gerberas, and the walls were decked out with red and white checkered banners on twine.

I bit into one of the maple-leaf sugar cookies and grimaced. "If only she baked as well."

Elizabeth laughed. "I can't get her to step foot in the kitchen, but maybe she'll listen to you."

"Why cook when you can have it catered?" Jayne joined us in the kitchen. "You don't think the cookies will impress?"

We shook our heads.

"The cupcakes?"

Elizabeth and I exchanged dubious looks.

Jane hopped on the counter and dangled her feet wistfully. "How am I ever going to get him to notice me?"

"Jayne," said her mother, "are you still trying to get Troy's attention?"

"There's no point," Jayne replied. "He thinks I'm just a kid. He dates cheerleaders and models. What chance do I have?"

"He's dating his age. And so should you. There are plenty of nice guys that you keep turning down."

"I don't want a *nice* guy."

"Now you listen to me, young lady. Troy might have somewhat of a reputation, but even *he* knows that you're out of bounds. So unless you want to get your heart broken, you'd best stop daydreaming."

Jayne pouted. "Can I at least go watch the fireworks with them tonight?"

"Who's going?" asked Elizabeth.

"Ryan, Ellen and Troy."

"Ryan and Ellen are a couple. Please tell me you're not thinking of this as double date with Troy."

"Mum!"

"You are!" Elizabeth shook her head and looked at me with a face that could only belong to mothers of teenaged daughters.

"What if Shayda comes with us?" asked Jayne. "It won't be a double date then, right?"

"I'm sure Shayda has other plans."

"No, she doesn't," replied Jayne. "Hafez isn't back until Sunday."

Elizabeth turned to me. "Have you ever been to the Canada Day fireworks at Ashbridges Bay?"

"No. I was going to catch it on TV."

"It's not the same. Bob and I stopped going because of the crowds, but you should go. If not this year, then next summer."

"Oh come! It'll be fun!" Jayne jumped off the counter. "Please, Shayda? Mum will let me go if you go, won't you?"

"Quit putting Shayda on the spot." Elizabeth opened the fridge and started stowing away the leftovers.

Behind her, Jayne clasped her hands.

'Please, Please, PLEASE,' she mouthed.

"Okay, I'll go."

"Yeahhh!" Jayne threw her arms around me. "I love you, I love you, I loooove you!"

I laughed, but it came out funny—embarrassed and awkward, and a little overwhelmed by the show of affection.

"Why don't the two of you go sit with Bob and Ryan?" I said. "I'll finish cleaning up."

"Are you sure?" asked Elizabeth.

"It's the least I can do."

"Thanks, Shayda."

Jayne watched her mother join the men in the backyard.

"Let me know when Troy gets here." She winked, before skipping out in her sassy denim shorts and crop top.

She was showing a lot of skin lately. Then again, it was her first adolescent crush and there was no stopping her. I admired her exuberance, the way she ran out to meet the world, expecting it to unravel to her dreams.

I put away the last pot and reached for the sliding door, stopping to smile at the scene before me. Ryan was chasing Jayne with a hose. She screamed and threw her flip-flops at him. The first one missed; the second smacked Ryan square in the jaw.

"Ohhhh, you're in for it now," he yelled.

Jayne ducked behind Bob's lounger.

"Shit!" said Ryan as he soaked his father instead.

Now it was Bob vs. Ryan.

"Cut it out." Elizabeth waved her arms at them. "Why can't we ever sit like a normal family and enjoy some quiet time together?"

The other three grinned and ganged up on her as she ran screaming to the other side of the pool. I couldn't tell what happened next because everything turned blurry. My palm rested on the air-conditioned glass, looking out at four happy figurines come to life.

I averted my gaze, focusing on the trees instead. If they hadn't been so dark and lush I might have missed it—a pair of eyes staring back at me in the reflection—a bright, brilliant blue, like the sky peeking through the leaves. Troy's silhouette was mirrored in the glass, standing behind me, but it was too late to hide my face. I dared not breathe or the tears that trembled on the edges of my lashes would fall.

The clouds moved and the leaves swayed, but on our side of that door, everything froze. I felt like a raw, exposed specimen under a microscope. But instead of cold, hard speculation, I found something else in his eyes, something unexpectedly overwhelming. I jerked away from the door, but he pinned my hand to the glass. His fingers covered mine, grounding me in an instinctual gesture of comfort.

For a moment, I fought against the disarming tenderness of a stranger, the shame of being caught in a moment of weakness. Then his arms circled my waist, pulling me away from the door, from whatever heartache he had witnessed in my reflection. The fight drained out of me. I turned into the shelter of his embrace, and he, not knowing, not asking, took me in.

Something changed in that instant. For me. For him. Like when the sun and moon align and day turns to night. They finally see each other's faces and hang, transfixed, even as their eclipse throws everything else into darkness. For those fleeting moments, everything made sense—the pattern behind the random trajectory of life, the infinite order beneath chaos.

I felt the warmth of sun-soaked soil under my feet, the joy of weaving through thorny lemon trees and chasing clouds of butterflies among spring blossoms. I felt like I was home again.

A loud splash jarred us back to reality.

I broke away, feeling like a star unfastened from the sky.

"I'm gonna get you!" We heard Ryan shouting from the pool.

Jayne shrieked and ran towards the house.

"Troy!" She stopped when she saw him, and slid the door open.

"Hi, Jayne." He stepped between me and her, allowing me a moment to pull myself together. "You guys ever lock your front door?"

"We've been expecting you." She hugged him, and held on until he unlinked her arms from around his neck.

"We?"

"I'm going too!" She grinned. "And Shayda."

"I see." He looked at me and then back at Jayne. "Is Ryan ready to go?"

"He needs to dry off. I got him good." She smirked.

"I'll let him know I'm here. In the meantime, why don't you go change?"

"What's wrong with what I'm wearing?"

"Bugs," he said without blinking. "We're going to be near the water. You better cover up."

"Fiiine." She sighed and stomped off, her pony tail swinging haughtily behind her.

Her absence left a hole that sucked up all the air in the room.

"I'm afraid I'm not dressed appropriately either." I tried to dispel the electric buzzing between us with small talk.

"You're fine. Exactly as you are," he replied, without taking his eyes off my face.

I smoothed my dress, feeling flush under his unwavering gaze.

"Hey." Ryan sauntered in, toweling his hair, oblivious to the tension he was cutting through.

"Is that you, Troy?" Bob asked from the backyard. "You kids better get going if you plan on making it."

"Soon as I change," replied Ryan, heading for his room.

"Don't stay out too late, you hear?" said Elizabeth.

"Yes, Ma." Jayne stepped out in a demure button-down blouse and jeans. "Come on!" She linked her arm with mine. "Before she changes her mind."

WE PICKED ELLEN UP ON THE WAY. WITH HER CINNAMON hair and warm smile, it was easy to see why Ryan was smitten. Their exchange was hot and flirty. I kept my eyes on an imaginary spot on the window, looking out as the sky darkened to a deep indigo.

We came to a crawling halt when we got to the lake. Pedestrians weaved between the stalled traffic; cars turned away from big, bold 'LOT FULL' signs.

"We'll never make it in time," said Ryan.

"Never say never." Troy steered us into a gas station. "We can walk it from here."

"They'll tow your car!" said Jayne.

"I'll go ask." He walked into the store, spinning his keys.

A few minutes later, he was back out. "Okay guys. We're good to go."

A middle-aged woman in a blue vest waved at us through the window.

"This one." Ellen laughed. "He can charm his way through anything."

We crossed the street to the beach, where people were already camped out on thick blankets, waiting for the show to begin. The smell of the lake mingled with hot dogs and fizzled-out sparklers. I trailed behind Jayne, wishing I had worn my flats. The boardwalk proved impossible in my kitten heels, so I stopped to remove them. The place looked different at night, but I was momentarily transported to another time. This was the spot I had come to the day I met Hafez. I closed my eyes, thinking of that young couple, of a time when possibilities were endless and whole worlds lay around the bend in the road.

When I opened them again, there was no sign of Jayne or the rest of the group. I stuffed my shoes in my bag, wishing I'd asked about a meeting point.

I was wandering aimlessly when an iron grip circled my wrist, spinning me around, into the solid wall of Troy's chest. I could feel his muscles tense as he braced me against the streams of people passing us by.

"Are you all right?"

I struggled to throttle the dizzy current racing through my veins. He had come back. He had picked me out from the vague mass of night shadows.

"You found me," I whispered.

"Of course." Like anything else was unimaginable.

At night, his eyes blazed like summer lightning. I felt something flutter inside me, something I thought was long dead. He took my hand and led me away from the crowd.

"Where are we going?"

"I know a place," he replied, cutting across the parking lot.

"What about the others?" I followed him past rows of tightly packed cars, into a residential alley.

"I lost them when I came back for you."

"I'm supposed to be with Jayne." I pulled my hand away. The gritty sidewalk dug into my bare feet.

"You always do what you're supposed to?" he asked, with the supreme confidence of someone who did exactly as he pleased. His eyes flashed with the hint of a challenge.

"I promised Elizabeth I'd keep an eye on Jayne." But it wasn't Jayne I was worried about. It was me. Alone with him.

We stood between rows of neatly trimmed hedges. The light from the street gave his face the craggy look of an unfinished sculpture, highlighting the cheekbones, the line of his mouth, the strong aquiline nose.

"Jayne is with Ryan. Which means she's safe. Now you can either follow me or find your own way back." He turned into the shadowy space between two houses.

"Wait!" I ran after him. "Insolent beast," I muttered.

"I heard that." But he kept walking.

We got to a dead-end, closed off by a chain link fence.

"Grab the top," he said, slipping my bag off my shoulders.

"What?" I blinked. "You want me to jump the fence? It says 'Private Property.'"

"It wouldn't hurt you to break a few rules now and then." He laced his fingers and hunched, giving me a sure foot-hold. "Quickly. Before the guard dogs come around."

"Guard dogs?" I scrambled over the top without further prompting, certain I had just cinched the World's Most Ungraceful Fence Vaulting award.

I heard a soft thud as he threw my bag over, and then we were both standing on the other side. A spasmodic trembling overtook me as I realized that we had just broken into someone's place.

He swore under his breath. "You're shaking like a leaf." His hands slipped around my arms, rubbing up and down in a firm, insistent rhythm.

"I'm f-f-fine."

Why? Why was I wearing a sleeveless dress that left my arms bare to his touch?

"There are no guard dogs, Shayda. And there's no one home. See?" He nodded towards the quiet bungalow. "We're just going to watch the fireworks and leave, okay?"

"No guard dogs? Wait a minute. You tricked me?"

"I embellished. A little. They have a chihuahua," he said. "You coming?"

I spluttered after him, across the grass to the private pier jutting out into the lake.

"Here we are." He gestured before us. "Best place to catch the fireworks." He slipped his shoes off and dangled his feet over the water.

I took in the wide vista spread out before us. City lights twinkled around the edges of the water as a warm breeze fanned across its inky depths. The gentle swishing of the waves calmed my nerves.

I dusted off a spot, a comfortable distance away from him and sat down. "How do you know about this place?"

"I'm familiar with the neighbourhood."

I dipped my feet in the water, letting it wash away the grainy bits of sand between my toes. Loud music blared from the deck next door.

"Looks like someone's having a party."

"Want to join them?" he asked.

Four figures lounged on comfy chairs, surrounded by a string of glowing paper lanterns. They were obviously having a good time.

"I like it better here," I said.

"You sure? In the dark?"

"That's the general idea, when you're uninvited."

"You hate getting into any kind of trouble, don't you?" he teased.

I jumped as the lights turned on behind us, followed by the sound of a door opening and slamming shut.

"Shit!" Troy jumped into the water, disappearing under the pier.

The sound of a dog's barking got louder.

"Jump, Shayda!"

I looked at him, then back at the house. I could make out the owner coming towards us.

"Come on." He held his hands out. "Now!"

I took a deep breath and plunged into the lake, gasping from the shock of icy cold water. He caught me swiftly, minimizing the accompanying splash.

"In here." He dragged me under the pier.

Our heads bobbed in the small space between the wood and the water as we listened to the creaking of the planks above.

"What is it, Nitro?" A man's gruff voice called over the dog's excited little woofs.

"Oh no!" I whispered. "I left my bag up there."

"I left my shoes." He laughed.

"It's not funny!" I panicked, my legs flailing in the water as I struggled to stay afloat.

"Shhh." He locked his arms around my waist and lifted me so I was straddling his thighs. "Put your weight on me. My feet are still on the ground."

"No, I'm..."

...fine, is I wanted to say, but I gasped as my curves settled against hard muscle.

Awareness zinged between us, catching us off guard. He inhaled sharply. I could feel the warmth of his body through layers of wet clothing. My dress floated around us like a white lily pad anchored by his physique. The lake grew unbelievably warm.

"Nitro!" Faltering steps stopped directly over us. "Get away from there." The speech was slurred.

"He's going to find us." I gripped Troy's shoulders as Nitro sniffed the corner where we'd left our things.

"Dad?" A girl called out from the party next door.

"Carol?" The man lurched to the edge of the pier. "What are you doing there?"

"Have you been drinking?" she asked.

"Yeah. You?"

Her friends laughed.

"You better not have," her father warned.

"Dad, I'm just catching the fireworks."

"Right. I'm going to head in soon..." His voice trailed off.

I felt Troy's weight shift and realized how long he'd been holding me up.

"I can manage now," I say.

But he pulled me back, one arm around my midriff, the other supporting the back of my knee. "I'm rather enjoying this."

He gave me that irresistibly disarming grin.

"It's really quite amazing," I said.

"What?"

"That you think you can get whatever you want by flashing a smile."

"She bites." The smile got infuriatingly wider. "I like that."

"And I don't like the fact that you have no boundaries. This is completely inappropriate."

"Is that what you're feeling right now? Inappropriate?"

"Yes!" I replied, trying to keep my voice low. "It's not right."

"It's not right we broke in or it's not right that it feels so good?" He stroked my back, his finger running over each vertebrae before his hand settled over the curve of my back.

"You still haven't asked me to let you go, you know." He braced me closer to the firm, unyielding contours of his hip.

I held still because I didn't want to give us away, because we had to be quiet. At least that's what I told myself. But all the while, a strange beast was unfurling in my veins.

Help, I beseeched the silver cross around his neck, but it just bobbed on its string of wooden beads.

Then the sky exploded in a thundering cascade of golden light.

"Wooh!" Carol's dad cheered. Nitro didn't sound too sure.

I broke away from Troy, my nerves more flammable than the fireworks. Large crimson stars burst in the sky, one on top of the other, followed by a flash of brilliant, white showers.

"Stop it!" I said as I tried to stay afloat in my heavy, sodden clothes.

"Stop what?"

"That!"

"I have no idea what you're going on about."

"Right." I swatted the shadowy mass by my side disbelievingly.

It swatted back and attacked my arm.

I stifled a scream and hooked both arms around Troy, latching on like a circus monkey.

"It's a duck. Relax. Probably just startled by the fireworks."

"Are you laughing at me?"

"No."

Another barrage of screeching lights rained down on us. The duck quacked loudly, glaring at us as it swam by.

"Okay, you're laughing at me." The corners of my mouth lifted in a reluctant smile.

"Maybe a little." He chuckled. "Now will you just relax so we can watch the rest of the fireworks?" He wrapped his arm around me, pulling me back into him, so we were both facing the spectacular display of light and color.

Massive blooms of pink and green exploded in rapid succession, descending in threads of sparkling silver. Spinning comets reached for the heavens, followed by a barrage of fast and furious explosions, each hanging momentarily in the sky, mirrored perfectly in the glassy reflection of the lake. And then the grand finale—an erratic cloud of red crackles with brilliant, white stars bursting all around.

I sighed as whisper soft clouds of smoke settled over the lake and disappeared like willowy ghosts. The distant cheering faded and the smell of sulfur hung in the air. Troy held on to me, silent, as we both looked out to the water. I felt strangely compelled to let the moment linger.

"Dad?" Carol's voice cut across from next door.

No answer.

"Dad?" she called again.

"What?" Her father grunted.

"Did you fall asleep?"

"No. You watch the fireworks and come straight home, all right?"

"Okay, Dad," she giggled.

"Come on, Nitro."

We heard the planks above us creak as he got up, but instead of retreating, he started singing a loud, bawdy song. He shuffled to the opposite side of the pier, turning away from his daughter.

And then a stream of water hit the lake.

"Ewww!" I watched, incredulous, as he emptied his bladder into the lake.

"Come on." Troy laughed and steered us away, towards a tired old canoe tethered to the shore.

"What are you doing?" I whispered when he lifted me into it.

"Stay down. I'll go get our things."

The boat smelled dank and musty, and the wood was slimy under my hands.

"Let's get out of here," I said when he returned, but he climbed in, deposited my bag and started putting on his shoes.

I watched the man and his dog disappear into the bungalow.

"They're gone. Let's go." I started getting out of the boat.

"Not so fast." He pulled me back in and tugged on the anchor. "We're going for a little ride."

"Are you crazy?" My voice rose a few octaves. "You're stealing his boat?"

"Trust me."

"Trust you?" I squealed. "You had me trespass on private property and jump into the lake like some fugitive. I'm wet as a mop, soaked to my skin; I've lost Jayne, been peed on, and attacked by a duck. And now you expect me to row away with you in a rotting old boat that's not even yours? I don't think so!" I planted my feet on the deck and stood with my hands on my hips.

"Sit down, Shayda."

The amusement in his voice set me off.

"I will not! I will not sit—"

"Suit yourself then." He started rowing.

I lurched and landed unceremoniously on my butt.

"Oh—!" I seethed, unable to find the right words to hurl at him.

Until he started steering us towards the neighbour's house.

"Are you mad? They'll see us!"

He continued rowing, his shoulders flexing as he paddled straight for their pier.

"What the hell?" A guy's voice called out from the deck.

Oh god. I hid my face in my hands.

"Troy?" A girl this time. Carol. "Troy, is that you?" She came around as he rowed us in.

The other three peered over the railing.

"Shayda?"

My mouth gaped open. It was Jayne.

"What happened to you guys?" she asked as Troy secured the canoe and helped me out.

"We took a little detour through Carol's place and ended up in the lake," he replied.

"We were starting to get worried," said Ryan.

"Are you all right? You're soaked!" Jayne exclaimed as we climbed up the stairs.

"What are you guys doing here?" I asked.

"Didn't he tell you?" Jayne shook her head. "This is Troy's place. We would have driven up if the traffic hadn't been so bad. I am so sorry we lost you!"

"Who's this, Troy?" Carol sidled up to him.

I felt like a dripping mess as she surveyed me with her salon permed hair and artfully ripped sweatshirt.

"This is my friend, Shayda," replied Jayne, bristling as Carol's hand lingered possessively on him. "Troy, your neighbour just showed up uninvited."

The two girls glared at each other.

"Why don't we go inside so you guys can dry off?" suggested Ellen.

"There's no need for *all* of us to go." Ryan pulled her back into his lap.

"There's no need for anyone to go." Troy extracted himself from Carol and pulled me away from Jayne. "Excuse us, ladies." He took me by the elbow and guided me up the stone stairs to the sprawling mansion.

I shrugged him off as he let me inside. Everything about the expansive interior spoke of old money, the kind that we had before the revolution.

We stopped at the base of a sweeping staircase. It looked like something out of a flamboyant television set, like Krystle Carrington or J.R. Ewing could come gliding down at any moment.

"Shayda, I—"

"Could I use your bathroom?"

"Of course. The guest en suite is up the stairs, second door to your left."

My foot had barely touched the first step before his hand covered mine on the banister.

"Aren't you going to ask why I didn't bring you straight here?" he said.

I thought of the heart-slamming moments under the pier. Climbing over the fence. Jumping into the water. Clinging to him like my life depended on it. And something snapped inside me. The cool, calm veneer I was trying to hold on to, cracked.

"I don't know, Troy. Maybe you're just a spoiled, rich kid who gets a kick out of making a fool of someone like me."

"Someone like you?"

"Look at me." I laughed. "I don't belong here, in your swanky place with your soaring ceilings and your gleaming floors. I don't know this culture, this lifestyle. I may not be sophisticated enough to play the kind of games you play, but that doesn't mean you get to humiliate me."

"Humiliate you?" He looked stricken. "I just wanted to spend some time with you."

"Why?" I tried to keep the hurt from my voice. "I'm not some carefree young girl you can drag around town with you."

"Haven't you ever done something just for the heck of it? Kicked up your heels and lived in the moment?"

"Living in the moment may work for you, Troy. The rest of us have to think about paying the rent."

"Really? Is that what was on your mind? Paying the rent?" He quirked an eyebrow in amused skepticism. "Are you telling me you didn't have any fun tonight?"

"You know what would have been fun, Troy?" I glared at him. "Fun would have been if you had actually brought me here instead of tricking me. Fun would have been hanging out on that deck, pretending I was just like everyone else for one evening. Fun would have been anything except this!" I gestured to my wet, wilted form.

The grand vestibule echoed with the sound of my shuddering breath.

"That's it. That's it, Shayda. Lash out at me. Heck, lash out at the whole world," said Troy. "I'll take the anger, the rage, any day over that awful, broken look you had on before."

Anger? Rage? The realization blindsided me. I couldn't remember the last time I was so furious, so openly unrestrained with my emotions.

"And you're wrong, you know," he said. "You look exactly like you belong."

A drop of water pooled at the end of his hair, hanging on precariously like a crystal bubble.

"You know your eyes turn almost black when you're excited?" He was so close that I didn't notice the little droplet going splat on my hand. "And your hair." He played with a strand. "Like Medusa. It gives you away, the part you hide so well." He traced my collarbone, letting his fingers play in the soft spot between.

I felt like soldered metal, glued to the spot by blazing blue irises. I wanted to jump back—from the touch, yes, but mostly the way he was looking at me.

"Roses." He closed his eyes and inhaled. "It's the damnedest thing. I smell roses. Every time I'm around you."

I stood there, not moving, not breathing, not wanting the moment to end. It was some kind of cruel spell.

"Shayda?" Jayne called from the door.

I jerked away from him before she entered.

"I thought you might need this." She held up my bag. "You have a change of clothes in here?"

"Um...no." I gripped the railing, trying to steady myself.

"You can borrow something of my mother's," said Troy. "They're not back until tomorrow. She won't mind."

"No thanks," I replied. "I'll just put my clothes in the dryer."

"No need. I'll have your dress dry-cleaned and—," He caught the expression on my face. "Right. Laundry's over there."

"What about you, Troy?" asked Jayne. "Want me take those wet clothes off you...I mean...em...*for* you?" She smiled, far from embarrassed about the slip.

"What's going on in here?" Carol followed, hot on Jayne's heels. "Can I get you some dry clothes, honey?"

Honey. Jayne rolled her eyes.

Dry clothes. Obviously she knew her way around.

"I'm fine." Troy ran his fingers through his hair. "Why don't the two of you just chill. We'll be out in a bit."

"Okay, darling." Carol dropped another endearment before she left.

'Okay, darling', Jayne mimed behind her.

"Jayne?" He arched an eyebrow.

"I'm going, I'm going."

"Wait." I called her back. "Maybe you should call Elizabeth and let her know you're going to be late. It's almost midnight."

"Sure." She shrugged and headed for the living room.

"Always the responsible one, huh?" said Troy.

"Always the troublemaker, huh?"

"Not my fault if girls fight over me."

"If you're done singing your own praises, I'd like to freshen up."

"Of course." He bowed mockingly, but I knew it was an attempt to lighten the tension still lingering between us.

I stomped up the stairs after him, leaving a trail of wet footprints on the mahogany, each wishing it were headed the other way—out the door and away from him.

12. FREE FALLING

PAST

July 2nd, 1983

I looked in the mirror expecting to see The Swamp Thing. It was me, only raw and wild, a reflection I wasn't familiar with. Instead of gracefully tamed layers, my hair had morphed into a riot of mad curls. My eyes had an odd sheen and my face was throbbing with color.

I sucked in my cheeks and examined my face.

Nope, I will never have high, chiseled Troy Heathgatesque cheekbones.

Stepping back, I cringed. My dress was clinging to every curve. I looked like a powerful opera had picked me up, dragged me through every aria between elation and agitation and dropped me, exhausted but oddly sated.

I stepped into the oversized shower and fiddled with the controls, shrieking as jets of icy cold water attacked me from all sides. There was a handheld shower, a ceiling mounted shower and several nozzles coming at me from the side panels. I tried again, paying more attention. Steam shower, rain shower, oscillating spray...I cycled through the options until I found a nice, comfortable setting.

I shimmied out of my dress and underwear, sighing as the water washed away the clamminess of the lake. The soap from the dispenser smelled like white gardenias. I felt a twinge of regret for using it to wash my clothes. The shampoo lathered into a rich, fragrant treat and the conditioner left my hair soft and silky.

Take that, Medusa, I thought, adding a second round in case she dared to rear her unruly head again.

I hesitated a second before slipping into a fluffy, white bathrobe and matching slippers. Skipping over the elegant selection of toiletries, I reached for the hair dryer. The faster I got out of here, the better.

Feeling more like myself with my hair hanging in graceful curves around my shoulders, I tip-toed down the stairs and put my clothes in the dryer. As I crossed the foyer, I caught sight of Troy in the kitchen.

He was chugging down a carton of orange juice, head thrown back, wearing nothing but a towel and the rosary around his neck. I squirmed, feeling like a voyeur, watching something primal and very, very intimate. I watched his adam's apple spasm as he drank greedily, not stopping to breath. His skin glistened, still wet from the shower, as beads of water ran down the flat planes of his abs and disappeared into the V barely covered by his towel. He drained the box, sated, and sighed with a satisfaction that sent a jolt of excitement through me.

"Why didn't you call?" Carol came into view.

He wasn't alone.

"I was at Ryan's."

"The nights too?" She pouted.

He turned to face her. "I didn't know we were still doing this."

"You're the reason I came home this summer. I haven't stopped thinking about you." Her voice dropped. "You were my first."

"And you regret that?"

"God, no." She ran her fingers over his chest. "I was hoping we could pick up where we left off." Her hands paused at the top of his towel.

"Carol." He lifted her chin so she was looking straight at him. "I'm incredibly lucky to have spent that time with you."

"But...?"

"But nothing. I thought we were clear about what it was."

"So I'm not your type?"

"You're not listening to me."

Carol walked to the other side of the island in the kitchen. All I saw now were her hands, clasped tightly on the counter.

"Life is just a bowl full of cherries for you, isn't it?" she said. "And you intend to taste every single one of them."

"Why not?" replied Troy, his muscles taut with restless energy. "You should too. You're young. Intelligent. Beautiful. There's so much of life waiting for the both of us." He leaned back against the fridge and regarded her.

"You really believe that." It was a half laugh, half sob.

"Carol—"

"Don't."

She was almost at the front door when he grabbed her.

"That's not how you say goodbye to a lover," he said.

And then he kissed her, like she was the most special thing in the world. She melted and clung to him. Who wouldn't? A kiss like that filled you up and left you with more than you had.

"Oh Troy." Carol cupped his face. Then she shook her head and let herself out.

He stared at the door after she'd gone.

"Was that Carol I just saw leaving?" Jayne burst in through the back.

"Yes," he replied.

"Finally!" She marched into the kitchen and pulled out a stool. "With Ryan and Ellen kissy-facing on the deck and you and Carol cozying up in here, I'm bored. And hungry."

"Don't look at me," said Troy. "I'm clueless in the kitchen."

"Fine." Jayne sauntered over to the fridge. "I'll just help myself."

It wasn't until she leaned over that I noticed she had undone the top two buttons of her blouse. She stuck her bum out before getting some pitas and cheese.

"Would you like something, Troy?"

He didn't miss the dramatic batting of teen eyelashes as she sidled past him, brushing against his bare, firm stomach.

His eyes followed her. "Come to think of it, I *am* kind of hungry," he growled.

He took the food from her and set it on the counter. "But maybe something we'll both enjoy?"

Jayne gulped as he moved towards her. She looked like she was about to swoon, but he shifted her aside and opened a drawer.

"What are you doing?" she asked.

"Patience," he said, as he walked over to the ice dispenser, letting cubes of ice collect into a bowl. "Now..." He took a small piece from the bowl and held it over her lips.

Seriously?

I rushed out of the laundry, but before I got to the kitchen, he let the cube slide down her neck.

"You need to cool off, squirt," he whispered, before dumping the whole bowl down her blouse.

"Ohhh!" Jayne squealed and hopped wildly around the kitchen. Ice cubes scattered all over the floor.

"Why you...!" She swung a jug his way, drenching him with cherry colored fruit punch.

"Oh yeah?" He challenged after the initial shock. He picked up a rapidly melting ice cube and threw it at her. She ducked. The two of them went slipping and sliding on the wet floor.

"Guys. GUYS!" I stepped in. "Stop it!"

"He started it!" Jayne pointed to her soggy blouse.

"She asked for it."

"What a mess." I surveyed the kitchen. "Jayne, mop. Troy, for heaven's sake, go put on some clothes. I'm going to get dressed and fix us something to eat so you can drive us back."

"Yes, ma'am." He grinned.

I turned away from the outline of steely thighs under his wet towel. Raspberry tinged water ran down his chest. He followed me into the laundry and watched while I got my clothes out of the dryer.

"Throw this in the hamper for me, will you?"

I turned around and caught the wet towel just in time.

"The robe looks good," he remarked. "Very sexy."

My jaw dropped as I followed the muscled contours of his back up the stairs, sleek and summer-bronzed, except for the pale patch of bare ass.

"Mmmmm..So good"

"It's just pita pizza," I replied.

Yes, just pita pizza, so why was I reacting to his rumbling approval as if we were lying on a pillow together? I fell back and started walking with Jayne.

The streets were empty but littered from the evening's festivities.

"You want some of mine?" Ryan offered his slice to Ellen.

"No, you have it."

"No, you."

Jayne rolled her eyes. "I'll take it."

Her brother glowered at her before wolfing down the whole piece. Then he rolled his napkin up and threw it at her.

"Poor Jayne." I laughed. "Not a good day, huh?"

"Oh, I had fun!" She grinned. "Thanks for coming along. Mum would never have let me go without you."

"You only came because of her?" asked Troy.

"Helloooo? You think she came for you?" said Jayne.

"I know at least *one* person who did." He shot her a cheeky look.

Jayne launched at him.

"Easy, squirt." He let her throw a few punches before hooking an arm around her. "Friends?"

"Friends." She laughed.

We found Troy's car under a flickering street light outside the gas station, exactly where we'd left it.

"Hop in. I'll be right back."

"Where are you going?" asked Ryan.

"I left the keys with Greta," he replied before stepping inside the store.

The air was hot and stifling in the car so we rolled the windows down and waited outside. Ryan and Ellen leaned against the hood, gazing up at the stars.

"What's taking him so long?" Jayne walked up to the door and peered in.

"Hey." She waved me over a few moments later. "Come look at this."

We pressed our noses against the glass.

At first I saw nothing but an empty store. Then two heads appeared behind the shelving. Talking? No. Moving. Gliding down row after row.

"Are they...are they dancing?" I asked as Troy maneuvered Greta through lines of haphazardly stacked toilet paper and air fresheners, up through the magazine section and back to the cash register.

Jayne giggled. "Come on." She pulled me in after her.

A male voice was singing to a carefree, flirty beat through the speakers.

"What's this song that's playing?" I asked.

"It's Tom Jones," Jayne replied. "Just Help Yourself."

We went unnoticed as Troy swept past us, smiling at the woman in his arms. It didn't matter that her green eye shadow had creased into the papery folds of her lids, or that her hair had de-pouffed under the weight of harsh fluorescent lights. In that magical moment, she was the belle of the ball, swept away from the ordinary. The dusty layers of time sloughed off and I saw her as she would have been, at her prom, or her wedding perhaps. She sparkled under the spotlight Troy shone on her, the moment he decided to steal a dance, while his friends waited outside.

"Me, me, me!" cried Jayne, the next time the two of them came around.

"Ah, we have company!" Greta let him go, still laughing, and started clapping to the beat.

Troy carried Jayne away, her head disappearing behind the stark white shelving. For a while it looked like he'd gone completely haywire, turning and bobbing through an empty store by himself. I heard her whoop of delight as he twirled her around, and then he was coming back our way again.

Jayne grabbed me while Troy pulled Greta in, and we ended up in a conga line, threading our way up and down the aisles, the three of us following his lead. Three shuffles, a crazy kick and a toss of our heads. And repeat.

Then he stole me away and we waltzed past the cooler with the milk and little cartons of half-melted ice-cream. I shrieked as he led me into a series of dizzy spins, one after the other, before drawing me back to him. I could smell the clean, spicy scent of his freshly showered skin as we returned to where Jayne and Greta were standing, doing their own versions of the twist. He joined them, competing for the most ridiculously exaggerated poses. Just before the song ended, he lowered Greta into a dip and planted the biggest smooch on her lips. She tottered unsteadily as she came up for air, her face split with the widest, brightest smile.

"Thank you, Greta." He picked up the car keys from the counter.

"Lordy." She laughed.

"You behave now." He wagged a finger at her as we left the gas station.

She waved, beaming at us through the smudged square of her window.

"Let's go, girls." Troy opened the car door.

Inside, Ryan and Ellen were lip-locked, legs and arms entwined in the back seat.

"Alrighty then." He shut the door and walked around to the other side.

"You go," I whispered in Jayne's ear. I wasn't getting anywhere near all that action.

"Hey!" Jayne elbowed Ryan. "Break it up. You're making us uncomfortable."

And by 'us', she meant me. Jayne was obviously amused and Troy was thoroughly enjoying my discomfort. The passionate duo pulled away reluctantly.

"Where to?" asked Troy when I got in the front with him. The sleeves of his t-shirt strained against his biceps as he put his seat belt on.

I gave him the address, feeling like the back seat might have been a better option after all.

"You're the furthest," he said. "We'll do Ellen, then Ryan and Jayne, and then you."

"Or you could just drop me off first, and them on the way back." The prospect of being alone with him made my stomach clench into a tight little ball.

"Us first!" declared Jayne. "Mum's going to be up waiting and I don't want to screw it up for next time."

"Right," replied Troy, turning on the ignition. "Anyone waiting for you, Shayda?"

I looked away, wondering where Hafez had spent Canada Day. Maybe he was at the wheel, eating up the miles to make his deadline, or maybe he had pulled into a truck stop to stretch out his legs.

When we got to Ellen's, Ryan walked her to the door. They disappeared in the shadows while we waited in the car.

"You're done for, mate," said Troy when he got back. "Whipped. Finished. Over and out."

"Just drive, will ya?" Ryan grinned. "Wait until it happens to you."

"Ha!" exclaimed Jayne. "Bet he's the first one dragged down the aisle."

"Oh yeah? Bet he's the last man standing."

Troy let them speculate, keeping his eyes on the road, but I felt his gaze on me every now and then.

THE SILENCE GREW THICK AFTER WE DROPPED JAYNE AND Ryan off. Suddenly, I was acutely aware of the way Troy's arms moved when he shifted gears, the way his legs controlled the pedals, the way the car purred under his command.

"You mind?" he asked, rolling down his window.

"No." I fished out a scrunchie from my bag and tied my hair back. It was still hot, but the night air cooled my fevered skin.

"Hey, Shayda?"

"What?"

He slid the scrunchie out of my hair and tossed it out the window. My carefully tamed mane sprung back into a mass of curls. I opened my mouth, shut it, opened it again, and swallowed the words. Then I unrolled my side of the window and shot him a sideways glance.

We started laughing at the same time, both of us looking equally ridiculous, our hair flapping in the wind as if we were free-falling into the night.

"Here we are." He turned into my apartment.

"I'll be fine," I said as he reached for his door. "You don't have to come up."

"I want to." He smoothed my hair behind my ear.

"Don't." I gripped his hand, holding it away.

The air throbbed as our eyes locked.

"Is it just me or do you keep everyone at arm's length?" he asked.

I let go of his hand, feeling foolish for reading more into the gesture.

Outside, a Canada Day party was going strong. David Bowie was rocking out the words to 'Let's Dance' with jittery breathlessness.

"Now if I were to do this..." He tugged me closer so our lips were almost touching.

My stomach flip-flopped. My eyes widened in alarm and I clamped my hand over my mouth. Then I was running out the door, fumbling blindly with the keys before racing through the lobby and jabbing the elevator button.

"Shayda!" I could vaguely hear Troy coming after me.

I ran for the stairs, taking two at a time as his footsteps echoed after mine through the drab, grey stairwell. I flung open the door to the third floor and made a run for the apartment, barely making it to the kitchen sink before throwing up all over it.

Troy rubbed my back as I retched and retched until there was nothing left.

"Can't say I've ever elicited that kind of a reaction before." He attempted some humor as I cleaned up. "And I've never met anyone who could hold it through six flights of stairs until it was good and proper to let loose."

My throat felt tight and exhausted. I rinsed the sink and splashed some water on my face, appalled that he had to witness that.

"Here." He led me to the couch and sat me down. "May I?" he asked, before kneeling to wipe the plastered hair off my forehead. "No one's home?" He glanced around the sparsely furnished space.

I shook my head.

"Stay right there." He walked into the kitchen.

I heard him moving things in the refrigerator. He returned with a glass of ginger ale.

"Here." He handed it to me. "Drink."

I took a few small sips, grateful for the cool bubbles that soothed my throat. This was the third time in as many weeks that I'd thrown up. My brows furrowed.

"You okay?" he asked.

I looked at him, flipping a calendar in my head.

"I think...I think I'm pregnant," I replied.

The night Ma died. My first time with Hafez. I had long run out of the birth control pills Dr. Gorman had given me.

"Wow." Troy slumped into the chair, looking pale, as if he were about to hurl too.

"Don't worry, it's not yours." My turn to attempt some humor, even though it felt like the rug had just been pulled out from under me.

"Shouldn't your...shouldn't your husband be here?"

"He's back tomorrow."

"You want to call him?"

"He's on the road. It can wait."

Troy got up and started pacing the living room.

"You should go," I said. "I'm fine. Really."

He went very quiet, like he could see just how hard I was shaking inside.

"I've never met anyone quite like you, Mrs....?" he said as I let him out.

"Hijazi. Shayda Hijazi."

"Well, Mrs. Hijazi." He gave me the kind of smile that begs a ribbon, the kind you want to wrap up and store away. "It's been a pleasure."

"Sorry I—," I started, but he shushed me with a finger on my mouth.

"You rest now."

I nodded, trying to get over the knot in my throat as I watched him walk to the elevator.

"I hope it's a girl," he said before stepping in. "With sunset red in her hair, like her mother."

"I don't have red in my hair."

"You do," he replied. "When the light hits it a certain way, like that morning I ran into you. Beautiful, fiery shades of red."

I shook my head and smiled. A charmer to the end.

"Goodbye, Shayda Hijazi," he said before the elevator closed on him.

"Goodbye, Troy Heathgate."

I shut the door, not knowing it would be twelve years before I saw him again.

13. WAIT

....

November 11th, 1995 (2)

A COLD WIND SWEEPS GREY LEAVES AROUND MY FEET. I GET up, hoping it will pick up my memories of Troy and take them wherever grey leaves go to die. I stop by the pond, with my hands in my pockets, and see a flash of color on the ground. I kneel and pick up a dead butterfly. Its wings cling stubbornly to their color, beautiful even though large sections of the scales are missing.

When the revolution started in Iran, Baba had thought we would be safer out of the city. Months later, when they came to our summer home, with torches blazing, Maamaan, Hossein and I fled to the hills. When it was quiet, and the black spires of smoke had lifted, we made our way down and waited for Baba in the barn. He returned at dawn, smelling of perfume and wine. I had seen a butterfly that day, in the ashes of scorched lemon trees, much like the one I'm holding, except I had trampled it in our rush to get to the barn. I watch the lifeless form in my hands now through a haze of tears.

A lone runner passes by, stops and tracks back.

"Shayda?"

I don't need to look up. Only one person says my name like that.

He kneels beside me as I nurse the butterfly.

"Look." I hold it out.

"It's not your butterfly," he says.

"I know. But it's dead, Troy. It died."

"Don't cry." He lifts my chin. "I can't stand it when you cry."

We're back on that sidewalk again, our eyes locked, except it's a different time, a different season.

He cups his palm over mine as a gust of wind threatens to sweep the butterfly away.

We stand up slowly, holding the Monarch between us, and walk to the edge of the pond. We lower our hands into the water and let it float away. We watch, reluctant to move even after it disappears, because we both know what happens next.

Don't go, I want to say.

"See you around, Shayda." He pushes the flyaway curls out of my face, but they don't stay. His smile is bittersweet as he plugs the headphones back in his ears.

I watch the back of his head, covered by a hoodie, as he takes off.

I make it half way to the parking lot. My throat is clenched so tight it's hard to breathe. I feel like I've left some part of me behind to die, to float away on some cold, glassy surface that will turn to ice.

No.

I turn and start running towards Troy.

Wait. Wait. Wait. Wait.

My words carry to him. Somehow. Because he stops and turns around.

I halt, a few feet away from him, my chest heaving. For a few seconds, we stand on opposite sides of an invisible fence. Then he tears through it, closing the distance, and I'm in his arms. He's lifting me up. And spinning me round. I'm laughing. Crying. Deliriously happy. Scared senseless.

When I come down, he's holding me, his forehead resting on mine.

"Your hands are so cold," he says.

We sit on the bench and he rubs them briskly. When he's warmed them up, he trails his fingers over my palms, up and down, before entwining them with mine.

"Here we are," he says.

"Here we are." I rest my head on his shoulder.

14. HOTEL ROOM

November 22nd, 1995

I CAN'T REMEMBER GETTING OUT OF THE CAR OR WALKING through the reception area. I don't recall what the hallway looked like or what room number he said. I sit at the edge of the mattress, the side closest to the door, and let my eyes follow the vibrant swirls on the carpet—wandering, drifting, straying. I can't bear to look at the bed, the chocolate headboard, the lamp on the night stand. *Him.*

He kneels on the floor and slides my boots off. First one, then the other.

"You okay?" He rubs my feet.

Am I okay?

I start laughing, a little hysterically. I don't think he has the slightest idea what it's taken for me to get here. I've crossed oceans and countries and continents. That was the easy part. But sitting here before Troy Heathgate now, I'm teetering on a knife's edge between honor and disgrace.

"Drink." He hands me a glass of water.

It works. I can't drink and laugh and cry at the same time.

"Just because you're here, doesn't mean anything." He takes the empty glass and turns on the TV. "We'll get room service, talk, watch a movie."

My eyes go round.

"Not *that* kind of movie," he laughs.

The warm chuckle melts my bones.

"No?" I feign disappointment.

He swats me with a pillow. I retaliate, swinging back with a hard whack.

"Really?" His eyes narrow.

And then we're rolling and tumbling on the bed, pillow fighting like kids at a sleepover.

Except we're not kids. I can feel the raw strength in his arms, the ripple of hard muscle under his shirt, his carefully controlled desire. We stop at the same time, breathless and flushed, the air between us pulsating with that crazy, hungry energy that eats up every sane thought in my mind. He reins himself in first.

"What do you want to watch?" he asks, leaning back.

"Doesn't matter." I prop up a pillow next to him.

He pauses at the music channel. Safe, comfortable, non-flammable. I have no clue what we're watching. I doubt he does either. He puts his arm around me and I snuggle in, like it's the most natural place in the world for me to be.

He's wearing faded blue jeans and a soft, white t-shirt. I've never seen anyone rock every day essentials the way he does. My eyes follow the long line of his legs. His toes are surprisingly pretty.

I smile.

"What?" he asks.

I shake my head and focus on the TV. "This must be a first for you."

118

"It is. The cuddling usually comes after."

"I meant getting a room and then having someone chicken out on you."

"Are you afraid, Shayda?"

"Of...?" I swallow, wishing he'd go back to pretending we're watching music videos.

"Of this? Of me?"

"No."

"Then what?"

"Of...me," I reply.

It's true. I don't know this person lying beside him.

We sit, separated by a tiny band of pale skin on my ring finger. For the first time in thirteen years, I've left home without my wedding band. I feel the tension, like spring coils compressed into the space between us, expanding and contracting with each breath we take.

He's waiting.

Let me in.

I move my foot towards his until our toes are almost touching. Almost, but not quite. The rise and fall of his chest ceases. He holds his breath. The TV drones on.

I can stop this right now, this crazy stupid insanity. Walk out the door and run like hell.

My foot brushes his. It's the smallest movement, but it's all he needs.

His hand slides into mine; our fingers entwine. His thumb draws circles in the center of my palm. We watch images flicker across the screen, but every nerve is focused on what our hands are doing. He traces up and down my fingers, lingering in the gaps between them, teasing, caressing.

Have I been touched there before? Surely I would remember this sensation, so simple yet so exquisitely loaded.

The back of my fingers run across his palm. He sucks in his breath as he feels my nails on his skin. The thinly stretched cord of control snaps.

He flips me on my back and pins my wrists over my head. I close my eyes, anticipating his kiss, yearning for it. But it doesn't come.

He sucks my fingers instead, one by one, like they're covered with the sticky, sweet filling of a freshly baked pie. His tongue traces the blue-green vein along my inner wrist, making me squirm against him.

I wait for guilt to set in. I wait for self-loathing to roll in. I wait for my feet to carry me to the door. But when his lips graze mine, whisper soft, I know this is what I've been waiting for. How long have I thought about this? How many weeks? Months? Years? His lips on mine. Like this. My fingers running through his hair. Like this. The hard, muscular length of him against me. I open my eyes and fall into the endless sky of his irises while Gloria Estefan sings 'Here We Are'.

In this moment, it doesn't matter that he is Troy Heathgate.

'Wealthy, debonair, visionary leader,' say the business magazines.

'Hazardous, womanizing, master of seduction,' says the trail of broken hearts.

No. In this moment, he is just a man, raw, primal, stripped of all the labels and titles—bare eyes, hungry mouth, intent on one thing and one thing only. Me.

If Troy Heathgate locks in on you, you're done for.

Clearly, whoever said that had made a very important public service announcement.

Troy's mouth is devastatingly insistent on my lips, building to an intensity that makes me cling to him as my world spins out of control. Yes. Yes yes yes. *This*. This is what a kiss should feel like. Like nothing else exists. All yearning and dizzy and falling and flying. Great big galaxies of want and wonder spiral inside of me.

"I've waited so long for this," he says in my ear.

I push a lock of hair away from his face. Such dark hair, such light eyes. The seductive pull of the devil, the redeeming touch of an angel.

He grabs a fist full of my hair and pulls, exposing my throat. I expect pain, teeth, fangs even. Happily. But he drops a tender kiss on the vein that pulses life into my heart. I feel the light stubble on his jaw as he nuzzles in.

"Mmmm. Roses." He moves his face back and forth against my neck, caressing my skin with his nose, his mouth, his cheek, the soft parts of his face, the ridges.

"Turn around," he growls.

No. Keep going. This is good. This is so good.

"Turn." He flips me over and swipes the hair away from my nape, continuing his sensual attack.

I was wrong. This is even better. I feel teeth. Sharp, little nips, followed by soothing tongue. Lips, soft, then hard. Fingers sliding down the back of my neck, tugging at the zipper of my dress.

"Shhh," he whispers when he feels me tense.

It's easier this way. Not having to look at him, my face buried in the pillow. I feel a slight chill as my dress starts to part, followed by the heat of fiery kisses. He makes a slow descent down my spine, exposing one inch at a time. When he gets to the small of my back, his tongue dips into the slight indentation. A moan escapes me.

"Ah." I feel the curve of his smile against my skin.

He holds down my hips as his mouth ravages the bundle of nerves I never knew existed. I buckle against the bed.

"Behave," he says.

How can the softest whisper be edged with steel?

He replaces his lips with the heel of his palm. The rhythmic, kneading motion feels even more intense, pushing the pulsating core of me into the mattress. Hot, unbidden images flash before me and I stifle a sharp, agonized breath into the pillow.

"Your skin..." He trails off, tracing the curve of my spine with knowing fingers. Up and down.

His touch feels like rain on parched earth.

"Now." He turns me over. "Let me look at you."

My arms cross instinctively against my chest, keeping the front of my dress in place. My face burns from the intimacy of being undressed by him.

"Hello, Beetroot." His mouth is hot on my skin as he nudges my bra straps past my shoulders with his lips.

His kisses move lower, caressing the exposed skin of my breasts. I cling to my dress, but inch by inch, it retreats. Who can resist to be disrobed so? With lips and tongue and lover's breath.

My fingers slide into the thick mat of his hair. I gasp as his mouth closes over my swollen nipple.

"Raspberry." He circles the peak with his tongue. "I wondered what color you'd be."

I give myself up to his hungry kisses, but he wants more. More. Cupping, kneading, sucking, teasing. Pulses of pleasure rush through me, pulling some primitive cord inside of me. I twist hard and fast against him.

A guttural sound vibrates from his chest. He pulls my dress off in a frenzied motion.

"This too." He tugs at my bra. His eyes are darker now, pupils dilated, burning with need.

I shake my head, holding on to the cups of my bra, even as my breasts spill over.

"Fine. I'll go first." His t-shirt hits the floor.

There are few men that are born just ridiculously sexy. One happens to be half-naked in front of me now. I take in the smooth expanse of muscle and sinew, the taut, flat stomach, the way the tattoos encircle his corded arms. I want to breathe the solid wall of his chest, to feel those arms around me. I want our legs entwined, our breaths mingled. I want to know his face in ecstasy.

His breath catches at the fleeting expressions on my face.

And then we're kissing madly. Hot, fevered, hungry. I feel the rough texture of male hair against my legs. When did he take his pants off?

Our eyes lock.

What is this madness?

I don't know. I don't know.

"God, you're so beautiful."

I bask. No. I glow.

He trails his hand down my body and dips his finger into my navel. Round and round, he traces it. The soft flesh beneath trembles. The back of his fingers stroke the space between my belly button and the top of my panties, back and forth. One finger slides under the waistband.

My stomach clenches. I can't control the shaking. My breath starts to come in short, shallow bursts. I place my hands on his.

Stop. Wait.

But he pins them to the bed and buries his face in my stomach.

Ohhh. So warm. So hot.

I feel his breath on my tummy, blazing a stream of promises across my skin. He grips the edge of my panties with his teeth and tugs.

God.

With my arms held to the sides and his weight on my legs, he holds me motionless. All of my senses zone in on the slow, slow descent of my panties. I feel the moistness of his lips through the fabric, the warmth of his exhalation, until little by little he exposes the pulsing, throbbing core of me.

The tremors intensify inside of me.

He lets go of my hands and splays his fingers across my trembling tummy, steadying me, holding me down, as his lips taste the throbbing button between my folds.

"Mmmm." The humming vibration rocks through me.

Then his hands slide under my hips and he claims me. Completely. With his nose and his mouth and his tongue and his lips.

My nails claw at the sheets. It's overwhelming, these sensations, so raw, so intense. I start pulling away from him, flexing my legs.

"Shhh...just a little more," he says.

How do I tell him? *Should* I tell him?

Troy, I don't know how to do this. I wish you'd stop because it frightens me. I wish you'd stop because if it doesn't happen with Troy Heathgate, God of All Things That Make a Woman Squirm, I'll know I'm flawed. Lacking. Defective.

I writhe against him, trying to free myself, but he has me pinned to the bed, completely at his mercy. Suddenly, I'm under Pasha Moradi, reliving those ugly moments of helplessness and terror. Troy's face disappears and everything turns dark.

I start kicking and fighting with everything I've got. The heaviness lifts off, almost instantaneously. When I can breathe again, and the darkness has dissipated, I find him watching me.

"I'm not going to hurt you." He holds his palms up.

I nod, shivering. My body is drenched in cold sweat. He strokes my hair, coaxing me into his arms. I lie on his chest,

124

listening to his heart. How could I mistake this beat for that monster's?

"You want to talk about it?" He half-kisses, half-talks against my forehead.

"I just..." I swallow the fist in my throat. "I have to go." I start pulling on my panties with as much grace as I can muster.

"You're not going anywhere until you tell me what just happened." Gone is the adoring lover. In his place is cold steel and ice.

"I can't."

"You can't? You can't what, Shayda? You can't trust me? You can't stand being touched by me? *What*, Shayda?" He spins me around hard against him so we're face to face, kneeling on the bed.

"I can't use you!" I can't use him to heal myself, to put together the broken pieces and make me whole again.

"*Use* me?" He lets out a deep, throaty laugh. His hold softens and he runs his hand up and down my arm. "Do I look like a man who can be easily used?"

Um...no. He looks...he looks...sinfully hot. How does he bring me from the depths of churning despair to a simmering bliss in ten seconds flat? And how did I miss these? Red briefs? Really? Who wears such sexy, bold briefs, that hit the thigh and leave little to the imagination?

"Like my trunks?"

Shit. I've been staring.

He takes my hand and puts it on his thigh. I stroke the fabric tentatively, feeling the muscle underneath.

"Ahhh." He closes his eyes. "I love when you use me."

"You think I'm naïve." I remove my hand.

"A little. Yes." He sits back and sighs. "It's one of the things I find disarmingly seductive about you." He runs a finger from my forehead, down the ridge of my nose, to my lips. "And just so you know, I love making you squirm and quiver and hot and wet." He slips the tip of his finger inside my mouth, stroking the soft, inner flesh.

"Why did you fight me, Shayda?"

"I just...I don't like being pinned down," I reply, resisting the urge to suck on his finger.

"No kidding." He traces the scar on my lip. "But look, I can do it hands free."

"Troy!" I pull him back up.

"Mmmm?" He starts nibbling my neck.

"I..."

"You...?" He props himself up and plays with a strand of my hair.

"I've never been able to orgasm with anyone." There. I want to die from shame.

"So?" The nibbling moves to my ear.

"Did you hear what I said?" *I'm no good. I suck at this.*

"I did. And I'm guessing you've had all of what—one sexual partner?"

I don't reply.

"Tell me something. Can you make yourself come?"

How can it be this quiet when so much blood is rushing to my face?

"Why, Beetroot!" His eyes dance with amusement. "I believe you can."

I duck under his chin, into the sanctuary of his chest.

"I still don't get your reaction," he says. "But it can wait. I know it took a lot for you to get here and I know why you came."

"Why?" I finger-doodle on his chest.

"For the same reason I did. Because you had no choice. Because you couldn't eat. Or sleep. Or think of anything else but this."

His lips capture mine in a long, drugging kiss.

Yes. I'm here because of this. And the lopsided tilt of his smile. And his infuriating confidence. And the way the air pulsates between us.

His arms come around me, wrapping me into the warmth of his body. "Shayda, if we're going to do this, there's something you should know. I don't do threesomes with shame or guilt or regret. You need to check those in at the door. They don't belong in bed. I intend to get to know everything about you—every curve on your body, every dirty, sexy thought, every dark, hidden spot. Everything. So as far as I'm concerned, we're off to a great start."

"But you didn't...you know..." There is no denying his raw arousal throbbing between us.

"Well, neither did you." He laughs. "I may not always be a gentleman in bed, but I do believe in ladies first."

"In that case, you're going to be very frustrated. Not to mention disappointed."

"Are you kidding me? I'm the luckiest man in the world."

"How's that?"

"Because I get to make your toes curl and your knees shake. I'll be the first to hear the kind of sounds you make when you come. Will you plead, Shayda? Will you moan? Or will you give me quiet little gasps? Whatever it is, Shayda, I can promise you one thing. It'll be mad and passionate. Because I don't believe that mediocre sex is worth having." He tilts my head and kisses the corner of my mouth.

"And just so we're clear..." He nips my shoulder. "There will be no stopping me next time."

15. BATTLE OF THE SHEET

December 15th, 1995

"APPLE CRUMBLE, CRÈME BRÛLÉE OR RED VELVET CAKE?"
Troy runs a lazy finger down my spine.

"Red velvet," I reply.

"You sure you don't want a proper lunch?"

I nod.

"One red velvet cake, one coffee," he speaks into the receiver.

"Don't you want anything?" I ask after he hangs up. "Or is that the price you pay for these washboard abs?"

"Did you know, anatomically, my abs don't end there?"

"They don't?"

"No, you have the six pack or the Rectus Abdominis here, and then the much overlooked Erectus Hominis, right here."

"Troy!"

"That's right, baby. Say my name." He smacks my butt playfully.

I laugh. He makes this easy.

"Kiss me." I sink my fingers into his hair.

It's always there, the fire between us, like glowing embers waiting to be stoked. One look, one kiss, one caress, and I come alive for him.

"Hold that thought," he says when there's a knock on the door.

I will never tire of the way he moves, lithe and graceful, the smooth ripple of muscle under warm, bare skin. He's been cautious since that first encounter. Sometimes we spend whole afternoons in bed just talking, our hands entwined, enjoying long pauses of blissful silence.

"How do you expect to eat when you're grasping that sheet so tightly with both hands?" He sits cross-legged on the bed and places the room service tray in front of me.

I pull the bed sheet closer around my chest.

"Suit yourself." He shrugs and takes a bite of the cake. "Mmmm. It's so..." He searches for the right word. "Moist. Not too sweet. Surprisingly light. And this icing...." He proceeds to swipe another great, big chunk. "Mmmm."

"Coffee? You take cream? Sugar?" He helps himself.

"Seriously?" I ask as he continues to devour everything on the tray.

"Why? Did you want some?"

"Of course I want some!"

"Then let go of the sheet."

"No!"

"You have beautiful breasts, Shayda. Gorgeous. You should be showing them off. In fact, I should be eating *this* cake off *those* breasts." He lunges for me.

"Watch it! There's hot coffee on the bed!"

"There's also an incredibly hot woman on the bed." He crawls towards me on all fours. "Guess who gets my attention?"

He tangles his fist in my hair and gives me a long, twisting kiss.

"I can see I'll have to feed you myself." He sits back and attends to me, one luscious forkful at a time. "Good?"

"Uh-huh." I could get used to this.

When I've had my coffee and the plate is empty, he puts the tray away.

"Still hungry?"

I shake my head.

"Good, because I'm starving." He looks at me with naked eyes. "Show me what you do."

"What?"

"You said the only way you can orgasm is if you do it yourself. Show me. How do you please yourself, Shayda?"

I wish the ground would open up and swallow me whole.

"Ah Beetroot, you never fail to make an appearance." He smiles. "I need to know, Shayda, so I can do what you like."

"I ...I already like what you do."

"Yes, but I want to catch that look in your eyes as you go over the edge. I want the ultimate satisfaction of knowing I'm driving you wild. It's only fair. Because I intend to thoroughly enjoy myself with you, to extract every last drop of pleasure, no holds barred." He takes my hand and guides it lower. "Show me."

Who knew the sweet, wanton power of words? A string of sentences transformed into moving, writhing images. I swallow.

"I can't."

"Why not?"

"Because I don't...touch myself."

He looks at me and lets it sink in. "Then how?"

"I just...I do it differently." I squirm. "Now can we please not talk about this?"

He doesn't say anything. When I peek at him, he's contemplating me with narrowed eyes.

"You're like a labyrinth, Shayda. But I will find my way and you *will* show me."

I burrow deeper into him.

"Do you know what you feel like?" His fingers follow the curve of my hip and slide under the waistband of my panties.

I suck in my breath as he parts the moistness between my legs.

"You're like a warm, wet, velvet glove," he says. "It's a little like this..." He closes his mouth around my finger and rolls it around. "But better. Tighter." His eyes darken with desire. "And a texture that I can't explain. Do you want to feel, Shayda?"

He guides my hand over my belly, distracting me with hot kisses as he slides my finger inside, next to his.

Ohhh.

"Move with me, Shayda."

We start a slow, rhythmic dance. He leads, I follow. Our fingers step in and out in unison, until I'm reeling from the raw intimacy of it.

"I...can't." I pull away, a strange hollowness aching inside me.

"You can." He takes my finger and sucks on it, savoring the taste of me. "You should." He props himself up and gazes at me. "Play with yourself, get to know how amazing you feel, how incredibly responsive. See this?" His thumb presses against my clit. "Ahhh this." He closes his eyes and flicks the little nub from side to side. "I intend to get to know this very, very well."

My hips buck involuntarily against him.

He pushes the hair away from my face. "Rub against my palm."

I writhe, twisting and turning, my face and neck flushed with desire. He nips my bottom lip, groaning as he feels me getting wetter. My thighs clench together and I start undulating against him in an age-old rhythm. He lets me ride the wave, higher, higher, but I lose the peak, an image of my shameless, greedy, cheating self, flashing before me.

"Don't stop, don't stop," he whispers.

But it's too late. I hide my face in the pillow.

"Hey." He tries to catch my eye, but I can't bear to look at him.

He gathers me to his chest and rocks me gently.

"I'm sorry." My voice is muffled and unsteady.

"Why?"

"You're not disappointed?" I trace the barbed wire tattoo around his arm.

"Disappointed? With what?"

"With me."

"Shayda." He sighs. "This is not some race to the finish line. Yes, I want to please you, but I don't expect you to become suddenly orgasmic. It takes time, and getting to know each other, and trust each other. Heck, does this feel disappointed to you?"

He brings me flush with the hard line of his arousal. "I am so hot for you right now, I might just pop this zipper."

I feel him through his pants and tug at them. "Take them off."

"You take them off." He says it quietly, but I feel every muscle in his body tense.

He's giving me the option to turn away, to pace this, control it.

I unbuckle his belt and pull. The leather slides out slowly, one loop after the other. I pause for a heartbeat, steadying my hands before undoing the button. My mouth is flush with his zipper. I hold my breath and pull the tab down.

"Come here," he drawls, kicking off his pants and underwear as he pulls me up so I'm lying on top of him. Then he rolls his pulsating manhood between our bellies.

"Ohhh," I gasp.

He places my hands over it, letting my fingers get acquainted with the length and girth of him.

"God." His head falls back as I stroke him from tip to base. "You're going to kill me with that light touch."

His hands cup my bottom, pulling me closer. I feel him becoming even fuller for me.

"Show me," I whisper.

"You want me to come for you?" he growls in my ear. "Is that what you want, Shayda?"

He sits me on the edge of the bed and stands before me, tall and proud and fiercely male. My eyes are level with his raging erection. Something wild and primal stirs in me as he starts moving his fist up and down his shaft in a slow, steady motion.

"Here." He massages the thin ridge along the underside of his penis. "And here." He rubs the ridge where the head meets the shaft.

I push his hands aside, mimicking his strokes, making twisting motions on the way down. One hand slides lower, cupping his balls.

A low rumble escapes him. He picks me up and pushes me further back on the bed.

"I'm going to come, Shayda."

I flick my thumb over the tip of his penis.

He cries out as he gives in to the spasms that rock his body, spilling himself on my tummy until he's spent and breathless.

His lips touch mine in a soft kiss, before he collapses on his back, taking me with him.

When his breathing returns to normal, he gives me that killer smile. "Don't look now, Beetroot, but you lost The Battle Of The Sheet somewhere between the District of Ohhh and the Region of Ahhh."

16. GUILTY LINGERIE

....

December 19th, 1995

"Please tell me we have everything." I flop on a bench, flanked by tall, golden urns of festive poinsettias.

"You're a terrible shopper," says Jayne, picking up the brightly colored bags at my feet. "One more stop. I need something for Matt. Come on."

I plod after her, mentally checking off every person on my list. Yup, I'm done. I've even got Maamaan covered, in case she decides to show for Christmas. She'll arrange herself like royalty and make sulky faces about adopting traditions that are not our own, but then she'll see the smiles on the kids' faces and secretly enjoy herself.

"I thought you said you needed something for Matt." I follow Jayne into a luxe lingerie boutique.

"It *is* for Matt." She winks. "He appreciates a well wrapped present."

The inside of the store is like a courtesan's boudoir—damask walls, plush chairs, gilded mirrors. One wall is covered with bra-thong-garter combos in jewel toned silk and racy lace. The other showcases waist cinching corsets and diaphanous negligees.

"This!" Jayne holds out a sheer chemise. "And this." She takes a hot number off the rack. "And this. And this, and this."

The salesgirl follows her through the store, collecting a pile of slinky under things, before showing her the fitting room.

"Don't you want anything? Something sexy to spice things up?" Jayne peers at me through the draped velvet curtain before disappearing behind it.

I think of the pink baby doll I had put on for Hafez, now quietly folded away. Then I think of the plain bra and panties Troy took off me, with his lips and his teeth, like he was uncovering the most exquisite thing he'd ever seen.

"This would look divine on you." The salesgirl brings me a metallic black showstopper with boob-sculpting cups that looks like it's designed to be ripped off in minutes.

"I don't think so," I reply.

"No harm trying, right?" She hangs it up before me.

I look away, but all I can think of is Troy's hand slipping under the gauzy chiffon, sliding the cheeky thong down my legs, undoing the silky ties...

I catch myself, caressing my stockinged calf with eyes half-closed. Shameless. Like a cat in heat.

"You know what? I think I'll try it on after all."

"Great. Let me know if you need a different size." The salesgirl smiles at me.

I hear Jayne come out of the adjacent room. "I'm going to take these four."

"Sure. Your friend is in the fitting room."

"Oh?" Jayne walks over. "Whatcha got in there, Shayda? Let me see."

"Jayne!" I shield myself as she barges in and draws the curtain behind her.

"Holy shit." She gapes at me. "Oh mama! I knew you were hiding beneath all those layers, but damn. You got it going on, girlfriend." She circles me, fixing the straps, pulling here, tugging there.

"I was just killing time. It's really not my style."

"Not your style?" She laughs. "You are so getting this!"

I look at myself in the mirror. "You think?"

"Um...YA!"

I hesitate at the register before pulling out my credit card. "It's so extravagant."

"Every woman should have something in her closet that makes her feel like a sex bomb. You just found your secret weapon, darling. Hafez won't know what hit him," says Jayne.

The thing about having an affair is that one minute you're having a Holly Jolly Christmas, and the next, Frosty the Snowman dumps a pile of guilt on you, so high, that you wonder if you'll ever be able to shovel your way out of it. And I deserve every bit of it. I should be used to lying. To Hafez, to the kids, to Jayne. But I don't know if it will ever come without this soul crushing weight. I feel like a total fraud as I take the bag from the salesgirl.

We head to the food court, barely managing to juggle the shopping bags.

"You're sure you don't want to join us over the holidays?" asks Jayne as we sip cinnamon spiced vanilla lattes.

"Yes. Hafez finally has some time off. I think he's just looking forward to some peace and quiet."

"It's a huge chalet, if you change your mind. Nothing but mountains and snow for miles and miles."

"Who's going?"

"Well, there's Matt and me. Ryan, Ellen, the kids. And two other couples. Maybe Troy. Ellen's been trying to play matchmaker, so if Ryan convinces him to come along, her friend will be there too. You know, surprise!"

"What happened to the girl he was with at Thanksgiving?"

"Who? Rachel?" Jayne shrugs. "Who knows? All I know is that everyone and their uncle is trying to fix that man up. I don't think Troy Heathgate is not going to be single much longer."

17. CALL ME

....

December 22nd, 1995

"You need any help?" asks Susan as I walk past the reception.

"That would be great." I hold the door open, juggling gift baskets and festively wrapped boxes.

Susan picks up the rest of the gifts. "Your clients really love you."

"I've come to know them over the years." I slide my things in the back seat and open the trunk for Susan.

"It's because you're good at what you do."

"Thanks. I love being a part of their milestones." I smile. "Enjoy the holidays."

"You too. See you in the new year." She waves goodbye.

I make it to the grocery store in time to grab the last of the turkey. The express line is a mile long. I push my cart to another check-out. The place is a zoo, none of the Christmas cheer here, just tired, harried shoppers, eager to get home.

My line stalls for a price check. The customer starts shouting at the cashier. I feel sorry for the poor girl. She wipes her brow and looks up. It's Marjaneh.

I watch as she rings through one person after another.

"Hello."

Scan, scan, weigh, scan.

Bag, bag, bag.

Ding, ding, ding, goes the register.

"Thank you. Merry Christmas."

Smile.

Next.

"Hello Marjaneh," I say when it's my turn.

She looks surprised to have someone acknowledge her.

"Hi, Shayda." There's no time for chit-chat.

I see the thin film of perspiration on her upper lip, the stains under her arms as she bags the turkey.

"Here you go."

"Thanks." I take it from her, and then I pause. "Listen." I reach for my business card. "If you ever think about doing something else, call me."

She takes it and shoves it in her vest pocket. "Merry Christmas."

Smile.

Next.

I GET IN THE CAR AND WAIT FOR IT TO WARM UP. THERE IS no snow on the ground, but the windows are frosty and the air is biting cold.

I hear a muffled chiming, like the ring tone of a cell phone. Strange. I don't have one, but something in the car is definitely going off. It stops for a while and then starts again. I rummage through the packages, letting the sound guide me, until I find a red box with a cell phone inside.

"Hello?"

"Shayda."

Shayda with the ahhh. In that rich, baritone, coffee-over-marshmallow voice. I feel the chill in my bones melt.

"You there?"

"Yes," I reply. "What's with the cell phone?"

"Well, I can't call you at home and I don't want to go through your receptionist every time I want to get a hold of you."

"I have a pager."

"Always on the cutting edge of technology." He laughs.

"But I didn't sign up for this."

"I did. It's in my name."

"So the bill comes to you?"

"Yes." He sounds like he's in a bar, or maybe some fancy restaurant, with tinkling glasses, and soft jazz playing in the background.

"I can't accept it."

"Humour me. Please."

The way he says 'please', like his tongue just licked the back of my knees.

"Fine. I'll hold on to it. For now."

Silence.

We're both thinking of the last time we were together. I can picture his fingers skimming the rim of his glass as he recalls how he played with my skin.

"Will I see you over the holidays?" he asks.

Arrows of anticipation shoot through me at the thought of it.

"I...uh...Hafez...the kids..."

"I understand." He spares me the agony.

I hear the striking of a match.

"What are your plans?" I ask.

He blows a puff of smoke away from the receiver. "I think I'll take Ryan up on his offer and join them at the chalet."

The chalet. Where Ellen is waiting to fix him up with her friend.

"Great," I reply, dying a little inside. "Have fun."

"I will." He takes a sip of whatever it is he's drinking. "And Shayda?"

"Yes?"

"I've programmed my number. Call me."

18. BROWNIES

....

January 1st, 1996

HAFEZ AND I CATCH THE COUNTDOWN ON TV. THE CITY skyline explodes in a dazzling display of fireworks as revelers huddle together to ring in the new year. Confetti covers Nathan Phillips Square in bursts of colorful celebration.

Hafez turns off the TV and heads for the stairs. It's a familiarity born out of habit, the comfort of not having to ask, of knowing when it's time to sleep or eat or wash the car.

I soak our coffee cups and turn off the lights. Natasha and Zain are already in bed. I stop by their rooms, wondering what this year will bring—maybe Natasha's first period or another loose tooth for Zain.

"Happy New Year." Hafez gives me a kiss as he leaves the bathroom. It's a tiny peck, the kind we've exchanged countless times before, but I feel like I've violated a sacred trust, touching him with the same lips that have kissed Troy. I shut the door behind him and lean against it. Then I walk to the sink and splash cold water on my face. The uneasiness lingers. I brush my teeth and step out.

"I'm going to call Maamaan," I say.

I tip toe downstairs and pick up the phone.

"I can't talk too long," says Maamaan. "I'm waiting for your brother to call."

"Go to sleep. They're probably out."

Maamaan will wait by the phone all night, but she will never dial Hossein's number. It's beyond her, akin to admitting a weakness.

"He doesn't care." She sniffs.

I can picture her in her nightie, standing by the kitchen table, tapping her fingers on the counter.

"Happy New Year, Maamaan."

"Our new year isn't till March," she reminds me.

"Happy New Year anyways."

She tells me how inconvenient it is that things are closed—her doctor, the convenience store, the food court where she meets her friends.

"One more day," I say.

"Zarrin is in the hospital again."

"What? When?"

"Last night," replies Maamaan. "It's not good."

"I'll pick you up tomorrow. We'll go see her." I pause. "And Maaman?"

"Yes?"

"When was the last time you had your mammogram done?"

"In May. You took me."

Some things are so mechanical, I don't remember. I hang up, thinking of my early days in Toronto, days spent with *Khaleh* Zarrin in her nutmeg scented kitchen.

"Food connects people," she said. "It brings us together. Nothing says love like the taste of home. These brownies are my personal creation. Remember me when you make them for your own family some day. It will remind them of you, a little bit of magic only you can create."

She showed me the secret to her fabulous recipe.

"Don't make them too often. Or your man will go rolly-polly." She puffed up her face and laughed long and hard, her round belly lifting up in little contractions against her apron.

I took *Khaleh* Zarrin some brownies a few days after her first chemo.

"You still make them." She smiled and took a small bite. "I bet Hafez hurries home for them."

But Hafez doesn't have a sweet tooth. Troy does.

My eyes linger on the coat closet. I can almost see the red box, stowed away in the corner.

Call me.

I turn on the cell phone. There is just one number under the contacts list. I select it and hold my breath.

The phone rings five times before he picks up.

"Hello."

I slink into the guest bathroom and shut the door.

"Troy." I can hear the loud kathumping of music behind him.

"Hold on." He puts his hand over the phone and says something. A door closes. The noise fades.

"Yes?"

"It's Shayda."

A pause, and then a soft, "Hey."

"Happy New Year," we both say at the same time.

I laugh. He laughs.

"I'm glad you called." The music comes back on at his end. There's muffled talking. "Listen, I have to go, but I'll be back in a couple of days. See you then?"

"Yes," I reply.

"Bye, Beetroot."

"Bye." I smile into the phone.

19. OPENING THE DOOR

January 4th, 1996

"Check it out." Jayne spreads the newspaper before me.

'First Kiss of the New Year,' reads the caption. 'Heir to Accord Hotels, Matt Cavelry, and his wife Jayne, ring in the new year with the first kiss of 1996.'

I smile at the photo. It's typical Jayne, standing out in the middle of a dance floor full of other couples. And then I see him, a few feet to the left—the casual, messy way he wears a suit, the turn of his profile...

"What's wrong?" asks Jayne.

"Nothing." I hand her back the paper, trying to erase the image of Troy with a tall woman in a bare-backed gown, his arms around her waist, his lips locked in a passionate kiss. A thousand black and white pixels come flying out of the page and attack me like raw edged shrapnel.

"You sure you're okay?"

"Yes." I collect my defenses. "I'm fine."

"All right then." Jayne looks me over. "I wish you'd come. We had a wonderful time."

I picture Troy skiing down the mountain, heading for the chalet after wards, the fire roaring, warm and toasty. Him and Ellen's friend. A wonderful time.

"I'm sorry. I have to get going." I pay for my half. "I just remembered I have an appointment." I leave a bewildered Jayne, sitting alone with her half-eaten lunch special.

Listen, I have to go...

The words echo in my mind. The muffled talking, how happy he sounded. It wasn't because of me or my call.

Silly, silly, silly Shayda.

He had to get back. To his date.

I drive downtown and park outside the building Bob showed me after closing Troy's commercial deal.

'Heathgate Group.' I follow the dots next to the listing... Suite 910.

The desks are empty. I make my way through the sawdust, the haphazard electrical wires, the drilling, the clanging, and then, more chaos—Troy, behind a glass wall, shooting hoops in his corner office. Who has a basketball net installed at work? How did I allow myself to get involved with a man who thinks the whole world is his playground?

I don't knock. I walk straight in.

"Shayda." His face lights up. Then he frowns. "What's wrong?"

"I just want to return this." I put the cell phone on his desk and turn on my heel, but he stops me in one swift move.

"What's this about?"

"You want to know what it's about?" My voice quivers. I walk over to his desk and unfold the newspaper. "This." I point to the photo. "This is what it's about, Troy."

"This?" He casts a cursory glance at the image. "You're worked up over this?"

But it's not just this. It's the things he doesn't see, the ghosts of my father and brother in that photo, staring back at me. Men who can never limit themselves to just one woman.

"I'm done, Troy. It's over."

I head for the door, but he grips my wrist and swings me around.

"Really? Just like that? Because you see me with another woman?" He tangles his fist in my hair and pulls my head back. "Do you think it's easy for *me*? To think about you lying in bed with another man, night after night?"

"He's not another man. He's my husband!"

"That's just it, Shayda! He's your husband. I can't compete. I can't demand. I can't win!" His breath is hot and harsh against my ear.

"Stop it, Troy. You're hurting me."

But he twists my hair tighter. "You think I *like* waiting on the fringes of your life, wondering when I'll see you? Maybe Christmas? Maybe New Year's? And when I do, you walk in here and throw *this* in my face?"

"You don't know anything." I spit out.

"No? Then tell me, Shayda. Do you make the same sweet sounds for him? Does the rose scent of your skin drive him fucking crazy? Do you soak your panties for him like you do for me? Tell me, Shayda. Godammit!"

It's not like that, I want to say. But I say nothing. Because that would open up secrets that are not mine to tell. And isn't it enough that I have already betrayed Hafez?

So I let him swallow the jagged pill, I let him wash it down with the bitter concoction of me in my husband's arms, sharing all the things that I share with him.

"I'll take you any way I can, Shayda," he says. "But everything else is off limits. You don't get to be married and keep me on a leash. And if you can't handle that, if you can't handle *this*," he waves the paper at me, "then we end it. Right here, right now."

Yes. That's what I came to do. End it. Ignore the sharp pain stabbing at my insides and hack away in spite of it.

So many chances to walk away, so many reasons, but they fall like dominoes around me, one by one, until I am standing in a circle without sense, with my cheating heart and my cheating soul. I bow my head; my shoulders slumped in defeat.

"Then leave him," he says.

"I can't. I can't just *leave* him. He needs me."

Troy's jaw clenches. "You can't leave him. You can't leave me. You can't handle the in-between. What do you *want*, Shayda?"

They tell you that an affair destroys everything, that there are no winners, that there is only heartbreak. I know this. And still I do it. Still I take his face in my hands and kiss him until he returns my fierce, desperate kisses with a fervor that pushes everything else aside.

"I'll learn to deal with it." I pick up the paper and throw it in the trash.

We cling to each other, trying to keep it down, this cocktail of raging, tangled emotions. I know it'll be like this every time I see him with someone else, like taking great, big nauseating gulps of poison, but I do it anyways.

I open the door and let it all in.

20. SHOW ME

....

January 10th, 1996

"WHAT'S GOING ON IN THERE?" TROY SOUNDS AMUSED, LIKE he's ready to barge through the bathroom door.

"Just a minute!" I reply, struggling with the garters on the sexy black number I picked up. The silk stockings go on easy enough, but these attachments...ugh.

Next time practice, genius. I make a mental note.

A few more tries and I give up. Good thing the stockings have a stay-up top. I draw a cat's eye with black liquid liner and add a smudge of gloss to my lips. Then I slip into red patent stilettos.

Sex in a shoe box, that's what the sales lady said.

How odd they looked in my closet, next to the line-up of plain, sensible flats. Like great, big exclamation points in the middle of a mundane sentence.

I check my reflection. Someone else stares back at me— bigger, taller, sexier. Someone so selfish, I have to look away. I take a deep breath and step out.

He's not hovering outside the door. What was I thinking? Troy doesn't hover. He expands, he occupies, he fills the space. And so, sitting on the bed, shirt off, laptop on, nothing but boxers and bare, smooth skin, he hits me with that rough, tender mix of masculinity even before he looks up. And then he does...

I love the way his mouth just hangs open. His eyes roam the length of my body. This is what great masterpieces must feel like on museum walls—like sighing, like climbing out of their rigidly stretched frames, and falling, boneless, into a lover's glance.

"Come here," he says.

I take a step forward. Six inch heels are not my friend. My arms flail out, grabbing the door frame.

The great works of art tut-tut their disapproval.

"On second thought, stay right there." He gets out of bed.

Six inch heels and Troy Heathgate. Not a good combination for the knees.

The heels bring me almost eye to eye with him. When I look at the sky, I will think of it like this—on fire, with crackling clouds of desire.

He angles his head and leans in, his lips are almost touching mine. He looks at me like that until I gasp, until I've seen all the things we're going to do, all the things that have come already alive, in the private corners of his mind.

He strokes my face and lets one finger linger under my chin, guiding me to him in a whisper soft kiss. He pulls away far too soon and stands back, teasing me, goading me.

I grab his bottom lip and suck on it greedily. Then I let go, catching it between my teeth before letting it slide out. He groans and pulls me hard against the muscled contours of his legs. My knees buckle, but he's already lifting me off my feet, one hand cupping my bottom, the other guiding my legs around his hips.

He pushes me against the wall, hard, and rocks against me, letting me feel every steel boned inch of him. I need his lips so bad, but he won't let me have them, just this mad, grinding dance. I grab on to his shoulders, feeling myself burn from the inside out.

"Please," I plead.

"Please what?"

I don't know what, so I rub my nose on his neck—my lips, my cheeks, my forehead. But it's not enough. I squirm against him, arching against his hips in slow, rotating circles. I feel the short, shallow rush of his breath as he tears my face away from his neck with a triumphant gleam.

Then he kisses me. The kiss I've been waiting for, mastering my mouth even as he carries me to bed.

"You have no idea how incredibly sexy you look," he growls, placing me on the sheets.

He kneels between my legs and kisses the inside of my ankle, resting my sharp, pointy heels against his chest. His hands caress my skin, down to the back of my knees, thumbs moving back and forth over the soft, sensitive spot. My shoes dig deeper, leaving little round dents on his skin.

"Planning on driving these straight through my heart, aren't you?" He slides his fingers under the arch of my foot and removes one red stiletto.

"You know..." He toys with the other one, clearly enamored. "Much as I adore these, I'd rather you skip them. I want to be the only thing that makes you all wobbly and weak-kneed."

The second shoe hits the floor.

His lips run down the sole of my foot through a fine layer of seamed silk. I shudder as his tongue darts over my toes, touching but not touching.

"Should we take these off?" His fingers splay over my stockings. "Hmmm?" He hums along the length of my leg until he gets to the band on my upper thigh. "Yes?" He starts peeling it off. "And this one too." But he holds on to the second stocking, winding it around his hand.

"Close your eyes, Shayda."

"What?"

"Close. Your. Eyes." He waits until they're shut and then blindfolds me with the silk stocking, tying a soft knot in the back.

"Now show me what you do."

"I..."

"Yes you can," he whispers. Soft kisses cover my eyes, my forehead, the corners of my mouth. "Yes you can."

With my eyes closed, all I can do is listen. And feel. The strength of his arms, the heart in his words. He's got me. And there's nothing I can't share here, in the circle of his embrace.

Still I hesitate, trembling like the last leaves of winter, until he starts whispering in my ear, words that make me twist and turn and fly with the wind.

I turn to my side, crossing my legs at the thighs and then again at the ankles, hooking one foot around, squeezing, undulating, letting his voice paint hot, erotic worlds in dizzy, rushing strokes. He spoons me, sliding one hand between my legs, feeling every movement I make without stopping the sensual string of sentences.

I push deeper into him. His thighs cradle the curve of my bottom. I feel him against me, excited, aroused, even as I start to lose control. His palm encircles my neck from behind and he tilts my head back, kissing me on the forehead. A sweet cord of tension snaps inside me. Ripples of mindless ecstasy flood through me. He holds on to me until he feels the tremors pass, until my body goes limp. Then he moves, letting me roll onto my back.

"Wow. You just squeeze your thighs?" He pushes the blindfold aside.

I cover my face with my hands as the reality of what I just did sinks in.

"Shayda." He nudges my palms aside with his face, his nose rubbing against mine. "Look at me."

I open my eyes.

"How did you learn to do that?"

"I don't know. By accident. I was pretty young. My parents were fighting at the dinner table. I was clenching my thighs, rocking back and forth on the chair. It was a coping mechanism I used all the time, but that day...it just happened."

"So you got off, for the first time, in front of your parents?"

"I never quite thought of it like that."

"Sneaky Beetroot." He laughs. "I love it. And I love that you shared it with me. God, that was such a turn on." His kiss chases away the last of my embarrassment. "And now, there's this rather...um...pressing matter at hand." He gives me a wicked smile.

"There is? I'm afraid I have to get going."

"Oh, you better get going all right." He takes my hand and guides it to his boxers.

"Troy?"

"Hmmm?"

"Does it bother you that we don't have sex?"

"We don't?" He closes his eyes as my hand slides over him. "Because it's always frigging awesome."

"Answer the question." I rake my nails down his thigh.

"Look at you. Digging your heels into my chest, scraping my skin off with your talons. What kind of beast have I unleashed?" He flips me over, letting me feel the hard, pulsating core of him. "Do you want to?"

"Do you?" I ask, thinking how magnificent he looks when he's turned on.

"Like you wouldn't believe."

"Are you afraid I'll fight you off again?"

He traces the line of my collarbone before his thumb circles my nipple. "I'm just breaking you in slowly."

"Breaking me in? What am I? A horse?"

"Uh-huh. My prized filly. Let me get my crop so we can go a-ridin'."

"A crop, huh?" I grab my discarded stocking and whip him with it. "How do you like it now?"

"That's it, baby. Let your inner freak out."

We start laughing. Then his voice drops.

"Come here." He pulls me down for a long, searing kiss.

It's not funny anymore. It's hot and urgent and throbbing.

My lips explore the planes of his neck, the smooth, broad expanse of male chest, his tight, flat abs, down, down, down. I hear his sharp intake as my breath warms the part of him that's twitching with need.

"Payback time." I smile, dodging the area altogether.

His thighs clench as I reach for my black stocking and wrap it around the base of his shaft. I pull one end at a time, letting the soft, wispy fabric run first to the left, and then the right, caressing his flesh in a silken loop. He groans as I move the stocking up and down the length of him, tugging on him, pulling, teasing.

"Yessss." His head sinks back into the pillow.

Watching him with his eyes closed, head tilted back and that look of utter rapture, I feel the heady thrill a woman feels, when a man who is always in control is about to lose it. Just for her.

The moment I wrap my lips around him, he lets his breath out in a long, slow hiss. My hands stroke him as my tongue slides up and down, focusing on the points he showed me, until he cries out.

When he's spent, he flings one arm possessively across me. I nudge his leg over my belly, until I'm completely anchored by his weight.

"Really?" he asks, eyes closed, a small smile playing on his lips. "You're not going to freak?"

"Really."

21. NO PROMISES

....

February 3rd, 1996

"Syntribation."

"What's that?" I open the pizza box and let the aroma invade Troy's office.

"Syntribation," he repeats. "The technical term for the way you masturbate."

"What?" I almost drop the lid.

"Masturbate." He grabs a slice and bites into it. "Does that word make you uncomfortable, Shayda? Because everybody does it. You do it, I do it, the whole world does it."

"I...um..." I peer intently into the pie-chart of colorful slices.

He pushes the curtain of hair from my face and laughs. "I wondered how long it would take today, Beetroot. I think we broke a record."

I pick a slice and put it on the napkin.

"Here. Let me show you something," he says.

I look around while he logs into his computer. Most of the work in his new office is finished. There are some odds and ends, but I only notice because there's no one around, none of the crazy hustle and bustle I hear when we're on the phone. It's a huge space, rows of cubicles, meeting rooms, and the white checkerboard of a commercial ceiling.

"Here we are." He turns the screen towards me.

"What's this?"

"This, my dear, is the future. The internet. You type in a search and the results come up, almost instantaneously." He pulls me into his lap. "See? Syntribate. When a woman masturbates by crossing her legs and rubbing her thighs together."

Somehow it doesn't feel so weird anymore—that word— as I sit in a lush leather chair, with his arms around me.

"So this internet...it's like a dictionary? A library of sorts?"

"It's much more than that." He lights up like he's been watching a fantastic game and people are finally joining in and catching up. "You'll be able to put your real estate listings on here, post photos, describe properties, reach out to a whole audience that you wouldn't otherwise get to interact with. On the personal front, you can stay in touch with anyone in the world, without stamps or long distance phone bills or telegrams."

"How's that?"

"Well, it's something called email. In fact, let's set you up with an account right now."

"An account? I don't think I'm ever going to use it."

"Maybe not right away, but now is the best time because you can get whatever name you want. This stuff is in its beta stages. You can be the first Shayda on Hotmail."

"On what? I don't want my name out there."

"It won't be out anywhere." He laughs. "You just give it to people you want to stay in touch with. It's like your phone number on the internet. You use it send and receive messages."

"I don't know about this."

"We don't have to go with your real name. Pick an alias."

"Like what?"

"Like hotmamma or browniebaker or hey, how about syntribater?"

I roll my eyes.

"Okay. We'll go with *the*syntribater. It sounds more bad ass, like 'The Terminator', except in the bedroom."

"We'll do no such thing," I reply, but he's already typing.

"Username: beetrootbutterfly." He pauses. "No. Something sexier." "Beetbutt...yes, that's it. Password... hmmmm...hereweare. Let's add some numbers... hereweare1996. You think you'll remember that? Aaaaand... voila! Shayda Hijazi, you are now officially beetbutt@ hotmail.com."

"Thanks. I can't wait to give that out to everyone."

"Yeah, you should add it to your business card. Hey, maybe we should register beetbutt.com before anyone...uh... grabs it."

I slap his hand away from my tush. I haven't giggled in years. "And what am I supposed to do with it now?"

"Check it for dirty emails from me."

"You're mad." I shake my head. "And I have forty-five minutes before I pick up the kids."

"Right." He looks at his watch. "Which means you have five minutes to finish your pizza and I have forty minutes to thoroughly, completely, utterly ravish you."

We reclaim our lunch, now cold and soggy, but it still tastes divine. Maybe it's because we're sitting on the floor, Troy leaning against the desk, me leaning against him, our feet stretched out in a double V before us.

We watch dust motes in the sun, streaming through the windows before us. The city bustles beneath, soundless behind the glass, little cars zipping in and out of concrete blocks of lego land.

"That's me." He points to the west, a distant spot near the lake. "Behind the tall building with the white roof."

I think of us in his loft, that sultry afternoon last summer; those five words he spoke.

I'm dying to kiss you.

We never meet there.

"A neutral spot. Not mine, not yours. A space between," he said.

And so we meet in a hotel room, a luxurious suite with thick drapes and a soft carpet and a padded headboard, that muffle voices and footsteps and reality.

"And that's you." His finger moves across the window, to the other end of town.

"You can't possibly make my place out."

"No." He wipes his hands and hugs me from behind, resting his chin on my shoulder. "But I like to imagine you out there, one of the lights in the night."

I think of him, standing by the blue of his roof top pool, looking across the lake, to a suburban house with a red door and a swing set in the back. I know what it's like to wonder because I do it all the time. Mundane things like the color of his bed sheets. When does he go for his run? What radio station does he tune in to? Is he in the car, listening to it, while he heads out to dinner with a date? Does he take her to his loft after wards? Does she hop in the shower with him in the morning? Does she dry herself on his towel?

The papers have stopped reporting on him. A few interviews here and there, but nothing on his social life. I wonder if he made a few discreet calls after I barged in here about that photo. I don't know which is better. Knowing or not knowing.

"Troy?"

"What?" He twirls a strand of my hair around his finger.

"Promise me you'll tell me if things start to get serious with someone."

"Why?" he asks. "Will you leave?"

I don't answer.

He doesn't promise.

It's not perfect, this thing between us, like trying to bring the two circles of our lives together, and living in the small, tight space where they intersect, everything else pushed to the circumference, until we step back inside our very different, very separate orbs.

I look at the time. Five more minutes.

I want this simple afternoon of cold pizza and dancing dust motes to stretch out forever.

22. HOOKAH COLA

....

February 25th, 1996

"Why don't you come and stay with us for a few days?" I ask.

"No." Maamaan dabs her eyes. "I'll be fine."

Always proud, stoic, removed. She leaves me feeling lacking and inadequate.

"I'll miss her." She sits down. Pouffff. Like a rapidly deflating soufflé, tired of holding her form. "She would have been happy. So many people."

"*Khaleh* Zarrin was a sweet lady. Her life touched a lot of people."

"And me?" asks Maamaan. "Who will come to my funeral?"

How different can two sisters be? *Khaleh* Zarrin—quick to laugh and eat and dance. Quick to forgive. And Maamaan —locking everything up in a tight closet, tucking the key in her bra, along with a stiff, white handkerchief and a $20 bill.

"I certainly don't want *him* there," she says.

"Baba came to pay his respects today. We can't begrudge him that," I reply, although it had come as a shock, seeing him after all this time. Didn't he know we needed notice? To shine and polish our armor; to take up our positions.

"Hossein should have been there. Why didn't he come? Is he too busy to attend his aunt's funeral?"

"It's a long drive from Montreal." I make excuses, not because I'm trying to protect Hossein, but because I can't stand the fits that Maamaan has, when that closet bursts open and I'm the only one standing in its path.

When I was small, I read a story about a Dutch boy who saved his country by putting his fingers in a leaking dam. He stayed there all night, in the cold, until help arrived. And so I tend to the cracks and the holes and the rips, even though I know that Hossein will never return.

"Here." I pour her some tea, in one of the dainty, gold-rimmed cup-saucer sets she insisted on bringing along from Iran.

"Ah." The first hint of a smile all day.

I know she is thinking of sun drenched parlors, and friends gathered in pink velvet arm chairs with high backs.

EVERYONE ADORED MONA KAZEMI. THE WOMEN WANTED to be on her list, invited to the lavish affairs she hosted. The men wanted her—her Sophia Loren body, a glance, a smile, a scrap of anything she threw at them.

But she remained faithful, even though it was common knowledge that Ali Kazemi went from one mistress to another. Then came the revolution. Baba lost his businesses, his estates, the posh cars, his investments. We moved to a squalid apartment on the other side of the city. Maamaan grew resentful. She had put up with the cheating, but a change in her lifestyle was not acceptable. It was Baba's job to provide for her and he was failing. The lower Baba fell, the more they fought. She slammed the door. He went out and got drunk. She broke the china. He had another affair.

When Baba and *Amu* Reza pooled resources for a new business venture, Hossein and I thought things would get better, and for a while, they did. Hossein escaped Maamaan's cloying grasp and I came of age. Of marriageable age.

"She's beautiful," said *Khaleh* Zarrin. She looked so modern in her white capris and bright coral lipstick. "Send her to me. Toronto has so many good Persian families. I'll fix her up like this." She snapped her fingers at 'this'.

Maamaan's eyes darted to Baba.

"I don't want to get married," I said to *Khaleh* Zarrin. "I'm studying to be a writer."

"Shayda, we've never interfered with your education. You've had the best schools and the best teachers. But writing is such a fickle career." Baba waved his hand dismissively. "And with all the censorship here, what's the point?"

"I don't want to go to Toronto."

"Not even for a holiday?" asked Maamaan.

We both knew it wouldn't be just for a casual visit. We couldn't afford that.

"Shayda, you have an opportunity. For a better life. And who knows? With one of you there, the rest of the family stands a better chance of getting out," said *Khaleh* Zarrin.

At least she had the balls to be up front with me.

They all fixed their eyes and hopes on me.

"ARE YOU SERIOUS?" SALOMEH PULLED ME ASIDE. "THEY'RE going to marry you off to someone you barely know?"

"It's not like you'll be picking your own husband either," I replied.

"No, but at least I'm having fun. I've been kissed." She smirked. "I know boys, I go out."

"You mean you sneak out."

Salomeh lived next door. I would see her wiggling in and out of the window, sometimes way past midnight, in a button-popping blouse and pencil skirt, like Rizzo from 'Grease'.

"Whatever." She shrugged and blew a pink bubble. "So you up for it or are you going to spend the rest of your single days scribbling in your journal?"

And so two days before I left, I snuck into Salomeh's house. Her parents were at a card party. The living room was smoky and dull. A girl and boy were dancing to American music, loud enough to hear, but not so it would draw outside attention. Three or four guys were messing around with hookahs. The rest of the girls sat on the couch, eating popcorn and staring at the wall like they were watching a movie.

"Where's Salomeh?" I asked.

They pointed me to the kitchen.

I walked in and saw her kissing a tall, lanky guy whose hands were way up her skirt. I joined the other girls on the couch. They giggled. Apparently everyone knew what was going on.

"You want to dance?" One of the guys came over and asked me.

All the girls looked at me.

"Sure," I answered.

It's what I was there for, right? To have fun. My first and last hoorah.

We danced, not touching, but every once in a while, his legs bumped against mine. I could feel the other girls watching.

"You want a drink?" he asked when the song ended.

"Yes, thanks," I replied, but I didn't follow him into the kitchen.

He came out, holding two glasses. "Want to sit on the stairs?"

I let him steer me away from the group.

"What's your name?" he asked.

"Shayda." I took a sip, a little hesitantly.

"It's only pop," he replied, like he expected me to be disappointed. "They didn't have anything else."

We sat there for a while, before he gathered the courage to lean in.

"You're pretty." He brushed his lips against mine.

He tasted like hookah and Coca Cola. Hookah Cola, the flavor of my first kiss. I think it might have been his first too. It was nothing like the romance books I'd been hiding under my bed, the ones I had passed on to Salomeh so Maamaan wouldn't find them when I was gone.

Our mouths shook hands politely.

Hello.

Hello.

We stayed glued for a few seconds, before I pulled back, which made his mouth look like he was slurping spaghetti.

And so it was done, the first kiss, that rite of passage. I don't remember his face, except that his nose was crooked, like he'd been in a fight, and that he looked surprised when I got up and left.

"ARE YOU LISTENING?" ASKS MAAMAAN.

"What?" I tune back in.

"Sugar." She holds her cup out. "I need more sugar."

Yes, more sugar to make the loss of *Khaleh* Zarrin more palatable. More sugar so Maamaan can sweeten the memories of those glorious days when she was queen.

166

"You're a good girl, Shayda." She smiles before losing herself in her gold-rimmed past.

Yes, Maamaan. A good girl.

23. THE GHOST OF NOWRUZ PAST

March 21st, 1996

"You look happy." Troy shuts the door behind me. His arms encircle my waist, pulling me close.

"I am. Nowruz Mubarak." For the first time in years, the shadow of another Nowruz has lifted.

"Now-what?"

"It means Happy New Year in Persian. Nowruz Mubarak."

He repeats it after me. I laugh. It's totally off. He tries again. I shake my head. Not even close.

"You know what?" His finger runs down the V of my dress, following the hint of cleavage. "You have me at a distinct disadvantage." He takes in my little black dress, the sheer sleeves, the deep neck-line. "Since when do you dress like this?"

Since you. Since I started feeling sexy and confident and attractive and hot.

"You don't like it?" I step away, pulling my pumps off.

"I love it." He comes after me, pulsing with that intense, exciting energy that surrounds him. "But then I'd love it even if you wore a sack." He corners me. "Know what else?"

"What?" I know he's about to pounce. My eyes dart behind him, looking for a way to prolong this delicious teasing.

"I love it more when I have you *in* the sack!"

He leaps; I dive on the bed, almost making it to the other side before he grabs my ankles and drags me back.

"This is for ignoring your very hungry, very ravenous lover for weeks." He sweeps my hair aside and bites the slope of my shoulder.

"Ow!" With my face buried in the sheets and his body pressing down on me, I know I won't be able to squirm away. But I have fun trying.

My movements ignite a low growl. He lets me wiggle against him, until I feel his erection pressing against me.

"You're in trouble now." He flips me over, his arms pinning mine to the bed.

He watches me closely, testing me, as his weight shifts over me, a little at a time. He lowers his face, slowly, so I'm staring into those hypnotic blues, waiting for his lips. But it's not a kiss. He gives me a long lick, from the base of my neck to my chin. I shiver as he follows the trail with his hot breath.

There is an urgency to him, coiled and controlled. He pulls my panties off and buries his face between my legs. I gasp at the raw contact, no teasing, no nudging, just an all-out assault on my senses. A very hungry, very ravenous lover.

"Troy." I try to lift his face, but he pushes my fingers away with his mouth. His tongue carries me to a rising crest of passion.

"Troy." This time I bury my fingers in his hair.

He looks at me, his eyes like twin lakes set ablaze, as my hips lift off the bed. He starts kneading my throbbing centre with his fingers and the heel of his palm, sending ripples of rolling pleasure through me. He watches my face, gauging my reactions. More pressure here, less here, honing in, zoning in, until his movements reflect the exact sensations I feel when I'm reaching for release.

"How...?" I gasp.

"I paid attention. When you showed me." He continues handling me, with maddening detachment.

I close my eyes as my senses circle around the exquisite vortex he's creating.

He pushes his knee between my legs and rubs it against me, hard against soft, rough against smooth. I can't control the rush of slick wetness that escapes me.

"That's it." He closes his eyes and leans his forehead on mine. His breath scorches my skin.

Did I start the kissing? Did he? He continues his erotic rhythm, even as his tongue plunders my mouth, forcing me to give up all of its secrets, the taste, the texture, the moist darkness. A flash of heat ignites around my pulsating core, radiating up into my belly and down to my thighs. I stiffen, afraid it will fizzle out, but he keeps going, fanning the flames with long, sure strokes, pressing up, letting go. A whiplash of pleasure bursts through me, ripples of searing, convulsing heat. I give myself up to it, hot, breathless, clinging madly to him.

"Take me in your mouth," he demands.

I open my eyes and gasp at the raw urgency of his gaze.

"Now, Shayda." It's a low throaty growl.

He watches as my lips close over him. And then he lets out a sound. Like a hot iron being doused.

I want to swallow him whole, all of him, his heat, his magnificent skin, his belly, his lips, his eyelashes. All of him.

After wards, we lay quietly. My face on his thigh, my hand still wrapped around him, my hair sprawled across his belly as he runs his fingers through it. The slow, sated touch of bliss.

"Beetroot."

"Mmmmm."

"That was..." He trails off, looking for the right word. "Come here," he says instead.

I settle into the crook of his arm. He takes my hand and kisses it. We let our palms slide against each other, touching, playing, stroking.

"Here we are," he says.

"Here we are."

"You know what this means, right?"

"What?"

"You just made the leap from relying on yourself, to learning how to take pleasure from a partner."

I turn scarlet.

"Sometimes I get the weird feeling that being intimate is completely new to you," he says. "I know it's ridiculous, but still. Your reactions...I can't quite put my finger on it."

This is the part where I tell him the truth. This is the part where I tell him about the Ghost of Nowruz Past. But I keep my mouth shut.

"You're an incredibly responsive woman. Incredibly beautiful—every curve, every fold, every inch of you. You hear me?"

I blink. I nod. I swallow through the tightness in my throat.

"And Shayda?"

I look at him through wet, spiky eyelashes.

"Nowruz Mubarak," he says it perfectly, with all the right inflections.

I laugh. He's back to being fully functional.

"So do you do anything special for your new year?" he asks.

"We used to set a ceremonial table to welcome spring and new beginnings, but we haven't done that for a while."

"Well, I hope you're ready for new beginnings, because this is just the tip of the iceberg." His voice hangs somewhere between a threat and a sweet promise.

24. PRETENDING

....

May 16th, 1996

"THANK YOU FOR SEEING ME." MARJANEH SITS DOWN AND clasps her hands in her lap.

"Sorry about the mess. We're getting some new equipment installed," I say.

"That's okay," she replies. "You said to come see you if I wanted to do something different. I'm not sure if you're still hiring any office staff, but I thought I'd check."

"We're not hiring any office staff."

"Oh." Her face falls.

"But..." I push my chair away from the desk and pick up a framed document. "I thought you might like to consider this."

"Your realtor's license?" She looks confused as she hands it back.

"Yes. This one's mine." I sit back down. "But what do you think about getting your own?"

"Me?" Her eyes widen. "You think I could do it?"

"Why not?" I reply. "There's nothing to stop you from taking the courses, and I can help you study for the exams. In the meantime, you can still hold on to your job. You might need to make a few shift changes, but I don't see any reason why you can't go for it."

"And if I make it?" She allows herself a moment of possibility.

"I'll talk to Bob. He's always looking for responsible, reliable people."

Marjaneh's eyes fall on my license. I know she is imagining her name there, in gold calligraphy.

I smile. It's a start.

"Are you...are you doing this because you feel bad about your brother?" she asks.

I know we're both thinking of Hossein's hastily scribbled note, the one he left on the kitchen table.

I can't do this anymore. I'm sorry.

I can still recall Marjaneh's face.

"He doesn't know," she cried.

She had been six weeks pregnant. For days, we searched for Hossein. He had quit his job, his friends were tight-lipped and his car sat in the garage, sullen and clueless. Maamaan went crazy, convinced she would have to support Marjaneh and the baby.

One evening, Marjaneh came home with dead eyes.

"Where were you?" asked Maamaan. "I have enough to worry about."

"You don't have to worry about me anymore." Her voice was flat. She walked past us slowly and mechanically.

"Are you all right?" I followed her into the bedroom.

She didn't answer. She pulled out a tattered suitcase from under the bed and started packing.

"Where are you going? You can't leave like this."

"Like what?" She gave me a cold smile. "I'm not pregnant anymore. I took care of it. It's no-one's problem now."

Looking at her now I feel ashamed of myself, of my brother, of my family. But that's not the only reason I'm happy to see her. I need to make it right—*Amu* Reza, the pebbles, my part in the whole thing.

"Here." I pull out a small box from my drawer and hand it to her. "I was hoping you'd come by."

She opens it and finds a smooth, white river stone, with the word 'BELIEVE' carved on it.

"Thank you," she says.

"Shayda?" Bob knocks on the door. "I'm sorry to interrupt."

"It's all right, Bob. I'd like you to meet Marjaneh. She's thinking of getting her realtor's license."

"Excellent." He gives her a firm handshake. "Good luck, my dear. Come see us when you're ready." Then he turns to me. "We need to get in here to install the new computer. And Troy's hooking us up to the internet too."

"Troy?"

"Ah, here he is. All done with my office?" asks Bob, as Troy's tall, lithe frame sends my heart into crazy somersaults.

I should be used to this by now. Seeing him in the flesh. But I can't control the lurch of excitement. The last few times have been intense—greedy, needy pleasure fests. Him, unrelenting, holding me up, holding me down, holding me to sweet staccato spasms, again and again. It's like all the mad, sexual energy that fuels his core has honed in on me and he just can't get enough.

"Hello, Shayda."

Another somersault.

"Hi, Troy."

The pretending is tough. Civility, when all I can think about is the way he cries out my name when he buries his face in my hair.

"And this is..." Bob trails off.

"Marjaneh." I say.

"Troy." He introduces himself to her.

She stares, a little dumbfounded, before snapping out of it.

"Hello," she replies. Then she turns to me. "I...uh...I'll see myself out."

There are two types of women in the world. Those who run far and fast from Troy Heathgate, and those who throw themselves at him. Indifference is not an option.

"It was good seeing you, Marjaneh," I say. "Tell Susan to give you some information about the accreditation process before you leave."

"I can do that," says Bob. "Come with me. I have a ton of stuff to get you started. Troy, you'll let Shayda know if you need anything?"

"I will," he replies. "Ohhh, I will," he repeats, an octave lower when they're out of earshot.

"You didn't tell me you were coming," I say.

"You always want to know when I'm coming."

Oh please no, I think. But it's too late. My face turns a bright shade of red.

"Aaaand my work here is done." He smiles. "Except for this thing I told Bob I'd look after."

He starts opening the cardboard boxes. His movements are deliberate and efficient, the muscled planes of his back flexing as he lifts the packages out.

"Where do you want it?"

"Huh?" *On the desk, against the wall, sprawled out on the floor.*

"Where..." he moves closer and breathes into my neck, "...do you want it? Your new computer."

"Um...right here is fine." I point to the space I've cleared on my desk. "Since when does Heathgate Group make house calls?"

"Since I get to see you."

There's no way I'm going to get any work done now.

"I'm uh...I need to go over some of this stuff with Bob." I grab the paperwork.

"Not so fast." His fingers circle my wrist.

"Troy...the door's open."

"So?" He captures the other one.

I wonder if he can feel my pulse quicken.

"Much as I'd like to throw you over this desk and have my way with you, I do have some measure of restraint," he says. "Promise me something before you go."

"What?" As if I'd be able to deny him anything.

"Your birthday. Next month. Lunch."

Lunch. Another word for our trysts, tangled sheets, fevered kisses. Slipping away from work and into his arms, learning just how delicious not eating can be.

"Fine," I reply. It's his birthday too.

"I'll hold you to it." He drops a kiss on each of my palms before letting me go.

I walk into Bob's office, still tingling. "You have a minute?"

"Sure."

"Marjaneh's gone?" I ask as I sort through the files.

Bob nods. "She seems nice."

"Yes," I reply. "She's my brother's ex-wife."

"Ah. They have any kids?"

"No."

None that survived.

We're half way through the paperwork when Troy shows up, leaning with a lazy confidence against the door.

"All done." He unrolls his sleeves and does up the buttons. "Now, about that promise you made me?"

I jump. What the hell?

"Hell, yeah!" replies Bob. "Liz has been looking forward to it all week. She won't feed me if I don't show up with you."

Oh. I relax.

"Why don't you join us?" Bob says to me. "I have no clue what's for dinner, but Liz will be thrilled to see you."

"Thanks, but I have to get home. We can finish another time." I pick up the folders.

"All right then," says Bob. "Troy, you think you could show me how this works before we leave?" Bob turns his screen around. "Shayda, you want to see?"

"You can show me tomorrow," I reply.

"Bye, Shayda." Troy grins, very much aware of the wide berth I give him as I leave.

Shaydahhh.

I return to my office and shut the door. I want to keep the smell of him from escaping. It's barely noticeable, the kind of thing only a lover would recognize, sparking associations that set the pulses racing.

I drop the papers on my desk. He's left the new computer running. The background is set to a close-up of a butterfly against a golden valley.

I sit back and sigh.

How long, I wonder, before this thing between us blows up in our faces.

25. SCARY CHERRY

June 17th, 1996

I'VE STARTED TAKING THE BUS ON THE DAYS I SEE TROY. IT'S safer than driving, especially on the way back, when my mind projects a play by play action of our time together, and I can't focus on much else.

But today, I regret not driving in. It must be disconcerting for my fellow passengers, when the woman next to them suddenly hides her face in her hands. Then she composes herself and sits back up. And what is that sound she keeps making? Halfway between a laugh and a gasp, a sharp intake, before her cheeks turn pink. Then she hides her face again. She squirms, crosses her legs, uncrosses them. She runs her fingers down her neck and under the collar. Then she laugh-gasps again and covers her mouth.

One by one, the people around me start changing seats. In my slightly delirious state, I find this hilarious. Then I flashback to Troy peeling off my dress and my stomach clenches. I grab a book from my handbag and try to concentrate on the words.

"More." I hear myself moaning. "All of you."

The words on the page float and fade before me.

WE HAD LUNCH—DECADENT DISHES SERVED WITH STEEL-domed covers. Steak, chicken, lobster, fish, pasta. Troy ordered one of everything. We're still learning. The little things. He knows every nook and cranny on me, but not my favorite dish. It doesn't matter because it's all changing. My favorite color used to be yellow. And now it's blue—all the different shades of it in his eyes.

"Happy Birthday." He leans across and kisses me when we're both very, very full.

"Happy Birthday," I reply, tugging on his collar to pull him closer.

His rosary trails on the starched, white tablecloth.

"Is there a story behind this?" I finger the beads.

"It belonged to my grandmother," he says. "She gave it to me when I was little. I used to wake up convinced there were monsters under my bed. She said, 'Hold on to this. It'll bring you light in the dark.' I've slept like a baby since."

"Are the two of you close?"

"She's gone now. But I have some great memories." He pushes his chair back and takes my hand. "Come with me."

We step out on the private balcony overlooking the lake. I lean back against him as the curtains flutter in the spring breeze.

"What do you want for your birthday?" I ask, convinced he'll have a list of naughty requests.

"I already have it."

His kiss is sweet. It unsettles me. Hot, demanding, insistent Troy I know, but this soft, vulnerable Troy is devastating.

"Come on." I drag him inside. "I have to be back in an hour."

But he lies beside me, stroking my arm, playing with my hair, perfectly content to let the afternoon slip away.

"You're pretty hot for a thirty-four year old," he teases.

"You have some pretty interesting thirty-four year old parts yourself." My hand slides down to cup him.

And that's how it starts. The first time he takes me, except he doesn't, not until he has me begging. And still he teases, parting me with the tip of his shaft, the shallowest thrust, the slightest nudge, and then he withdraws. He rubs himself on me again. Tease, tease, tease. Until I'm achy. And hollow. And throbbing with need.

His lips and tongue and fingers and palms take me over the edge. Again. Again. But it's not enough. I want to melt with him. I want to hold him in my core, in my being.

When I wrap my legs around him, digging my heels into his flesh, urging him, goading him, he finally gives in with low growl.

"Hold on," he says, retrieving his pants.

I hear the rip of foil. When he turns around, I put my hand over my mouth.

"What is it?" he asks.

I shake my head.

"Are you...Shayda, are you *laughing*?"

I burst out, unable to hold it in any longer. "It's...it's red." I point to the condom.

"It's cherry."

"It looks so...angry. Scary cherry."

"Shayda. Never, *ever* point to a man's penis and laugh."

"I'm sorry." I giggle. "It's just...I've never seen a condom on before. It looks so..."

"Angry. Scary Cherry. I get it," he replies. "Of all the scenarios I imagined for this moment, and trust me, I've thought about it a lot, I never figured *this* would be your reaction."

"You thought..." I wipe the tears from my eyes. "You thought what...?"

"Awe. Amazement. A swoon. You know, the usual."

"Well, it doesn't look like my reaction was taken too personally."

"Maybe not here." He points to the source of my amusement. "But up here? Up here, I'm screwed. Scarred for life. I'm going to need a lot of very intensive therapy."

"Poor baby. Anything I can do to help?"

"You better get started on that therapy right away."

He groans as I stroke him. It feels weird, the plasticky sheath encasing him. My hands are tentative as I explore its filmy texture.

"Wait a sec." He stops me. "You said you've never seen a condom before?"

"I said I've never seen it *on* before."

"So you're on the pill?"

"No."

"What then?"

"Well...I don't...Hafez is out of town so often..."

"Right." He cuts me off.

The mention of my husband's name is like a splash of cold water. We lie on the bed, together, but separate.

A little sob escapes me.

"Don't." He gathers me in his arms. "You're ruining a perfectly fine moment."

"What moment?" I scoff.

He frames my face in his hands and looks at me. "This one."

And just like that, he pushes everything else aside.

There isn't an inch of me that he doesn't taste. From the space between my brows, to the hollow of my navel, to the sweep of my spine, to the arches of my feet. When he finally settles his weight between the cradle of my thighs, I close my eyes, alive only to the searing sensation of him sliding into me.

"You're so tight." He hisses, as the first long, slow plunge meets my flesh.

"Ahhh," I gasp, half pleasure, half pain.

"You all right?" His voice is gruff with the hard edge of passion.

I nod, thrusting my hips up, wanting more, but he pulls out instead.

"I just want to stretch you out," he says, when I start to protest.

He slips two fingers inside me and starts moving them in a maddening rhythm, in and out, side to side, round and round. His thumb plays with my clit, as he watches me take shallow, frenzied breaths.

"Do it," he says, in that familiar, intimate way.

I roll to my side and start a rhythmic clenching of my thighs, with his fingers still inside me. It's not long before he feels me contracting around him. With a muffled grunt, he flips me over and enters me again, swallowing my cry of pleasure with his mouth.

This time there is less resistance. He plunges deeper, letting my walls accommodate to his fullness, even as he feels the last ripples of my orgasm pulsing through me.

"Unhh." He slides his hands beneath my hips, lifting me, burying his hot flesh between my legs.

My lips form a soundless 'O' as I take in the full, thrilling hardness of him.

"Wider," he commands, nudging my thighs apart.

I wrap my legs around him as he sinks deeper into me.

"You have no idea how good you feel." His eyes are wild and feverish as he looks at me. Then he rocks against me, holding himself up by his forearms, anchoring his fingers in my hair.

Yes. Yesssss. I bite into his shoulder, inhaling the scent of his body. I've never been more conscious of anything in my life, never realized I've been walking around with this deep, vacant hollow that he fits into so perfectly, so completely.

He is by turns gentle and savage—slow, sensual grinding one moment, followed by quick, hard stabs. Each shift makes me cling to him, blood roaring in my ears, until I feel him straining against the last shreds of self-control. And still he waits.

I take his face in my hands so he can see what I'm saying. Then I rotate my hips and push against him.

"Shaydahhh." He lets go with a primal growl.

I feel the first rush of ecstasy jerk through him. His fingers grip my hips, holding me still as he empties himself inside me. He shudders violently, dazed by the intensity of his release before burying his face in my shoulder.

We stay like that for a while, catching our breath. It's too soon to face each other, like the first moments after a head-on collision, shaken by the raw, unexpected force of it.

"God. I love everything about you," he says when he can speak again. "These long, dark lashes, your glowy, golden skin, the way you smell. Roses, always roses. Pink roses. Like your lips."

He traces the line of my nose with his finger. "I love this dent over your mouth, the way your smile fills the corners." He stops at the silver scar on my bottom lip.

If he asks me now, I'll tell him everything. Anything.

But he kisses the spot in silent communication of all the things he can't voice.

"What?" he asks when he catches the spasm in my throat.

"Nothing." I play with the rosary around his neck. It helps me bite back the tears. "I have something for you."

"You got me a birthday present?"

I nod.

"Fuck. Now I feel like shit."

He's given me the best gift of all and he doesn't even know it. He's pulled Pasha Moradi out by the roots and cast him out of my soul.

"I made you some brownies," I say.

"Where are they, woman?"

"I don't feel like getting up." My arms flop to the side.

We lie in silence, listening to the drone of a boat on the lake.

"So what are you doing tonight?" he asks.

What he's really saying is: *I want to know what it's like. For you to go home and celebrate your special day with your family. The real people in your real world.*

I'm not sure if I should tell him.

Who am I trying to protect? Him? Myself? My family?

"Nothing," I reply. "It's a school night. We might go out for dinner on Saturday."

I don't ask him what his plans are.

When I try to imagine his night, or the night after that, or the weekend ahead, I see phantoms with faceless bodies. They're all glossy and dazzling—young, free, fun and firm.

"So how about those brownies?" I ask, glad I cut them into neat little squares so I don't have to touch this double-edged sword that swings between us, slicing through me when I least expect it.

26. CALL HIM YOURSELF

June 18th, 1996

"I can't believe it's been a year already," says Jayne.

I can't believe it either. A year ago, Troy had been like a passage in a book, the kind you remember and recall. And then he was real and more powerful than any words on any page in any story could convey.

"Happy anniversary." I give Jayne a hug.

"And happy birthday to you! A day late, but you were too busy to meet me for lunch yesterday," she chides.

"Sorry." *I was celebrating a mutual birthday in ways that still make me catch my breath.*

"So?" she asks after the waiter takes our order. "Spill."

"What do you mean?" I ask.

"Oh, come now," she says. "Something's going on. Your hair, your skin, even your eyes are different. You look positively radiant. Did you get something done?"

"What? No." I laugh. "Nothing like that."

"Then what?"

"I'm just...I don't know, happy." I twirl my glass, hoping the tinkling ice-cubes will stop the full flush I feel coming on.

I'm happy. And sore. My skin is chafed from Troy's stubble, and I ache when I move—the joints where his hips fit, my inner thighs, my waist where he held on.

"Well, whatever it is, it sure agrees with you," says Jayne.

"So how's the new place coming along?" I take a sip of my water and change the subject.

"It's amazing!" She lights up. "We should be ready for a house-warming soon, but you have to join us at the cottage first. We're hosting a small barbecue to celebrate our first anniversary. August long weekend."

"I'll check with Hafez," I reply.

"No checking. You're coming."

We spend the rest of our lunch catching up. It's nice and yet weird, like I'm wearing another skin beneath my own, another pulse that's flowing, separate from the Shayda who's sitting here. A Shayda I have to keep from the world.

"Heading back to the office?" asks Jayne as we pay the bill.

"No, I'm taking Maamaan to the clinic."

"Everything okay?"

"Just a routine screening," I reply.

MAAMAAN IS WAITING ON THE PORCH WHEN I ARRIVE.

"I hate these appointments." She plops her handbag on her lap and shuts the car door.

I smile. She wears a hat to anything she considers important. Weddings, funerals, parties. And mammograms. Today, it's a wide-brimmed ivory hat with a pink ribbon. Her winter hat is a deep burgundy cloche with felt flowers that she embellishes with an assortment of brooches if she suspects she's been seen in it before.

The mammogram doesn't take long.

"That wasn't too bad, was it?" I ask on the way back. She hmphs and stares out the window.

We stop at a bakery to pick up her favorite pastries, a reward for having her breasts squished and flattened and compressed and x-rayed. 'Mishandled' is the way she likes to put it.

In her kitchen, we settle down to what has become an annual tradition after one of these trips. I set the table while she makes tea—not the regular, everyday tea, but the kind on the stove, with real tea leaves and the careful simmering of milk and water. When the mixture is just the right shade, she adds a few strands of saffron and sugar.

"To Zarrin." She clinks her cup against mine.

"To *Khaleh*," I reply.

Only when she has sipped all her tea and finished her pastry, does she remove the hat.

"Call Hossein," she says.

I get up and start dialing the number. Then I stop, put the phone on the table and sit back down.

"Call him yourself."

Maamaan stares at me for a while before collecting her face. Then she clears her throat and picks up the receiver.

27. TWO SHADES OF RED

July 6th, 1996

"WHAT IS IT?" I ASK, IN THE QUIET AFTERGLOW OF PASSION.

Troy takes my hand and entwines his fingers with mine.

"I wish I could hold your hand outside this room, go for a walk, sit on a patio, watch the world go by."

I snuggle closer, to stop these simple, ordinary wishes from seeping between us, wishes that live and die in these four corners.

"Are you coming to Jayne's barbecue next month?" I ask.

"I'm in New York that weekend." He shifts so he's lying on his side.

I feel a stab of tenderness—the tousled hair, the sleepy sensuality in his eyes, the way he looks at me with that intense, soulful gaze.

"I love your after-sex face," I say, tracing the line of his jaw.

"Oh yeah?" He pulls me closer so I can feel him stirring. "How about my before-sex face?"

"But you just...we just..."

"Shut up and kiss me, Beetroot."

What starts as soft and gentle, quickly becomes urgent.

"God, I love the way you taste," he says. "You get so wet and your clit..." He licks me with slow, broad strokes before switching to a burst of rapid, stomach-clenching caresses.

"Your clit gets so swollen." He places his tongue beneath the mass of throbbing nerves and slides it up with soft, wet strokes.

Desire explodes at the pure, uncensored delight he takes in me. I wiggle my hips, hoping to ease the tension. He cups my butt and lifts me higher, deepening the red hot attack on my senses.

My fingers claw at the bed sheets.

"Not yet." His voice is muffled, but his eyes seek mine.

When he slips his finger inside, I throw my head back, unable to keep contact.

"Look at me." He slides his body over mine. "Look at me as I take you."

He sheaths himself with a condom before prying me open and settling deliciously into my core. A ragged cry leaves his mouth as he sinks into my ready wetness. My hands grip his shoulders as he eases out, almost all the way, and then back in.

"So good." His eyes glaze over as he looks at me.

He thrusts into me, slowly, rhythmically, building me up, until I'm arching my hips, giving in to that explosive need. He grips my hipbones, his strokes coming harder and faster.

"Come with me," he says. "Come with me, Shayda."

"I can't."

"You can. Like this..." He moves behind me, drawing my back to his chest so we're both resting on our sides. "Now." He slides into me. "Squeeze, baby."

I double cross my legs and start with long, slow contractions of my thighs. It's a different sensation, having him embedded in me, fuller, thicker, but I find my rhythm and thrill to the deep, guttural sounds that escape him. I arch my back and grind back against him.

"Wait. Hold still." He sucks in some air, fighting to pace himself. "You first." His hands clamp down on my hips.

I abandon myself to it, riding the pleasure to its pinnacle as he wraps his arms around me. I come hard, spiraling around two worlds—the hard, magnificent length of him and the twisting, pulsing bud of need.

He takes my ear into his mouth and stifles a moan as he feels me contract around him.

"I've got you." He holds me tight, as he gives in to his own passion, in short, jerky gasps.

We collapse against each other. I close my eyes, knowing I have never felt more connected to anyone and it kills me, that it's wrong.

"Shayda?"

I refuse to look at him. He gathers me in his arms and lets me cry into his chest. There are no questions, just the softness of his fingers stroking my hair. The minutes tick by, but we stay locked together.

"I'm glad you don't have to rush off," he says.

"Me too," I reply, drawing little circles on his chest.

"I'll be right back." He excuses himself to use the bathroom.

When he comes out, I'm wrapped in a sheet, painting my toe nails.

"What color is that?" he asks.

"This is..." I turn the bottle over and read the label. "Ablaze."

"I love it."

"The shade?"

"The shade is very sexy on you, but also the fact that it's never plain 'red' with you women. It's strawberry red or candy-apple red or habanero red."

"And I love that it's all about food with you guys. Strawberries and apples and habanero. I think this is named more for an emotion or a feeling."

"Ah, so ablaze, aflame, aglow, astride..."

"Astride?" I laugh. "That's not a feeling. That's a position, Mr. One-Track-Mind."

"I can behave. Occasionally." He stretches out on his tummy. "Give me your foot."

"Have you done this before or am I going to get goopy nails?"

"You'll just have to trust me."

As it turns out, he has an incredibly steady hand. He paints thin strips of shiny color with rapt attention. Troy Heathgate, treating my toes like they're the center of his universe.

"What?" he asks when I giggle.

"You just focus," I reply, wanting to do nothing more than shower him with big, squishy smooches.

"There." He sits back, admiring his handiwork.

"Not bad." I stretch my legs, wiggling my toes before me. "You have hidden talent."

"I have many hidden talents." He rests the soles of my feet on his chest and blows on my toes in a way that makes me want to curl them up.

"Let's go sit on the balcony," I suggest.

We can watch the world go by from there.

"Not so fast." He gets the robes from the bathroom and helps me into the one that says 'Hers'. Then he picks me up and carries me to the over-sized patio chair. "We don't want to ruin your toes."

"You spoil me," I say.

He drops a kiss on my nose and settles into the chair beside me. A dazzling view of the water stretches out before us.

"Do you always ask for this suite?"

"I ask for the best." He says it with no trace of pretentiousness. "Come sit with me."

I curl up next to him. It's like we can't go too long without the feel of the other.

"I won't be able to see you for a while," I say.

"No?"

"The kids are home for the summer and Hafez is taking some time off."

We watch sea gulls swoop down into the water, and the bobbing sails of boats across the lake.

"Troy?"

"Hmmm?"

"Don't think I didn't notice."

"Notice what?"

"No red condoms today."

"Never again." His eyes crinkle at the corners.

"No more Scary Cherry?"

"No, but I kinda like the way that sounds. You may be on to something, Beetroot."

"What do you mean?"

"I mean like a cosmetic company that manufactures just one shade of red. I can totally see women with Scary Cherry lips and Scary Cherry toes and Scary Cherry cheeks."

"You're crazier than I thought." I laugh. I'm crazier than I thought too. About him.

"I wish you'd kept the cell phone," he says.

"Hey, we have our work email set up now. You can message me."

"What about beetbutt? Have you logged in recently?"

"beetbutt@hotmail.com?" I laugh. "I'd forgotten about that."

"Maybe I should leave a reminder so you don't forget." He gives my bottom a good spank.

"Ouch!" I rub it in sore indignation. "I think that's my cue to leave."

"Stay." He pulls me back. "I'll kiss it better."

I stretch out on top of him, feeling his hand slide under the robe. "I really have to go."

"But we're in the middle of expanding our line. We now have two viable shades of red: Scary Cherry and Beet Butt."

"I. Have. To. Go."

"You can't. Your toes aren't dry yet."

"They've been dry for ages." I laugh.

"Fine, but don't say I didn't warn you," he says as I step inside.

I'm almost dressed when he comes in and helps me button up.

"I blew off a major meeting to see you today," he says. "You're no good for business."

"You don't say." I lift the hair away from my neck, letting him fix my collar.

"Uh-huh. You're hazardously distracting." He brings his hips into full contact with mine.

"And you, Mr. Heathgate, are completely insatiable."

"Completely." He grins before handing me my handbag. "Have you ever thought about getting your broker's license?"

"Me? Do what Bob does?" I laugh. "I'm fine with being an agent."

"Don't settle for fine, Shayda. You're a fantastic negotiator. I think it's because you're so good at making everyone happy. You should look into it."

He gives me a long, slow kiss goodbye, the kind that will stay on my mind. I linger, not sure when I'll feel the full, firm crescent of his mouth on me again.

I walk into the hallway, straightening my skirt as I wait for the elevator. A man walks out, but I'm too busy smiling at the shiny red paint peeking through my open-toed shoes.

"Shayda."

I freeze.

Baba.

"What are you doing here?" he asks, holding the elevator open.

"I was just...dropping off some papers." How easily the lie rolls out of me.

"Ah, for a minute I thought I'd caught you in the act. You know, the apple doesn't fall far from the tree." He laughs like it's an absurd inside joke, because it's something that can never be.

I want to scratch his eyes out. Because he's right. I made sure I married someone as different from him as possible. I never expected that I'd be the one who would turn into him.

"I didn't know you were in town," I say.

He shrugs. "You know how your mother gets when she finds out. Why am I here? Who have I come to see? It eats her up inside. I can feel her curses raining down on me."

I nod. "Well, see you around."

He pushes the door aside as it starts to close. "Listen Shayda, I...uh..."

Oh dear god. Not here. Not when Troy can come striding out of the room at any minute.

I watch as Baba fumbles. I notice the age spots on his hands, the way his lids droop on his eyes, like a tired, crinkled roof, sliding lower every year.

"Maybe we can meet for coffee while I'm in town?" he asks.

I see us sitting across the table, sugar cubes and awkward silences, like two strangers stuck together on a train.

"Sure," I reply.

Baba smiles. I know he won't call. He knows he won't call, but it's not about that. It's about me accepting his olive branch. And how can I not, when I am trailing in his footsteps myself?

The door closes, separating our worlds—the Apple and the Tree.

28. TSUNAMI

....

August 4th, 1996

"Are you kidding?" asks Ryan. "You're going to serve us year-old cake?"

"It's a tradition," replies Jayne. "And it's been carefully preserved. I didn't even have to re-frost it."

"I don't know." Ryan eyes the thawed out top of Jayne and Matt's wedding cake. "Can I just get another hamburger instead?"

"Ellen." Jayne turns to his wife. "Can you talk some sense into my brother?"

The deep, heavy rumble of a motorbike cuts her short.

"Holy shit!" Ryan gets up as the fire-engine red steel and chrome machine rolls into the driveway. "I'll be damned!" He races off towards it.

Tough boots, snug jeans and a wicked black leather jacket—trouble cruising for a place to land. Even with the sleek, dark helmet, I know the sexy, assured way Troy carries himself—feet planted wide, the broad measure of his shoulders, the chest that cradles my cheek.

"Who's *that*?" asks one of the guests.

"Down, girl," says Jayne. "There's a waiting list."

"Does it look like I care?" she replies.

"That's a Ducati 916," says Hafez, more interested in the hardware.

The men make their way, gathering around the bike like schoolboys around a shiny, new toy.

"Helllllooo?" yells Jayne. "Cake-cutting going on here!"

"Come on, guys," says Matt. "Before my wife serves my head instead of cake."

"Hello, Jayne." Troy gives her a peck on the cheek. "Making a splash as always?"

"Sorry. Bad timing?"

"You'll just have to make it up to me," replies Jayne. "Maybe a ride on that sexy thing after wards?"

"You got it, Mrs. Cavelry."

"Happy Anniversary!" We clap as Jayne and Matt cut into the cake.

My eyes find Troy's over the cheering. I'm immobilized by the rawness he pins me down with. That intense sexual tension, yes, but something else, a slow inner smoldering, like a heart on fire.

"Where are Natasha and Zain?" I ask Hafez.

"In the back with the other kids. Matt set up a trampoline and a sprinkler to keep them busy."

"I'll go check on them." I need to get away, to breathe. I'm completely unprepared to see him.

"Shayda." Jayne stops me. "Would you mind rustling some lunch up for Troy?" She turns to him. "I should let you go hungry for showing up so late, but there are lots of leftovers inside. Tell Shayda what you want."

Tell Shayda what you want. I almost laugh at the irony of it.

"I thought you weren't coming," I say as he follows me into the kitchen.

"I rescheduled New York."

I can feel the heat of his body behind me as I open the large foil dishes. Hamburgers, chicken, corn on the cob, colesla...

His hand halts mine as I reach for the plate, pressing my palm flat against the counter. His other arm comes up from behind, circling my waist.

"Troy—"

He swings me around and captures my lips in a rough, savage kiss, branding me with his possession, rendering me defenseless. I push against him, but he forces one leg between mine, slanting his mouth to deepen the kiss. His hands slide into my hair, tugging my head back, plundering my mouth with his tongue. Blood roars through my veins, a rushing boom-boom-boom, drowning out where I am, who I am. My body ceases to struggle.

"Why haven't you returned any of my calls?" His lips press against my temple.

Because I'm scared. Because each time I see you, it's a little more overwhelming Because I'm afraid it'll build up to a tsunami-like crescendo and come crashing down on me.

I cling to him, inhaling the rich, intoxicating smell of him and wind and leather.

"Hello? Anyone here?" A woman's voice asks from the entrance.

We break apart at the sound of approaching footsteps.

"Hey!" It's the girl who was admiring him outside. "I hear you want some lunch." She holds out her hand. "I'm Tanya."

"Troy."

"So did you find anything yet?" She looks at me, then him, and then the counter.

"You know what? I'm going to leave the two of you to it," I reply. "I have to check on the kids."

Troy's eyes narrow, but he doesn't say anything. He slides out of his jacket and gives Tanya that knees-to-jello smile.

"I think we'll manage just fine," he says to her, without looking at me. "Won't we? Tanyahhh."

I leave the kitchen, my heart dragging like a wet rag behind me. I follow the trail of kids' laughter outside, but there's no sign of Natasha or Zain.

"I can't find them." I say when I return to Hafez.

"Here." He hands me his half-eaten cake. "I'll go take a look."

Troy comes out of the house laughing, with Tanya literally eating out of his hand—carrot sticks or celery or whatever's on his plate. The two of them sit under the tree, away from the rest of the party. I know what he's doing. He's wringing my wet rag of a heart until it's all twisted and turned, punishing me for keeping us apart.

The cake tastes like saw dust in my mouth. I laugh at something Matt says, because everyone's laughing, so it must be funny.

Don't look, don't look, I tell myself, but my eyes wander back to Troy...the exact moment when he leans over and kisses Tanya.

A high pitched shriek comes from the lake. Everyone pauses.

Then we hear it again.

"Natasha!" I drop my plate and start running towards the water.

She comes crashing through the trees.

"Natasha! Are you all right?"

"It's Zain. He's in the water." She catches her breath. "We were playing on the boat and he fell over."

I can't get to the dock fast enough, my heart hammering against my ribs. Heavy, urgent footsteps follow me.

"He can't swim," I cry.

"Keep her here." I hear Troy's voice. And then a splash.

Hafez catches up to me.

"Zain." I point to the water. "He fell in."

Another splash as he joins Troy. Matt and Ryan peel off their shirts and dive in.

My knees buckle and hit the hot, splintered wood. I'm vaguely aware of Natasha crying beside me.

One by one, heads come up in the water.

Oh please. Oh please. A flicker of hope bursts to flame each time someone emerges, but no Zain. They come up empty, gasping for air before diving in again.

Every second passes like a time-bomb, ready to detonate inside me, spilling my guts all over the dock.

It's my fault. My fault, my fault. I was kissing Troy in the kitchen when I should have been looking for Zain. I was distracted by petty jealousies while my son fell in the water. I dropped him at Maamaan's to spend an afternoon with my lover. This is my punishment. This is my tsunami. Except it's claimed Zain, not me.

My breath comes in heart-wrenching sobs. How odd it sounds in this serene setting, with the wind rustling through the pines, as if it were just an ordinary afternoon. How can the water look so sparkly? Why is the sky still blue?

There is a loud, sharp intake as someone breaks through the water. Two heads. Oh god. Yes. Yes. I make out Troy's form, swimming back towards us, towing Zain to shore.

Hafez helps him out of the water and they lay Zain's body on the dock. His lips are a sickly blue and his eyes remain closed. Troy places two fingers on the inside of Zain's wrist.

"Call an ambulance," he says. "Now!"

"My baby." I crawl up to Zain's limp form.

Troy puts the heel of his palm on Zain's breastbone. "Hafez, keep his head still."

"1,2,3,4,......" Thirty fast, hard chest compressions. An endless stretch of eternity. Then he covers Zain's mouth with his and pinches his nose, tilting his chin up as he gives him a breath. Once, twice. He places his ear close to Zain's mouth.

Back to 1,2,3,4.....Each number feels like a quick, sharp stabbing of my soul. Hack, hack, hack, hack. The cross around Troy's neck sways. Life, death, life, death.

"Come on." He gives Zain another rescue breath. "Come on!"

Pink foam sputters out of Zain's nose and mouth on the next round of compressions. It's not clean, like in the movies. It's ugly and slimy and mucusy. He hurls lungfuls of water with each chest press. He takes a breath, but sucks the water back down. Cough. Sputter. Horrible popping, gurgling sounds. His eyes open, teary and bloodshot.

Troy rolls him to his side. More water. More wretched gasps.

"Get me some blankets from the boat," shouts Troy. "Where's that damned ambulance?"

He lifts Zain up from behind, arms around his waist, and squeezes. More water. Hafez covers Zain with a blanket and Troy lays him down again.

The paramedics arrive, intubate Zain and start pumping out more water. I think of his tiny lungs, swollen, like two bags of water, and sob convulsively.

Troy puts his arm around my shoulder. "He'll be all right." He looks exhausted, drained, completely spent.

"Thank you," says Hafez.

I move away from Troy and reach for my husband. We follow the paramedics into the ambulance. Troy stands outside as I huddle into the cramped interior with my family.

The door closes and we drive away. I know Troy is watching, but I don't look back. The shiny red paint on my toes is all chipped and cracked.

29. FOUR YEARS LATER

July 29th, 2000

ZAIN WAS BORN DURING A THUNDERSTORM.

It was the spring of '86 and it had been raining for three days. Hafez was away when my water broke. Bob drove me to the hospital while Elizabeth looked after Natasha.

"Are you sure you don't want me to call anyone?" she asked.

"Just try Hafez again."

I labored for sixteen hours. Zain was much harder than Natasha, or maybe it just seemed that way because I was alone. The lights went out when he came into the world. The first time I saw his face, was between flashes of lightning. Maybe that's why he's afraid of thunderstorms. When he was young, he would put his arms around me and bury his face in my belly.

"Make it go away, Mum," he'd whisper.

Now he finds other ways to stay close. Today he shuffled around and asked if I could make hot chocolate, the kind he likes, from scratch.

There is a certain comfort in watching milk come to a boil, a simple pleasure in breaking pieces of chocolate and seeing it melt in expanding swirls as I stir the pot.

I sit with Zain and Hafez at the kitchen table, as the steam rises from our cups and fogs up the windows.

"Can we stay with Grandma tonight?" asks Zain, strumming his guitar.

"Yes," replies Hafez.

"No," I say at the same time.

"Well? Which is it?" asks Zain.

"Dad isn't here next weekend," I reply. "You can go to Grandma's then if you want to."

"But—"

"Zain." Hafez looks up from his newspaper. "What your mum says."

"But she never lets me go anywhere."

"She's scared." Natasha walks in and pulls up a chair. "You know, because of what happened."

"But that was four years ago. And I know how to swim now."

I look at my children. Natasha, sixteen, almost as tall as me, but much more opinionated than I was at her age. I like that. I want her to have a voice. And Zain—at fourteen, his face is starting to change. We came so close to losing him. He has my curly hair and Hafez's big, round eyes.

"Next weekend," I reply. "You can go to Grandma's next weekend."

"Did you see this?" Hafez spreads the newspaper out on the table. "There's an article here on Troy."

My heart still rams into my chest at the mention of his name. I look into my hot chocolate, waiting for the moment to pass.

"Let's have a look!" Zain grabs the business section.

"Heathgate Group is expanding its international offices to Mexico and Hong Kong. The company, which has thrived under the leadership of founder and CEO, Troy Heathgate, is set to step into the international arena..." Natasha trails off. "Look, there's a photo of him too."

I pick up the empty cups and start washing them.

"How come we don't see him anymore?" asks Zain.

"He's a busy man," replies Hafez. "I think the last time Mum and I ran into him was two years ago. Right, Shayda?"

"That's right."

Two years, five months, two weeks and two days. The Valentine's Day ball that Jayne had organized.

I managed to avoid him all evening, except for that moment on the dance floor when I looked over Hafez's shoulder and our eyes met. I didn't see who he was dancing with. Didn't know, didn't care. They were playing Lionel Richie's 'Oh No', and for those few moments we were the only two people in the room.

He looked so handsome in his tuxedo, like Richard Gere in that opera scene from 'Pretty Woman'. I remembered what it felt like to dance with him, my hand clasped in his, breathing in that heady, exciting air around him. I wished the song would end. Who plays this on Valentine's Day? Three minutes of pure lyrical hell, of pretending I could breath, that my feet weren't lead, that my heart wasn't choking, gasping, sputtering pink froth.

Later, when Hafez made his way over to Troy's table, I said I had to use the bathroom. He looked at me funny. He couldn't understand how I could be so indifferent to the man who had saved our son. Indifferent, he said.

"Mum." Natasha turns off the tap. "You've been washing the same cup for the last five minutes."

"Oh." I stare into the sink. "Just a spot I can't get out."

The phone rings as I'm wiping my hands.

"Hello." Hafez picks up. "When?" He looks at his watch. "No, no. I'll be there. Yeah. Okay."

"What now?" I ask.

"One of the drivers can't make his shift. I have to go."

"Can't you get someone else to cover?"

"No one's available on such short notice. I'll be back Wednesday night." He kisses me on the cheek.

"And off again on Friday," I remind him. "I thought owning a business afforded us certain privileges."

"It's a new contract. We start missing deliveries and there are ten other companies waiting to swoop in."

"I know." I sigh. "I'll see you Wednesday."

I watch him back out of the driveway.

I wonder when he'll stop running.

30. DARK SPELL MASTER

August 4th, 2000

Jayne and I come to a faltering halt in the middle of downtown traffic.

"Damn it." She hits the steering wheel. "Damn it, damn it, damn it!"

"I don't get it. It's a brand new car," I say.

"It's not that." She thunks her head on the wheel.

"Then what?"

"I forgot to get gas."

"You're kidding."

She shakes her head. "The light's been on for a while."

"Seriously?"

"Seriously."

"Now what?" I ask. "Hafez is out of town. You want to call Matt?"

"Um...NO! He's always going on about how he has look to after me."

"Which is so obviously *not* the case." I roll my eyes.

"I know we have some kind of emergency roadside assistance..." She flips the dashboard open and a pile of papers fall out.

"I'll get them." I start picking them up.

"Sweet Jesus!" she exclaims.

"What?" I come up and hit my head.

"I'll be right back." She dashes out of the car and crosses the street, waving her arms about like a mad woman. I rub my head. What is she up to now?

It takes me a second to figure out who she's running to. Troy Heathgate. In the flesh.

My heart brakes mid-breath. No. Nonononono. Then I realize we've stalled not too far from his office.

I watch as Jayne points to the car, talking animatedly. His face breaks into a smile. God, I've missed that smile. He hands his briefcase to his associate and crosses the street.

My stomach twists into a knot as he opens the door and gets in. He freezes when he sees me, one leg in, one leg out.

"Shayda." With the ahhh.

"Hello, Troy."

He's sporting a five o'clock shadow that makes his sharp features look even more rugged. His hair is shorter, but just as thick and unruly. That dangerous, electric vibe is still there, throbbing, hot and hard between us.

"Troy?" prompts Jayne, reeling us back to reality.

I look away, even as the blood pounds in my ears. Will I ever stop being so aware of him?

He turns on the ignition. Nothing.

I watch his fingers—all the places they've been, all the ways they've made me moan and squirm.

"You've got to be kidding," he says to Jayne. "No gas? There are at least three gas stations within a few blocks of here."

She shrugs, not about to admit anything.

"I'll have one of my guys look after it." He makes a call and hangs up. "Can I drop you off somewhere? Looks like we're in for a hell of a downpour."

"Could you?" replies Jayne. "That would be absolutely darling of you!"

Great. How absolutely darling of you, Troy.

I follow the two of them to the parking lot.

"Wow." Jayne gets in the passenger seat. "Nice sports car. Hey, you still have the Ducati?"

"I do." He flips the driver's seat down for me to slide into the back. His arms steady my waist as I get in. We pull back instantly.

"You still owe me that ride, you know," says Jayne.

There's a horrible silence as the three of us recall that day, why Jayne never got her ride. August 4th, four years to the day that Troy dragged Zain out of the water.

"Hey, is this a Bose stereo system?" Jayne tries to lighten the moment. "Check it out!" She turns on the radio.

I envy her the blissful freedom to breathe and talk and think around him.

He starts the car and the engine roars to life as the first drops of rain start to fall.

"Just in time," says Jayne. She babbles on about the weather and her trips and the events she's planning.

I'm thankful for the chatter. The car smells of Troy, and new leather—dark, masculine and sexy as hell. It's low slung, with a quietly powerful engine and a sleek instrument panel.

"Oh hey. I love this!" Jayne cranks up the volume.

I catch Troy watching me in the mirror, his eyes the only points of brilliant blue on this grey day. Bryan Adams is reminiscing about his lover in that perfectly raspy voice. 'Please Forgive Me', he sings. The light turns green and Troy breaks contact, but his knuckles are white as he grips the steering wheel.

"This is me!" announces Jayne as he pulls into her driveway. Lightning flashes across the sky. "Thank you, Troy."

"I'll get off here too." I grab my handbag.

"Shayda, it's pouring. Troy will drop you home. You don't mind, do you Troy?" asks Jayne.

"No." He stares straight ahead.

Jayne gets out and folds the chair down. "Hop in the front, Shayda. Quick, I'm getting soaked!"

I do as I'm told, aware of how ungraceful I must look, scrambling out with my skirt hitched up.

"Bye, Troy. Thanks again! Sorry we couldn't do coffee, Shayda. I'll call you." Jayne pulls her jacket over her head and runs to the porch. As soon as she's inside, I open the door.

"Where do you think you're going?" asks Troy.

"I'll take a cab," I reply, pulling out my umbrella.

"For God's sake, Shayda, I—"

His words fade as I bolt out of the car. The wind whips my hair and I stumble blindly towards the road. A hard yank pulls me back.

"If you think I'm going to leave you here in the middle of a bloody thunderstorm, you're fucking crazy!"

He hauls me over his shoulder and starts walking towards the car. I splutter with indignation. My umbrella goes flying into the street. I watch as it gets swept off into an upside down world.

"Get in and *stay* in." He deposits me like a sack of potatoes on the seat.

"I'll ruin the leather." *I don't want to be alone with you.*

He gives me a chilling look as he gets in the driver's seat. I hear the sound of the automatic locks.

"We need to get out of here." He puts the car in reverse as Jayne draws the living room curtains, peering at us through the window.

His arm goes around the back of my headrest as he pulls out of the driveway. He's drenched; his shirt is clinging to the hard planes of his chest and his hair is dripping wet. An unbidden memory of him, fresh out of the shower, towel slung around his hips, flashes before me.

"You made me lose my umbrella." *I hate sitting so dangerously close to you.*

Why is Bryan Adams still singing this stupid song? How long is it anyways? I switch the radio off. Now it's worse— just him, me and rhythmic swishing of wipers splashing the rain this way and that.

Troy ignores me until we come to a stop sign. His weight shifts and he leans over, his mouth inches from mine.

Oh god, he's going to kiss me.

"Seat belt." He buckles me in.

Relief.

Disappointment.

"You need to dry off." His hands go back to the wheel. "There's a towel in my gym bag. In the back."

I reach around, feeling for it, but I can't find it.

"It's on the floor, behind your seat." He turns into an empty parking lot. "Here." He gets the bag and hands me a towel.

I smell him on it. The rich, sensual scent of his skin brings back flashes of bare, sweaty moments and tangled sheets.

"Damn it, Shayda. Dry off!" He grabs the towel and starts rubbing it briskly over my hair.

"I can do it myself!"

"Fine." He tosses the towel back at me and turns the car off.

"What are you doing?" I ask, alarmed as he removes his tie and starts undoing his shirt, one button at a time.

"What does it look like I'm going?" He slips out of the wet shirt and digs into his gym bag. "I'm changing."

I'm hit with the brunt of raw masculinity, the corrugated leanness of his abdomen, his nipples hard from the rain. I don't breathe until he's safely covered up.

"I'd offer you the t-shirt, but I sense you won't be as free dispensing with your blouse." His eyes fall to the top that's clinging to me like saran wrap. I hold the towel closer, shielding myself.

"Don't worry, Shayda." He rakes his hand through his hair. "I'm not going to take you like some depraved, dejected fool. You've made it very clear that you can't stand the sight of me."

Can't stand the sight of him? I hold back the crazy laughter that threatens to break free.

He reaches into the dashboard for a cigarette, and places it between his lips.

"Don't," I say.

"What do you care?" His eyes challenge me.

Lightning illuminates one side of his face.

Damn you, Troy. Why do you have to be so heart-breakingly handsome?

"Just don't." I remove the cigarette from his mouth.

It's a simple move, but it brings back all the other times I've done it before—a hotel room with soft, fluffy pillows, foggy mirrors in the bathroom, him zipping up my dress and leaving hot, smoky kisses on my back.

He watches me put the cigarette away, like he's battling his own army of flashbacks.

"Your hair is still wet." I hold up the towel, expecting him to take it, but he leans forward and puts his face in it.

I wipe his hair, wanting to kiss the thick, dark strands. I wipe his eyes—eyes that know all of my secrets. I wipe his cheek, the one he liked to rest on my belly. I can't bear touching him and yet not touching him, so I remove the towel from his face. But it's a mistake, like I've removed a mask. His eyes are bare, naked, like he's been running for a long, long time and now he's finally here, looking at me, tired, weary, and very, very thirsty.

Please don't look at me like that.

He lowers his gaze, picks up a strand of my hair and twirls it around his finger.

"I miss you," he says to it.

It's barely audible over the sound of the storm raging outside, but in here, it's like a roaring crescendo.

Why do his words have the power to turn my world upside down?

Why do will and shame and guilt and sense fall by the wayside when I'm with him?

Because you love him, comes the answer.

You love him.

You love him.

It echoes like the clap of distant thunder.

How many women have loved him and been left by him? How many have sat with him on a rainy night and felt like this? This gut-twisting, soul-wrenching thing he does to me? What does it matter, this sad, useless love, when it would destroy all my other loves—my home, my family?

"What happened that day wasn't your fault," he says. "Stop punishing yourself, Shayda."

I take a long, slow breath, feeling my resolve falter.

"I think you better take me home," I say.

He nods and starts the car.

I don't need to give him directions. I wonder if he's circled this block before, driven by my house, debated what world lies beyond its red door.

"Looks like you beat everyone to it," he says as we approach. All the lights are off.

"The kids are at Maamaan's and Hafez is away."

For a moment, he looks at me without unlocking my door. The air turns thick with possibilities.

"Well..." My fingers tremble as I reach for the handle.

I have one leg out the door when he pulls me back.

"Shayda...I'm sorry."

I know he's apologizing for kissing a stranger under a tree, the day Zain almost drowned, but all I can feel is the rough pad of his thumb caressing the inside of my wrist. And he doesn't even know he's doing it.

"Goodnight, Troy." I turn and dash for the front door, a wobbly mass of tangled nerves. I am in love with a ninth degree dark spell master.

The rain is a welcome relief from the hot, steamy car, but it does nothing to wash away the imprint of his touch. My hands shake as I fish for the keys. I glance back, half expecting him behind me. I get in and lean against the door, holding my breath until I hear him drive away.

31. FLY, DAMMIT, FLY

....

August 5th, 2000 (1)

"DID YOU MAKE IT HOME ALL RIGHT?"

No, Jayne. I slipped up somewhere between your place and mine.

"Yes." I reply.

"Can you believe it? Running into Troy out of nowhere?"

"Did you get your car back?"

"I did. With a full tank of gas, a Petro-Canada gift card, and not a whisper of it to Matt. That man." She laughs. "You know, I haven't seen him in ages. He just dropped out of the scene. No girls, no booze, no parties. But damn, does he keep getting better looking or what? He must be what now? Forty?"

"Thirty eight."

"That's right. You guys share the same birthday. How weird is that?"

"Any news from Bob and Elizabeth?" I ask.

"They're having a fabulous time. Dad's been so relaxed since you got your broker's license. Has it been busy without him?"

"Yes, but Marjaneh's really picking up."

"I'm glad. So what time are you there till today?"

"I'm just getting ready to leave."

"Are you sure you don't want to join us tonight?"

"Maybe another time. I'm actually looking forward to some alone time."

"Call if you change your mind."

"Thanks, Jayne." I put the phone down and collect my things.

"Delivery for you." Susan buzzes me.

I switch the lights off and step into the reception.

A small parcel is waiting for me—a generic, cardboard box with no markings except for my name.

I leave the office and get in the car. It's a scorcher of an afternoon. The seats have been baking in the sun. I picture Hafez on the road and hope he's keeping hydrated. I switch on the a/c and reach for the package. When I nudge the packing paper aside, I freeze. Inside is a fold-up umbrella, like the one I lost last night, except in red. I get out of the car and open it. A single butterfly, a few shades darker than the umbrella, is printed on one side. It's fun and playful and vibrant. It makes me want to go out and dance in the rain.

I choke back a sob. This is what he does to me. Open up the windows of my soul and push me out.

Fly, dammit, fly!

I get back in the car, trying to overcome the choking sensation in my throat. I think of spending an empty night in a dark house, of waking up to cereal and cold milk, of doing the laundry, and being good and right and dutiful.

But I drive the other way, through tear-blurred streets to Troy's office.

'HEATHGATE GROUP' in gleaming gold letters, now occupies four floors. I get in the elevator and press the top one.

Please be there. Please be there. I may never have the courage to do this again.

"Miss? MISS! May I help you?" I barely hear the receptionist trying to stop me.

There is only one office and it's closed off behind dark wood paneling. I swing the door open and step in.

There he is. One hand in his pocket, the other holding the phone to his ear, looking out of the floor-to-ceiling window. No basketball hoops. Just stark lines, gleaming steel and sleek white furniture.

He turns around at the commotion and fixes his pacific blues on me. His eyes narrow as he scans me.

"Sam, I'll call you back," he says before hanging up.

"I'm sorry, Mr. Heathgate, she just—"

"Thank you, Tina. That'll be all." He dismisses her.

We're alone.

It's so quiet, I can hear the thundering beat of my heart. Now what? I hadn't thought this far. We stare at each other across the room. His hair is disheveled, like he's been running his fingers through it. And he's wearing the same t-shirt from last night.

"I got the umbrella," I say.

"Good."

"Doesn't look like I'm going to need it today."

"No."

"Well." I fumble with my hands. "I just came by to say thanks."

I pivot on my heel and open the door.

He's behind me in two long strides, pushing it shut.

"Don't go."

I stare at the grain of the wooden door, the smooth texture, the small open pores. I can feel his breath on my neck, but he doesn't touch me. He just stands there, hands braced on either side of me. Then he steps back and heads to the bar across the room.

"Can I get you some coffee?"

I let my breath out and turn around.

He pours me a cup and holds it out. When I don't take it, his lips twist in a wry smile and he places it on the counter. "Here."

Where our hands won't touch.

"Thanks," I reply.

"Cream? Sugar?" He adds just the right amount.

"Aren't you having any?" I ask.

He pours himself a cup and stares into it.

He looks worn, haggard. The ready laughter that lived in the corners of his mouth is gone.

"Troy?"

"Yes?"

"I don't want coffee." A hot tear rolls down my cheek.

"Don't, Shayda." The muscles on his forearm tighten as if to stop himself from reaching out.

"I don't want coffee. Or cream. Or sugar."

"I know, baby. But it's all we got."

I clench my fist until my nails leave red crescent marks on my palm. "We've got today."

"What are you saying, Shayda?"

"I'm saying, we have now. Here. Today."

He goes very still. "Quit fucking with me, Beetroot."

"I'm not. If you still..." I barely manage to lift my voice beyond a whisper.

His brow furrows. "I don't know, Shayda. I'd have to check my schedule."

My heart sinks. What was I expecting? StupidstupidstupidShayda.

He walks over to his desk and buzzes his assistant.

"I think I'll just get going." I tuck my chin and head for the door.

"Tina," he says into the receiver, "clear my calendar for the day."

I halt in my tracks and spin around.

He has the biggest smirk on his face.

Oh yeah?

I hold up three fingers.

"Hold on." 'Three days?' he mouths silently. "Tina, clear my calendar for the next three days." He nods. "I know. Reschedule them." He studies me thoughtfully. "And Tina? Take the rest of the day off."

He hangs up and sits back in his chair.

"What?" My pulse beats erratically as he steeples his fingers and regards me.

"Don't ever do that again."

"Do what?"

"Barge into my life and expect me to drop everything for you."

"Don't send anonymous packages to my office then, and pretend like you didn't mean to summon me."

"Touché." He measures me with an appraising look. "You grew a pair. I like that. Now come here so I can kiss you like I've been dying to since the moment you walked in."

The first kiss is gentle, a soft re-acquaintance of our lips, as if we're gliding on a dream, careful not to wake ourselves out of it. The second sends the pit of my stomach into a wild swirl. He ravishes my mouth with an intensity that is both frightening and exalting. I wind my arms around his back, molding my curves to his body, giving myself up to it. When my senses are completely short-circuited, he lifts his mouth and gazes into my eyes.

"You put me through hell, you know."

"We both knew it couldn't go on forever."

"And yet here we are, Shayda." He sighs. "What exactly are we doing?"

"Three days." I drop my chin to his chest. "I haven't thought beyond that."

"Three days, huh?"

I squeal as he puts one hand under my knees and picks me up.

"We better get going then. You, my dear, have a lot to make up for." He grins and carries me out of his office.

Tina has left and the building is quiet. We cross the lobby and head for his car.

"Someone will see us, Troy. Put me down!"

"Not a chance. You've taken off on me too many times." He ignores the stunned looks from passers-by. "Besides, it's so much easier when I don't have to throw you over my shoulder, kicking and screaming."

"Caveman," I say when he deposits me in the passenger seat. "Where are we going?"

"My place. For now."

"I thought your place was off-limits."

"You made a three day exception. I'm doing the same."

WE TAKE THE PRIVATE ELEVATOR TO HIS LOFT. THE DOOR opens and closes. We don't notice. He has me against the wall, his knee between my thighs, my fingers in his hair, our lips locked in a hungry kiss. It's not until the second 'ding', when the elevator hits the basement again, that we come up for air.

"You're so fucking distracting." He presses the button to the loft again and goes back to nuzzling my neck.

"Stop swearing."

"Stop swearing, stop smoking, stop drinking. That leaves just one other option." He cups my bottom and pulls me in suggestively. "It'll have to make up for everything else." He slides his hand under my thigh and wraps my knee around his waist. "I hope you're ready because once we get up there, you're all mine. To do with as I please."

I give silent thanks that he's holding me up or I'd be on the floor, a puddle of quivering anticipation.

This time we make it out of the elevator. He opens the door with one hand, reluctant to let go of me.

"Here we are." He stands behind me.

I look around. He's turned the empty, industrial space into a warm, cozy den.

"Here we are." I smile and turn to him. "The place looks fantastic."

"You like it?"

I nod. "And what a find. You must have a great realtor."

"I did. The best. But she has this nasty habit of taking off on me." He leads me in and shuts the door.

"Sit." He pats the lush leather love seat before picking up the socks and newspapers strewn around the place.

Cute. I'm expecting him to drag me to the bedroom and he's playing the gracious host.

"Have you had lunch?" he asks.

As if on cue, my stomach rumbles.

"That would be a no." He laughs. "How about I whip something up? You like pasta?"

"Since when do you know your way around the kitchen?"

"You'd be surprised at all the things I've learned since... well, since I stopped going out as much. The most important of which is—always start with some good music." He points the remote at his stereo system. The smooth, smoky voice of Lenny Kravitz fills the air.

"How about you chop, I cook?" He hands me the cutting board and a knife.

"Let's see." He opens the refrigerator. "Basil, avocado, garlic—" He pauses and tosses it back inside. "No. Let's skip the garlic." He gives me a wicked smile. "Cherry tomatoes, parmesan...I think we're set."

"You shouldn't store your garlic in the fridge," I blab, so I can pretend that being with him in such close proximity isn't turning my insides to mush.

"No?" He steals a long, slow kiss. "You should come over and straighten me out."

Damn, now my knees are entering the State of Eternal Jellification. I rinse the avocados and get started.

"How do you want them?"

"Like this." He holds my hands from behind and shows me. "Peeled...halved...pitted."

He makes each word sound ridiculously sexy.

'I belong to you', chants Lenny Kravitz. The beat is rhythmic and seductive. We work in silence, or at least we pretend we're working, and not thinking about tearing each other's clothes off. I feel the soft, smooth flesh of the avocado as I peel it. His hands stay on mine, echoing my movement, his breath caresses the back of my neck. We rinse the small, round tomatoes, feeling the water run through our fingers.

"Halve," he whispers, guiding me as we cut through the plump, juicy centers.

I swallow. When he said he'd whip something up, I didn't think it would be this hot, frenzied need in me.

"Basil. Chopped. Coarse." He picks up a stalk and runs it up and down my arm as I struggle to keep the knife straight.

"See what distraction does?" He nips my ear lobe.

Cooking with him is an exercise in raw sensuality. But I know I'm not the only one this is affecting. I can feel his arousal pressing up behind me.

"I think you need to cool off, mister." I cup my hands in ice-cold water and splash it on him.

"Ohhh!" He stares at me disbelievingly, his mouth wide open.

Both of us look down at his pants. I got him where it counts.

"You little minx!" he growls and lunges for me, but I dart to the other side of the counter.

He stalks me with deadly deliberation, his muscles flexed and ready to pounce. The perfect hunter. Except for that wet spot on his trousers. I giggle.

"Gotcha!" He grabs me by the hips. "You have *any* idea how much trouble you're in?" He plops me on the counter. Tomatoes and avocados go rolling off the top.

"A whole lot of trouble?" I ask, barely able to breath.

"A whole, whole lot." His hand slides under my bottom and he brings me closer to the edge of the counter so I can discern exactly what 'a whole lot' feels like.

"I love when you wear a dress," he says into my neck, as he strokes me over the lace of my panties.

"You're so wet," he whispers. "But it's payback time. I want you soaked right through, like what you did to my pants. You hear me, baby?" He pauses and holds me with burning blue eyes. "I'm going to take you to bed and we're not leaving until you give me exactly what I want."

I nod, feeling like a finely stretched piece of string, about to snap at the slightest tug. My legs lock around his hips as he lifts me off the counter. His mouth claims mine, driving me dizzy with desire.

We barely make it to the living room, a tangle of arms and legs and withheld passion. We claw at our clothes, ripping, shedding, discarding.

"Damn it, Shayda, I wanted to do this right," he says as he lowers me to a soft, full rug and reaches for protection.

"You mean like candles and rose petals?"

Why are we talking when we should be kissing?

"I mean like feed you first." He laughs as my impatient hands pull him down.

His lips close around my nipple and I let out a ragged sigh. He plays with it, tugging, pulling, teasing. He moves further down my body, blazing a trail of kisses over my tummy, his tongue dipping into my navel. My hips raise off the floor as he buries his face between my thighs. I feel the wetness trickle down my thighs.

"Mmmm. Good, Beetroot," he says. "But I want more. Give me more." His tongue teases me through the thin mesh of my panties, giving me a taste, but not quite enough.

"Ohhh." I twist one way and then another, my fingers sinking into his hair.

The sound inflames him. He rips off my panties and presses his mouth into me. I buck against the white hot sensation.

I clutch his shoulders and urge him back up. There's a hot, gnawing emptiness that only he can fill.

"Take me now," I say.

"No." He looks up, singularly bent on sending me over the edge with his mouth and his tongue.

"Now, Troy." I invite him in. It's a move I know he can't resist.

He kneels between my legs. "Is this what you want? Tell me, baby. Say it." He teases me with the tip of his passion.

"Yes. Yes!" I hear myself say. I have never been so tightly wound up, so naked in my need. My fingers close around the long fibers of the rug, pulling and tugging.

He turns me on my side, ready to take me like that, allowing me the freedom to move, to work myself to orgasm.

"No." I turn back around "Like this." I lock my legs around his waist.

He snaps, giving in to the primal need in my eyes. He lifts my hips and buries himself inside me. One deep, hard thrust. Like coming home.

Our eyes lock, mouths opening in a silent 'ohhh' as my walls stretch to accommodate the rock hard length of him. It's exquisite, this connection of our bodies, this open, honest confession of all the things that remain unspoken.

He shifts, penetrating me from a higher angle, pressing against my clit with the base of his shaft and his pubic bone. I moan as he starts rocking, rubbing back and forth against that quivering bundle of nerves, until I explode in a whiplash of ecstasy. It's different, this release. It reaches deep inside, wave after wave of breath-sucking contractions. His head snaps back as he feels my insides clutching and releasing around him.

"Yes." He pushes me higher. Once, twice, until I'm falling, floating, collapsing in his arms. He catches my cry in his mouth as he spills into me.

We lay spent and exhausted on the rug, letting our hearts catch up. He takes me in the crook of his arm and plays with my fingers.

"What was that?" He smiles at me knowingly as I look away. "Come on, Beetroot. You got some 'splaining to do."

"You know exactly what it was."

"Oh, I do." He grins. "That's the first orgasm you've had without having to syntribate when I'm inside you. Holy shit! I want to shout it out from the rooftops."

"*You* want to shout it out?" I laugh. "I believe that's *my* prerogative."

"Listen to you. Cutting me out of your moment of glory. I am your Lord of Orgasms, baby! And it starts getting even better from here."

"What are you talking about, Mr. Heathgate?"

"One step at a time," he replies. "I don't think your tummy is willing to wait while I educate you further. Those are some fearful growls coming out of there."

He's right. I'm starving.

I watch him slip into his underwear, admiring the naked lines of his body.

"You better get up before I pounce on you again." He slips his t-shirt over my head.

"Damn. You're sexy as hell, Beetroot. Your messed-up hair, your swollen lips..." He comes in for a taste, his fingers splayed softly on my waist.

We follow the trail of hastily discarded clothes back to the kitchen. An image of my kids' rooms flashes before me as I pick them up.

"Don't," he says softly.

It's amazing how he can read the simple turn of my face or the line of my shoulders.

I fold everything up in a neat pile and watch as he plugs the blender in.

"Avocados," he requests.

"Basil."

"Olive oil."

"What?" He looks puzzled when I start laughing.

"I feel like I'm in an operating theatre. Scalpel. Gauze. Forceps. Anything else I can do for you?" I ask suggestively as my arms slide around him.

"Quit molesting the chef, devil woman. Especially if you want to be fed." He turns on the blender and puts a pot of water to boil.

I wander into the living room and pick up a picture frame.

"My parents," he says.

It's so odd, filling in these pieces of his life—two happy, weathered faces, beaming back at me through a pane of glass. He has his father's hair and his mother's eyes.

"You get along?" I ask.

"They were worried about me for a while. Thought I was just drifting through life, that I could never commit." He adds some linguine to the pot. "They're relieved some of that is behind me now. My work helps. I still get to do new things, see new places, meet new people." He drops a handful of pine nuts into the blender.

"I don't see them as much as I'd like," he says in-between the pulses. "They're away most of the year, traveling, seeing the world."

"Are you an only child?"

"Yep. The sole beneficiary of all their love and affection."

I put the frame away and look around. "So what's it like? To have it all?"

"Like flying. Soaring. Until you come across the one thing you'd give it all up for, and can never have."

I suck in my breath.

"Come give this a try," he says.

"Mmmm." I love the rich, creamy texture of the pesto, but I'm even more enamored with how delighted he looks that I like it.

I open the fridge and take out a few cloves of garlic. "If we're going to do this, we might as well do it right."

"I couldn't agree more."

Our eyes meet over the whirring of the blender and I get the distinct impression that we're talking about something entirely different.

"Would you mind if I made a quick call?" I ask.

"Phone's right over there," he says.

"I have my cell."

"You? A cell? Next, you'll be telling me you check your email too."

"Shhh. I'm calling my mother."

Zain picks up. "Hey. We're watching the 'Star Wars' Trilogy."

"Are you having fun?"

"Uh-huh."

"Have you had lunch?"

"Uh-huh."

I smile. Clearly, 'Star Wars' is winning the battle for attention.

"Put Natasha on," I say.

"She's watching it too. She says hi."

"Does anyone want to talk to me?" I laugh.

"Here's Grandma." Zain hands her the phone.

"The kids are fine," says Maamaan. "We'll see you on Monday."

"Call me on my cell if you need anything, okay?"

I say goodbye and call Hafez. His voice mail picks up. I struggle at the beep. Words seem fake and inadequate. I hang up without leaving a message.

"Ready to eat?" asks Troy when I return.

He looks so endearing, standing in his boxers, holding out a beautifully assembled plate of pasta, topped with a sprig of basil. All muscle and carefully hidden heart.

"That looks divine," I say.

"Eat on the terrace?"

"Sure." I pick up the plates and head outside.

"You know half your ass is hanging out in that t-shirt, right?"

I plop the food on the patio table and pull on the hem.

"Ha. Gotcha!" He laughs.

How can I not love him when he's like this?

He brings out some bread and a bottle of sparkling water.

"It's beautiful out here," I say. An unobstructed view of the water stretches out before us.

"You've seen it before."

Yes, but not like this, with no underwear and a full serving of Troy Heathgate on the side.

I lift the hair off my neck. "It's so hot."

"Want to eat in the pool?" He starts setting our food at the edge.

"You eat in the pool?" I ask.

"Why not? It's my pool," he replies. "I can eat in it. Hell, I can pee in it if I want. Don't worry," he laughs at the horrified expression on my face. "I don't. I don't pee in the pool, for heaven's sake."

"I don't have a swimsuit."

"So? We'll go au naturel." He starts undressing.

More of the horrified expression.

"Fine. I'll keep the boxers on. You swim in the tee."

I hover, undecided.

"Let's go, Beetroot!" He picks me up and starts walking down the wide, round stairs.

My arms circle his neck. I shiver as my butt comes in contact with the water, and cling on tighter.

The next instant, he lifts me higher and dumps me unceremoniously into the pool.

"Ohhh." I gasp as I come up for air, shocked, dazed and utterly exasperated. "What did you do that for?"

"Sometimes you just need to take the plunge." He dives in, and surfaces next to me.

"You always do that." I shake my head. "Headfirst into everything."

"And you're always one toe in, one toe out. Now eat."

He twirls a forkful of pasta and holds it out for me. I open my mouth, but he teases me with it, letting my tongue reach for it before he gives it to me.

"Mmmm." I savor the texture of the linguine, coated in thick rich sauce, the tartness of the tomatoes, the sharp, salty cheese. "Good."

He feeds me, and himself, between nibbles of crusty bread dipped in seasoned olive oil. It doesn't dawn on me until I've had my fill that my top has been riding up, leaving my bottom completely exposed. I tug on the hem, trying to make it to behave.

"Leave it." His voice is gruff and throaty. "I find it incredibly erotic to catch glimpses of you naked."

He smiles as color sweeps across my face. "Are you done, Beetroot?"

I nod as he pushes the food away.

"Turn around," he says. I feel one arm slide over my waist, encircling me from behind. The other plays with my curls as I lean back against him.

We watch clouds float over the shimmering water.

This is as good as it gets, I think. Warm sun above me, strong arms around me.

I glance into the water and freeze. He sees it at the same time. A thin, wispy strand of bright red.

His body goes tense. "Did I hurt you, Shayda?"

"No." I close my eyes and make a mental calculation.

"It's the beginning of my cycle," I say. "I guess this ruins our plans for the weekend." I start getting out of the pool, but he pulls me back.

"Are you kidding me?" His arms tighten around me. "That's not what this is about. It doesn't make one hell of a difference to me." He nibbles the back of my neck. "Besides, just thinking about not having to use any protection with you is getting me rock hard." His fingers slide under my tee and circle my breast. "Can I tell you something?" he mumbles against my throat.

"What?"

"You're not going to like it."

"Since when has that stopped you?"

"True." He yanks my t-shirt off and brings me skin to skin with his chest. "When we were hiding under that pier, this is all I could think about."

"I know," I reply. "And I was praying to this cross." I touch it again.

"God, Beetroot. You have the most impeccable sense of timing. If you're not laughing at my penis, you're reminding me of my grandma's rosary."

"What's wrong with your grandma's rosary?"

"Nothing. It's just not the best time to bring up my grandma. She may be out there. You know...watching."

"You don't like being watched? Come on, Troy. Let your inner freak out."

"My inner freak, huh?" His teeth sink into my shoulder and I lose track of my thoughts.

He leads me to the edge of the stairs and sits on the middle one. The water reaches up to my knees.

"Straddle me, Shayda." His voice is thick as he kicks his boxers off. "One knee here." He places it by his right hip. "The other here."

I glance at the tall buildings on either side of us.

"They can't see." He suckles my breast. "And if someone's watching from the water, all they'll see is this beautiful, golden back, bobbing up and down." He runs his finger down my spine.

A snapshot of us, entwined like that, floats before me. I press my hips into him as dizzy spirals of longing rush through my body. He lifts me up and lets me sink slowly into him.

"Ahhh." We gasp at first contact.

It's bare and raw and more intimate than ever before.

"God, you feel so good." He throws his head back, sucking in his breath.

I slide lower, but stop midway, unable to take him in any further.

"Easy. Put your hands here." He guides my palms to the stair above him, placing one on either side of his shoulders. "Now lift yourself, up and down. That's it, Shayda" He buries his face between my breasts, his hands kneading my flesh in round, circular motions.

I find a slow, rhythmic motion, rising and falling, but I'm still not able to take all of him. He holds my hips still and raises his pelvis, burying himself in me, millimetre by millimetre.

"Ohhh." I gasp at the fullness, the feeling of complete possession.

"Now move. Up and down, round and round, side to side. Whatever feels good, baby." His hands slide over my butt, mimicking each motion as he says the words. "Yes. Just like that."

I rest my forehead on his as we rock to an age-old rhythm. He tilts his head back and kisses me. And kisses me. A crazy yearning-churning-burning builds up inside. I press harder into him, trying to relieve the coiled up tension.

"Lean back and rub against me here." He presses his hand down on my pubic bone and keeps the pressure going.

I shift until I feel the hot, hard length of him pushing up against the front of my inner wall.

"That's it," he groans as I start to move, trailing up and down that part of me.

"Ahhh." I gasp each time the tip of his shaft hits a particular spot. "What's that?" I ask breathlessly.

"Your g-spot." He fixes an intense gaze on me. "Keeping going."

"Nnnnh...I feel like I'm going to pee."

"Don't stop." His voice is rough and urgent. "Bear down on it."

"I can't..." The pressure is intense.

He takes over, pushing against me, hard and fast, while his thumb strokes my clit, side to side.

The tension builds unbearably, almost painful in intensity. Every muscle in my body tightens before I burst like a balloon, gushing around him. The contractions come in dizzying waves of pleasure, radiating from my lower belly to my thighs, my calves, my toes, my nipples. I tilt my head back, arching my back, weeping uncontrollably as it rolls through me.

A muffled groan escapes him. He explodes in convulsive release, his fingers digging deep into my hip bones. He buries his face between my breasts, carrying my weight as I collapse against him. Faint pulses still run through me, keeping me from slipping into complete exhaustion.

"Fuck!" he says, when his breathing returns to normal.

He moves plastered tendrils away from my face.

"Troy?" I murmur, my eyes still closed.

"Mmmm?"

"I think I peed in your pool."

I feel the laughter bubble up in his chest.

"That wasn't pee."

"I know. I read Cosmo. Occasionally." I link my arms around his neck. "I just never thought the whole squirting thing would happen to me."

"Well, you're learning by leaps and bounds today, aren't you?" He shifts and pulls out, wrapping his arms around my waist. "Something's different, Shayda. What is it?"

My throat clenches. I hide my face in the crook of his neck and sigh.

I'm finally facing up to my feelings for him.

"We have this one weekend," I say. "Let's leave everything else behind."

32. LEVEL SEVEN KANOODLING

August 5th, 2000 (2)

"Where are we going?" I ask.

"Wherever the road takes us." He keeps one hand on the steering, the other on my thigh.

We stop at a drugstore outside of town. He follows me into the feminine hygiene section.

"Seriously?" I ask, thinking how comical he looks against daintily arranged boxes of Tampax and Midol and Canesten.

"I'm not letting you out of my sight," he replies.

"Put that down." I smack his hand.

"Evie's Extra Vinegar Douche. Shouldn't this be in the fish and chips aisle?"

"Would you just go buy a newspaper or gum or something?" I hiss. "I can't be seen with you."

"Who are we going to run into here?"

"You never know."

"Hey. I know exactly where we should go." He pauses and peers over my shoulder. "Gentle glide tampons? And these have wings. There's some serious aeronautic shit got going on here, Beetroot."

I turn around and glare at him.

IT'S LATE AFTERNOON BY THE TIME WE GET OFF THE highway.

"Hamilton?" I ask as he takes the exit.

"There are a whole bunch of cool vintage stores here."

"I wouldn't have pegged you for a vintage kind of guy."

"It's not for me," he says enigmatically.

We park outside a cluttered shop with wind chimes on the door.

"Welcome to Ken & Judy's." A ruddy complexioned man with a grey beard and kind eyes greets us. "The trinkets are here, gizmos there, thingamabobs in the back and the whatchamacallits over here. Anything else, just let me know."

"You have any wigs?" asks Troy.

"Sure." He points to the back. "My wife will meet you there."

"What do we need wigs for?" I ask as we weave our way through over-stocked racks.

"You said we can't be seen together. So pick a disguise, Beetroot, because we're not staying in this weekend."

Worn velvet curtains drape off an area labeled 'WIGS' in a barely legible scrawl.

"Hello," says a big, busty woman in a sing-song voice. She ties one curtain back and turns on the switch.

I gasp. It's like being hit with a giant spotlight. The back wall is covered with a high voltage vanity mirror. The counter overflows with mannequin heads sporting all kinds of wigs—red, blond, long, short. Old-world perfume bottles with atomizers and ornate tassels sit on gilded trays.

"I'm Judy," says the lady, dusting off a cushioned stool with gold legs. "Which one of you is looking for a wig?"

I pick up a headful of tresses and hold them against Troy. "I think the ringlets would look fabulous on him."

"Hmmm." Judy stands back and surveys him. "With his bone structure, he'd be absolutely dazzling in the Farrah Fawcett."

Troy takes a step back. "I'll...uh...leave you ladies to it." He ducks under the curtain and beats a hasty retreat.

"How long have you two been married?" asks Judy, after we stop laughing.

I glance at my ring. "Not too long."

"He *is* dazzling. You make the perfect pair." She smiles. "So what kind of wig are you looking for?"

We go through the options and settle on a sleek, chin-length bob with straight bangs.

"Very chic," says Judy. "And I love the red undertones on you."

"Can I leave it on?" I ask, turning one way and then another in the mirror.

"Of course," she replies. "Do you need any clothes?" she asks as we step out of the little room.

"As a matter of fact, I do. This trip was so last minute, I didn't have time to pack."

"Well." Judy rubs her hands. "I have just the right stuff for you."

In the end, she sets me up with a hand-picked wardrobe for the entire weekend. I come out of the dressing room in a cream, grecian jumpsuit with a gathered waist and flared legs.

"Oh yes!" she exclaims. "And try these." She brings me a pair of strappy gold sandals. "Boy, is he ever going to do an about take when he gets a load of you."

"Where is he?" I ask.

"I'll go get him."

She returns alone. "He's next door, looking at some cottage rentals for the weekend," she says, as we walk to the counter.

"Thanks for all your help." I hand her my credit card.

"Your husband's already looked after that." She hands me my bags. "Stop staring, Ken," she says without looking at him.

"You look smashing, love." Ken smiles at me. "My Judy has a magic touch." He gives his wife a big squeeze. "Yes, indeed. Magic."

We turn at the sound of wind chimes as Troy enters the store.

"Is she ready to go?" he asks, walking right past me.

"Ready and waiting," says Judy.

"Well, I got the cottage." He swings the keys before her. "The one Ken recommended. They said..."

He stops mid-sentence and goes very still, like he's just felt the hair on the back of his neck stand on edge. Then he swings around.

"Beetroot?" he asks, looking like he's been punched in the gut. "Bloody hell!"

He scans me from head to toe. The blunt cut of the wig accentuates my cheek bones and the bangs draw attention to the almond shape of my eyes. With the high, cinched waist, my legs look like they go on for miles. The soft, creamy fabric accentuates all the right places and brings out the golden hue of my skin.

"Damn! Come here, you." He pulls me in and gives me a big kiss. "And so the butterfly emerges."

I bask in the warmth of his embrace, my heart bursting with something I can only identify as silly, absurd happiness.

"Is this everything?" he asks, taking the bags from me.

I nod.

"Enjoy the cottage." Ken and Judy wave as we leave the store.

"That was so much fun," I exclaim, as we put the bags in the trunk. "I can't wait to show you what I—"

He cuts me off with a passionate kiss, slamming me hard against the car.

"I fucking love you," he chants with hot breath in my ear, before claiming my lips again.

Cars honk as they drive by. A man passes by with his dog. Somewhere, a jackhammer is drilling the pavement. Wind chimes tinkle in the breeze. The soft whirring of pigeon wings. A kid laughs at us. And there, in the bustle of mid-town, our lips cling in silence, until the edges of our bodies melt, until my mouth knows the taste of his soul.

When we finally come up for air, I open my mouth, but he silences me.

"I just couldn't not say it anymore." He leans his forehead against mine and closes his eyes.

I cling to him, not caring that the whole street can see me crying.

"Troy?" A man interrupts. "Troy Heathgate?"

"David?" Troy turns around and breaks into a genuine smile. "It's been years. Good to see you, buddy!"

They give each other the man-hug, affectionate slaps on the back.

"Is this guy giving you a hard time?" his sandy haired friend asks when he sees me wiping my eyes.

"David, this is BeetButt," says Troy.

"Beet what?"

I jab Troy with my elbow.

"Beetroot," he says. "This is Beetroot."

"That's uh...that's an unusual name."

"It's her stage name," replies Troy.

"Oh? Are you in show biz?" asks David.

"Best pole-dancer this side of the border," replies Troy.

My cheeks turn red, but David knows better.

"Good luck with this one, hon," he says. "Listen." He turns to Troy. "I have to run, but I hope you're going to stop by before you leave."

"Will do. Maybe tomorrow night."

"Great. I'll see you then."

We get in the car after he leaves.

"Pole-dancer?" I swing my bag at Troy.

"Well, it's not entirely a lie, you know. The way you danced around my—"

"Troy!"

His phone rings and he switches to the dignified, composed businessman.

"Tell them a video conference is the best I can do this weekend." He listens and scribbles a note. "Tomorrow then."

"Everything okay?" I ask when he hangs up.

"Just putting out some fires." His eyes soften as they settle on me. "You ready to go?"

I nod. "So where's this cottage?"

"Niagara-on-the-Lake. It's about an hour away."

I sit back, watching the landscape roll by. Evening settles around us, covering rows of carefully tended vineyards with a blanket of stars. The reflections of street lights and cars in my window meld into ghostly forms, glimpses of the past, whispers of the future, until I see Troy and me in the middle of a busy street.

I fucking love you.

I put my hand up to the glass, but the image disappears.

"You all right?" he asks. "You've been very quiet."

"I'm fine." I turn away from the window. "How do you know David?"

"David and I go way back. I moved to New York after college and David was my room-mate until I got my own

241

place. We used to drive down here all the time. His dad owned a pub in Niagara Falls. David's taken over. Maybe we can stop by tomorrow night?"

"Sure," I reply.

I want to run my fingers over the stubble roughened planes of his face and tell him what I know I shouldn't. So I take his hand in my lap and close my eyes.

"Shayda." He rouses me when we get to the cottage. "We're here."

It's too dark to see anything, but when we get inside the cabin, the view is spectacular. The moon is shining through the windows in the living room. Its reflection falls on the lake like thousands of silver fish. Troy opens the french doors to the deck and we step outside.

"It's beautiful," I say.

Tall trees surround the little cottage, locking us in a private oasis. The shoreline dips gently into the water. A barbecue. Adirondack chairs. A hammock swaying lazily between tree trunks.

Two people. One weekend. So much love to squeeze into this space.

We step back into the warmth of the cabin, the weathered paint, the worn wood, the homey kitchen, the hutches filled with knick-knacks collected over the years. Suddenly it's awkward, standing together in this lived in, domestic space, like something that could have been our own.

"I think I'll go take a shower," I say.

"And I'll go get us some take-out," replies Troy. "Any requests? Need anything before I leave?"

"Just this." I frame his face in my hands and kiss him.

When I step back, his eyes remain closed.

"Damn. I forget everything when you do that," he says. "Uh..."

"Dinner." I laugh.

"Right." He picks up his keys.

"Troy!" I shout after him.

"Yes?"

It's just the two of us, but I run up to him and whisper it in his ear. "I need a change of underwear."

He laughs. "I hope you're okay with utility underwear because I doubt the sexy stores are open."

"Granny knickers are fine."

"Know what's even better?" He cups my bottom. "No underwear, just this plain, juicy ass."

"Go." I laugh, pushing him out the door. "Oh, and I need a toothbrush. And a hairbrush. Is there toilet paper in the bathroom? Troy? Troy!"

But he jumps in the car before my shopping list starts unraveling. I shut the door, grinning.

I fish my phone out of my handbag and take a deep breath before calling Hafez.

"Hello." He picks up.

Please don't ask where I am.

Please don't ask what I'm doing.

He doesn't.

"I just talked to the kids," he says. "Natasha's working on her assignment and Zain—"

"Zain's probably been watching TV all day."

"Actually, he was playing Bingo with Maamaan and her friends. And winning too."

We talk for a few minutes. My family is fine. The world has not fallen apart. All I have to do is make it back in one piece.

By the time Troy gets back, my wig is off, I'm fresh-faced out of the shower and wrapped in a towel.

"I don't have pajamas," I say, as he appraises me.

"You're saying this isn't a planned seduction? You didn't intend to greet me like this?"

"Nope."

"Too late," he says, dropping the bags and kicking the front door shut.

We wrestle on the big shag rug. Well, I wrestle. He pins my hands over my head and laughs as I kick and twist and try to wriggle away. We've come a long way.

"Enough." He kisses me, effectively immobilizing me. "You need to eat if you plan on keeping up with me."

He takes out two candles and a bottle of wine from a plastic bag before handing it to me.

"What's this?" I ask.

He looks around and whispers, "Underwear," in my ear.

I laugh. "And what should I do for pajamas?"

He unzips his weekender and gives me a clean t-shirt. "This looks better on you than it does on me."

DINNER IS THE TWO OF US, SPRAWLED OUT ON THE RUG, digging into cardboard boxes of kung-pao chicken, and peking duck, and beef with broccoli, and chow mein.

"Like this." He picks up the rice with his chopsticks and shows me how it's done.

"Like this?" I catch his nose between my chopsticks and twist.

"You're not going to have any wine?" he asks after we stop goofing around. "This place has amazing ice wine."

"I don't drink."

"I know. I just thought you might like to try. Good thing I didn't go with that for a plan of seduction." He pours himself a glass.

"Oh? So exactly what plan did you go with?"

"Hey, I bought you a Hanes three-pack. Everyone knows that scores some major kanoodling."

"Noodles before kanoodles," I say, finishing the last of the chow mein. I stretch and stifle a yawn.

"Why don't you go get ready for bed? I'll clean up here." He snuffs out the candles and starts picking up the leftovers.

"You sure?"

"Well...I'm hoping it'll up the kanoodling factor."

"You're terrible," I say. *I love you.*

I give him a great, big hug and go to brush my teeth. I'm exhausted, but I've never felt more alive. My cheeks are flushed and everything inside feels like it's zinging and singing and buzzing.

I get into bed, snuggling into the smell of freshly laundered sheets. That's when it hits me. I'm going to be spending the whole night with Troy. No furtive glances at the clock. No rushing off to pick up the kids or head back to work. My heart pounds at the thought of us in bed for hours and hours.

I listen to the water running as he hops in the shower, the flushing of the toilet, him spitting into the sink as he brushes his teeth. Ordinary, everyday sounds that are so extraordinarily intimate.

"Hey." He slips into bed with me.

I smile, trying to stay awake. I don't want to miss a minute of this.

"Close your eyes." He kisses them shut. "Let go." His fingers stroke my brow, back and forth. "Let it all go." He smooths the hair away from my face.

I feel myself slipping away. "No kanoodling?" I murmur.

"What do you think this is? We're talking level seven kanoodling." His voice starts to fade.

Lying in his arms is the best place in the whole world.

33. TELL ME

....

August 6th, 2000 (1)

DAWN GLOWS AROUND THE EDGES OF WEATHERED WHITE
shutters. It takes me a few minutes to realize where I am.
Troy's arm rests around my waist, our legs criss-crossed
under the sheets.

Soft light falls on his face, growing brighter by slow
degrees. With his eyes closed and the angular planes of his
face relaxed, he looks angelic. Angelic with morning stubble.
Or maybe that's just me, looking at him through the lens
of my heart, against the halo of the rising sun. My gaze
follows the line of his mouth, his absurdly thick lashes, the
lock of hair that's fallen over dark, arched brows. I close my
eyes, storing away this moment, this portrait of him, in the
'special' archives of my heart.

I stroke the warm wooden beads around his neck,
letting my fingers trail to the barbed wire inked around his
bicep. He stirs and fixes sleep-drenched eyes on me.

"Hey."

"Hey." I smile, loving the sound of his waking voice, low and gravelly.

We look at each other, a little wonder, a little disbelief, on matching pillow cases, learning each other's morning breath and weirdly, yearning it. My lips brush his and I draw his bottom lip into my mouth, sucking on it.

He growls. "You know what you are?" His finger traces the curve of my lips before he slides it into the warm, wet cocoon of my mouth. "Pure sensuality. Begging to be explored."

I swirl my tongue around the tip of his finger and get rewarded with a low moan. My lips find his ears, his jaw, his chin. His throat clenches as he feels the swell of my breasts on his chest. I push his hands away as they slip under my t-shirt. It takes a second before he catches the gleam in my eyes. Then he lies back, reining in his passion, willing to yield to my exploration.

My fingers follow the bunching muscles of his shoulders and I graze his throat with my teeth. My tongue encircles his nipple, teasing the sensitive area around it, blowing hot breath over wet kisses until he bucks against me. I move slowly, letting my lips skim the hard slab of his belly, dipping my tongue into the groove of his stomach.

His fingers twist into my hair, urging me lower, but I push them away. My hand slips under the waistband of his boxers. He inhales sharply as I brush past his crotch and start rubbing against his inner thigh. His muscles tense as I slide the boxers off him and release his throbbing erection.

I ignore his hot, engorged flesh and press my mouth to the other thigh, moving it back and forth, little nips here, soothing tongue there, delighting in the texture of his skin and the feel of tight, toned muscle. I cup his balls in one hand and let my nails scrape gently against them.

He makes a sound in the back of his throat, like a big male cat. I look at him and feel a surge of heady power. His eyes are closed, head tilted back, fingers splayed out on either side of the bed. I purr and purse my lips, letting him slip inside my mouth, swishing my tongue over his head. His hips lift off the bed as I take him in deeper, deeper still, until I can't fit any more. My hands wrap around the rest of him.

He shudders as I let him pop out of my mouth and take him back in, my hands sliding and twisting around him. My head bobs up and down as I relish the wet, slurpy sounds my mouth makes against his hot, hard flesh.

"Fuck!" He grabs my hair, holding it off to the side so he can watch me through slitted eyes.

Our eyes lock and he grows even bigger, his head expanding with the cresting swell of passion. I move my hand to his balls, scratching lightly, applying gentle, circular pressure, until I feel him tighten. My mouth moves faster as his muscles tense up.

"Shaydahhh," he groans, his thighs trembling as he fights to prolong the pleasure.

I pull my mouth away, stroking him in a tightly clenched fist.

He snaps and yanks me up until I'm stretched out on him, mouth to mouth. His hands plunge into my hair, holding me at the angle he wants so his lips can ravish me. His tongue sweeps my mouth as his hips buck against me, in thick, hot spurts.

"Ohhh." He squeezes my bottom, convulsing in sweet release.

I feel the slamming of his heart against mine, the tremors running through his body, and I taste the sweet, sweet satisfaction of pleasuring him.

"It's better than a thousand chocolate snickerdoodles," I say.

"What?" he asks, still lost and breathless.

"Your face. When you come."

He thinks about it for a second. "You know what you're like?"

"What?"

"A giant bundt cake."

"A *bundt* cake?"

"Yeah. Your face goes all bundt-cakey, like the big 'O' in the middle. It's so fucking sexy."

I shake my head.

"What?" he asks.

"My lover thinks I'm a bundt cake."

"Say that again."

"My lover thinks I'm a bundt cake?"

"I love when you call me your lover," he growls.

IT'S ANOTHER FEW HOURS BEFORE WE MANAGE TO DRAG ourselves out of bed.

"Farm fresh eggs, homemade preserves, strawberries, peaches...You picked up a lot more than take-out last night."

"I stopped by a farmer's market." He kisses me on the cheek. "You want tea or coffee?"

"Tea," I reply, watching the oil sizzle on the frying pan.

"What's wrong?" he asks when he catches my frown.

"I don't know how you like your eggs."

His arms encircle me. "Fuck the eggs. Tell me what's wrong."

"It *is* the eggs," I reply. "It's just...being so close and yet not knowing anything about you."

He switches the stove off and turns me around. "I like veggie omelettes. I like my steak medium rare. I could eat a whole pan of your brownies. I like rock bands. Cordless drills. Monkeys. I love 'The Godfather'. My bike. I don't like that color when you mix green and brown. And I absolutely hate being possessed by a goat."

"That's the worst."

"Right? When you can't stop bleating and you're pooping pellets all over the place."

I rest my forehead against his chest and smile.

"Are we okay?" he asks, playing with a stray tendril.

"As long as you don't start pooping pellets."

"I'll do my best." He grins.

We have breakfast on the deck, under a cloudless sky, to the sound of loons and gently swaying trees.

"It's even more beautiful in the day."

"You like it here," he observes over the rim of his cup.

"I've always wanted a place by the water," I say.

He gives me a look that catches my heart like a flick from barbed wire.

I SLIP INTO THE YELLOW DRESS THAT JUDY HELPED ME PICK out. With its flowy skirt, halter neck and nipped-in waist, it's pin-up perfect for a sunny day. The white bird print adds a touch of whimsy that makes me smile.

Troy stops in the middle of his conference call when I walk into the living room. His eyes follow me into the kitchen as I tidy up.

"Fine," he speaks into the phone, "but I want to see the reports. Have them couriered to my office."

I look out the window, washing the dishes, listening to his voice, without listening to the words. If a parallel universe existed, this could be our life.

"You were wearing a yellow dress the first time I saw you."

I spin around and find him leaning against the wooden beam by the counter.

"And you were wearing a grungy sweatshirt."

"You smelled like roses." He pulls me away from the sink. "No. Wait. Don't say it. I was reeking of sweat." He laughs.

His arms wrap around me and we shuffle around the kitchen to a silent waltz.

"Shayda." He strokes my hair. "Are you ever going to tell me?"

"Tell you what?"

He stops moving and traces the scar on my lip.

"It was a long time ago," I whisper.

"I know." The tenderness in his expression stuns me. "I knew something was up when you fought me off that first time. But I didn't know what until after Zain's accident. You wouldn't take any of my calls. I had no news. I was going out of my mind. I looked you up, and there it was."

"You looked me up?" I frown. "But it happened before Zain was born."

"A man died, Shayda. That kind of stuff doesn't just go away. And the sick, twisted fuck is lucky he's dead. I couldn't think straight for days. I'm so sorry for what he did to you."

He did worse to Hafez. But you won't find that in any archived news article.

In a strange way, Pasha Moradi was responsible for bringing us together. He is the reason Bob offered me the job, how I came to meet Troy, why I'm standing here today, in the circle of his arms. Had it not been for a monster, I would never have known this glorious love. And yet, had it not been for the same monster, Hafez would be whole and our relationship might have taken a different turn.

"It's funny." I start half-laughing, half-sobbing. "Life is funny."

"Shhh." He rocks me gently.

When I'm done, he wipes my cheeks. "I've changed my mind," he declares.

"About what?"

"About being possessed by a goat. I'd much rather poop pellets for the rest of my life than see you cry."

"I'd rather we skip both." I break into a smile.

"Agreed. You know what else?" He grabs my hand. "We need to get out of here and make the most of this beautiful day."

WE FOLLOW THE RUSTIC TILES PAST THE GAZEBO, TO THE long, narrow strip of sand that hugs the lake. The shoreline is tucked away between tall pines on either side. Lounge chairs rest in shady spots.

"What's that?" I point to a circle of grey pebbles with a white 'X' painted on it.

"Beats me." He stands in the middle, inspecting it.

"The water is so clear," I say, pulling him towards it.

We take off our shoes and wade into the lake. It sparkles with a million diamonds, cool, calm and serene.

Holding hands with him, walking in the sun, the swishing of the waves—the making of a perfect moment.

"So what are we doing today?" I ask.

"I thought we'd go into town, do a little sight-seeing, maybe some lunch."

"Mmmm." I stand on tip toe and taste his lips.

"Mmmm." He holds the back of my head, deepening it.

He lowers me to the ground without breaking the kiss, or maybe I pull him down with me. It doesn't matter. The pebbles on the beach, the water in the lake, the sun in the sky, fade away.

"Yessss," he hisses between hot, breathy kisses as I rub against the outline of his desire.

I unzip his jeans and free him, gasping at the hard, sinewy weight of him. My need for him turns fierce and urgent. I give in to the whirl of raging emotions and kiss him with reckless abandon. He pushes my panties aside. I barely notice him pulling out the tampon before he embeds himself deep inside me.

"Ahhh." I drag his mouth back to mine, clutching his shoulders, digging little crescent marks into his skin with my nails.

He pulls the hair back from my forehead, holding my face motionless as he starts a relentless rhythm that rocks my whole body.

"Tell me." His eyes pierce mine with a ferocious need.

I moan, squeezing my eyes shut, but he presses his thumb and forefinger into my cheeks, squeezing until my lips purse open.

"Tell me," he rasps, harder and faster, driving to a harsh staccato drive.

The intensity builds up to a fevered pitch. White hot bolts of lightning shoot through me. I wrap my legs around him as my toes curl in ecstasy. "I'm yours, Troy. Yours."

"Mine!" He lifts my ankles over his shoulders and slams into me, his body shuddering with a jarring release.

"Mine, Beetroot. All mine." he says, kissing the corner of my mouth as he spirals down from the heights of passion.

After wards, he flips me over so I'm lying on top of him, and brushes the sand off my back. Then he wraps both arms around me like he's never going to let go.

34. CRUSHED ROSES

August 6th, 2000 (2)

"Turn," says Troy, holding the shower head over me and letting the water trickle down my back.

Gritty sand gathers around my feet. "I think I have half the beach in my hair." I laugh.

"It's the price you pay for your sexy curls, Medusa." He hands me the shower and lathers up my hair.

"Heyyy!" I laugh as his soapy hands move lower, cupping my breasts. "There's no sand there."

"I'm not taking any chances," he replies. "The only thing I want chafing your nipples is this..." His teeth graze a soft peak before he soothes it with his tongue, sucking on it until I moan. The steamy stall feels hotter as he moves to my other breast, catching a droplet of water before it slips from the rosy tip.

"Your breasts are so incredibly yummy. They make me forget how sore you must be." He steps back and smiles as I turn crimson at the thought of his hard, urgent possession by the lake.

"My turn." I take over and start soaping him.

The hard, warm muscles of his pecs glisten under the water. My hands slide across the tightness of his abdomen, and lower, to long, powerful thighs.

"You better stop, unless you want to keep waddling like a duck."

"I'm not waddling like a duck!"

"You're right. It's more of a penguin shuffle."

"Troy!"

"But it's the sexiest penguin shuffle ever. You have no idea how much it turns me on, knowing I'm the cause of it." He lets me feel just how true that is. "But I think you need some time to recover, Beetroot." He turns around, giving me his back.

I gasp.

"What?" he asks.

I trace the long red lines my nails have left down his back.

"Ah. Well, I didn't get away scot-free either." He laughs.

WE STEP OUT OF THE SHOWER AND INTO FLUFFY, WHITE towels. I dry myself, watching him wipe a circle off the steamed-up mirror. He shaves the old-fashioned way, with a brush and shaving cream, applying lather in swirling motions until his face is covered.

"That is so hot," I say, watching his very male ritual.

His razor halts mid-stroke as our eyes meet in the mirror. He completes the stroke, elongating his neck, making me want to press little kisses along the exposed flesh.

"Come here." He turns around and anchors me between his legs.

The fresh, male scent of him is amplified by steamy heat, sending a hot zing to the pit of my stomach.

"Will it always be like this?" I ask.

"Always." He hands me the razor.

"I don't think I can do it."

He takes my hand and guides me. "Keep your hand steady, keep the razor angled. Like this."

We do the first few strokes together. Then he lets go, giving me his cheek, his chin, his neck, all the while watching me with eyes that make me want to lick him all over. His hands stay on my hips and he sits very still, his breath fanning my face in an incredibly erotic way.

"Again," he says. "This time, feel with your hand first." He takes my palm and rubs it against his skin. "Feel how the hair grows, then shave in that direction."

I close my eyes and memorize the planes of his face, the space between his nose and lips, the line under his jaw, the feel of rough stubble, the patches of smooth skin.

"I get it," I say.

I get this face. I get the man behind this face. I get the love rushing to my fingertips.

"Shayda." His breath is soft and warm. Always the way he says it, like wind in my hair. He leans his forehead on my chest.

I kiss the top of his head. Then I reach behind him and draw on the foggy mirror.

"Come on." I pick up the brush and start lathering his face. "We need to finish what we started."

This time, my strokes are smooth and steady. I hand him a towel and turn him around. "What do you think?"

At first he doesn't notice it. He splashes cold water on his face and looks in the mirror again. That's when he sees the writing in the lower left corner.

BB♥SC

His fingers touch the pane, leaving two smudges underneath.

"I knew that." He smiles. "But it's nice to have it in writing." He turns to me with a gaze that makes my heart hammer against my ribs. "Beetroot Butterfly, you just made Scary Cherry the happiest man in the world."

"Wow," I remark as we drive down Queen Street, past charming inns, boutiques and elegant architecture. It's like a glimpse into a well-preserved 19th century village.

"It isn't called the prettiest town in Ontario for nothing." He covers my hand with his. "You haven't been here before?"

I shake my head as he backs into a parking spot.

"In that case, we'll have to take a trip back in time."

I turn down the visor and adjust my wig in the mirror. "Where are we going?" I ask, slipping on the classic aviators I picked up at Ken and Judy's.

"Somewhere where that outfit is going to feel a little out of place," he replies.

I look down at myself. Frye harness boots in vintage leather, black jeans and a heather grey t-shirt with 'The Beatles, Liverpool 1962' printed under a photo of the group. "I thought you said you like it."

"I said I *love* it! You look like a sexy rocker chick."

"But?"

"But nothing. It's perfect." He smiles with a devilish gleam in his eyes. "Come on." He tucks my arm under his and leads me down the strip.

Baskets full of colorful flowers hang from old-fashioned lamp posts, lining beautifully maintained heritage buildings. We walk past eclectic shops, outdoor cafes and charming window displays.

"Oh, look." I peer into a store, admiring a claw-footed bathtub with brushed nickel legs.

"That's just begging for you, me and bubble bath."

"You have a totally one track mind."

"I think that's already been well-established," he grins.

At the intersection of Queen and King Streets, he pulls me into an elegant red brick building with an ornate victorian façade. The sign reads 'Prince of Wales Hotel ESTABLISHED 1864'.

I take off my sunglasses and let my eyes adjust to the interior. The lobby oozes old world charm with rustic paneled walls, inlaid wood floors and paintings in gold frames. A lady at the front desk looks up and smiles.

"Afternoon tea for two," says Troy.

"You have reservations?"

"No, we—"

"Mr. Heathgate?" A man's quietly controlled voice interrupts.

Troy turns around. "John. How nice to see you."

"If I may, this way please." The silver haired man takes over from the front desk staff and escorts us across the hallway.

"This is our Victorian Drawing Room." He smiles at me, completely overlooking how my attire clashes with the posh décor and decadent chandeliers. "If you give me a minute, I'll have a table ready for you."

Troy lets his hand rest on the small of my back while we wait, oblivious to the stares of every woman in the room. Even in his casual clothes, he exudes an easy confidence that allows him to command any environment. Including this elegant space, filled with a colorful collection of tea pots, old parlor antiques, and portraits of British nobility.

"Follow me." John returns and whisks us to a little sun room overlooking the street. "Enjoy." He bows and leaves us with a menu.

"Did he just click his heels?" I smile.

"I wouldn't be surprised. He's very efficient."

"You've been here before?"

"Not for afternoon tea, but yes. I've hosted a number of corporate events here. My staff appreciates these getaways and it's a convenient spot for both my New York and Toronto offices."

"And now you'll have to find a suitable spot in Mexico and Hong Kong."

He puts the menu down. "Have you been stalking me?" His thumb rubs the back of my hand.

"Maybe. A teeny tiny bit."

"This day just keeps getting better." He sits back and smiles.

A smartly dressed waiter takes our order. We select tea from a long list of the finest loose leaves, and find ourselves sipping on a perfect brew.

"Pinky up, Beetroot."

I laugh, sticking my little finger out. Never in a thousand years would I have pictured Troy Heathgate sitting in an ornately carved chair, holding out a flowery little tea-cup.

Bite-sized cakes and pastries arrive, little sandwiches piled high on silver-tiered servers and piping hot scones fresh from the oven.

"Lemon Curd Tart with Almond Crust, Milk Chocolate Crème Brûlée with Mandarin Orange, Chocolate Dipped Shortbread." The waiter points them out. "And the sandwiches: Egg Salad and Dill on Marble Rye, Salmon Salad on Fennel, Cucumber and Goat Cheese Pinwheels. And of course, clotted cream, churned butter and strawberry preserves." He smiles. "Can I get you anything else?"

Troy looks at me, but my eyes are fixed on the table. My pinky droops in disbelief.

"I think we're all set." He laughs.

"Oh. My. God," I whisper after the waiter leaves, filling my plate with all the little goodies. "This one and this one. Maybe this too? Yes, and this. Definitely this."

"I'm glad we're sitting by the window. I want the whole world to see." Troy grins as he watches me eat.

"That you're having tea with a pastry-devouring gremlin?"

"That I'm with the most beautiful woman in the world. A woman who, when she allows herself, savors life with all of her senses."

I blot the corners of my mouth with my napkin and clear my throat.

"I would like some more tea, please," I request in the most upper crust accent I can muster.

"With pleasure, me lady." He plays along until our laughter provokes arched brows from the other patrons.

"There's something wrong with your Beatles t-shirt," he remarks.

"And here I thought you were staring at my breasts."

"George Harrison, John Lennon, Paul McCartney." He points them out. "But the guy on drums looks nothing like Ringo Starr."

"It's not. That's Pete Best. Ringo replaced him later in 1962."

"The year we were born."

"Hence the t-shirt."

"So it's not just some cool t-shirt you randomly picked from the vintage store?"

"I'm learning to collect things that mean something." Like today. These moments, carefully plucked and tucked away in my book of life, like pressed roses.

We finish our tea in the sparkling atmosphere of another world, another time.

"So what would you like to do?" asks Troy, steering me through the door. "Shopping, sight-seeing—"

"Mr. Heathgate!" John catches up as we're about to leave. "I trust you enjoyed your tea. I have arranged a complimentary horse and buggy ride for you and your companion. If that's something you'd like."

"That's very generous," replies Troy. "Companion?" He turns to me. "Horse and buggy ride?" He holds out his arm.

"I would love to." I smile, linking my arm with his.

"This way please." John leads us past the tulip garden and introduces us to a formally dressed coachman in a cravat, vested coat and black pants. "Tom will be your guide today."

Tom tips his hat and assists me into the carriage. Troy says something to John, who beams and stands by while Troy gets in next to me. The seat is upholstered in plush red velvet. Brass lamps adorn the sides of the carriage and a leather canopy shades us from the sun.

"All set?" asks Tom, as he maneuvers our carriage out of the hotel.

The magnificent Scottish Clydesdale clip-clops past John as we wave goodbye.

TOM REGALES US WITH INTERESTING TIDBITS ABOUT THE town as we saunter along. The gazebo adorning Queen's Royal Park was featured in a murder scene in Stephen King's 'The Dead Zone'. Ghosts and haunted houses abound. The headless soldier. A house that makes cameras go crazy. Sobbing Sophia who lost her dashing British hero in battle, and wanders the halls of Brockamour Manor, her sobs reverberating through the town at night.

I lay my head on Troy's shoulder as we listen to the tales, our carriage winding along the water front and through the picturesque streets of Old Town.

"You okay?" he asks, stroking my hair. "He's not scaring you with these ghost stories, is he?"

"Nothing scares me when I'm with you," I reply.

It's almost sunset when we make our way back. A golden glow surrounds us, rosy and warm, like the feeling in my heart.

We dismount outside the Prince of Wales Hotel. Troy tips the coachman while I pet the beautiful horse. He puts his nose in my palm and sniffs.

"Can I give him a treat?" I ask.

"Sorry, miss," replies Tom. "Treats make him nippy, but if you keep your arms by your side and let him get close, he gets very affectionate."

I stand still and let him nuzzle my neck with his nose, laughing as his breath tickles my face. Then he gives my wig a big lick, leaving a trail of wet goo. He stares at me, looking a little confused.

"It's not real hair," I say. "Bet it doesn't taste too good, huh?" I stroke his neck.

"Hey." Troy hugs me from behind. "This is making me very jealous."

"You, Mr. Heathgate, have to learn to share," I reply.

Then I cringe as the words sink in. Isn't that what he's been doing all along? Sharing me.

THE STREET LIGHTS ARE ON BY THE TIME WE GET TO THE car.

"Want to swing by Sweeney's before we head back?" asks Troy.

"Sweeney's?"

"David's pub. I told him we might check it out tonight."

"Sure." I buckle up. "I'd love to see it."

We follow the signs to Niagara Falls and take the Victoria Avenue exit. Sweeney's is located in a low-key plaza with a drug store on one side and a dry cleaners on the other.

"Here." Troy grabs my jacket from the back seat. "It's getting chilly."

"Could we make a quick stop at the drug store first?" I ask, slipping my arms into the black leather sleeves. The cropped moto jacket with its zippers and spiked shoulders is like nothing I've owned before.

"What do you need from the drug store?" he asks when I get out of the car.

"A vinegar douche," I reply. "Kidding." I laugh at the look on his face. "Some lipstick. I didn't bring any."

I stop at the make-up section while Troy discovers torturous looking girly gadgets.

"What's this?" he asks.

"Eyelash curler."

"And this?"

"A comedone extractor."

He turns it back and forth a few times before giving up. "You see anything you like?"

"Still looking." I open another tester.

"I like this one." He hands me a bold, crimson lipstick.

"Red?" I make a face. "I never wear red."

"You should. With those lips, you'd positively sizzle."

"Since when are you an expert on make-up?"

"I don't have to be an expert. I just know your face." He closes his eyes and visualizes it. "Yes. Red lips look super hot on you. Too bad they don't have a nice shade of Scary Cherry or Beet Butt."

"Crushed Roses." I read on the bottom. I apply the color and blot my lips.

The ruby red pout instantly transforms me into va-va-voom territory. I stare at my face in the mirror.

"I knew it would look good," says Troy, "but fuck! We're so getting it." He snatches a silver tube off the shelf.

"It's not too much?" I ask, running my tongue over lips.

"Oh, it most definitely is." His eyes fall on my wet, scarlet lips. "But that's the point." He hands the lipstick over to the cashier. "It makes me want to..."

With blunt intimacy, he proceeds to tell me exactly what he wants to do to me. I try wriggling away, acutely aware of everyone around us, but he holds on with one arm around my waist.

"Cash or charge?"

"Charge." He gives the cashier his card and goes back to whispering hot, dirty things while the line-up behind us grows longer.

"You're terrible." I say when we get outside.

"And you're not walking like a penguin anymore. I say we skip Sweeney's." He stops by the car and yanks me to him. "I don't think I can wait any longer. All I can think about are these insanely hot lips." His thumb traces the shape of my mouth. He pulls down the lower lip and slides it inside, rubbing the rough pad over my tongue.

"Troy! You made it."

We jump apart, thankful for the dark parking lot. Obviously David didn't see much of what was going on.

He ushers us into the dimly lit pub and holds out his hands. "Ta-da!"

"Wow." Troy looks around, taking it in. "It hasn't changed a bit, you lazy bastard."

"Eh?" David walks around proudly. "My old man would have been pleased."

The interior is all wood, exposed brick and dark patterned carpeting. Comfy, mismatched furniture is arranged in little seating areas—a large four seater couch in the back, two over-sized Victorian chairs around a slender coffee table, a few booths against the wall and three televisions mounted in random spots on the wall. Apart from the L-shaped bar with stools for patrons and a make-shift stage with various musical instruments, Sweeney's could easily be a rec room in someone's basement.

We slide into a small booth and David squeezes in with us. "Sorry, long weekends are busy."

"The locals always loved this place," says Troy. "You still make those wings?"

"Are you kidding? That's Pop's legacy. They'd kill me if I stopped serving them."

"Well, I am definitely going to have the wings then."

"Awesome. And what can I get for you...er...I know it's not rhubarb...or radish..."

"Beetroot," I laugh. "Pop's legacy for me too."

"Two orders of chicken wings, coming right up."

We watch David disappear into the kitchen.

"We used to spend a lot of weekends here, goofing around, pretending we were helping," says Troy. "His dad was a super nice guy."

"David has the same barbed wire tattoo around his wrists," I remark.

"We got them done together. He was going through a rough patch. Slashed his wrists one time. I found him in the bath tub." Troy's eyes follow David as he comes back to the dining room, balancing orders, laughing, chatting. "He got the barbed wire tattooed on his wrists to remind him never to cut through it."

"And you?" I ask.

"I was drunk." He laughs. "I went with him and woke up the next morning with tattoos around my biceps."

"You don't like them?"

"I don't regret them. I thought getting a tattoo was like an initiation into a tough-guy society. All macho and manly. But there are other, immensely more *virile* activities."

"So no more tattoos?"

"Not unless I feel the drastic need to express myself."

"I like it." I run my fingers over the ink. "This and your cross. They remind me of love and sacrifice and redemption."

He watches my mouth as I say the words and I get the distinct impression that he's miles away, playing with a trail of red lip prints.

"Troy? Are you listening?"

"What?" He refocuses.

A waitress arrives with our food, wet-naps and a complimentary basket of kettle chips. "David said to bring over the special hot sauce." Her eyes linger on Troy.

"Thanks," he replies.

"Let me know if you need anything else, love." She winks before walking away, her hips sashaying seductively.

It's like I'm not even here. I roll my eyes before digging into the wings.

They're smothered in a tangy, buffalo-style sauce; crispy on the outside and so moist on the inside that the bone slips right out.

"You like?" Troy is already half way through his bucket.

"Delicious. I can't believe I'm so hungry after that tea."

"Good. Eat up."

"What's that look for?" I ask.

"Just thinking."

"Of?"

"Well, if you must know..." He wipes his hands, one finger at a time, slowly and precisely. "I'm thinking of you and me and kinky stuff." He gives me a look that turns my panties wet.

"Can I get you folks some more?" David stops by our table.

"No thanks. That was fantastic," replies Troy. "Listen, it was good seeing you."

"What? You're not leaving, are you? Karaoke starts in two minutes. You have to do your thing."

"I don't think so." Troy laughs. "It's been way too long."

"Nonsense. It's like riding a bike. Come on. It'll be fun."

Troy looks at me. "I think we better get home."

"This guy." David squeezes his shoulder. "He used to bring the house down. Have you heard him sing?"

I shake my head.

"Do it," he says, pulling Troy up. "Do it for old time's sake. Hell, I'll even go the first round with you."

"Go." I smile, trying to reconcile a crooning Troy Heathgate with the one I know.

David drags him off to the stage.

"Ladies and gentlemen." David turns on the microphone. "We're going to start off with..."

There's a muffled discussion. David holds his hand over the mike. Troy shuffles over to the karaoke machine and starts scrolling through the selection. The two of them stand there—yes, no, yes, no. It's hilariously disorganized, but no-one seems to mind.

"Okay, here we go," announces David over loud, screeching feedback.

Troy picks up the second microphone as a dry harmonica riff introduces the number.

"Love, love me, do...you know I love you," they start singing in unison.

The lyrics are simple, the beat is catchy. Troy and David play off each other, singing to the crowd. A few of the diners clap along. The mood is jovial, but I push my food away and blink, trying to fight the tears.

I know why Troy picked that song.

Love, love me. Do. The Beatles. 1962.

An English band for the English tea we shared, for the year we were born, for the t-shirt I'm wearing, for this happy, stolen weekend, for the simple words and the intricate truth behind them.

So please. Love me. Do.

Troy catches my eyes as the song comes to an end.

"And now," says David, "I'm going to ask Troy to sing the one song we were so sick of him singing that we used to boo him off. Oh no, no, no." He pulls Troy back on stage. "This song…." He turns to the crowd. "I have to tell you the story behind this song. You see back then, Troy had a thing for this mystery woman. He never told us who, but after he'd had a few drinks, he'd crawl up on stage and sing his heart out. You ready to do it again, buddy?"

"I don't know, man." Troy shifts uncomfortably, even as everyone cheers him on.

David sets him up with a stool. The lights dim. A single spotlight falls on him. He looks at the microphone, holding it with both hands. Alone on stage, in his black jeans and grey t-shirt, he looks oddly vulnerable, the cross on his rosary gleaming in the light.

This time there is only the faint chord of a guitar before the lyrics kick in.

"Ain't no sunshine when she's gone…" Troy's voice resonates, warm, sexy, soulful, filling the room. Conversations halt, drinks are put down, people sit up.

He continues, eyes closed, oblivious to the stillness, the absence of fidgeting. The smoky ballad comes alive, reaching across the room, infusing the air with a truth that makes my hair stand on edge.

He reaches the 'I know, I know, I know' part.

Twenty six times in a single breath.

"Yeahhhhhhh." Someone applauds.

I know, I know, I know....

I know the mystery woman is me. It's been me all along. All these years. I clench the edge of the table as it hits me.

The music fades as Troy comes to the end of the song. His eyes open and he looks at me. Under the spotlight he's all black and white and grey. Except for his eyes. This is what the earth must look like from space. All shiny and pure and blue.

There is silence for a few moments. And then, one by one, people start to get up. The clapping grows louder as Troy weaves his way to our booth. He stops, a few feet away.

I cross the distance between us and throw my arms around him, kissing him with all the crazy joy-pain-love inside me.

"Woohooo!" We get cat calls and wolf whistles.

Troy grins, and kisses me harder.

35. 'X' MARKS THE SPOT

August 7th, 2000

I BRUSH MY TEETH AND CHECK MY PHONE. 1:11 A.M. ZERO messages.

It's hard to believe we've been here for just two days. I feel I've lived lifetimes, like a giant, where everything big has become small and I can see farther, breathe deeper, live larger.

I find Troy on the deck, leaning against the railing, looking out at the moonlit lake.

"Why are you smoking?" I hop on the wooden rail and stub his cigarette out.

He keeps his eyes on the water as the trail of smoke disappears into the night.

"Come with me." He lifts me off the railing, wraps my legs around his waist and carries me to the hammock.

We lie side by side. Crickets chirp. Waves lap up to the shore. Glittering stars stud a velvet sky.

"The moon looks bigger here," I say.

He brings my hand to his lips and speaks in the space between my knuckles. "One more day."

I sigh. It was so much easier in that other world. If you were a woman, you didn't expect happiness, so you didn't chase after it. If you found it, you held on to whatever scraps you could get. And if you collected enough, you could stitch together a cloak and get through life intact. But this. Having the freedom to make choices. It makes you greedy. It makes you want more when you already have enough.

We don't sleep that night, except for short, little pauses, drifting in and out of a crazy thirst for each other, falling exhausted, waking parched. Maybe the sun won't come up. Maybe we can make this last forever.

I STIR WHEN TROY UNTANGLES HIS FEET FROM MINE.

"Go back to sleep." He tucks the covers around me. "I'm going for a run."

"How?" I mumble, too tired to lift a finger.

He laughs, before I drift off. But it's only for a while. He's back, jumping on the bed, minutes later.

"Get up. Get up, Beetroot!"

I protest as he pulls back the sheets.

"Hurry." He grabs the blankets and holds my jacket out for me.

"Where are we going?" I ask, fumbling into it.

"The 'X' on the beach? I just figured it out."

Dewdrops kiss my feet as we run to the lake. He grabs cushions from the chairs and throws them on the circle of pebbles. I sit cross-legged next to him, still half-asleep. He wraps the blanket around us and points to the lake.

"Look."

I blink. The sun is still a soft, hazy ball of red, peeking over the horizon. It rises slowly, painting the water with strokes of shiny, vivid gold.

I catch my breath, realizing that we're seated directly in the line of that magnificent sunrise. As the rays grow longer, they reach for us—now a few metres away from shore, now touching the sand, now creeping up to our feet, now kissing our toes.

"Ohhh." I close my eyes and feel the warmth color my eyelids, like a tank being filled from the bottom up.

Our hands entwine under the blanket. We laugh—stupidly, deliciously happy.

I look at his face and suddenly, I know.

His gold tipped eyelashes tell me, the curve of his smile tells me, the way my heart beats tells me.

"Yes," I whisper.

"Yes what?"

"I know what I have to do."

It's not a choice anymore. It's time to take a stand.

He squeezes my hand in silent understanding.

The sun floats over the water, a red balloon of hope and joy, tethered with the weight of things to come.

WE'RE ALMOST READY TO LEAVE WHEN HIS PHONE RINGS.

"Hello?" He listens for a second before his face lights up. "Hey, Ma." He sits down. "I'm good. Scratch that." His eyes fall on me. "I'm great."

I smile and go back to tidying up the kitchen.

"Bali?" He laughs. "So you finally got to see the monkey temple?"

Snippets of his conversation float into the kitchen.

"When are you planning to visit? No, I'll be in Mexico then. Hong Kong over Christmas. I hope so."

"Yes, we met," he continues. "Would you quit, Ma? I don't need you to fix me up with the Ellas or Bellas of this world. Yes. I'm flaming gay. That's just a smoke screen. No, I don't need anything from there. Okay then, maybe a silk scarf for my coming out party. Fine, I'll get it myself. You're mean. Let me talk to Dad."

He chats for a little longer. "Miss you too. Yeah. Love you."

I wipe my hands and take one last look out the window. He walks up behind me and we stare at the swaying trees and shimmering water.

"Whatever happens, we'll face it together," he says.

It's bittersweet, standing at this crossroad.

"Come on." He pulls me away.

We're both quiet on the drive back. Outside, motorists honk and music blares on the slow moving highway. Long weekend travelers returning home. The shiny, sleek tresses of my wig peek out from the bag at my feet.

The parking lot outside his office is empty, except for my car. How can it sit, so still and unaffected, as if nothing has changed?

"Here we are." Troy turns the engine off.

"Here we are."

He brushes the hair away from my face. I close my eyes and lay my cheek on his palm. Then I collect my things and slip from his car into mine.

One world is waiting to be folded and put away, another is fluttering in the wind, like a sweet-smelling dress on a clothes line, longing to be put on.

MAAMAAN DOESN'T NOTICE. THE KIDS DON'T SEE IT. Is there nothing on my face to give it away?

I drive home listening to their incessant chatter.

Grandma trimmed my bangs. Do you like them?
Natasha has a boyfriend.
I do not.
Do too. You were all lovey-dovey on the phone. For hours,
Mum.
Zain was gambling.
It was Bingo! And I won fair and square.
Twenty quarters.
Yeah? So?
So you took money from old ladies. Mum, he took money
from Grandma's friends.
You're a snitch.
What's for dinner?

They stomp upstairs, blissfully oblivious, leaving me standing in the living room.

I place my keys on the counter. The red light on the answering machine is flashing. 4 new messages. I press play.

"Hello, Shayda. This is Dr. Gorman. Please give me a call when you get in."

I jot down the number. The rest of the calls are hang-ups.

I look at the time. 6:30 p.m. Should I call or wait until tomorrow?

I dial the number.

A woman picks up the phone.

"Hi, may I speak with Dr. Gorman?"

"Honey!" she calls him.

Damn. It's his personal line.

"Hello?"

"Dr. Gorman, it's Shayda Hijazi."

"Shayda. Yes. I've been trying to reach you. There were some abnormalities in the mammogram. It's probably nothing, but I'd like to schedule a follow up."

My knees go weak. "Yes, of course." I sit down. "I'll call my mother and make an appointment."

There's a pause at the other end. "It's not your mother's mammogram I'm calling about, Shayda. It's yours."

36. I CHANGED MY MIND

August 18th, 2000

THE DOORBELL RINGS REPEATEDLY. FOLLOWED BY LOUD thumping on the door.

Natasha. So impatient.

"Coming, coming! Now what did you what forget?" I swing the door open.

My heart screeches to a slamming halt. "Troy." I turn pale. "You...you shouldn't be here."

"No?" He storms past me into the house. "Where should I be, Shayda? Waiting by the phone? Staking out your office? Checking my email? Where the *fuck*, Shayda?" His fist slams into the console table, so 'fuck' is an obscure, jarring thud, like some censored song on the radio.

"I changed my mind."

"You changed your mind. Just like that?" He starts pacing the hallway. "And when were you were planning to tell me exactly? When, Shayda?"

"I made a mistake." My voice quivers. "I got caught up in the moment. We were alone, we were away. It was...it was all an illusion."

"An illusion?" He pulls me hard against him. Our bodies collide, knocking the breath out of me. "Is this an illusion?"

His lips assault mine.

"And this?" His hand slides under my dress, claiming my thigh.

"What about this, Shayda?" He pushes my panties aside and slides two fingers inside.

"Tell me, Shayda. Tell me this is all in my head." He shoves me against the door and deepens his strokes. "Tell me this is nothing." He rubs his fingers on my neck, leaving the unmistakable trail of my reaction.

"This is you, Shayda." His finger slips inside my mouth. "Your taste, your smell, your skin, your touch." He grabs me by the hair and pulls my head back. "Tell me you're not real, Shayda. Tell me!"

I feel the gathump gathump of his heart. Our breath comes in short, shallow gasps. His eyes darken, black holes pushing sky blue irises to the edges of raw emotion. Hunger. Anger. Love. Pain.

The shrill ring of the telephone rattles my shattered nerves. Troy keeps me pinned against the door. The answering machine picks up.

"Hi, Shayda. It's Lisa from Dr. Mason's office."

I free myself, and run to the phone.

"Your mastectomy has been scheduled for September 12th.."

...something, something, something. Beeeeep.

No. Nononono.

I sweep the answering machine off the counter. It breaks in big, black plastic pieces. I swing around to face Troy, my chest heaving.

"Are you happy now? You still want to hang around? Watch them cut my breasts off? Maybe you'd like to see my bald head? Huh? Hold a bucket while I puke my guts out?"

With each question, I shove him back towards the door. He offers no resistance, letting me pummel him with my fists.

"Get out, Troy!" I hold the door open. "I can't stand your butterfly dreams or your perfect love or your perfect world. You hear me? I can't stand it!"

The look on his face. Like I've sucked the soul right out of him.

It kills me. It absolutely kills me, but I don't want him to count on a life with me when I can't even count on life itself. I don't want to drag him through that hell.

"Go!" I give him one final push and turn away.

Stillness. Then I hear the door shut.

My shoulders slump. The spirit drains out of me.

I did it. I finally did it. I pushed him away. For good.

I fall to my knees and double over on the floor, wrapping my arms around myself, like a newborn yanked out of the womb, cold and naked and bloodied.

"Don't." The softest whisper.

My eyes swing to the door.

He never left.

I want the earth to open up and swallow me whole. I want to hide. But he doesn't let me. And he doesn't help me up either. He stretches out on the floor and lies next to me.

"I'm not going anywhere," he says. "I told you. Whatever happens, we face it together. I know you're doing this to protect me, but I'm not going to let you shut me out, Shayda. Not again. I won't let you."

He tucks his arm under my neck and rests my head on his shoulder. He doesn't want me to see his face. He doesn't want me to watch him stuff his pain inside.

We lie on the floor, not caring that the door is unlocked, that anyone can walk in and find us like this. No one cares if, after a storm, they're washed ashore naked. Only that they are alive.

37. EVERY WOMAN IMAGINES IT

September 27th, 2000

NATASHA PROPS UP A PILLOW AND SLIPS INTO BED WITH ME. "Marjaneh called. She says she'll be dropping by a little later."

It's been this way since I got back from the hospital, Natasha turning into my constant shadow, to make up for some irrational guilt over still having breasts.

Zain hovers by the bed, feeling left out by the female bonding.

"Get in." I pat the other side of the bed. It's still difficult to raise my arm.

"Does it still hurt?" He nestles in.

"It's much better." His gentle concern makes me smile. "How's high school? You like it?"

"S'okay." He shrugs.

"Natasha, do you keep an eye on him?"

She shrugs, mirroring his expression.

Hafez walks in, carrying a tray with a bowl of soup, crackers, water, medication.

"This is nice." He rests it on the night stand and squeezes in next to Zain. "Who wants to watch some TV?"

"Go back, go back," says Natasha. "That was Seinfeld."

"Hey, that's the one where Jerry steals the old lady's bread." Zain laughs.

"Marble rye." We chant in unison.

Hafez smiles at me over Zain's head. The things that bind a family.

The doorbell rings.

"I'll go." Natasha hops out of bed.

"Zain, go sit on the chair. Let Mum eat." Hafez places the tray on my lap and brings the spoon to my mouth.

"I can do it."

"Let me," he insists.

He's been a rock. He's helped me into my clothes, put my hair up in a pony tail, made appointments, dropped the kids to school, cooked, cleaned, folded the laundry. And now, he's made me soup.

I can't stand it. I want to weep and shout.

"It's good," I say, taking the spoon from him, hoping these moments slip by unnoticed, when I push away his kindness, his unquestioning attentiveness. I don't want him to take time off, I don't want him to take care of me.

"I called your mother," he says. "She gave me the recipe. She wants to come stay with us for a few days."

"No need. I don't want her going to any trouble."

"Shayda, she's your mother. She *wants* to help."

Natasha enters the room, her face obscured by a bouquet of colorful balloons.

"Another delivery for Mum." She places it on the bench by the foot of the bed. "This one doesn't have a note either."

Towering over the bright, metallic balloons is a single, red, heart shaped one.

"Now you can't even see the TV," says Hafez.

"No," I reply. "Leave it." I take my pain killers and push the tray away.

"I tell you what. I'll give you fifty dollars," says Jerry Seinfeld from behind floating reminders of Troy.

"Take it and run, Jerry. Run!" says Zain.

THE ROOM IS DARK WHEN I OPEN MY EYES AGAIN. HOSSEIN and Marjaneh are sitting stiffly, side by side, as if they would rather have picked another time to avoid running into each other.

"How have you been?" asks Hossein.

"Fine," she replies. "And you?"

"Good."

They don't say anything for a while.

Then Hossein clears his throat. "Are you all right? I mean...life." There is an odd tenderness to his voice.

Marjaneh gets up and walks to the window. "What was wrong with me, Hossein? That you had to leave?" she asks.

"Nothing." My brother sighs. "It was me. We happened too...easily. Our families fixed it, we went out a few times, and then everyone started making plans for us. I never had the chance to *yearn* for you."

Marjaneh nods, and continues staring out the glass pane. "I hate that they couldn't tell if it was a boy or girl. When I want to mourn, I have no face, just some formless tissue that would have turned twenty-two this year."

Hossein goes to her and takes her in his arms. She goes limp, like it's finally all right to let go, to be comforted by the man who betrayed her. "I'm so sorry, Marjie."

I can't tell if they're crying. The moment is so private that I pretend I'm still sleeping.

"Don't close yourself off because of what I did," says Hossein.

"I did. For a while." she replies. "Then I met someone who showed me that there are men who stand by their families no matter what."

"I'm glad," says Hossein. "Is it serious?"

"He doesn't know."

"You haven't told him?"

"No," she says. "I seem to fall for men I can never have."

She tenses when Hafez comes into the room with two cups of tea.

"Thanks, Hafez," says Hossein, draining his cup. "I'm sorry, I have to get going. Would you let Shayda know I came by?"

"I will," replies Hafez.

"Bye, Marjie."

"Bye, Hossein." She holds her tea without drinking from it. "They took everything?" she asks Hafez.

"The tumor was in her right breast, but given her family history, her best option was a double mastectomy."

Marjaneh stares at her hands. Every woman imagines it for a horrifying second.

"The good news is that there is no lymph involvement. Her tests are clear."

Marjaneh continues to examine her fingers.

"Hey," I say.

Her eyes come up. "Hi, Shayda. How are you feeling?"

"Much better. I hope I haven't left you in a lurch. I can't thank you enough for looking after everything at work."

"I'd still be working the checkout lines if it wasn't for you." She squeezes my hand. "Everyone sends their love. Bob says he'll be in again. Maybe tomorrow."

She stays a little longer. "Let me know if I can help," she tells Hafez at the door.

"Time for your medication," says Hafez after she leaves.

"Already? They make me so groggy."

"You need the rest."

My cell phone rings as I'm swallowing my pills. Hafez picks up. For a moment, I panic.

"Yes, hold on." He hands me the phone. "It's your father."

"Baba?" I sigh, relieved.

"Shayda, Hossein told me you had surgery."

"Yes. I didn't want to worry you. I'm fine."

"Cancer is not fine! You know what happened to Zarrin."

"We caught it in time, Baba. I have to go through some chemo, but the doctors are taking good care of me."

Hafez goes downstairs, giving me some privacy.

"I'll be in town next month," says Baba. "Promise me we'll meet up."

"Yes." I know we'll do it this time.

Nothing revives the cup of life more than a caustic splash of death.

I hang up and check my messages. Two voice mails from Jayne. Five text messages from Troy.

5 a.m. in monterrey. thinking of u, beetbutt

guess what? just saw a goat

in meetings all day. how r u doing?

message me!!!

business dinner. you would love the chapulines

Simple texts that scream 'I MISS YOU'.

He was adamant about canceling his trip.

"Work can wait. I want to be here. With you."

"But you won't be. I'll be at home after the surgery. It's not like you can come visit. It's taken you months to set things up for Mexico. Go. I'll be right here when you get back."

The red balloon sways before me. I can hear Natasha, Zain and Hafez having dinner downstairs.

hey, I text.

Five seconds later, he replies: *BB!!!!*
love the balloons
u got them
yes & the roses & the red velvet cake...u need to stop
how are the incisions?
they're coming along. what are chapulines?
grasshoppers
ewww
what did the doctor say?
pathology report is clear
the drainage tubes still in?
no. & stitches have dissolved
good. it's hell not being with u
sorry, have to go now. N coming up
ok. u rest now

I turn the phone off and put it under my pillow.

"We cut some fruit for you." Natasha places a plate beside me.

"Natasha, how do I look?" I ask, tucking my hair behind my ear.

"You look fine." She views me through the eyes of a daughter. It doesn't matter that I'm in a button up granny night gown or that my chest is as flat as a seven year old's.

"You know your friend's mother? The one who's a hairdresser?"

"Yes."

"Does she make house calls?"

"I'll ask. You want her to come over?"

"Yes. I would like that." I want to do girly things. Hair and make-up and mani-pedis. I want to look pretty. Maybe then I'll start feeling like a woman again.

38. RED REBOZO

....

October 2nd, 2000

Jayne meets me outside the prosthesis store. A
woman's silhouette coming out of a pink circle, arms
outstretched, spans the sign. The store window features
mannequins with wide strap bras, pink ribbon decals and
a large, flashing 'WELCOME' sign. I pause at the door,
thinking of our trip to the lingerie store and brace myself for
how different this will feel.

"Come on." Jayne takes my hand. "Let's do this."

We walk in and exchange relieved smiles. It's not so bad.
It looks just like a 'normal' store, racks displaying matching
bra and panty sets, swimwear, hats, scarves, jewelry.

"Hi, you must be Shayda." A cheerful lady greets me
from behind the counter.

Yes, the boobless one who made the appointment to get
fitted for new boobs.

"I'm Kelly." She comes around. "I'm so glad you brought
a friend. It's more fun that way."

Jayne's eyebrows shoot up. "Fun?"

Kelly laughs. "Think about it this way. You can get breast forms that are bigger, smaller or perkier than what you had. You get to choose from teardrop, triangle, heart shapes. Silicone, foam, fiberfill. The choices are endless and our mastectomy bras come in neutrals, pastels and a variety of sexy colors, so you don't feel like you're giving up anything."

Her outlook is refreshingly empowering. I like her right away.

She ushers us into the private fitting room. Jayne stays with me, but I keep my back to her, not wanting her see my chest full on. It's not long though, before Kelly nudges my body around, taking measurements at strategic points on my chest and around the rib cage.

Jayne holds a wobbly smile, keeping her eyes on my face, although there's no way to avoid the angry lines slashed across my front, screaming, 'Look at me, look at me!'

With the bra fitting done, Kelly notes the shape and drape of my chest, and has me try on me a variety of prostheses. In the end, I opt for silicone forms with a self-shaping inner layer. We pick a nude seamless bra with molded cups and breathable mesh pockets to insert the breast forms. The straps are softly padded and the extra support makes me feel more held-in and secure.

"I think that looks just right," says Kelly. "But you need some fun, sexy bras, maybe a matching set? I'll be right back."

With the new bra and breast forms in place, I button up my blouse and look in the mirror, feeling like I can finally walk into a room without being painfully self-conscious.

"Look, Jayne. No more Frankenboobs."

My smile freezes when I see the tears pooling in her eyes.

"Oh, Shayda," she cries, giving me a big hug.

We stand in front of the full-length mirror, me consoling her, as she sobs uncontrollably into my shoulder.

"It's okay," I say.

"I'm pregnant," she announces and clings on tighter.

"What?" I step back and look at her.

"I'm finally pregnant!"

We start laughing. And crying. And laughing.

When Kelly returns, we're holding on to each other's shoulders, hopping up and down.

"Well, that's one way to test your prostheses," she says.

I leave with new bras, panties, a padded swimsuit, vitamin E for my scars and a wedge cushion which Kelly says will help me sleep better.

"You don't have to go home yet, do you?" asks Jayne.

I look at my watch. I have an hour before I meet Troy. "Let's go into that café."

We cross the road and find a cozy table by the window.

"So when's the big day?" I ask.

Jayne rubs her belly. "It's going to be a spring baby. Late March, early April. And of course, you are going to be the godmother."

"I'd be honored. But you do know I could be called on to check out at any time."

"And so can anyone else," she chides. "So? Tell me."

I do my best, leaving out the husks, the tough, tasteless bits that stick in your mouth, begging to be spit out. Like lying under bright surgical lights, feeling like a still-alive frog about to be dissected. The phantom pains that fool you into thinking you still have your breasts, until you reach for them. Wishing you could keep the thick, white gauze on forever so you don't have to face the deformity below. Crying in the bathroom because your scars are puckered and bruised, and not at all like the nice, clean lines you imagined. How 'okay' becomes your personal mantra. 'Okay,

okay, okay,' while you're waiting for them to tell you if they got it all. 'Okay, okay, okay,' when you notice skin folds on the side of your body because the tissue under your arms is now just hanging. 'Okay, okay, okay,' when your backside is gaping through thin, paper gowns and you would give anything for a blanket.

I don't tell Jayne any of that. It doesn't pair well with the strawberry and spinach salad or the grilled chicken or anything else on the menu.

"You didn't opt for reconstruction?" she asks.

"It's a possibility I may consider down the road." I reply. "It would mean more surgeries. Tissue expanders, permanent implants, nipple reconstruction. For now, I just want to give my body the chance to heal."

Jayne nods. "I'm planning a New Year's Charity Ball with Matt's mum. It would be wonderful if you spoke about your experience. You know, raise awareness."

"You know me and public speaking. I don't know if I can share something like this with a room full of strangers."

"No pressure. Just something to think about."

"Sure," I reply as we say our goodbyes. "And we definitely have to talk about a baby shower."

"I'm glad you're back," she says before driving off.

I glance at my watch.

On my way, I text Troy.

I take a deep breath and check my face in the rear view mirror. I'm filled with anticipation and dread. *Okay, okay, okay.* I start the car, wincing a little as I turn the wheel.

HE BUZZES ME INTO THE GARAGE. I REACH FOR THE DOOR to the elevator when it swings open. We stop at the same time.

He moves first, pulling me inside. The door shuts behind us. He scans me from head to foot, like a parent checking a newborn for ten fingers and toes.

"God, I've missed you." He envelopes me in a tender embrace.

We step into the elevator, still locked together. The afternoon sun glints off the dark wood in his living room. He seats me on the couch, takes my boots off and places my feet on his lap. His fingers knead them with a strong, steady pressure.

I smile.

"What?" he asks.

"You did that the first time I met you in that hotel room."

"I remember."

"I always wondered why you insisted on meeting there."

"Because I was selfish," he replies. "I figured we'd have a wild, passionate fling. Get it out of our system, get on with our lives." He strokes the top of my foot. "I didn't want reminders of you here, in my bed, in the kitchen, on the couch. But it didn't matter. My place. Or the hotel. You were in my head. I couldn't stop thinking about you." He pauses. "That reminds me—I got you something while I was in Mexico."

He walks into the bedroom and comes out with a gorgeous shawl.

"It's a rebozo." He places it around my shoulders.

"It's beautiful."

The rich, crimson fabric feels like a soft blend of cotton and raw silk.

"You must have read my mind," I say. "I was wishing I had something like this when I was in the hospital." I pull the ends and wrap it around myself.

Something jingles on its hand-knotted fringes.

"What's this?" A set of keys are tied at the edge.

"The keys to my place."

I stare at them quietly.

"I don't want you to have to buzz in," he says. "Walk in, walk out. Anytime you like. And while you're at it, feel free to make whatever changes you like. I want the place ready for when you and the kids move in."

"About that..." I weigh the keys in my hand. "There's something you should know." I take a deep breath. "Hafez has been amazing. Beyond amazing. Through all of this. And the kids...I need time to ease out of it."

"How much time?"

"I know Hafez won't fight me for the kids. He's away so often. But I can't just uproot them and move in here with you."

"Fine. We'll find a place close to their school. Keep them in a familiar environment. This place was never permanent, anyways. I've always wanted kids, Shayda. Always. I would love them like they're my own."

"That's not it, Troy. I need to do it alone for a while. Without Hafez, without you. The divorce will be difficult enough. I want to introduce the kids to the idea of having you around slowly. One thing at a time. What I'm saying is... we need to hold off a little longer."

Silence.

I hold his scalding gaze for as long as I can.

"Troy—"

"Unacceptable."

"But—"

"It's not up for debate, Shayda. I refuse to wait any longer. I almost lost you, dammit! I am not wasting any more time, and I'm not going to let you do it either. I will have you by my side, in my house, in my bed, so help me god!" His eyes flash with steely determination.

"And if I don't agree?"

"Are you waiting for a ring, Shayda? Is that it? Are you afraid of creating a bad impression on the kids?"

"I just want to do the right thing."

"Well, it's a little too late for that, don't you think?"

I flinch like he just slapped me in the face. This is not how I anticipated our first meeting after my surgery.

"I deserved that." I start pulling my boots back on.

"Shayda—"

"No! I get it. You didn't sign up for this." I gesture to my chest. "If you're looking for a way out, there's no need to be cruel. Have the balls to say it. Tell me I'm not woman enough for you anymore."

Troy clamps his jaw tight. "If that what's you think, then you might as well leave. Don't expect me to indulge you so you can feel fucking sorry for yourself."

The way he says it sends cold chills to the centre of my soul. He's right, of course. I want to be coddled and reassured. I want to be told I'm still beautiful, still desirable. Instead, he's holding out my discarded self-esteem, insisting I dust it off and put it back on.

"You know the one thing I regretted when the anesthesiologist told me to start counting back?" I say.

He keeps his face turned away.

"I thought, 'What if I don't wake up from this? I never told Troy I love him. I never really said the words.'"

His breath escapes in a long exhale.

I frame his face in my hands. "I love you, Troy."

I say the words to him, but a dam breaks loose inside, releasing gallons of soothing salve that heal my wounds from within.

He puts his arm around me and draws me in.

"We both want the same thing, Shayda. Let's not fight."

I sigh and settle into the warmth of his chest. "I'm scared, Troy. I'm scared I'll do all this, turn everything upside down, only to have the cancer return. And then what? It will all have been in vain."

"If we base our decisions on all the things we're afraid of, we would be paralyzed with fear. We'd never have the guts to love, or hope or dream, or have kids, or swim in the ocean. And that's what makes us human, isn't it? What carries us through it all?"

"But it's not right to be selfish about it either. I don't want to ruin their lives, or yours, Troy."

"There you go again, hogging all the responsibility, deciding everyone's going to fall apart before giving us the chance to react. You didn't get here alone, you know. There were inherent problems in your marriage right from the start."

There are no more secrets. I've told Troy everything, including the whole, dark truth about Pasha Moradi.

"Yes, but it wasn't Hafez's fault."

"It wasn't your fault either," he replies. "You tried to make the best of a difficult situation, and so did he. Maybe it's time you put some faith in Hafez. Maybe you'll find out that as much as you want him to be happy, he wants the same for you. So quit with the long face. It's not like the fate of the entire universe is resting on your shoulders."

"Ouch. Talk about deflating a woman's ego." I laugh.

"I'm just saying. You've been through enough. Give yourself a break, Beetroot." He smiles. "You want something to eat?"

"No. I had lunch with Jayne. I got fitted for breast prostheses today."

"Is that what you're wearing?" He traces the edge of my collar.

I tense, not ready for him to see.

He pulls away, just a fraction, enough so I can breathe again.

"What's it like?"

"These? They're are made of silicone—"

"That's not what I mean."

What's it like to face your own mortality?

"It makes you think," I reply. "The big things, the small things. The dreams, the regrets."

"Like?"

"Well, big things like wondering if you'll ever see your kids graduate. Small things that you never get around to, like a trip to the South Pacific. Falling asleep in an overwater bungalow to the sound of swaying palm trees. Snorkeling unexplored reefs, dipping your feet into waterfalls that cascade over volcanic cliffs. You revisit your dreams, the ones you lose along the way. At one time, I wanted to be a writer, to touch someone with words, to inspire."

He listens to me quietly. "And the regrets?"

"I have none now." I say, kissing him softly.

39. DEFENSELESS

October 9th, 2000

IT'S THE MONDAY OF THANKSGIVING WEEKEND. I LIE IN bed, wondering what Natasha and Zain are doing up so early.

"I'll go take a look," says Hafez, after a particularly loud clang from downstairs.

He doesn't come back, but the tinkering stops. I close my eyes and doze off.

"Breakfast!" yells Natasha.

I shuffle out of bed and head down.

The table is set with scrambled eggs and french toast and fresh strawberries.

"Looks great." I sit down to still faces. "What's wrong?" I look around the table.

"Surprise!" Zain jumps up with a cardboard sign that says 'HAPPY'.

Natasha grins and gets up, holding 'ANNIVERSARY!' Then Hafez. '# 18'.

Zain puts his arms around me. "Happy Anniversary, Mum."

"I was sure you were going to come down before we were ready!" Natasha laughs, kissing me on both cheeks. "I'm glad Dad did though. I was going to boil some eggs and Zain had microwave oatmeal ready to go."

"All that noise for boiled eggs and oatmeal?"

"We had to make the signs too!" says Zain.

"Well, thank you. This is very special."

How could I have forgotten?

"Happy Anniversary, Shayda." Hafez gives me a kiss.

"Happy Anniversary, Hafez."

I'm a fraud.

I drown my french toast in maple syrup, but it still tastes like cardboard.

"Last night was fun," says Zain. "I can't believe Grandma invited Grandpa for Thanksgiving dinner."

"I can't believe Grandma actually acknowledged Thanksgiving," Natasha replies. "You think the two of them were in on it together? Like 'Let's do something nice for our daughter'?"

"The possibility of losing someone you love will make anyone rethink their priorities," says Hafez.

"Is that why you're not gone as often?" asks Natasha. "To spend more time with Mum?"

"I feel like I've been given a second chance. To spend more time with all of you." Hafez picks up my hand.

I swallow my orange juice, keeping my eyes on the plate.

"I liked meeting Kayla and Ethan and Summer yesterday." Zain helps himself to more eggs. "Although I couldn't understand a word when they switched to French."

"They were probably talking about how obnoxious you are," says Natasha.

"Natasha," warns Hafez.

She giggles. "Honestly, I can't remember ever meeting Uncle Hossein's kids. And Aunty Adele. She's very pretty."

"Is that why Uncle Hossein left Marjaneh?" asks Zain.

"I think Marjaneh is very pretty too." Hafez puts the cap back on the maple syrup. "Are we all done?"

"I like Aunty Adele," Zain continues. "But I feel bad for Marjaneh. It's not nice to lose your family."

"Don't worry, son." Hafez ruffles his hair. "Nothing like that is ever going to happen to us."

I get up and start clearing the table.

"Let me." Hafez starts taking things from me.

"No!" It comes out much harsher than intended. "Sorry." I put the plate down. "I just...I need you to stop hovering over me."

Hafez backs off. The kids turn on the TV, leaving us alone in the kitchen. My reflection stares back at me from the kitchen window as I wash the dishes. My cheeks are orange, there's green on my chin and my forehead is half red, half yellow. Fall colors from the park behind us. They make me look fragmented, like a patchwork quilt sewn together from different pieces.

"I was thinking we could go out later. Just you and me. For an anniversary lunch," says Hafez.

"Everything is closed today."

"Not everything," he says. "Wear something warm."

"WE'RE WALKING?" I ask.

"It's not too far," replies Hafez.

"The park?" I say as we cross the street.

"Go sit on the bench," says Hafez. "I'll be right back."

He returns ten minutes later with a greasy paper bag held horizontally. Inside are two slices of hot pizza.

"You remember? That first Christmas we were married? We walked around and shared some pizza?"

The day he picked the red onions off for me.

"I told you I would do everything I can to make you happy."

"It was a long time ago." My throat constricts.

"Yes," he replies. "A time before Pasha Moradi. We didn't have much but we had each other."

My tears drop on the deluxe vegetarian, with roasted red peppers.

"I want to go back, Shayda," says Hafez. "I want to go back and start over. I'm starting therapy. Next week."

I look at my husband's face. He wants to try. He wants to leave the ghosts behind. So many years, I waited for this day. And now that it's here, I want to make it stop.

Don't go. Don't try. Don't make this harder for me.

"That's great," I reply.

Stop thinking about yourself, Shayda. He needs this, to heal, to become whole.

"I'm glad." I manage a smile. But a part of me is furious with him.

Why now, Hafez?

The worst thing I can do is leave him. Not when he's so close, when he's finally reaching for help.

It's not fair! Another part screams. *IT'S NOT FAIR!*

I get up. "I think I'll go for a drive."

"I'll go with you," says Hafez.

"No!" Again it's too harsh. "I just need some time alone."

We walk back to the house in silence. Hafez stands on the side of the driveway, holding two slices of cold pizza, as I back out.

I feel like I'm running away when I'm most needed, but I can't stay. I need to clear my head. What do I do with this life that's been spared? How do I spend it? Here, with my family, being a good mother and a good wife? Loving them as they deserve to be loved? Or there? With Troy? Tingling with anticipation at the dawn of each new day, feeling more alive than I ever have?

The tires squeal as I step on the gas, leaving a trail of spinning gravel behind.

"TROY!" I SWING THE DOOR TO HIS LOFT OPEN. "TROY!"

I walk in, turning corners—the kitchen, laundry room, pool, library. No Troy.

I take my jacket off and slump into the sofa, burying my face in my hands.

"Shayda?"

He's standing in the hallway, a towel slung around his hips, his hair wet from the shower.

He's never looked better.

I rush to him, throwing my arms around his neck.

"I'm slipping away, Troy."

"What hap—"

I don't let him finish. My mouth devours him.

"I need you. I need you so bad."

"Are you sure this is all right? A month after your surgery—"

"It's fine." I yank his towel off and sink to my knees, taking him into my mouth, all of him, as far, as deep as I can.

"Shayda..." He leans back on the wall, trying to slow me down.

I suck his balls. I lick his shaft. I wrap both hands around him. With each bob of my head, each flick of my tongue, I reclaim my power, my femininity, my hacked up body. My hunger for him unleashes a shameless, greedy beast. I moan at the taste of the first bead of his arousal, rubbing the tip with my thumb, spreading it around.

His thighs tremble. His fingers clench my shoulders as he gives in to me. "Don't stop. Don't stop. Don't fucking stop."

I swirl my tongue around the edge, under the head. He jerks. I look up and find him watching me with an intensity that shoots electric arcs of desire straight between my thighs.

"I've missed you," he whispers hoarsely.

I keep my eyes on him and keep going. He tugs my hair, signaling his climax, but I keep my lips wrapped around him, pushing my face further between his legs.

"Unhh!" He pounds his fists back into the wall.

The immensity of his explosion fills my mouth. I wrap my arms around his clenched buttocks until I've milked every last drop. The gagging sensation is overwhelming, but I don't want to waste a single drop. I want to absorb all of him, every last bit of his essence.

He leans back against the wall, trying to catch his breath.

I let him slip out of my mouth, holding him with my hand, while I run my face back and forth over him. I don't want to let go. I don't want it to end.

He slides lower, inch by inch, dragging his back down the wall, as if he can't hold up any longer. He tucks the towel around himself and pulls me into the crook of his arm. We sit like that for a while, our eyes closed, listening to each other breathe.

"You turn me inside out." His voice crackles with emotion.

Then he looks at me and frowns. "Is everything all right?"

"I'm fine." *Now that I'm with you.*

"I'm glad you're here," he says. "There's something I want to show you."

He leads me into the bedroom and turns the light on.

What used to be a window seat is now converted to a custom desk, set flush against a view of the lake.

I've always wanted a place by the water.

On the desk is a leather bound notebook, a laptop, fine sheets of cotton vellum, notepads; pens, pencils, sharpeners, erasers—neatly arranged in mini silver pails.

I wanted to be a writer, to touch someone with words, to inspire.

Four colorful photos hang on the wall, arranged in a two by two configuration: an endless stretch of blue, blue sky melting into the ocean; a bungalow on stilts, perched above a tranquil lagoon; colorful fish nibbling on coral; a fern-bordered waterfall surrounded by red and pink flowers.

...a trip to the South Pacific. Falling asleep in an overwater bungalow to the sound of swaying palm trees. Snorkeling unexplored reefs, dipping your feet into waterfalls that cascade over volcanic cliffs.

"You like it?" he asks.

This is what it feels like when someone wraps up your hopes and dreams, and presents them to you on a sunny afternoon.

There is nothing to hide anymore. When love looks at you, when it truly pins you down and stares into your soul, it renders you defenseless. And in that moment, in that state of humbling nakedness, it makes you completely invincible.

I reach down the front of my blouse and undo the first button. The rest come apart easily. I shrug out of it and unzip my pants, letting them fall around my ankles. My bra drops to the floor, heavy with the fake breast forms. I stand before him in my panties, letting him see me for the first time.

He doesn't flinch, but he doesn't cover it up either. His fingers trace the jagged incisions. The left one is squiggly, veering up and then taking a downward swoop. The right cut is longer, extending under my arm.

"God, Shayda." He drops to his knees and pushes his face into my stomach, as if trying to find comfort in the soft roundness there.

You have beautiful breasts, Shayda.

I should be eating this cake off those breasts.

His arms go around my waist, pulling me closer. I feel his shoulders quake. Quick, short, soundless heaves. Of helplessness. Of being unable to protect someone you love.

When he's done, he gets up. The power is back on. I see will and strength and determination in the set of his jaw.

"Come here." He pulls me into bed.

His kisses are long, languid sips of lips and tongue and hope.

At first.

Then he takes me hard, without a shred of tenderness.

I know what he's doing. He's punishing my body for turning on me.

Take that, you evil, insidious sickness.

You can't have her, you rogue, renegade, diseased cells.

He flips me over and claims me from behind, one hand holding my face down to the mattress, the other digging into my hips. He chases the demons away, fast and furious. And in that exorcism, the darkness disappears.

I cry out as brilliant white light explodes around me, shattering into a billion jagged shards. But he keeps going, like he's on some mindless, frenzied quest. When he finally reaches his release, he pulls out and comes on my back, panting, heaving, covered in sweat.

"Shit," he says between shallow breaths. "I wanted it to be more special." He rolls me over and enfolds me in his arms.

"It was exactly what I needed," I reply, nuzzling into his chest. "I'm tired of everyone handling me with kid gloves."

"Oh? Why didn't you say so? I've been waiting to introduce the leather paddles and restraints."

"Really?" I laugh. "It didn't look like you were going to stop for anything."

"Quiet wench, or ye shall be punished some moreth."

"Moreth? I think Shakespeare just rolled over in his grave."

"Thankfully, I'm not the one who'll be writing on yonder desk."

I turn to my side and look at the little corner he's carved out for me in his room. The late afternoon sun filters through floaty curtains, turning it into a golden, ethereal space.

"I love it," I say.

He tucks his arms around me and we watch the clouds cross the sky.

"They're white," I say.

"The clouds?"

"Your bed sheets. I used to wonder what color they were."

"Are you telling me you used to picture me in bed, Beetroot?"

"I did."

"For future reference, I'd rather you picture me without the sheets. Are we clear?"

"Clear."

We close our eyes, feeling the sun on our skin.

"So when do you start the chemo?" he asks.

"Next week," I reply.

We lapse back into silence.

"Troy?"

"Yes?"

"Are they really ugly?"

"What?"

"My scars."

He turns me on my back and kisses them gently. "They're your battle scars, Beetroot. A testament to your strength. But I never imagined anything so harsh. I'd be lying if I didn't admit that it's going to take me some time to adjust to your noobs."

"My noobs?"

"No boobs. And I don't just mean physically. I mean in my head, because I fantasize about you *all* the time. So do I go with boobs or noobs? What's the proper etiquette?"

"There's no place for etiquette in fantasy." I play with his fingers. "You think I should get implants?"

"Get them, don't get them. It won't change the way I feel about you. You are pure delicious, through and through."

I lift the bed sheet over our heads, letting the light filter through the soft cotton, while we hold hands in our private little fort.

40. NEW GIRL IN TOWN

October 29th, 2000

AMBUSH HUGS. THAT'S WHAT I CALL THEM. HUGS THAT catch you unawares.

It's part of Hafez's therapy, a daily exercise in intimacy. The rules are simple. You start with one minute and work your way up. Face each other, no talking. Your bodies have to touch. No space in between and no 'there, there' pats on the back.

"Bye." I say at the top of the stairs, one hand on the banister.

He comes out from the bedroom and ambush-hugs me. "Bye."

I don't tense up like I used to. Somewhere between the mandatory hugs, I realized that it's possible to love two people in two completely different ways. And I can allow myself, I can allow Hafez, the simple comfort of closeness, of acceptance, and not feel like I'm cheating on Troy. I wonder what the therapist would make of my twisted mindset.

The hugging is nice, a daily disconnect from incessant thoughts and guilt and worry, a tribute to our nights up with sick kids, of raking leaves in the backyard and taking out the garbage. It's the few seconds after that are awkward. The removing of hands, re-zipping of faces. Hafez knows something is wrong. He's known since the day I left him standing in the driveway. But I'm too exhausted to take it on right now.

THE CHEMO HAS TAKEN ITS TOLL ON ME. BRUSHING MY teeth hurts. Long cuts extend through my gums. I rinse out toothpaste and blood. When I look at my face in the mirror, I realize how much of it I've taken for granted, how the bits I've paid only passing attention to make up such a big part of my identity. Like my eyebrows and my eyelashes. I miss them. Even more so than my hair. My reflection reminds me of an egg—smooth and bland. And blank. When I'm surprised, I look blank. When I frown, I look blank. When they said I'll lose my hair, I pictured a bald head. I didn't think about *all* my hair.

It started nine days after my first chemo. I woke up with long, curly strands on the pillow. Then they collected in the shower drain. My hairbrush. The towel. In a perverse way, it intrigued me to tug gently on a tuft of hair and watch it come out.

Zain accompanied me to the hairdresser's. If I was going to lose my hair, I wanted to do it on my terms. I think it was the first time the hairdresser had to shave a woman's hair off. She had this pained expression, like I was asking her to break some professional code. She was supposed to make me look pretty, dammit.

"I want to shave mine off too," said Zain.

There was no talking him out of it. And so the poor lady had two bald heads walk out of her salon, noggin to noggin, in shining solidarity.

The eyebrows and eyelashes came later. After vaseline-smeared chapped lips and kleenex-stuffed bloody noses. Taste went, smell increased. Taste returned, vomiting started. Some days I lay face down on the couch, too tired to turn over. Other times, I put on my Beetroot Butterfly wig, and walked to the park. The wig was mostly for other people. It put everyone at ease. I took it off when no-one was around so I could feel the sun soak into my scalp.

"WHO CALLED?" I ask HAFEZ, AS I PUT MY COAT ON.

"Dr. Hardy's office. They want to see you next week."

My physician, my surgeon and my oncologist. They stay on my mind as I drive to Jayne's. Sometimes I see them as characters in a video game. A trinity of warriors, wielding surgical steel swords, summoned to a bloody tournament to compete against evil tumors and dark, inexplicable shadowy things. Mortal Kombat.

Two cars are already in the circular driveway when I pull up to Jayne's place. The house backs onto a lush ravine, with tall trees holding on to the last of their fall foliage.

"Perfect timing," says Jayne as she hugs me. "You remember Matt's mother, Charlotte."

"Of course." I smile at the bird-like woman with the perfectly coiffed hair.

"Dear." She takes my hands in a motherly gesture. "Thank you so much for doing this. I'm sorry I have to rush off." She turns to Jayne. "Take care of my grandkid." She pats Jayne's tummy and says goodbye.

"Come on in." Jayne pulls me inside after she's gone. We cross the gleaming marble floor into the formal dining room.

"I'd like you to meet Gabriella. She's the newest member of our committee. Gabriella, this is my dear friend, Shayda."

We shake hands across the dining table. Gabriella is stunning, with porcelain skin, silver blond hair and eyes the color of polished pewter.

"Look at you two," remarks Jayne. "It's like having summer and winter at my table. I don't think two people could look more strikingly different."

"I know." Gabriella considers her arms. "I'm so pale I could pass for a ghost." But her voice is warm and light, like she's perfectly comfortable in her skin. "I would give anything for that delicious golden tan."

"It's not a tan. Shayda's like this all year long," says Jayne, scrunching up her nose. "I know." She looks at Gabriella. "It's disgusting."

We laugh and chat over a selection of Jayne's latest cravings: cheese on rye with thinly sliced zucchini pickles.

"You're lucky you weren't here yesterday. It was cottage cheese with BBQ sauce and ketchup chips."

Gabriella laughs. "Remind me to keep tabs on the menu for our New Year's Ball."

"Hey, I'll have you know I'm a perfectly fine hostess." Jayne feigns indignation. "All of my events garner rave reviews."

"I can't argue with that," replies Gabriella. "I've been over the figures for the last two events. I'm so excited to be a part of it."

"And. AND." Jayne pauses for effect. "We have an awesome line up of speakers this time, starting with this one."

"What? I'm the first one on?" I ask.

"Think about it this way," says Jayne. "Once it's done, you get to sit back and enjoy the rest of the evening."

I look at her dubiously.

"Here," says Gabriella, pulling out the agenda. "Let's go over the options."

She walks me through the sequence of events, the timing, the presentations. Her confidence soothes my jittery nerves.

"So? What do you think?" she asks.

I think of the reclaimed dreams Troy dug up and hung for me on his bedroom wall. Perhaps there is more than one way to reach out and inspire people.

"I'll do it," I reply.

"Fantastic! We have a rehearsal the day before. I would love to see you there. In the meantime, if you think of anything else, here's my card." She gets up and collects her kelly green leather satchel. "Jayne, thanks for the pickles." She gives her a cheeky grin. "It was lovely meeting you, Shayda."

I glance at her card: 'Gabriella Kensington CFA, Financial Analyst.'

"I like her," I say when she's gone.

"Isn't she great?" says Jayne. "She's smart, she's funny and we're incredibly lucky to have her. It was Troy's mother who convinced her to join the charity."

"Troy's mother?"

"Yes. She's also on the committee." Jayne leans forward. "She's been trying to set them up for months. To be honest, I think that's part of the reason Gabriella took on the position. The girl has a massive crush on Troy. I mean massive." Jayne holds her arms out wide. "If you thought I was sweet on him, you should see the look on Gabriella's face when he's around. She's ten years younger, but can you imagine the kids the two of them would make? Ugh. But anyways, tell me how *you're* doing."

Her voice fades as realization hits me.

Gabriella.

Ella.

The same Ella that Troy's mother mentioned when she called him at the cottage.

41. A FAIRY TALE. KIND OF

November 11th, 2000

Troy's loft has become my sanctuary. With Bob insisting I take some time off, and both kids in high school, I have whole days to myself when Hafez is away. My favorite days are like this, when I'm chasing words on the desk in his bedroom, and I hear the front door open. These chance intersections, unplanned and unscheduled, make me feel like we're real, like the intangible between us has turned into a common space that we can walk in and out of.

I listen to the sound of his footsteps, stopping at the kitchen counter, the cushioned thud as he lowers his briefcase and lifts the plastic dome covering the plate. Steak, medium rare, mini roasted potatoes, sauteed vegetables. I know his favorites now. But he doesn't pull up a stool and dig in. He walks over to the stove and I hear the scrape of metal as he finds the rack of brownies, still warm from the oven. I can almost hear his smile.

The tearing of a paper towel. Two, maybe three pieces of brownies. He walks down the hallway and into the bedroom, placing them on the night stand. With his back turned to me, he reaches for his cell and punches a number.

"Hey," I answer on the first ring.

He swings around.

Winner of the biggest, sexiest grin ever.

"Hey," he says into the phone before turning it off. "I didn't see your car."

"Visitor's parking. I thought I'd surprise you," I reply, surprised by my own reaction at the sight of him, the way his jacket hugs his shoulders, his undone collar, his face rough after a long day.

His phone rings. He glances at the number before picking up.

"Sam? Yes. Got them. The initial figures look good. I'll go over them tonight." He taps long fingers on the night stand. "I need that confirmed. Okay. Call when you have it."

"Hong Kong?" I ask when he hangs up.

"Uh-huh." He downs a brownie in one bite.

"When?"

"Mid-December." He stretches out on the bed and props himself up on his elbow. "Why so far?"

"I'm writing."

"What about?"

"A prince."

"So it's a fairy tale?"

"Kind of."

"Can I read it?"

"No! It's not ready yet." I flip the cover down on the laptop.

"How do you know I haven't read it already?"

"Because it's triple password protected," I reply smugly.

"You forget I know a thing or two about security."

"You would hack into my computer?"

"I could." He throws me a wicked smile. "But you keep distracting me." He swings his legs over the side of the bed and rolls my chair over to him.

"Still too far." He lifts me off the seat and onto his lap.

"Hello, Beetroot Butterfly."

"Hello, Scary Cherry."

We fall back on the bed, kissing softly.

"Still tired?" he asks.

"On and off."

"No more cooking and baking. You're supposed to be resting," he says.

"It gives me something to do," I reply.

"I think you know what you *really* have to do."

"And I will, as soon as I'm done with the chemo."

"You're just putting off the inevitable, Shayda."

"I know, but Hafez is just starting to get the help he needs, Troy. I don't want to throw him a curve ball. This next little while could be crucial to his therapy. I owe him that much, at least until I'm done with the chemo."

Troy sighs and slips off my wig. "How much longer?"

"A few more rounds."

He nods and kisses my bald head. "So can you stay?" he asks.

"Ten, fifteen more minutes."

We lie side to side, studying each other's faces.

"I met Gabriella."

"Gabriella?"

"Ella. Gabriella."

He gives me a blank stare.

"The girl your mum's been trying to fix you up with."

"Ah. Gabriella," he replies. "We went out a couple of times."

My heart does a jealous hop. I think of the two of them sharing popcorn in a dark movie theatre. "What happened?"

"Well..." He runs his hand over the curve of my hip. "I was somewhat preoccupied."

"But we weren't...together."

"Yeah, I don't get that either. She was hot. Man, when I think back—ow!" He tears me away from his neck and rubs the teeth marks. "Marking your territory?"

"You bet."

"So where did you meet Gabriella?" he asks.

"At Jayne's," I reply. "She asked me to speak at the New Year's Ball, and Gabriella's on the committee."

"Ah." He rubs his chin.

"What?"

"I just figured out why my mother wants me back in time for New Year's. She told me she has tickets to some fancy bash. They'll be in town for a few weeks over the holidays. Which reminds me, I told them they could use the guest bedroom."

I slip my hand under his collar and feel the rosary around his neck. "I never thought about your parents' reaction."

"When I tell them about us?"

I nod.

"You just look after your end of things. I'll take care of the rest. How are things at home?"

"Okay." I lie.

Hafez's therapist said we should list ten qualities we like about each other. I wanted to tear up his list. He likes how loyal I am, how trustworthy and unselfish and giving. How much I value family.

Sometimes I feel like I should just tell him. Everything. Other times I want to protect him, just a little longer, from the upheaval that will undoubtedly follow.

"So are you going to do it?" asks Troy.

"Do what?"

314

"Speak. At the New Year's event."

"I said yes, but I get so anxious every time I think about it."

"You have to stop running from the things that scare you, Shayda." He fixes those dreamy eyes on me. "The only way to feel truly alive is to start living fearlessly."

42. THE BIG 'O'

December 31st, 2000

NATASHA ADJUSTS MY WIG AND STEPS BACK.

"Perfect!" she declares.

"It seems so undone." I look in the mirror, twisting my head from side to side.

She rolls her eyes. "It's supposed to look like that. All sexy and tousled and just thrown together."

"Sexy, huh?"

"Yes, Mum. I can say the word, you know." She laughs. "Trust me, the hair balances your gown perfectly. Not too casual, not too formal. You look amazing!"

"Thanks to my fabulous hair and make-up artist." I give her a hug.

"Careful, careful." She air-kisses my cheeks instead. "We don't want to smudge anything."

"I think you've done enough smudging."

"It's a smoky eye and it makes you look like one of those glamorous movie stars, like Anouk Aimee. Big hair and dark eyes."

"Anouk Aimee?" I ask. "How do you know about her?"

"You know Grandma is a big fan of those old Fellini movies," she replies, handing me my earrings. "She borrows them from the library and we have movie marathons."

"Hmmm...I'm not sure they're entirely suitable."

"Oh, Mum!" Natasha shakes her head. "Okay, turn. Let me see."

I do a little pirouette for her.

"Shayda, we need to get going—" Hafez walks in, sees me and halts in his tracks.

"You look...beautiful." He says it haltingly, like a long forgotten poem that's coming back.

"Doesn't she?" says Natasha, fixing the delicately draped fabric of my gown.

Sheer overlays float around me, and the diagonal ruching plays up its asymmetrical style. The soft shade of pink is a perfect guise for the harsh reality of twin scars across my chest.

"I feel like I should have brought you flowers." Hafez hovers by the door.

"Aww, you guys," says Natasha, "it's like you're going to prom. So cute."

The doorbell rings.

Natasha turns red.

Like mother like daughter.

"He's early." She makes a face to cover it up.

"Do you think it's wise?" asks Hafez as we watch her bounce down the stairs to greet her date.

"She's sixteen, it's New Year's eve, and Nathan's a good kid," I reply. "Besides, Zain will be here. We couldn't ask for a better chaperone."

"You're hoping he'll snitch."

"Not really, but it doesn't hurt for Natasha to think so." I laugh.

"You really do look...really lovely."

I feel a surge of tenderness for Hafez, looking so out of his element in a sharply pressed suit and tie. His nails are clean, like he's spent hours scrubbing the grime out from under them, and his hair is slicked back like that first time we met.

"And you look very handsome." I smile. It doesn't quite reach my eyes, not because I don't mean it, but because I want to protect him. From myself. "Thanks for coming. I know it's really not your thing."

"Well, speaking in front of a crowd isn't your thing either. But you're still doing it." He looks at me with a mix of pride and reserved affection. "Are you ready?"

"Ready as I'll ever be."

Downstairs, we find Zain firmly entrenched between Natasha and Nathan on the couch.

Hafez can't help but smile when he catches my eye. "We're off, kids. Be good."

Three heads turn around.

"Hi, Mr. Hijazi, Mrs. Hijazi." Nathan gets up.

He's much taller than Natasha, although they're in the same class. Green eyes, hair that's too long, a black t-shirt with 'LINKIN PARK' printed across the front.

"Hello, Nathan," I reply. I can see why Natasha likes him. There's a soft confidence about him that's rare in boys his age.

"You look nice," says Zain.

All I can see are his round eyes staring at me over the back of the sofa.

"Wait." Natasha jumps up. She gets the camera and huddles Hafez and me into a corner.

We smile, as much for the camera as the absurdity of having her fuss over us. The strained tension of the last few months dissipates under Natasha's directions.

"Dad, closer. No, no. Your hand here. Mum, look up. Now look at Dad. Now smile. Look here. Both of you. No teeth. Okay, teeth."

Click, click, click.

"Dinner's in the oven." I remind her as I slip into my coat. "Don't forget to watch the countdown."

"See you next year," says Hafez as he locks the door behind us.

It's a sharp, chilly evening. The crunch of snow echoes in the stillness as we back out of the driveway.

"I've been thinking," says Hafez when we're on the highway. "It's been ages since we went on a family vacation. We should plan something for March break."

I stare ahead. Three months into the future. "Is that what your therapist recommended?"

"No, I just thought it would be nice for the kids." He takes my gloved hand. "And for us."

We take the downtown exit. Brightly lit skyscrapers tower around us.

"Has Dr. Harper said anything about how long she expects you'll be in therapy?"

"There's no definite time frame." Hafez signals, turning into an underground parking lot. He presses the button and takes a ticket.

No definite time frame. I watch the neon yellow gate rise slowly. No easy entry or exit point.

"So? What do you think?" Hafez parks and turns the engine off. "Any place particular you'd like to go? You've always had a thing for the South Pacific..."

No. Not the South Pacific. The South Pacific is four square frames on Troy's wall.

"...but it's too far," he continues. "Maybe when the kids are older. I'm thinking the Caribbean. Or even—"

"Hafez." I hold my hand up. "There's something I need to tell you."

I can't bear to look at his face. I focus on the stark brick wall ahead. "I can't do this anymore."

The headlights of another car pass us by.

Hafez traces the steering wheel with his fingers. "I'm making progress, Shayda. It's tough, but you know what keeps me going?"

I look at him, the planes of his face blue from the fluorescent cast of underground lights.

"That feeling when you came into my life. Like for the first time, I was worth something. The way your face lit up when I walked through the door, like you'd been waiting all day for me. It was like coming home, even though home was a pull-out couch in my parents' apartment." He lets out a ragged sigh. "Being with you healed me, Shayda."

I feel my throat seize.

"And then Pasha Moradi came and took that away. And even though he's gone, I've been letting him take all the things that are important to me. My childhood, Ma, my self-esteem. I won't give him any more, Shayda. I won't let him have you. I should have done this a long time ago. But I'm doing it now, Shayda. I can do this. All my life I've fixed things. Stalled engines, flat tires, chipped wind shields...Give us some time, Shayda. Don't give up on us, not when we're so close."

I reach for his clenched fist. "I'm not the faultless, blameless woman you make me out to be, Hafez."

"You're everything good in my life," he says. "Don't you see? I want to make it right."

Tell him.

Tell him, tell him, tell him.

320

He deserves the truth.

"Hafez—"

"Look," he says. "We don't need to make decisions right now. It's a big night. We can talk about it later. Let's get you inside, okay?"

I nod, but something in my expression makes him pause.

"I can't remember the last time I told you I love you," he says. "I do."

I PUT ASIDE MY PREPARED SPEECH AND BARE MY SOUL TO A room full of elegantly clad strangers. It feels cathartic, this uncensored confession, this facing of my fears, like opening up my heart and letting some blood out so it doesn't choke on itself.

My voice touches the twenty foot ceilings, the magnificent domes and pillars, the iron-laced balconies, and bounces back to me. My eyes settle on random faces. On this table, Bob, Elizabeth, Susan, Marjaneh, Hafez. On that, Jayne, Matt, Charlotte, Gabriella and other function representatives.

At the ten minute mark, I get the signal to start wrapping it up. As I end with a note of gratitude to all the people, organizations and resources that helped me make it, the door opens. A man in a rumpled suit walks in, and I forget what I'm saying.

Troy is back.

And he looks like he's come straight off the sixteen hour flight from Hong Kong. His eyes are tired, but they're glowing, like the sight of me is food for a hungry heart.

"...and all the people I can't even begin to name. You know who you are. Thank you." I conclude, my heart pounding, breathless at the sight of one guest, where three hundred left me nervous, but unmoved.

He claps like I just won an Oscar, and I barely notice the standing ovation as I walk off the stage. The evening changes, like a spark has ignited the room. I glide back to my table, trying to keep him in sight.

"You were wonderful," says Hafez.

When I look up again, Troy has disappeared.

The speeches continue, with Jayne introducing each guest. She looks adorable in a slinky black maxi dress, accentuating her baby bump. By the time desserts roll in, the presentations are over and the room is humming with conversation. Glittering chandeliers are dialed back up and the band starts to play.

"Elizabeth!" A silver haired woman with a pixie haircut stops by our table. Her dress is simple but immaculate, a portrait of regal style in tones of silver and mint. She looks vaguely familiar.

"Grace, my god, it's been ages." Elizabeth gets up to greet her.

Bob follows, gallantly planting a kiss on her hand. "Did you bring Henry or has he been too much of a nuisance lately?"

"Henry's at the table. He'll be thrilled to see you," she replies. "And you, my dear..." She fixes brilliant blue eyes on me. "What a marvelous speech."

"Grace, this is Shayda, and her husband, Hafez," says Elizabeth.

"Would you mind very much if I borrow your wife for a moment?" Grace asks Hafez. "I know Henry would love to meet her."

"Not at all." Hafez stands as I get up.

"You have a well-mannered fellow," she remarks, leading Bob, Elizabeth and me through the maze of tables.

"It's important, you know, no matter what young people think today. Ah, here we are."

A distinguished looking gentleman in an impeccably tailored suit and thick-rimmed glasses smiles as we approach.

"Bob, Elizabeth! How wonderful to see you. And I see you've rounded up my favorite person of the evening," he says to his wife. "How do you do? I'm Grace's husband, Henry." He shakes my hand. "Please, sit." He gestures around the empty table.

"We sent the kids off on an assignment." Grace winks at Elizabeth.

"And how's that going?" she asks.

"We're hopeful, aren't we, dear?" Grace turns to her husband.

"We're meddling," he replies. "We've been very patient, but—"

"Here they are." Grace shushes him, her eyes on someone behind me.

I'm about to turn around when I hear Troy's voice.

"Your donations have been made, courtesy of the Heathgate Group." That rich, velvet-edged baritone.

My eyes fly to Grace and Henry. The photo in his living room. Grace, only with longer hair. Henry, minus the glasses. I've been making small talk with his parents.

Troy has obviously seen me because he stops directly behind me, resting his hands casually on the back of my chair. His thumb strokes the back of my neck, slowly, imperceptibly.

I suck in my breath.

"Shayda! I've been looking all over for you." It's Gabriella, her arm linked daintily around his. Dressed in a ravishing gown that tapers to a seductive V in the small of her back, she looks absolutely spectacular. The black lace plays peek-a-boo with her pale skin, making her silver-blond locks look luminous.

"Troy, this is Shayda," she says.

He hasn't shaved all day. A lock of jet-black hair is tumbling over his forehead. No tie, a wrinkled shirt. And he's still the best looking man in the room.

"We've met." He doesn't shake my hand. Or smile. It's like he's hanging on to the frayed ends of his patience with the distractions, the people, the noise.

"You know each other?" asks Grace.

"They do," replies Bob. "Shayda works with me. Troy purchased his loft through her."

"Small world." Henry smiles. "Please don't mind my son. He's a little grumpy today."

"Troy, why don't you and Ella go dance?" Grace pipes in. "The band is really fantastic. It'll cheer you up."

"No, thanks." He pulls up a chair for Gabriella and takes the one next to me. "I'd like to sit for a while. If it's all the same to you." He looks pointedly at his parents.

"I think I'll get back to my table now," I say.

He seizes my wrist under the table, keeping me rooted. *Don't go.*

"But you just got here," says Henry. "I've been meaning to ask you..." He launches into a discussion about my experience with the health care system, what I liked, what I'd change.

I listen, but all my senses are focused on Troy's fingers, making zig-zag swirls on my palm. He stares into his drink, nodding now and then as Ella carries on a conversation with him.

"It's a far cry from Sweeney's, eh?" A man slaps Troy on the back.

I freeze.

Troy squeezes my hand, steadying me.

His friend, the one we met on our weekend away, takes a seat across from me.

"Hi. I don't believe we've met. I'm David," he says.

"Shayda," I reply.

It's been four months, and my face is skinnier now from the surgery and chemo. He can't possibly make the connection.

"You look familiar. Have we met before?" he says.

"Troy! How nice to see you." Hafez's voice makes me snatch my hand away from Troy.

"I'm sorry to interrupt." Hafez looks around the table. "But I'd like to have my wife back now."

"Of course," laughs Henry. "I've been taking up all her time."

"It was lovely meeting you, Shayda," says Grace.

I say my goodbyes while Hafez catches up with Troy. If I could put seven oceans between the two of them, I would, but I wait, withering under David's scrutiny, until Hafez escorts me back to our table.

"Almost time for the countdown." Marjaneh points to the clock.

The music picks up and couples crowd to the dance floor. I take a deep breath, wishing Troy hadn't come, my initial delight smothered by the weight of the masks we have to wear. David's presence reminds me of the fake and phony that I am.

"They make quite the couple," says Hafez.

"Who?"

He tilts his head to the dance floor.

A jolt of bitter jealousy rushes through me when I see Troy with Gabriella. The thought of watching him ring in the new year with her is unbearable.

"Come on, guys. What are you waiting for?" Jayne and Matt pull us from the chairs.

"I need a few minutes," I say. "Hafez, why don't you go with Marjaneh and Susan? I'll join you in a bit."

"You sure?" he asks. "You want me to get you something?"

"No. I just need to use the ladies room."

I walk past the dance floor, trying to look as if it doesn't matter that Gabriella has her arms around Troy, that she's smiling at him with her perfect lips, flipping back her perfect hair. Her perfect breasts are pressed provocatively against him.

The restroom envelopes me in dark walls and soft lighting. I take a deep breath, thankful for the empty stalls. Everyone is counting down the minutes to midnight.

A half-choke escapes me.

Pull yourself together. Crying and smoky eyes don't go together.

I look in the mirror, feeling washed out, faded, like I'm going to disappear. I turn my purse upside down on the counter. Mints, phone, keys, pen. A chic silver lipstick. My fingers close around it. Crushed Roses. Yes, that's what I need. War paint.

The door opens, but I pay no attention as I swipe the rich crimson color over my lips. There. I put everything back in the purse and take a final look. That's when our eyes meet. In the mirror.

My heart ceases and then picks up like a runaway train. He followed me.

I swing around, wanting to scratch his eyes out. For showing up. For dancing with Gabriella. For turning me inside out.

I reach for the door, but he stops me, his eyes intent on my lips. He always liked this shade. I see the raw hunger in his gaze, the torment of separation, the yearning for relief. He hooks his arm around my waist, pulling me up against

326

his chest, but I push him away. We stare at each other, neither one willing to back down.

I unbuckle his belt.

Is this what you want, Troy?

I kneel and unzip him.

The countdown begins. 10...9...8...7...

I put him in my mouth—his briefs, his aching, straining flesh, all of it, in one hungry swoop

...6...5...4...

I look at him, my mouth full of clothed cock.

Do you like that? Mmmmm. Can you hear the humming in the back of my throat?

...3...2...1...

Good.

I want it to resonate all the way through to your soul.

Outside, the world explodes with colorful streamers and confetti.

HAPPY NEW YEAR!

I straighten until my lips are a hair's breadth away from his. The band starts playing 'Auld Lang Syne' as our mouths meet in a crushing kiss.

Then I open the door and walk out, leaving him in the restroom. With a big red 'O' around his briefs. Marked, dazed and thinking of no other woman but me. Perfect breasts or not.

43. A DOUBLE BETRAYAL

January 3, 2001

"You need a good spanking," says Troy.

"You deserved it." I lean back against the headboard. "You knew you'd be paired off with Gabriella. You knew all I could do was watch. And still you came. Without even giving me a heads up."

"All I could think about was seeing you again." He shifts the pillow on my lap so he can look up at me. "You looked so beautiful in that dress, Shayda. Like a rose in a sea of black. My parents loved you."

"They loved my speech. I'm not the one they have in mind for you, and I can't say I blame them." My fingers play with his hair. He has two whorls on the top of his head. His hair grows in circular patterns around them—one going clockwise, the other anticlockwise. "How long are they staying?"

"A couple of weeks." He nuzzles my tummy. "We'll have to meet here until they're gone."

"I don't mind." I look around the hotel room. It hasn't changed much. "This is where it all started."

"Hardly," he replies. "It started long before this, when stars were mere particles in swirling clouds of dust. And every event since has conspired to bring us together."

"You should go away more. It brings out the poet in you. Give me moreth!" I smile.

He tugs my hair, pulling my face down for a kiss.

"I've missed you," he says. "And you know what else I missed?" He gets up. "I missed the chance to dance with you. It took me a while to...uh...recover, after you left me in that restroom. By the time I got back, you were nowhere to be seen."

"The kids were home alone."

"You ran away, Beetroot. Admit it."

"Fine. If you admit that you wouldn't have asked me to dance, even if I'd stayed."

"You're right. It would have been too obvious. I can't hide the way I feel when you're in my arms. But..." He turns on the radio. "You still owe me a dance."

It feels so familiar, so right, the circle of his arms, his chin brushing the top of my head, our feet moving to an easy rhythm.

"I like this," I say, when a slow, moving ballad comes on.

"It's a band called Bread. 'Baby I'm-a Want You.'"

"We're dancing to a band called 'Bread'?"

"Shhh. Just listen."

I let my hands slide down his back, following the hollow of his spine. My lips brush his collar bone.

"Kiss my neck and we're done," he growls. "I'm throwing you on the bed."

"Neanderthal." I say. "I should have known. You knocked me down the first time we met."

329

"You make it sound like you need insurance against me."

"I do. You're dangerous. And you leave bruises. And your words disrobe me, and your kisses destroy me."

"Works both ways." He massages my waist. "Unbutton my shirt."

"What?"

He takes my hands and puts them on his chest. "Undress me."

I start working my way down slowly, one button at a time.

"What's this?" I ask. "Did you get another tattoo?"

"Keep going."

When I reach the hem, I push the shirt off his shoulders and gasp.

Running horizontally across his entire chest is a tattoo of sharped, spiked barbed wire, much like the one around his biceps, except with his arms down, it looks like one solid line splicing through.

"I thought you shouldn't be the only one with interesting battle scars," he says, shrugging off his shirt.

I run my fingers over the tattoo. He did this for me. To honor the zig-zag gashes where my breasts used to be.

"Your chest! Why would you do this? It's not safe. Getting tattoos abroad." I need words. Something, anything to hold back the dam of emotions surging through me. "You're completely reckless, Troy! I don't—"

He shuts me up with a knee-buckling kiss.

"I love you, Shayda," he says. "I miss you everywhere I go. I want to see you turn your nose up at chapulines in Mexico. I want to walk Temple Street Market with you when I'm in Hong Kong. I want to share every sunrise and every sunset and every second in between with you. I want your laughter and your breath and your blood and your bones.

You're the one thing that centres my soul. I may circle the whole world, but you'll always be home, Beetroot."

I feel his heart racing under my fingers.

"Marry me, Shayda," he says. "I couldn't bear to see that look on your face again, that complete self-loathing when David showed up."

Unplanned, unrehearsed, his speech catches us both by surprise.

Say yes! The barbed wire tells me.

Don't give up on us, says Hafez. *Not when we're so close.*

You should find yourself a boyfriend, says Maamaan.

It's not nice to lose your family, says Zain.

It's like you're going to prom, says Natasha.

I always wanted kids, says Troy. *Always.*

You know what happened to Zarrin, says Baba.

I close my eyes.

It's sunny, but I'm in bed and my bones are cold.

Grace and Henry come in, wearing hospital masks. They give me a bouquet of roses, thorns and all. *"You should have let him go, dear."*

"How could you keep it from me?" asks Jayne.

I look out the window. Maamaan, Baba and Hossein are collecting fallen apples under the tree.

Natasha and Zain hold up a handmade card. Four stick figures with giant heads, torn in half.

Hafez cuts himself. *"Make sure Ma sees this, okay?"*

They all stand around my bed, waiting.

My hair falls off. Troy takes a broom and sweeps it away.

My skin turns grey. He smiles and rouges my cheeks.

Gabriella waits by the door. The blue-eyed baby in her arms starts to fade.

I take Troy's hand.

Everyone disappears.

The Angel of Death walks in.

He wrangles me away from Troy.

No.

No more of living in the shadows.

If we base our decisions on all the things we're afraid of, we would be paralyzed with fear.

I wrench myself away from the cold, deathly grip of despair, from all the worst-case scenarios, from guilt, from shame, from all the heavy chains that have shackled my soul. It's time, time for me to make the journey of a thousand miles, time for me to take a leap of faith. I stand at the edge of the abyss and hesitate.

Fly, dammit, fly, says Troy.

I smile and spread my wings, gliding, soaring, rising over a golden valley where lemon groves lie cradled in the warmest, softest earth. I feel like I am home again. Because I choose love. I choose faith. And hope. And happiness. And dancing dust motes in the sunlight.

"Yes!" I open my eyes. "Yes, Troy."

"Yes?" he blinks. "Yes?" He lets out a big whoop and crushes me. He totally, completely crushes me.

We start laughing—dizzy, giddy laughing.

"I don't have a bloody ring," he says.

"I don't care." Like any of that matters.

"Shayda Hijazi...no, no. Shit, I don't know your maiden name."

It's so absurd, we laugh some more.

"Kazemi," I reply. "It's Shayda Kazemi."

"Kazemi. Hijazi. Whatever the fuck it is." He takes off the rosary around his neck and wraps it around my wrist. "Shayda-soon-to-be-Heathgate, if I could handcuff you to me for the rest of our lives, I would. But this will have to do for now. You are mine, bound to me, tied to me, from this day on. And don't you forget it."

I feel his rosary around my wrist, warmed by his skin, and I think of how far we've come.

The almost-touching of our toes in this room.

Lather on his face.

Red nail polish.

A hammock by the lake.

The clip-clop of a Scottish Clydesdale.

His nose between my chopsticks.

All these things, all these things, break open, like a bag of marbles, rolling and rattling down the corridors of my heart, a river of shiny, bright lanterns, illuminating the way.

"It's true," I say.

"What is?"

"What your grandmother said."

It'll bring you light in the dark. It wasn't the rosary she'd meant. It was love, pure and simple.

"It keeps the monsters at bay." I smile. "I wish I had something for you."

"Oh, but you do."

"What? What can I give you when you've already bound yourself to me for life." I trace the beautiful tattoo around his chest.

"Put on your red lipstick, Shayda. You make a hell of an 'O' with that. I'll take that ring of eternity any day over gold and silver."

"Yes, sir."

"And finish the job this time, woman."

I STEP OUT OF THE REVOLVING DOORS, MY INSIDES SPINNING. The wind feels icy as it hits my lungs, but I breathe deep. I feel like I've finally shed all the dark, dull layers that have weighed me down.

I start walking towards the car, knowing I've got this—whatever comes next.

"Shayda."

I stop. "Hafez?"

He straightens from the light post he's leaning on.

"What are you doing here?" I ask.

His cheeks are wind-whipped and dry, like he's been in the cold for way too long.

"I had to see for myself."

That look. The look he'd given his father the day Pasha Moradi died.

Do you think I didn't know?

"I came after you," he says. "How many New Years have we rung in together, Shayda? Did you think I wouldn't miss you?"

I feel my world tipping over, the porcelain family he gave me slipping over the edge and smashing, like a shattered snow globe.

"I saw him follow you into the restroom," he continues.

"Hafez—" I reach for him, but he steps back.

His eyes are dull and tortured. A double betrayal. First his father. Now me. We were supposed to love him, but we crushed his soul.

"Go back inside, Shayda. I'm setting you free." He starts walking away from me, walking away from the pain, too broken and battered to stand and fight.

"Hafez. Wait!"

He turns, halfway across the street and gives me a bitter smile. "I didn't forget, Shayda. I told you I would do whatever it takes to make you happ—"

The loud blare of an air horn sweeps the rest of his words away. His body catapults into the air as a truck slams into him. He lands, several feet away with a sickening thud, his blood spilling like black ice on the asphalt.

334

It's only when the truck comes to a screeching halt and the driver jumps out that the reality of the collision sinks in, and I race to his limp form.

44. LIGHTING THE CANDLES

January 10th, 2001

I've learned to block out the incessant beeping of Hafez's monitor, the shrill announcements over the intercom, the chatter of food trays on a cart. I wish I could do the same with the constant screaming that's going on inside of me, the kind no-one can hear.

Torn.

This is what it feels like—like every fibre of my soul is being ripped apart, limb separated from limb, all my insides being scraped out.

My heart is breaking for Hafez, lying on the hospital bed.

My soul is bleeding for Troy, waiting in the wings.

It's been a week since the accident, and every day, every hour, has put my new found bravado to a gruelling test. On the one hand is the 'me' who responds automatically to all the years of conditioning, of doing the things I'm supposed to do, and feeling the things I'm supposed to feel; and on the other is the 'me' who refuses to live a lie.

I dial Troy's number again.

The first night he called, I flung my phone across the room. We had done this to Hafez. Troy and I.

It was so easy to slip into that dark, sickening spiral of guilt, to punish myself by pushing Troy away. Because I felt I deserved that awful, searing pain it brought, to deny myself the one person I wanted to be the most with.

But when Hafez opened his eyes for the first time in days, I realized we had both been touched by death, and we had both been given a second chance. It was time to release ourselves from this constant cycle of pain, to stop holding on to ideals we both yearned for, but that always remained out of our reach.

I hold my breath as Troy's phone rings.

No answer.

I debate about leaving a message.

Hey. Sorry I haven't called. Hafez was in an accident. I've been camped out at the hospital. The doctors say he'll be fine, but he has a concussion and a fractured femur. I haven't abandoned you. I'm yours—bound to you, tied to you, just like I promised. I just need to be here for now.

No. I hang up. No message. I need to see him, tell him face to face.

I call his office.

"Mr. Heathgate is out of town on a personal leave of absence. Would you like me to direct your call to his assistant?"

"When will he be back?"

"He didn't say."

I twist the rosary around my wrist. Then I try his cell again. I could listen to the sound of his voice over and over again.

"Call me back, Scary Cherry." I say.

My phone remains silent.

March 21st, 2001

"WHEN ARE THEY COMING?" ASKS ZAIN, PLUCKING HIS guitar strings.

"Soon," I say. My voice sounds distant and removed.

In some ways, Hafez and I have spent more time together in the last two months than we have in our entire marriage. Helping him get back on his feet, driving him to physio, sitting together quietly in the evenings, we've come to realize what we have. And what we never will.

"I should have told you the truth about Troy before I got involved," I say.

"I should have told you the truth about Pasha Moradi before I asked you to marry me," he replies. "I should have opened up about my past, given you the choice, Shayda. Neither one of us was an innocent party."

The accident enabled Hafez to re-evaluate life, to move past the hurt and see the real issues in our relationship. We've come to a mutual understanding, that it's time to let go of all the things that have crippled us, kept us locked in place of pain. It's a move in the right direction, for both of us, but it means nothing to me without Troy.

There's no way to track him down. No one knows where he is or when he's coming back. He's cut himself off, and I burn in a private hell, day after day, hoping he'll show up soon.

Natasha turns the TV off. "I still don't get why." Her voice is hoarse with frustration.

"Mum and I decided it's for the best," says Hafez. "When I'm settled in my new place, we'll see each other all the time."

"But why today? It's Nowruz!"

I think she made some kind of a pact when Hafez came home—to revive a discarded tradition. She spent days setting up the Haft Seen table. How could she have known the ghosts that her beautiful arrangement dredged up? She gave up when the movers dropped off empty cardboard boxes. The candles on the table remained unlit.

"I think the movers are here," says Zain, peering out the window.

I pull the curtain aside as a wheel-trans bus parks by the curb. The attendant lowers the ramp and wheels an old man out.

"It's not for us." I let the curtain fall.

A few moments later, the doorbell rings.

"Yes?" Hafez opens the door.

"Hafez Hijazi?" inquires the man.

"Yes."

"Your father asked to see you." He wheels a living skeleton into the living room.

Natasha and Zain stare, open-mouthed. They have never seen their paternal grandfather. I try to look beyond the oxygen mask and tubing, but all I can make of Kamal Hijazi are his watery, cataract eyes. Hafez has turned white, his feet rooted to the floor.

Pedar gazes at Natasha and Zain before moving on to me. Then his eyes settle on Hafez.

He says something, but his speech is garbled and his body jerks to one side.

"He had a stroke a few years ago," says the attendant, leaning lower so Pedar can speak in his ear.

They exchange some words.

"He wants you to have this." The man unclenches a brown paper bag from Pedar's fingers and gives it to Hafez.

Once again, Pedar says something to his attendant.

"He wants you to open it."

Seconds pass as Hafez looks at his father. All the times he imagined Kamal Hijazi over the years, I know he could not have pictured this—this trembling sack of skin and bones, an oxygen-pumped collection of wrinkles and veins and shriveled mass.

Hafez reaches into the bag and pulls out a set of figurines. The base is broken, but the three silhouettes, worn and faded, are still intact.

Me, Kamal and little boy Hafez, Ma had said.

The father figurine is chipped, but that isn't what catches my eye. Pedar has blackened its face, with paint or a sharpie or a crayon. I can't tell.

Hafez's grip tightens. His father is saying he is sorry. In his own way.

Pedar makes another sound. He lifts one hand off his knee and holds it there with tremendous effort, looking at his son.

Hafez nods and accepts his gift.

Then the attendant wheels Pedar back out of our lives.

The four of us watch him get back into the van. When the ramp is raised and the door slides shut on Kamal Hijazi, Hafez reaches for my hand.

"Zain, put this on the Haft Seen table, next to ours." He hands over Ma's figurine. "Natasha, go get the matches." Then he turns to me. "I think it's time we lit the candles."

His smile is thin but free, as if the muscles holding it have become unshackled, and his face must learn how to wear it anew. It's an echo of that first smile, the one that's always stayed with me. I see a lifting of the gates again, a slow release of the dark things that have plundered his soul.

We gather the children, Zain on one side and Natasha on the other. One by one, Hafez and I light the candles, watching as the wick catches fire. With each flame, a lightness grows, bit by bit, between us.

"Nowruz Mubarak, Hafez," I say. "Here's to new beginnings."

"Nowruz Mubarak, Shayda," he replies. "To new beginnings."

THE ELEVATOR CAN'T GET ME TO TROY'S LOFT FAST ENOUGH. I feel like a bubble of joy, about to burst into rainbow sparkles.

"We just got back from lunch with Troy," said Jayne when she called.

"He's back?" I asked.

"For a bit. I think he's heading back soon."

My hands shake as I fumble with the keys to Troy's place. I know he stormed off because of me, because he thought I'd shut him out yet again. I have so much to explain, so much to make up for, but he's back and that's all that matters. I can't wait to tell him how much I've missed him, to shower him with all the mad, irrepressible love fizzing inside me, to tell him I'm his—free and clear.

"Troy?" He's left the door unlocked. I step inside and freeze.

The place has been stripped bare. All the furniture is gone. His TV, shoes, pots, pans—everything.

No. Not everything. I walk into his bedroom and feel a hard punch to my gut. He's left the South Pacific, the dreams he gave me, as though he had no more room to carry them. They stare at me through square black frames, hollow and colorless without him.

I make my way through the emptiness, clutching at the walls in the hallway.

No.

I'll find him. I'll make this right.

I straighten and start heading for the door when it opens.

And there he is.

He sees me and halts.

Relief washes over me. "I thought I'd missed you. I thought you'd gone."

He picks up the last box in the living room and starts walking out again.

"Troy." I race after him. "Troy, wait!"

But he's already out the door.

I spin him around and reel from the look in his eyes.

Troy's eyes, yes, but without any of their bright, brilliant warmth, still blue, but frozen like the arctic wind. Locked down, impenetrable; every door, every window, nailed shut. I feel a howling in my soul.

"Troy, I'm sorry. Hafez was in an accident. I—"

"I know. There's always something, Shayda. You *promised* me, you bound yourself to me. And all that changed the moment you stepped out of that room. I get that you wanted to be there for him, but you turned me off— like a fucking switch. Just like that. I'm done, Shayda."

How different it sounds. Shayda without the 'ahhh'.

I stagger back from the pain of it. He might as well have ripped out a chunk of my heart and crushed it with his bare hands.

"You don't get to yank me around anymore," he says. "Not after everything I've laid bare for you. I don't want you or your dead promises or your mind-fucking, poison kisses."

"I can explain—"

"Get out of my way, Shayda. I have a plane to catch." He storms past me, into the elevator. His face is all angles, harsh and drawn out, and his breath smells of tobacco and booze.

"Troy, I—"

He stops me. With a single look. His face hardens, cheekbones locked in tight rage. A nerve leaps in his cheek.

I always thought I'd be the one to get hurt. Troy Heathgate, my strong, invincible lover, could never break.

The veils are gone. I see myself now. I am Jerry Dandridge, the vampire from 'Fright Night'. I have been feeding off him and now he's shutting the door on me.

"Goodbye, Shayda Hijazi," he says as the elevator closes on him, blowing out every window in our borrowed house, built on borrowed time. It collapses around me, a cloud of dust and shattered glass.

Goodbye, Troy Heathgate.

I lean back against the door, knowing I've broken something deep and precious, something beyond repair. I double over and crumble to the floor.

45. FADED

....

August 6th, 2001

THE COTTAGE LOOKS THE SAME EXCEPT PARTS OF IT HAVE been upgraded. The old couch has been replaced with a sleek, but comfortable sofa. There's a flat screen TV on the wall and new appliances in the kitchen. The counter is smooth, black granite, but the cabin retains its warm, cozy feel. The bathroom has been renovated too: a deep Victorian tub with gilded feet, separate shower stall, fancy faucets, fresh paint. Everything has changed except for the mirror.

BB♥SC. That's what it said, in foggy letters, one sunny, stolen weekend.

The online ad featured a picture from above, a satellite image, but when Amy sent me more photos, I knew. I held my breath as I scrolled through the gallery. The wooden beams, the weathered paint, the stone tiles leading down to the lake.

Our cottage.

I wanted to sit in the hammock again, to dip my feet in the water, to curl up in bed and wake up to the call of the loon. Everything about it called me back.

Come, come. 'X' marks the spot.

I called Amy the next day and booked it for the week that Hafez had the kids over.

I needed time to heal, to sleep in, to watch the moon. I felt like I had just come off a ragged rollercoaster—the shock of cancer, surgery, chemo. The divorce. The shock of losing Troy.

It's been months since he left for New York, but it still hurts like a wound that just keeps leaking. He won't return my calls. I logged into beetbutt@hotmail.com for the first time, and found messages from him, every year on our birthday, since we set it up. Every year except this one. I think of my own silent tradition, of baking brownies for him on that day, even if they never got him.

'I miss you,' I typed and hit 'send'.

No answer.

Each time I drive by his work, I die a little. Each time I think of that empty loft, I reach for his rosary. The silver cross is worn from years of sitting in the nook between his collarbones. Every wooden bead is like a memory of us, round and whole, but pierced through the middle. At night I count on the beads.

Come back to me.

Come back to me.

There are moments when I forget, like last week, when Hafez came over and we played board games with Natasha and Zain. They seem to be handling it well, although sometimes I catch them eavesdropping when I'm talking to my oncologist on the phone. They almost lost me; they almost lost Hafez. I think they're just thankful to have both their parents, even if it's not under the same roof.

"Hey, you want to join us? We ordered pizza and Nathan's brought a movie." Natasha poked her head in my room last night.

"Thanks, but I just want to get some writing done. Are you all packed for tomorrow?"

"Yep. So's Zain. Dad's taken the week off so he can take us camping. Nathan's parents are letting him come too. This is turning out to be an awesome summer!"

"I'm glad," I said.

"So what are you writing?"

"Just bits and pieces...of life."

I want to finish what I started in that sunny corner of Troy's bedroom; the letters I wrote for him, about him. Because I didn't want him peeking into my life through the tiny windows of our time together. And even though he's gone, he will always be my prince, my fairy tale, the happily-ever-after that eluded me. Maybe when I finish this, I'll be at peace. And so I keep typing, on the silver laptop he gave me.

I get it out of the trunk, along with the rest of my luggage and let myself into the cottage. The air conditioning is on at full blast. I unzip my bag and remove the red shawl Troy got for me. It wraps around me like a hug from a cherished gift.

I walk out to the hammock and doze off to the sound of soft, swishing waves. There is some magic here, this little spot in this big, big world, that heals me. Perhaps it's the memories we made, Troy and I, some seeds of happiness, still scattered in the air.

I stir as the sun starts to set, and head back in. For the first time in months, I'm famished. I get dinner started before checking in with Hafez and the kids.

It isn't until I hang up that I see it—the photo on the mantle, above the fireplace

It can't be.

I make my way over and pick up the frame.

It is.

I feel a fluttering inside me.

I'm a realtor. I can get to the bottom of this.

I turn on my laptop and start searching.

It doesn't take too long to find it. I note the name on the transaction and I'm torn between giddiness and a sick sense of grief. I pick up the frame again, but it slips from my hand and crashes on the floor.

Crap. I broke it.

I start picking up the pieces and find something sticking out behind the photo. It's another print, a faded image from years ago. I miss it the first time, but when I look again, there it is. Staring at me in the face. I sit down in stunned disbelief. All this time, all this time, the one thing that could have changed it all.

I might have started sobbing at the grand cosmic joke I was holding in my hands, but a surge of determination shot through me. I was going to make it happen. It *had* to happen. Because I had proof that it was meant to be. I start laughing at the inevitability of it.

Troy Heathgate, you don't stand a snowball's chance in hell.

46. A WICKED GAME

....

August 7th, 2001

MIDTOWN MANHATTAN IS A LIVING, BREATHING ORGANISM that pulses to its own beat. The lights, traffic, architecture, surround me as I make way to the 'x' on my street map.

Heathgate Group is housed in an imposing building with soaring glass doors and a lobby that features striking artwork, reflected off polished floors.

I head to the restroom first, squaring my shoulders as I look in the mirror. Maybe I should have picked something more conservative, but the leather jacket from Ken and Judy's makes me look tougher than I feel. And I'm hoping the slouchy vintage boots mask my wobbly knees. My hands are unsteady as I apply the lipstick. Crushed Roses. Red hot lips are my man's weakness, and I need every advantage for this confrontation. I stand back and take a deep breath. Then I head for Troy Heathgate's office.

"Do you have an appointment?"

His receptionists are stunning. Beyond stunning. I want him to fire them all.

"No, but I've come a long way. I'm sure he'll see me."

They refrain from laughing in my face. They're beyond professional too.

"He's in a meeting so it might be a while. Are you sure you don't want to make an appointment for another day?"

"I'll wait. As long as it takes." I take a seat on a gracefully upholstered leather chaise, trying to get a grip on my thundering heart.

The reception area is buzzing like a hive. So many people. So many offices. The incessant ring of telephone calls, hushed conversations, not so hushed conversations, endless sheafs of paper collecting at the photocopying station. Every minute that passes cranks up my nerves, until I'm coiled so tight, I spring off the chair and head for the coffee machine. I'm half way there when I see him, through the glass panels of the board room.

He's let his hair grow, as if he can't be bothered with such mundane tasks as getting it cut. Sexy stubble outlines his jaw as he absently taps a sleek, silver pen against the solid wood conference table. He looks like a bad boy who's behaving just so he can make it to recess, a bad boy who completely relishes getting out of that tailor-made suit. The thought turns my insides into mush.

I'm here to claim this sexy, passionate beast of a man.

I don't know if I can do it.

You can.

You must.

The meeting ends as I stand there, leering. I make a dash for my chair as the door opens, and then I wait. And wait.

The room empties, but Troy doesn't come out. One of the girls goes in to see him.

I twist the rosary around my wrist, waiting, waiting, waiting.

"He'll see you now." She finally comes out, and leaves the door ajar.

I put one foot in front of the other and step inside the room.

The vast length of the conference table separates us. Troy remains seated at the other end, his hands clasped before him. Damn. He always looks better than I can ever picture in my head.

"What can I do for you? Shayda...Kazemi." He reads my name from the note his assistant left him.

"I was hoping we could talk." Suddenly, I'm acutely aware of my cropped hair, that's slowing growing out after the chemo.

"So talk." He gestures to the seat near the door, the one furthest from him.

"I'd rather stand." I need the advantage of height, even though my legs feel like toothpicks, about to snap under his piercing glare.

"Suit yourself."

"You didn't tell me you bought the cottage."

"I wasn't aware I needed to keep you apprised of my investments."

"I rented it for the week."

"Yes, my property manager forwarded the info."

"Amy? Amy is your property manager?"

"Shayda." He taps the pen impatiently. "Why are you here?"

It's now or never, Shayda. Now or never.

"Because I love you. Because I miss you. Because I was empty before you and I'm empty after you. Because the only time I've felt truly alive is the time I've spent with you." *I'll rip my guts out, spill my soul all over this table. Anything, anything to get through to you.*

Steely-eyed silence.

"I do recall asking you to marry me," he says. "But then you had a change of heart."

"It's always been you, Troy. Always."

"Let me get this straight." He leans forward. "You think you can march in here with your hot lips, in that sexy outfit, and expect me to just roll over? Because you're bored and lonely now? Because you've decided you'd like to have me around, after all?"

"Don't do this, Troy. Not when we're finally here, at this perfect intersection; when we're finally free to be together."

"What makes you think I'm still free?"

"I don't care!" The intensity of my admission catches me off guard. But it's true—I really don't care. "*Make* yourself free. You're mine, Troy. And I'm not giving up without a fight. I've learned that I matter; what I want matters. So here I am. I get that you're hurting—I get that you want me to hurt too. And I'm sorry, Troy. I'm sorry for shutting you out. Time and time again. But I *know* you. Every cell, every edge, every fibre of your being. You miss me just as much as I miss you."

His expression doesn't change. He's completely bulletproof.

"Do you know what this is?" I place the picture I found at the cottage in front of him.

He throws it a brief glance. "It's a photo of me, from years ago." he says. "I'm rollerskating with my neighbour, Carol, on the boardwalk by my parents' place."

"It was tucked away behind your parents' photo. The one from your loft. You remember, you had it on the shelf in your living room?"

"You came all the way here to show me this?"

"Look again, Troy."

He gives it another scan, but this time he pauses. "Is that...is that *you*?"

Bingo. Upper right hand corner, behind the roller-skating duo, sitting on the grass with my knees to my chest, looking at their backs. My face is blurry, but there's no mistaking it.

"It was you, Troy. The day I went looking for a sign. I saw *you*. I wanted to be the girl holding your hand, I wanted us to be that couple. We were like two stars converging around the same axis, but with paths that missed each other by a fraction of infinity. And so we passed each other by. Don't let that happen again, Troy."

He focuses his magnetic blues on me. Then he pushes the photo away with lethal calmness. "I told you, Shayda. I'm not free."

"Kiss me, Troy." I splay my hands on the table and lean in. "If there really is no room for me in your heart, I'll know. I'll walk out of here and you'll never see me again."

My pulse skyrockets as his face comes closer, but his lips never get to mine.

"I don't have to prove anything to you," he says.

I feel his hot breath on my cheek. Then he gets up and holds the door open.

My heart sinks.

Gabriella. Ella.

I should have known.

Oh, fate. What a wicked, wicked game you play.

I walk past him, crossing the threshold back to my world, with a crushing sense of defeat. I feel like I've just lost the biggest presentation of my life.

Repeat after me.

I will not break down in front of all these people.

I will not.

Will not.

Break down.

Incredibly, my legs hold up. They carry me through all the noise and chatter outside the board room. All I want to do is find a quiet corner so I can fall apart.

"Wait." I hear Troy calling over the commotion. "I believe you have something of mine."

I turn around and find him standing by the reception. "Sorry?"

"You have something that belongs to me."

I feel the heaviness of his rosary around my wrist.

Oh god. He's going to strip me of everything. No reminders.

I feel all eyes on me as I walk up to him and hold my wrist out, waiting for him to unwind the rosary from my hand.

He grabs it by the cross and pulls me roughly, almost violently, to him. And then his mouth crushes me, hard and unrelenting, parting my lips with fierce domination. He devours me with a single-minded hunger, until my limbs start to tremble. I feel an explosion of joy, relief, tears, laughter, surging through me. My arms go around him as I drink in the savage sweetness of this kiss, our first, truly free, toe-curling, mind-blowing kiss.

We come up for air, breathless and a little dazed.

And then all hell breaks lose, as everyone starts clapping.

My face turns a bright shade of red.

"Don't you ever, *ever*, walk away with what's mine, Beetroot," he says.

He looks so endearingly comical, in his sharp suit with red lipstick smeared all over his face.

"I thought you'd put up more of a fight, Scary Cherry."

"I lose it. Every time you barge into my office. Every fucking time."

"Heyyy—"

"I know, I know. Stop swearing. Stop smoking. Stop drinking..." He looks at me expectantly.

"Which leaves just one other option." I laugh.

"Let's get out of here, Beetroot."

47. GIVE ME EVERYTHING

August 8th, 2001

I HAVE ALWAYS LOVED THE COTTAGE AT NIGHT. SOFT candlelight casts a golden glow on the walls. I sit in the tub, leaning against Troy, our legs stretched out before us. He dips the sponge in warm, soapy water and squeezes it down my back.

"So when did you do all this?" I ask.

"I put in an offer when we got back from our trip."

"And you didn't tell me?"

"I thought I'd surprise you. It was going to be the place you always wanted by the water."

"How could you not tell me? I'm your realtor," I tease.

"You're a pain in the ass." He bites my shoulder.

"So do you come here often?"

"I came in to check on the renovations. That was it. I couldn't stand being here without you. I rented it out, hoping that someone might find the same magic we did here."

"I am so glad I came across the ad." I don't want to consider the other possibilities, of skipping that random

355

moment that brought me here. Then again, I know that somehow, someway, we'd be still be here, maybe not in this exact moment, but at some other junction in life, because we belonged together. "Is this the same tub we saw in that store?"

"No. That one sold. But they got me the next best thing."

He runs the sponge down my arms and back up to my nape. "I like this Halle Berry thing you've got going on." He tugs at my short curls.

"Halle Berry, huh?" I laugh. "For a while I felt like Humpty Dumpty. No hair. No eyebrows."

"You've lost a lot of weight, Beetroot. I'm going to have to fatten you up."

"Mmmm." I turn around and kiss him. "I like the way this tastes. I could devour a full, eight course meal of this and still have room for more."

He lets out a low growl and runs his hands over my slippery skin.

"Eight course? You mean eight inches." His head falls back as I stroke him. "Not here, Beetroot. I want to fuck you properly, thoroughly—so completely, in so many different ways that this little tub isn't going to cut it."

And that's exactly what he does. He takes me to bed, still wet from the bath, and he tastes me, and teases me, and pleases me, until I'm a hot, writhing mess of desire. And then he obliterates me, unleashing his raw sensuality, feeding on my skin, my nerves, my lips, even as he rides me higher and higher. He thrusts me to the edge of the bed, until my head is hanging off the side, as he claims me from behind. Then I'm on my back, my ankles on his shoulders, my hips lifted off the bed. He turns me on my side and takes me again. And again.

"I want it all," he grinds out through clenched teeth. "Give me everything, Beetroot."

And the last bit of reserve, the last unclaimed piece of my soul, gasps in sweet agony as a million glowing stars shatter around me. Nothing held back. No inhibitions. Every part of me is wholly, magnificently free to love this man as he deserves.

My breath comes in a long, shuddering sob as Troy abandons himself to his passion and collapses with a ragged cry.

48. WINGS

August 9th, 2001

I OPEN MY EYES AND LET THE FEELING SINK IN: TROY'S cheek nestled between my shoulder blades, his arms around my waist, his thighs cradling mine. Warm breath against my skin. Life feels so precious, that every battle, every scar, seems worth it. I slide my hands over his and breathe with him.

When I wake up again, he's making breakfast. I listen to the sizzle of eggs in the pan, the tinkle of a stirring teaspoon, the 'ding' of toasted bread.

"Morning." I wrap my arms around his neck, and feel my body protest with the best kind of soreness.

I want him again.

"It's not going to work." He forces a plate between us.

"What's not going to work?" I nibble on his ear.

"These distraction tactics of yours. I'm still going to make you finish your breakfast."

I make a face.

He makes me finish.

WE PUTTER AROUND THE COTTAGE. ME IN A BORROWED t-shirt; him in checked boxers and those damn impressive pecs.

"Come on, Beetroot. Time to get ready," he says.

"Where are we going?" My head is on his lap, feet on the couch.

The photo of his parents is back on the mantle, in a new frame, next to the first pic of Troy and me, on the boardwalk.

"Have you been to the Butterfly Conservatory?"

"No."

"Then you're in for a treat."

"I don't want to go," I reply.

"Why not?"

"Because butterflies are meant to thrive and dance and fly free. I don't want to see them pinned behind some plexiglass."

"Agreed," he smiles. "Now are you going to get ready or should I forcibly evict you from my lap?"

I drag my feet to the bedroom and change into jeans and my Beatles t-shirt.

"You still have it?" He tugs the hem fondly. Then he frowns. "You're practically swimming in it now."

WE TAKE THE QUIET BYROADS THAT FOLLOW THE NIAGARA River, at times obscured by a thin line of trees, at times opening up to breathtaking views of the surrounding landscape. I ride tucked in behind Troy, my fingers locked around his chest as we pass a panorama of red, orange and gold maples. Between the trees, the river runs pale blue, like a silver snake, past vineyards and beautiful homes.

I love how our bodies sync together, leaning into winding curves, as we cruise along. Pressed up against his back, I feel a lightness of being that defies the heavy jacket and helmet.

He pulled them out of storage this morning, along with matching gloves and boots.

"I got them done for you when I bought the cottage. I always pictured us doing this one day."

The jacket fits a bit loose, but I'm stoked to go on my first motorcycle ride.

"Hold tight!" he shouts over the hum of the engine when we get to an open stretch of road. "Ready?"

I nod.

He twists the throttle. The Ducati picks up, zipping down the tree-lined route at full speed.

"Woooo!" I squeeze my arms around him, letting the giddy thrill of exhilaration race through me. I feel invincible, shielded, in the shadow of his broad back and shoulders.

He slows down as we turn off a tree-lined street. Sitting amidst the immaculately groomed grounds is a giant greenhouse full of tropical plants with paths that meander through a rainforest-like setting. The Butterfly Conservatory.

"Oh!" I exclaim, as thousands of butterflies float around us, flying freely among lush, exotic blossoms.

They land on fruit plates and dishes of honey and water tucked along the walkways so we can watch them feed.

"Like it?" he asks as I walk ahead of him, my arms spread wide, hoping one of them will land on me.

"No pins," I laugh.

I stop to read one of the signs. "It says not to touch them. The scales on their wings are so fragile, they'll come off like powder on our hands, potentially reducing their lifespan."

"Hard to believe that most of them live just two to three weeks," he remarks.

"Except for the Monarchs."

"Yes. They have a long way to go."

"The journey of a thousand miles."

"An eternity for a little thing."

We stand in the warm, moist greenhouse, while droplets of water condense on the windows and run down like little streams.

"Have you seen a Monarch hatch from its pupa?" asks Troy.

I shake my head.

He leads me to the emergence chamber, where butterflies come out of hanging cocoons, unfurling their wings and taking their first flight.

"Those are Monarchs." He points to jade green chrysalises with gold trim. "See the ones that have turned transparent?"

I gasp as I notice the black and orange wings folded inside, revealing a brand new butterfly. "Look at that one! It's starting to split open at the bottom."

We watch as the butterfly breaks free of its case and greets the world backwards, with tiny, shriveled wings. It sits on the empty shell and begins to open and close its wings, inflating them with a reservoir of fluid from its swollen abdomen. As the wings expand, the body takes on normal proportions and the butterfly rests.

"In a few hours when its wings are dried and hardened, it will take its first flight," Troy explains. "Like that one over there."

He points out a newly emerged butterfly that is flapping its wings slowly, and then faster and faster, before rising up gently. The new Monarch floats in the air for a few seconds and then joins the hundreds of free-flying butterflies in the conservatory.

"That was beautiful," I whisper.

Troy hugs me from behind as we stare after the butterfly, no longer able to follow its flight as it blends in with the rest.

"If the cancer comes back, remember me like that," I say, resting my cheek on his. "I feel like I've made my journey, like I've come a thousand long, impossible miles, but now I can fly free and weightless, disappearing where breaths go, where so many souls have gone before."

He doesn't reply.

Everywhere, exquisite butterflies float in the warm, moist air, spreading iridescent wings on leaves and flowers.

"Nothing's going to take you away from me." His arms tighten possessively around me. "When we get back, we're getting married. And then we're going to live happily ever after. You hear me, Beetroot?"

I nod, through the lump in my throat.

We make our way to the exit, savoring the feel of our hands clasped together.

"Look, Troy. This one's a brilliant blue!" I approach a butterfly that's drinking from a puddle of water on the path.

We crouch on the ground to examine it.

"A Blue Morpho," he says.

We watch it from opposite ends. My breath catches as I note how its exquisite wings are the same color as Troy's eyes.

"Beautiful," I say.

"Nothing holds a candle to my Beetroot Butterfly."

I smile, realizing we've been watching each other, our cheeks pressed to the stone tiles.

"Don't move," I whisper. "There's a butterfly on your shoulder."

The corners of his eyes crinkle. "Fifteen years and you're going to use that line on me now?"

"Eighteen," I say. "And there really is a butterfly on your shoulder."

"What color?" he asks.

"It's a Monarch."

Troy lies quietly and lets me watch it open and close its wings.

"I wonder how far yours got," he says.

"All the way to the Great Spirit."

"How do you know?"

"Because my wish came true. I found my wings, Scary Cherry."

49. RAINBOWS & WATERFALLS

August 10th, 2001

WE MERGE INTO TRAFFIC HEADED FOR THE FALLS. THE power of thundering water, as it pours over from the Great Lakes, is awe-inspiring. A fine mist covers our visors as brightly lit casinos and multi-storey hotels come into view. Troy pulls into a private parking lot and takes off his helmet.

"Everything set?" he asks the guard at the security station.

"Yes, Mr. Heathgate. Dale is waiting for you." The guard lets us in.

"Are you going to tell me now?" I ask when he unstraps my helmet.

"Patience, Beetroot."

Dale walks us to a concrete circle marked with a big 'H'. A bright blue helicopter with shiny rotor blades awaits us.

"A helicopter tour?" I almost jump up and down.

Troy grins and ushers me inside. "The last time we were here, we didn't quite make it to the falls."

I feel my cheeks flame as he straps me in. How can this man still make me blush?

"Is it just us?" I ask, eyeing the empty seats as Dale starts the engine.

"Just us." He puts on a baseball cap and holds my hand as we take off.

The timing is perfect. The setting sun paints the sky with bold strokes of pink and gold. Below us, rainbows appear and disappear as we skim over vast clouds of mist. We soar past the Whirlpool Rapids and the American Falls to the Canadian Horseshoe, spellbound by the majesty and power of the spectacle below us.

"A lot of the water from the Niagara River is diverted by dams and stored in underground reservoirs for power plants," Dale informs us. "What you see going over the falls is only a fraction of it."

His commentary continues as we circle the falls and then fly over the Rainbow Bridge.

"Don't forget your picnic basket," he says.

Troy opens a wicker basket lined with quilted plaid, and pulls out a blanket. We spread it between us and dig into an assortment of drinks, gourmet sandwiches, fruit, cheese...

"A bundt cake?" I ask.

"Special request," replies Dale over the drone of the blades.

Troy looks at me like he's completely clueless and bites into a drumstick.

We follow the river over picturesque gardens and fruit orchards. I huddle under the blanket, soaking in the spectacular aerial views as the sun dips below the horizon.

"Hot chocolate?" Troy opens the thermos and hands me a mug. "One more time around the falls, Dale."

We get there just as the kaleidoscope of nightly lights come on, turning the thundering water into a rainbow of colors. I rest my head on Troy's shoulder, settling in. It feels good, sharing this with him, a powerful force that can't be held or grasped or contained.

"Hey, Troy?" I say.

"What?"

I take his baseball cap and throw it out the door.

For a moment he stares at me, mouth hanging open. Then he laughs so hard that Dale throws us an inquiring glance.

50. NO MORE DISGUISES

August 11th, 2001

WE SPEND THE DAY REVISITING FAVORITE PLACES. Afternoon tea at The Prince of Wales Hotel; strolling down Queen Street; a trip to the cluttered vintage store in Hamilton.

It's good to see Ken and Judy again, to listen to the wind chimes and look out the window to the busy street.

I fucking love you, Troy had said.

"How did you like the cottage you rented last year?" asks Ken.

We look at each other and smile.

"It worked out pretty well," says Troy.

"There's another lovely place by the river. Remember, Judy?"

"Oh yes. The one in the woods. A bit of a drive, but absolutely enchanting."

"Save it for the next couple that comes in," says Troy. "We already bought our little patch of magic."

"You did? Congratulations! So anything particular you're looking for today?"

We pick up a matching Beatles t-shirt for Troy and I get a pair of silver starfish hair clips for Natasha.

"No wigs?" asks Judy.

"No." Troy kisses the top of my head. "No more disguises."

BY THE TIME WE HEAD BACK, THE STARS ARE OUT AND THE sky is steeped in inky blue.

"You still use this laptop?" asks Troy when he spots it on the table.

"That's how I tracked you down, once I saw your parents' photo."

"You spied on my property records? With the very laptop I gave you? That's not very nice, Beetroot."

"All is fair in love and war." I reply. "Need I remind you, you lied to me."

"About what?"

"You said you're not free."

"I'm not. I'm bound to you. Chained, wired, and branded, with your stamp across my chest. For life. I believe that earns me eternal kanoodling." His hand explores the hollows of my back. "So did you finish the story about the prince?" he asks.

"I'm still working on it."

"Are you ever going to let me read it?"

"All in good time" I stand on tip-toe and kiss him.

"Keep that up and we can forget about dinner." He steps away reluctantly. "I'm still on a mission to fatten you up, you know."

"But you make it so much fun to burn up the calories."

"Grrrrr. You're the queen of distractions." He smacks my butt. "You want to eat out on the deck tonight?"

We set the table outside and turn on the mini-lanterns on the ledge.

Troy holds my hand as we eat, his eyes lingering on my fingers.

"What?" I ask, as he studies them intently.

"I can't get enough of this. Bare fingers, mine to put a ring on. I'm trying to picture what would suit you best."

"I already have something in mind. And it's not gold or diamonds."

"What are you thinking, Beetroot?"

"I'll tell you when we get back."

"I can't wait to tell my parents."

I push my food around half-heartedly. "They'll never have grand-kids, Troy."

"They'll just have to make do with one deliriously happy kid. And two amazing step grand-kids. You gotta admit, that's a pretty sweet deal. Besides, we're in our late thirties, Shayda. We've paid our dues. It's time to start thinking about what makes *us* happy."

He balances me out so perfectly, it feels like we're two pieces of a puzzle falling into place, part of a beautiful picture that was always meant to be.

I pull my shawl closer, feeling the chill of the night settle around us.

"Let's go inside," says Troy.

"Not yet." I don't want to give up this night, this moon, this last bit of magic before we head back.

"Then let's get you warmed up." He holds his hand out and leads me to the gazebo.

I lean against the latticed railing and watch as he turns on the patio heater. The tall column fires up a stunning flame, providing instant warmth. Troy opens a built in panel and punches a few buttons. Soft music surrounds us.

"You know what we didn't do this time?" I ask.

"What?" He wraps his arms around me.

"Chicken wings and karaoke."

"Easily remedied."

We dance as he sings Duran Duran's 'Come Undone' to me—something about an immaculate dream made breath and skin, in that sexy, breathless tone that sends goosebumps tingling all over me.

"I was listening to this when I saw you that day, by the pond," he says.

The day I found the dead butterfly. The day that changed it all.

"Nice karaoke. But what about the chicken wings?" I ask, drunk on this moment, the look in his eyes, the silver reflections on the lake.

"Got those covered too." He takes a hold of my bony elbows and flaps them.

"Troy!" I laugh.

"I love you, Beetroot Butterfly."

"I love you, Scary Cherry."

51. LAUGHTER

....

August 12th, 2001

I SIT UP IN THE MIDDLE OF THE NIGHT, DRENCHED IN COLD
sweat.

"What's wrong?" Troy gets up.

"Crap!" I shake my head and bury my face in my hands.
"Crap, crap, crap!"

"Shayda? What's wro—"

"How am I going to explain this to Jayne?" I crawl into
his arms

We fall back on the bed and start laughing—silly,
absurd, convulsing chuckles. He rolls me over and puts his
ear on my chest.

"What are you doing?" I ask.

"Listening to you laugh."

I sigh and stroke his hair. "She has a baby now."

"Jayne?"

"Yes. A little boy."

"Good. She won't give a crap, crap, crap." He smiles.

At least, I feel him smile, because it's too dark for me to see. So I trace his mouth and let my hands wander over his face, savoring the curves, the contours, the bones beneath his skin, the smoothness of ear lobes, the orbits of his eyes.

When I wake up again, the first rays of daylight are just peeking through the shutters.

"Going for a run?" I ask Troy, sleepily.

"Not today." He snuggles into me. "Today, everything I need is right here."

We drift off again, only to be woken up by the sound of the front door slamming shut. Then a dog barks from the living room, followed by the pitter-patter of little feet.

"Fuck!" Troy sits up in bed. "Fuck, fuck, fuck!"

"What's wrong?" I ask.

"I forgot to tell Amy—no more rentals."

The bedroom door opens. Four pairs of startled eyes stare back at us. Mum, dad, a little boy and the family pet.

Troy and I look at each other.

Caught naked under the covers.

"I don't give a fuck, fuck, fuck," I whisper in his ear.

"Excuse my fiancée." Troy gives our unexpected guests a lopsided smile. "She has a real potty mouth."

We fall back on the bed and start laughing.

"Say that again." I pull the bedsheet over us.

"Excuse my fiancée?"

"I love when you call me your fiancée."

52. THE WINDOW

....

May 10th, 2010

I can't believe it's been been nine years since that morning at the cottage, nine years that I could go back and relive over and over again, because they have been the most enriching, the most expansive years of my life.

"I hope it doesn't rain," says Natasha, looking out of the arched window.

"If it does, they have the sun room and the tent ready to go." I knot the sash around her waist. The bright fuchsia adds a pop of color to her soft ivory dress.

"I know, but I've always wanted an outdoor reception."

"And that's exactly what you'll have." I adjust the starfish clips that hold up the whimsical flower crown on her head. With dainty white cherry blossoms and baby leaves woven through delicate vine, it makes her look like an ethereal woodland creature.

"Beautiful." I sigh. "My baby girl is all grown up."

"Can you believe it?" She smiles as I admire her reflection in the antique mirror.

The bohemian dress hugs her figure and falls to her feet in layers of soft tulle. Its stunning low back is edged with silk rosettes. Lace cap sleeves accentuate her shoulders. She looks like every woman should on her wedding day—glowing, radiant and sublimely happy.

"Oh, Mum." She catches me wiping a tear for the umpteenth time. "It's Nathan. *Our* Nathan. I'm married to my best friend."

"And it's about time." I sniff. "Oh, I almost forgot. I have something for you."

I give her a small gift bag and a large one. She looks inside the first and lets out a squeal of delight.

"Your butterfly umbrella?"

The one that Troy gave me.

"It's yours now." I say. "I hope you don't have to use it today, but if you do, it'll help you dance through it all. All of your rainy days."

"And this?" She pulls out a crimson coat from the bigger bag. "Oh my god! It's the coat that Dad bought you. Remember when I used to play dress-up with it? Now I can take all those memories with me to our new place. Thanks, Mum. I love them both!"

It's an old coat and a used umbrella, but I am giving her little pieces of my journey, two things that brought me the same kind of joy that I wish for her.

"I hate to interrupt, but everyone's waiting." Jayne walks in with her four year old in tow. "Look Sophia, doesn't Natasha look beautiful?"

"She's a mini-you," I say, admiring her daughter. Red hair, an elfin nose spattered with freckles, and arresting green eyes.

"She might look like me, but inside? She's a little devil. Nothing like her older brother."

"Like I said, she's a mini-you." I laugh. "Why didn't you bring her and Brady yesterday?"

"And risk them ruining that elaborate set-up you had?"

"The sofreh aghd?"

"Whatever you call the traditional Persian wedding spread. I've never seen anything like that before."

"It was beautiful. And so was the ceremony. And it was all Mum," says Natasha, "But I'm glad it's done. I just want to start my life with Nathan."

"Awww." Jayne and I move in to give her a hug.

"Careful, careful. We don't want to smudge anything," she says.

We laugh at what's become her trademark line. From fashion shows to TV sets, to weddings to photo shoots, Natasha is renowned for her meticulous make-up and special effects skills.

"Where's your maid of honor?" asks Jayne.

"Terri went to get my bouquet. She'll be right back."

Jayne looks around the room and sighs. "I'm so glad you chose to get married here. I remember this room like it was yesterday."

I remember it too. Staring through the half-open door as Troy and Jayne kissed in front of this very window; dancing with him in the great hall after wards; the tipsy, barely-there kiss he left on my neck. All these years and I can still feel the ghost of its imprint.

"Wait till you see the sunken garden. It looks magical," says Jayne. "Let's get you seated, Shayda. Everyone's waiting." She picks up her daughter. "I'll signal for your entrance, Natasha."

Jayne and I walk through the meandering pathways to a cobblestoned area, shaded by a giant oak canopy. Green and yellow paper lanterns hang from the branches like bubbles full of bright, suspended wishes. Directly underneath the magnificent setting is the head table, with a punchy centerpiece of lemon & lime colored pinwheels, and mason jars glowing with candles.

"It couldn't be more perfect," I say to Jayne. "You've made her dream come true."

"Just keep your fingers crossed that it doesn't rain," she replies, looking up at the gathering clouds.

I feel pacific blues on me as we enter, and can't help but smile. The weather doesn't stand a chance when Troy is around. He's a gloom-dispersing dynamo, and he keeps getting sexier with the passage of time. The years have chiseled away the planes of his face so that the only points of softness are his lips, lips so sensual, no man should have them. The thick, rough tangle of his hair shows a liberal smattering of grey, and the years have etched crinkles in the corners of his eyes, but it only grips at my heart.

He clasps my hand as I take my place next to him, with Hafez and Zain standing on my other side.

"About time, Mrs. Heathgate," he drawls.

My heart still takes a little leap everytime he calls me that.

We had a quiet ceremony at the cottage, a sunrise wedding by the 'x' on the beach, in our matching Beatles t-shirts. There was no exchange of rings—we had barbed wire tattooed around our fingers instead.

Maamaan sat in the front with Baba, Hossein and his family. She hmph'ed because it was too early and not traditional enough, but she wore a brand new hat with tall feathers that Bob had to part through to see what was going on. Elizabeth sat next to him, with Jayne, Matt and little Brady.

"Disgusting," Jayne had said when I told her the truth.

Her best friend and her first crush.

"I'm sorry, Jayne." I said.

"You should be. How could you waste all that time? I would have cavorted off with him that very first night. I mean, that body, those eyes." She fanned herself dramatically. "So is he as good in bed as he's reputed to be?"

"Jayne!"

"Come on! You *owe* me. Big time."

Grace and Henry had welcomed me graciously into their family.

"We always knew it was going to take a very special gal to win his heart," they said.

Hafez had attended with Marjaneh.

I smile at her across the family table. Hafez's steady affection has done wonders for her self-esteem, and the kids have filled the void she felt about not having any children. She lavishes Hafez with all the nurturing she had locked up inside, and he, in turn, has been transformed. He walks taller now, as if a great burden has been lifted off his shoulders. Opening up to Natasha, Zain and the rest of the world about his past has been a liberating experience.

Troy and I set up the Haft Seen table with the kids every year, and invite Hafez and Marjaneh over. I added a figurine of them. It sits besides three others: the original one of our family, Ma's broken one, and a new one of Troy and me. Next Nowruz, I will add Natasha's and Nathan's, and hopefully some grandkids soon. Each new addition, is like a new world, full of hopes and dreams. I finally understand Ma and her sparkling glass cabinet.

My heart swells as Natasha and Nathan make their way to the front. I never thought I'd live to see this day. Ten years is a damn long time in the cancer world. I remember passing the five year mark. 1,825 cancer free days. My doctor called it remission. I called it my bonus, my 'more', an extension to witness both my kids grow up, to see Hafez heal, to fall asleep in the arms of the beautiful man by my side—every freaking, unbelievable night. He's my secret weapon, the love that fuels my 'more'.

"No rock band t-shirt today," he whispers. "They one-upped us."

I laugh. Nathan has ditched his usual gear for a dashing grey suit, white shirt and a bright fuchsia tie that matches the sash on Natasha's dress.

"Pink," they said, while planning the big day. "For you, Mum."

"Can I get you anything?" I ask Maamaan when lunch is served.

"You're just checking in to make sure Baba and I aren't at each other's throats, aren't you?"

"Not at all." I smile. "I'm counting on Hossein to do that."

"So far so good," he reports. "We've put away all the sharp objects."

Maamaan doesn't look amused. "I still say Natasha should have married a nice Persian boy."

"When are you going to stop looking at the world like that?" asks Baba. "You can't put a leash on the heart. Hell, we eloped, Mona. See Farnaz and Behram over there? They work. Hafez and Marjaneh too. But Hossein here? He followed a different path. No disrespect, Adele."

"None taken," she replies. "Did you see your ex, Hossein?" She points to Marjaneh. "Let's go say hello."

"You see? Now there's a woman who is completely secure," says Baba after they leave.

"Are you saying I wasn't?" counters Maamaan.

"If I thought you were, I would have brought a date."

"A date." She rolls her eyes. "You mean an escort."

"Um...here come the children." I intervene. "Kayla, you watch Grandma. Ethan, you watch Grandpa. And Summer, see that pitcher of water? Don't be afraid to use it if these two get out of control."

They laugh. Even Hossein's kids know that this is the best it's going to get with Maamaan and Baba.

"Shayda." Someone taps my shoulder.

"Farnaz! I'm so glad you made it. It's been ages. Where's Behram?"

"He's talking to Hafez. How have you been?"

"Good. And you?"

"Busy. We just sold the first restaurant. You remember, the one on Pape?"

I laugh. "How could I forget? If it wasn't for you guys and that place, I don't know where we'd have gone."

"It was nothing." She shakes her head. "You have to come see the new place."

"Still souvlaki and baklava?"

"It's what we do best." She laughs.

"Ladies and gentlemen..." The announcement interrupts our conversation. "If you could all please take your seats. It's time for the bride and groom's first dance. We'd like to call Troy and Zain to the stage, please."

Troy winks at me and accepts the microphone. I swear no man fills out a suit better than him. Today he's wearing a bright yellow and green tie that matches my yellow dress and his larger than life personality.

"It's the first color I saw you in," he said, when we went shopping for a dress.

Zain sets himself up on a chair next to Troy, and starts strumming his guitar.

Natasha and Nathan take the floor, dancing to a fun, playful melody that Troy and Zain have written, especially for them. Between my husband's sexy vocals, and my son's stirring notes, I feel the seams of my soul start to come undone.

Hafez reaches for my hand across the table, as we watch Natasha dance with Nathan. Our little girl. His other hand clasps Marjaneh's.

I like that we can sit like this, simply and honestly. It hasn't always been easy, and it's taken many years, but we can finally do this, without blame, without static.

We have an infinite capacity to love, but when you wrap up your love and give it to someone, they expect all of it. And that's what you think too—that you're giving them everything you've got. You really do. Until you realize that love is end-less, bottom-less, boundary-less. The more you give, the more gushes out. It spills over, refusing to be contained in neat little parcels, swelling like a river after a flash flood. And in the end, it doesn't matter which part was whose, because in the end it's all one, like streams merging into the ocean. My love for Troy, my love for Hafez.

We clap as the song ends. Then Nathan gets his mother and Natasha grabs Hafez. The DJ takes over and Zain pulls me to the floor.

"That was beautiful," I tell him. "I hope you're taking notes, because you're next."

"Yeah, good luck with that." He laughs. He has those soulful puppy eyes that girls find irresistible. Goofy, but endearing at the same time.

"Mind if I cut in?" asks Troy, dancing up to us with Terri.

"Um...yeah. Sure," Zain mumbles, but gives Troy a thumbs up when Terri isn't looking.

Troy has always been his hero. Since the time he jumped into the lake after him.

"I want to do what Troy does," he said when it was time to choose his college courses.

"Geek." I can still hear Natasha's reply. "He runs a multi-million dollar corporation. You should be so lucky!"

I watch her dance and smile.

"Are you happy, Shayda?" asks Troy.

"Don't ask me what you know is true..." I say as we glide through the dance floor.

"Is that your answer or are you just singing along to this tune?"

"I thought you like karaoke," I tease. INXS's 'Never Tear Us Apart' is playing in the background. "You asked me the same question at Jayne's wedding."

"And you didn't give me an answer then either."

I laugh. As if there is any doubting it now.

"You know your ears lift up when you laugh? The teeniest bit," says Troy. "And if I watch real close, I can catch the hidden groove on your left cheek. But you have to be smiling really wide, cheshire-cat wide. like you are now, for that elusive sucker. It always hits me right in the chest—boom—when I score that one dimple."

"I don't have a dimple."

"Natasha." Troy turns to her as she's gliding by with Nathan. "Tell your mum she has a dimple when she smiles."

"Where?" She looks at me. "I've never seen a dimple."

"Maybe it's just for me then," says Troy. "Like the roses."

He nuzzles his face in my neck and takes a deep breath.

"You two are nuts, you know that?" says Natasha. "I hope we're just as happy when we're old."

"Who're you calling old? Forty-eight is prime time, right Beetroot?"

My breath still catches when he looks at me. I think maybe that was it all along. He always looked at me like he really saw me. Me, the empty woman with half eaten dreams and flaws and desires. And he filled me up.

He looks at me and I blossom, like a flower in the sun.

"Any age is prime time when I'm with you," I reply.

He laughs and hands me over to Nathan. Then he sweeps Natasha off in a mad whirl.

"You think it worked?" asks Troy, when we're seated at the table.

"They're still dancing," says Ryan.

We watch Zain with Terri, Ryan's and Ellen's eldest. They've spent many summers together, but it's just starting to turn into something more.

"They're so shy, they need a little prodding," says Ellen. Then she laughs. "I can't believe we've turned into those match making parents we swore not to become."

"Well, I for one am glad that our efforts at match making didn't get too far." Grace laughs. "I've never seen Troy so happy."

"And it all started by the sidewalk outside our home," says Elizabeth.

"Hmph." Maamaan butts in. "They crossed lines they shouldn't have, and we all know it."

There's an awkward silence before Troy gets up and holds his hand out. "Dance with me, Mona."

"How many times have I told you not to call me that? It's disrespectful. I prefer Maamaan,"

"But it's so sexy. Monahhh. Just like you. And if you weren't so sour, you could have any man here on his knees with a wiggle of your hips."

Maamaan's jaw drops. I brace myself for what's about to follow.

"Come on, baby," Troy prompts her. "Let's cha-cha."

She doesn't respond for a long, strained minute. Then she smiles, a big, flaky, completely un-Maamaan like smile and takes his hand.

"Well, I never..." Bob stares after them, completely gob-smacked.

The rest of the table erupts into laughter.

THE PHOTOGRAPHER ARRANGES US BEFORE A CASCADING fountain: Natasha, Nathan, Zain, Hafez, Marjaneh, Troy and me. Now both sets of parents and step-parents with the bride and groom; then some mother and daughter portraits.

My favorite shot is the one of Natasha with her two dads and Zain. Zain is standing behind her, on the ledge of the fountain, with his hands on her shoulders. Troy is on one side of her, and Hafez is on the other. It's one of those moments that sears itself in your heart, where you realize that somehow, miraculously, through all the mistakes you make, through all the hurt and pain, happiness can still find its way through the cracks in your heart.

I watch as Hafez and Natasha take their father-daughter portraits. Then it's Troy's turn. He behaves for the first few photos and then he scoops Natasha off her feet. She shrieks and throws her arms around him. Zain photo bombs them just as the photographer clicks.

"Ha!" Hafez claps, his face lit up with a wide smile—the smile that I've always loved on him, except it's there more frequently now, and comes more freely.

I know he will always be grateful to Troy for saving Zain, but their mutual respect has turned into an easy camaraderie. It always warms my heart when I see their two heads together, discussing business or family or the latest Leafs game.

I get called back for more photos as friends and family join in for group shots. Natasha holds out her hand as the first drops of rain start to fall.

"Oh no," she says. "We have to hurry."

We cycle through the last of the photos as the thunder rolls in.

"I'll go get the umbrella," I say, heading back to the room where Natasha got ready in the morning.

I spot it on the tufted bench by the window, a little patch of red against the grey sky. I look out, to the fountain centred in the window's arched frame, and press my palm to the cool glass pane.

The rain has started to come down now. Nathan is holding his coat over Natasha's head. Jayne's kids are running around, squealing with delight. Grace, Henry, Bob and Elizabeth are making a dash for the door. Maamaan is still standing, regal and proud, for the photographer, even as the feathers on her hat start to wilt. Baba is staring at her ass. Hafez, Marjaneh, Zain and Hossein are laughing at him. The rest of the party is in complete chaos. I can't tell who's who because everything turns blurry.

"Oh god. Not again."

I turn around and find Troy standing behind me.

"Look at all these happy figurines, Troy." Big, fat tears spill down my cheeks.

"You're a strange one, Beetroot." His fingers lift my chin, turning my face up. Then he kisses me, so deep that I feel like I'm being absorbed into him. I shut my eyes, feeling my body arch towards him.

Everything narrows down to this moment, this aching, unexpected 'more', so sweet that I tilt my head back, wanting to drain all of life's precious, honeyed nectar. We're back to where we started. Right here before this window. Except the impossible has happened. I'm the one in his arms now, his rosary around my wrist, a ring of blue-black wire around my finger.

"So." His breath leaves goosebumps on my neck. "Here we are, Mrs. Heathgate."

"Here we are." I smile and lace my fingers through his.

53. LETTERS FOR MY LOVER

June 17th, 2012

From:scarycherry1962@hotmail
Sent:June-17-12 8:20:30 AM
To:beetbutt@hotmail.com

Happy 50th, Beetroot Butterfly. Like your bungalow on stilts?

From:beetbutt@hotmail.com
Sent:June-17-12 8:21:15 AM
To:scarycherry1962@hotmail

You know I love it. And I have something for you too. Remember the story about the prince? I'm emailing it to you. Happy Birthday, Scary Cherry.

From:beetbutt@hotmail.com
Sent:June-17-12 8:24:06 AM

To:scarycherry1962@hotmail

Beetroot Butterfly to Scary Cherry. Why so quiet, Scary Cherry?

From:scarycherry1962@hotmail
Sent:June-17-12 8:27:30 AM
To:beetbutt@hotmail.com

I'm reading, woman. So I was the prince? This is *our* story.

From:beetbutt@hotmail.com
Sent:June-17-12 8:28:10 AM
To:scarycherry1962@hotmail

You like?

From:scarycherry1962@hotmail
Sent:June-17-12 8:35:18 AM
To:beetbutt@hotmail.com

You totally censored the dirty bits. There was *way* more action, Beetroot. You need to work on those before I get this published.

From:beetbutt@hotmail.com
Sent:June-17-12 8:36:06 AM
To:scarycherry1962@hotmail

Those letters are just for you—you'll do no such thing!

From:scarycherry1962@hotmail
Sent:June-17-12 8:36:48 AM

To:beetbutt@hotmail.com

Why not? You just gave it to me. It's mine. I can do whatever the fuck I please with it. And I'll be sending the first copy to your mother. Now pass me another brownie.

From:scarycherry1962@hotmail
Sent:June-17-12 8:38:49 AM
To:beetbutt@hotmail.com

Helloooo? Bee-hee-troot. If you're not going to feed me, you'll have to find other ways to keep me entertained.

From:beetbutt@hotmail.com
Sent:June-17-12 8:38:53 AM
To:scarycherry1962@hotmail

Stay where you are, Troy! No, Troy, n

HE TAKES THE LAPTOP OFF MY LAP KISSES ME. "WE MADE IT, Beetroot."

I look out the window, at the setting sun and the swaying palms. The whole week has been a slice of heaven: our own thatched roof villa, perched over a pristine lagoon with expansive panoramas of mountain peaks and endless ocean. Colorful fish and spotted turtles glide past the glass panels on the floor. Flower-decorated canoes deliver sumptuous meals to our deck—trays laden with exotic fruits in the morning, and extravagant full-course dinners under star studded skies.

I smile and look at Troy. I was right. His eyes are all the shimmering shades of the water in the South Pacific.

We drink in each other's faces, the lines where there were none, the subtle changes in our eyes, the kind that happen on the inside, removed from the passage of time.

"What's wrong?" I trace the tattoo on his chest.

"Just thinking."

"About...?"

"Your test results will be waiting when we get back."

"Someone once told me that the only way to feel truly alive is to start living fearlessly."

"An enlightened soul, no doubt."

"His body's not too bad either." I ogle his powerful, bronzed physique from under my lashes. "I've stopped waiting for those results, Troy. Every year we stress over them and every year we get another extension. And maybe our luck will hold, and maybe it won't. But it's no different from anyone else. No one knows how many tomorrows they have. That's what makes it all so precious." I lean over and give him a kiss. "Besides, we have a special kind of magic." I dangle my rosary-wrapped wrist in front of him.

His thumb caresses the beads. "Tired?" he asks when I stifle a yawn.

"Someone kept me up most of last night."

"Are you lodging a complaint, Mrs. Heathgate?"

"I will, if you don't follow up with the same tonight." I pat the pillow, but feel sleep catching up to me.

"Hey." He slips into bed with me.

I smile, trying to stay awake. I don't want to miss a minute of this.

"Close your eyes." He kisses them shut. "Let go." His fingers stroke my brow, back and forth. "Let it all go." He smooths the hair away from my face.

I feel myself slipping away. "No kanoodling?" I murmur.

"What do you think this is? We're talking level seven kanoodling." His voice starts to fade.

Lying in his arms is the best place in the whole world.

ACKNOWLEDGEMENTS

To the first person who read my first novel—Michelle Wolfson, of Wolfson Literary Agency. Sometimes we just need someone to believe in us before we can believe in ourselves. Thank you for igniting the spark.

I am indebted to Sara Izadi, Talia Farahmand and Setareh for their enthusiasm and hard work on the book trailer.

Didi H, thank you for swaying me from the George R.R. Martin School of Total Annihilation. We saved a lot of kleenexes!

To SueBee, my sincere thanks for the generous advice and insight.

Tasha B—the world's best beta reader—you rock!

To the girls club: YD, NM, SM, TV, RL, WLR, AD, SB, ADW, SA, JG, MK, EL, WC, ZA, FN, MM, HZ, SQ, SV, RI, KS—thank you for so many years of love, support and friendship.

My deepest gratitude to my parents, siblings and family. You add spice, humor and a dash of madness to my life. Without you, my world would be colorless.

To my son, for bestowing endlessly creative titles to cheer me on. No, you still can't read this book.

And finally, to my husband, who always has bigger dreams for me than I can possibly have for myself. You are the glue that holds me together. You help me weather the tough times and make the good times shinier.

ABOUT THE AUTHOR

LEYLAH ATTAR IS *A NEW YORK TIMES, USA Today and Wall Street Journal* best selling author, who writes stories about love—shaken, stirred and served with a twist. Sometimes she disappears into the black hole of the internet, but can usually be enticed out with chocolate.

Connect with her at
WWW.LEYLAHATTAR.COM

Other titles by Leylah Attar:

From His Lips: a 53 Letters Short Story
Select scenes from the full length novel, narrated from the hero's point of view—raw and uncut.

The Paper Swan